Sign up for our newsletter to hear
about new and upcoming releases.

www.ylva-publishing.com

OTHER BOOKS BY LOLA KEELEY

Major Surgery
The Music and the Mirror

SLAMMED

LOLA KEELEY

DEDICATION

For Lisa-Marie,

Two decades as bezzers; consider this me
signing up for at least another two.

INTRODUCTION

This novel is set in the world of women's professional tennis, but a few details have been changed along the way.

First of all, instead of the real-world overlap of the International Tennis Federation and the Women's Tennis Association working together, the governing body for tennis in this book is simply the Global Tennis Association (GTA). Think of them as Big Tennis, and you'll have the right idea.

As for real players, I've tried as far as possible to leave them out. Some of the fictional players are clearly influenced by careers you might recognise, though. The record Elin is attempting to beat is set at the number of slams Steffi Graf won in her career, which is twenty-two. Although Margaret Court won more (twenty-four), she didn't win all of those in the Open era, and I wasn't comfortable using a public and unapologetic homophobe as a point of reference. So please, if you can, forgive that slight fudging of the numbers.

Hopefully most of the terminology is explained or contextualised, but the main thing you need to know as a tennis newbie is that the grand slam tournaments are four held every year: Australian, French and US Opens, and Wimbledon. Winning these is amongst the very highest honours for pro players.

For most tournaments, the players are also seeded. The most on-form player coming into the tournament will be the number-one seed. The rest are ranked below that according to their recent record. Only a certain number are seeded, and the unseeded players can end up anywhere in the draw. The reasoning behind this is to spread the best players across the bracket, so that the very best don't meet each other in the first couple of rounds. If they all played in the first couple of days and half of them went out, it would reduce excitement and viewing for the rest of the tournament. That's why it's a big deal if an unseeded player makes it further in the tournament—they've usually done it the hard way!

CHAPTER ONE

FIFTEEN THOUSAND PEOPLE MADE A lot of noise.

The simple fact of their existence made it so: breathing, hearts beating, the soft-squashed gasp a person made when sitting down too heavily, or the squeak of their rubber-soled shoes against the concrete floor. Plastic chairs groaned on their hinges, throats were cleared, and that was before a single conversation, from the mutters between close friends to the shouts from one corner of the space to another.

But on Centre Court at Wimbledon, when the umpire called for, "Quiet, please," that was exactly what they got.

That quiet closed in around me, serving in the semi-final as the clock ticked over from afternoon to evening. The match had already been delayed by warm summer rain, the kind that appeared out of a faintly grey sky and soaked people to the bone without them realising. At the first drop, we had been postponed. Covers rolled out over the grass so quickly it seemed they were protecting from something far more dangerous than a little rainwater.

Then the roof closed, slow and mechanical like a spaceship in some clunky sci-fi show I'd watched growing up. With it sealed, with the weather shut out, everything sounded different. Echoes bounced in strange ways, and suddenly all those people at a safe remove seemed to be right on top of me.

I shook my head. *Focus, Elin.* What did a little change or two matter? I took a steadying breath and reminded myself that the tennis stayed the same.

The previous point had been decided with a furious rally, and I'd won when a last desperate lunge was backhanded into the net. I'd waited politely for my opponent to pick herself up and dust herself off. Her once-pristine white T-shirt, mostly sweated through like my own, bore green marks and sandy smears from where she'd hit the ground. I wiped at my own shirt in sympathy, ball for my next serve already in my hand.

I only had twenty-five seconds to make the serve, so I bounced the ball straight down at my feet. One. Two. The weight of it felt familiar against my palm, fresh from its precisely chilled can, in peak condition for being hammered against the ground just as hard as either one of us could hit it.

I closed my eyes for just a second and waited for the feeling to settle over me. Sure enough, it came rolling in just like the tide. I'd done this before, maybe a million times. I released the ball upwards, no blue sky above it that time, just the industrial surface of the closed roof. No matter, my other arm was already in motion, the movement as natural as breathing.

With the kiss of contact, my serve was unleashed. Not my hardest or fastest, but the women's game wasn't dominated by serve prowess in the same way as the men's. I could have risked serving an ace, effectively a shot that no mortal player should have been able to return. Aiming exclusively for those could lead to double faults though, and so it was a calculated choice each time.

I could barely feel my racquet in my hand. It was an extension of my arm by now, no matter how many different ones passed through my bag and my palm every day, every week. The custom grip I'd been using since I was fourteen and still playing in the juniors was moulded to the exact bends of my fingers, and the calluses I developed always fit within its grooves. Like a wedding ring worn for years but still felt after it had been removed, so too did I have my own phantom accessory, the slight heft of the graphite frame always with me even when I was far from the court or a kit bag.

We hit another long, hard rally, and I felt a twinge of complaint in my right calf as I stopped short to win the point. Damn, that would have to be looked at to make sure it didn't develop into a proper strain, or worse, an actual muscle tear.

For a moment, as I moved to serve again, I realised that I didn't actually have to. Somehow, in all the years I'd been playing, it never occurred to me that the entire act of playing in a match was voluntary. If I set my racquet down right then, in that moment, and walked off court, no one could have stopped me.

Fortunately for my wandering thoughts, I had been drilled too well by my coach over the seasons. Countless sessions with my therapist had focused on moments like these. Now in that final stretch of a match, I knew I had the stamina and technique to win almost by default. How hard that was usually came down to my opponent, and that was when I realised my real advantage.

It was bad form to admit it, to even think it in the first place, but ask anyone who ever won a tennis match and they would nod in recognition. The two of you were out there, alone in effect despite the umpire and the line judges and the kids who chased the loose balls around. That was what the world shrunk down to: one person competing against another, with only one winner possible. What any winner could have admitted—confessed, really—was that at some point on the road to victory, they could see their opponent settle for defeat.

That moment? Seeing the loss in their eyes even as they stared defiantly back over the net? That was what kept me going, made me want to compete and bring home as many trophies as they could throw at me. Maybe I should have said something humble, about playing for the love of the game, but it would only have been a lie. That look, the one I saw radiating back at me in that moment, said that yet again I'd won. Now all that remained was to clinch those last two points and let the umpire confirm what we both already knew on court.

I had won, and on Saturday afternoon I would be playing in front of royalty, celebrities, and millions of people all around the world, for a chance at yet another Wimbledon Ladies' Singles title. Taking a moment, I smoothed down my white skirt and plucked the white T-shirt away from my skin where sweat was making it stick uncomfortably.

I unleashed the ball again, ready to finish the formalities and be declared the winner for all on Centre Court to hear. The crowd watched on in silence as I wore the woman on the other side of the net down, stroke by stroke, sliced backhand by sliced backhand.

By the time the umpire called it—"Game, set, match, Miss Larsson"—I was already at the net, arm extended for the handshake of congratulations and commiseration. Mostly I just wanted to get back under cover of the locker room, out of sight of the roaring crowd who somehow seemed closer than ever.

One more match, I told myself. Then I could rest, then some things would be optional again. I just had to behave myself for two more days. What could be easier than that?

CHAPTER TWO

ALL I WANTED TO DO was to have one drink in peace.

Not too much to ask, surely? But it certainly seemed to be an impossible quest that Friday night. I'd been careful in my choices, taking a cab into the centre of London, a bustling city where anyone could get lost without really trying. I picked a hotel with a famous bar but excellent security, frequented by people who ended up in the morning papers, but the paparazzi shots were always out on the street, never inside.

Like I said, careful.

I suppose I had to be, since technically my face was recognisable. So people liked to tell me, anyway. I had found that like most people in this world, a hood pulled low made people gloss over you when they looked. Much better than baseball caps and sunglasses. That passed for a disguise back in LA, which I mostly called home, but in London it was a neon sign screaming, *Look at me!*

Instead, I dressed like any other woman in her thirties hitting the town. Little black dress, killer heels—not the hoodie that I would have preferred at all. I could always hide my face behind my hair, just about. One of the few perks of letting all that blonde hair grow out, even though I'd been longing to cut it short since my teens.

The bar was everything I remembered from my previous, less-incognito trip there. Dark in all the right corners, the blueish glow from the bar enough to get you served, but the strange colours meant nobody really looked like themselves. That's why I thought I was safe to perch on a stool there, to stay in the thick of things instead of retreating to a lonely corner. After all, that was why I'd come out in the first place: to drown out the maddening quiet of my rented room.

Of course, being in a bar meant men hit on me. Not because I was anything special, trust me. Blonde, female, with a pulse was basically a bat signal to a lot of guys who couldn't read the signs—like the fact that I had checked out more women than they had. Still, it was almost good practice to keep knocking them back. I backhanded their approaches like I returned serves over the net.

Which is to say, I did it really well. Just like I return serves really well. Because that recognisable face I mentioned? Might have something to do with the whole professional tennis player thing. Not that I bought into it, but London during Wimbledon fortnight was tuned into the world of racquets and balls in a particular way, making my trip out on the town particularly risky, since my goal was not to be noticed.

Still, I liked my odds. A city of eight million people, the blurring effects of alcohol, and the fact that nobody in their right mind would expect me to be out on the town the night before playing in the Ladies' Singles final.

The main event on the second-last day of the tournament, the final was one of the crown jewels of two weeks of tennis mania tucked into the Southwest corner of the city. A person, particularly an elite athlete with an impressive career behind her, would have to be in an especially strange mood to do something so foolish the night before such a major event.

Well, hello. I'm Elin Larsson and apparently I'm a fool.

It didn't take long for my entourage, by which I mostly meant my coach, Britta, to notice my absence. Instead of hotels, which weren't plentiful close to the Wimbledon courts, we rented huge luxurious houses for two weeks every year that I played this tournament. All the other players had been doing the same in recent years, preferring the illusion of home comforts over sterile, identikit hotel rooms. Which meant it hadn't taken Britta very long to discover I wasn't in fact having an early night with a face mask and some meditation exercises. At least in a hotel, my door would have locked.

Did I mention that Britta—for all her coaching awards, not to mention the books and videos—was also my mother? Some would say that job came first, but I also wouldn't have been shocked if she had drills for my backhand worked out while I was still in the womb. I just knew better than to ask questions like that anymore.

Anyway, there I was in the blissful semi-anonymity of being out in public and ignoring the messages lighting up my phone, when a tall brunette took the last empty barstool, the one next to mine. I suppose I could have ignored her, but hey, only human. I took a long, careful look at her in profile, and I felt that half-click of recognition as I looked at her face. Maybe she was someone famous too.

And in a very cool, composed sort of way, I choked on the olive from my martini.

I really was having just the one drink to relax me a little. I planned to stick to sparkling water the rest of the night, a drink so bland and pointless that it felt more like a punishment than anything else. I envied the people around me ordering doubles, or cocktails full of different spirits and a ton of sugar. Even the guy yelling about his rum and Coke had me idly wondering when the last time I'd casually ordered a soft drink was.

During all that, she caught me staring, of course. Or maybe the choking caught her attention, but I was grateful for the thump between my shoulder blades all the same.

"Thank you," I managed to gasp, and her concerned look gave way to a tight smile. "Can I buy you a drink?"

"Well, I think you just ruined martinis for me."

"Sorry."

"Just stay away from the nicer Scotches if you're planning to choke again. Those I would really miss."

Her accent was soft, wrapped around her consonants like syrup. I couldn't claim to know where it came from, though I'd have guessed Italy with a gun to my head.

"Then at least let me buy you one of those for saving my life. Or more like my dignity, I suppose."

"True, it wasn't very dignified." She flagged down the bartender. "I'll take your most expensive single malt. She's paying."

"Make it a double," I added, because I was not about to be outdone. "And a sparkling water for me."

"Scared yourself with the martinis too?" she asked, turning more towards me. There really was something familiar about her face.

"I'm not a big drinker," was answer enough. "I'm Elin, by the way." Offering a hand was awkward and a little hopeless, but she shook it anyway. It made that smile of hers a little bigger.

"So formal. Antonia, but please, everyone calls me Toni."

Something pinged at that too. A memory half-forgotten, itching at the back of my skull just to irritate me. Did she work for the All England club? Maybe one of the sponsors? They were all in town, having a great time on expenses. These past two weeks I had shaken more hands than ever, posed for more selfies than anyone could ever want to see. I signed giant novelty tennis balls on court and tried to show up for any charities that invited me, matches and training permitting.

"Have we met?" I'd learned over the years not to prolong the agony. Once, I'd have tried to hang in there and pick up a few clues, but if I didn't get it from a first name then I knew the blank was never going to fill itself.

"Just once, in Paris. I don't expect you'd remember, though."

"Sorry, I'm bad with faces. Even worse with names."

Our drinks came, and she took a large sip of her drink. "Not bad."

I didn't know one end of a whisky from another, but I knew when I was being teased. "So, Toni…"

She was saving me from myself by interrupting. "Listen, I was going to string it out a little longer, not let you know that I know who you are. I even had this whole joke about how they call you the Ice Princess and the ice in my drink…but you should know that the guy at the end of the bar is a gossip columnist for a big tabloid here. And he gave you a second glance like he knows you from somewhere."

Shit. The last thing I expected was an actual journalist. Maybe a fan with a mobile phone, but everyone in the bar seemed far too cool for that sort of thing. Never mind that players went out before big matches all the time, but with my public reputation as the quiet one, the resident good girl of tennis, they'd have a field day.

And that was before you considered the reaction from my mother.

As the bartender passed, I fished some cash from my purse. Plucking another twenty on top of the bar bill and tip, I risked leaning in to ask, "Is there a back way out of here? Maybe a staff entrance I could use?"

He took the extra money and nodded to the opposite end of the bar from my unwelcome journalist. "That way. Anyone stops you, just say Jimmy sent you. Leads right out into the side street."

"You're a lifesaver."

I suppose I shouldn't have been surprised that when I stepped down from the stool and headed that way, Toni followed right along. She actually took me by the elbow and steered me towards the barely visible door on the far side of the bar, apparently concerned I wasn't moving fast enough. I could keep up with Olympic runners on sprints, but that evening I was sluggish, almost slow. I blamed the heels.

The door opened into a space with duller blue lights, like something out of a bad sci-fi movie. We jogged down the corridor, her hand never leaving my arm, and as we reached the first turn, normal fluorescent light greeted us at last.

We never got a chance to explain our presence, because nobody intercepted us between there and the door out into what was an alleyway at best. Calling it a side street suggested it was somewhere people might willingly walk down or that cars could drive down. This was a horrid place, full of industrial bins and cobbles shiny with rain. At least the wet pavement could be explained by the damp weather and not what it distinctly smelled like.

By that point I was definitely moving fast enough. I practically dragged Toni out of there, to the safety of the main street and the potential of flagging down one of those iconic black London taxis.

"Thank you," I said, trying not to be disappointed that she finally let go once we were on the pavement. "I hope I didn't interrupt your evening. I just have a big day tomorrow and thought a little time to myself might be nice…"

"I get it. I didn't get a chance to say back there, but I'm on the tour again this year." Oh. Implying that previously she hadn't been? I was caught completely off guard. Maybe that was why she looked so familiar at second glance. I hadn't just been staring because she was so damn pretty with those high cheekbones and expressive dark eyes that seemed to play a news ticker of her feelings as she silently worked through them. I envied her the transparency. Lately I only expressed emotion over missed points and bad line calls.

"So when we met in Paris…?" I asked, suspecting at least part of the answer.

"You put me out in the second round at Roland Garros. Straight sets, 6-1, 6-0. I suppose you do that so often that it's just a statistic, but it was a big day for me. Thanks for letting me win that first game, by the way. Saved a little bit of my pride."

"Let you?" I couldn't help but scoff. "I never let anyone win anything. It's possible it took me until the second game to be fully warmed up. But, uh, sorry about that. Also for not recognising you tonight. You must think I'm some arrogant bitch."

"With a career like yours, I don't think you'd have the storage space to remember every poor girl you ever sent crying back to the locker room. At least I got a kiss on the cheek at the net when you were done demolishing me. I'd have been even more bummed to just get a handshake."

There was that sparkle in her eyes again. Maybe saving me from the press hadn't been her only motivation. I hardly dared entertain the idea. Tennis I could do. Flirting? There wouldn't be trophies for that any time soon.

"So since you know where I'll be tomorrow," I began, because once the idea had struck me, I had to speak up instantly or lose the nerve, "any chance you might be in the same place?"

Toni laughed. "You mean will I be on Centre Court at Wimbledon? It's funny, but they don't give out tickets to the people dumped out in the second round."

"I have one to spare," I said, because I did. Three, in fact. "As long as you don't mind sitting in the box. The cameras can be…" I was going to say *too much*, but I didn't want to sound spoiled about all the attention. "But the Royals will be in. My Swedish ones and the local ones. That will pull focus."

"Well, I'd be an idiot to turn down a free ticket, right?" Toni stepped closer, and just when I began to think a kiss might be in my future, she stuck her hand out instead. She hailed a taxi, and miraculously for a Friday night, the first one with a light on actually stopped.

"Just go to the collection window at the ticket office, I'll put one under your name." It occurred to me then I had only a vague grasp of her surname. "Actually, could you just remind me…"

"Antonia Cortes Ruiz," she said, close to my ear, and the soft *S* with the rolled *R*'s made for a very pleasant sensation. "Now get some rest. I don't want to come all the way to watch you lose tomorrow because you were too tired from choking on martinis."

"Deal." I didn't say that I felt more awake than I had all day. Instead, I got into the taxi, wondering what it might be like to be the kind of person who asked Toni to get in alongside me.

Turned out I wouldn't get to know, because the door closed behind me and she simply waved from the pavement.

"Where to, love?" the driver asked.

"Bathgate Road, please. SW19." I hoped that by not saying the *W* word he wouldn't make the association. But there it was: the flickering glance back to the rear-view mirror as we pulled into traffic.

"Wimbledon?" he said, and I nodded without making eye contact. "Here, has anyone ever told you that you look a bit like—"

"I get it all the time," I said, faking a laugh. "That would be nice, huh?"

He accepted the denial at face value; people always do. It's easier to accept that the unlikely isn't really happening. "Would be nice to have her money, that's for sure."

I rested my head against the inside of the cab, feeling the vibration of the tyres against the road rattling through my head, that strange tickling that seemed to go through my teeth. Traffic was slow as drunken revellers spilled into the street and buses competed with other taxis for places to stop. Soon, though, we were heading for the river and quieter roads.

When the orange lights started to blur, I let my eyes close for the rest of the journey. I hoped it would prevent any conversation, the awkward questions that I never knew how to answer. London sped by outside, but I didn't see any of it.

CHAPTER THREE

I ALWAYS WOKE UP FAR too early on the day of a final, though these days it was just force of habit. Years ago it had been pure nerves; often I'd hardly been able to sleep at all. I'd been a jittery, jumpy wreck of a girl, barely able to hold my racquet right or answer a simple question.

That soon went, with practice. The regular, manageable amount of anxiety still fizzled and crackled in my veins, but I had learned how to seem completely cool on the outside, to seem like a major final was just any other three sets of tennis.

Sitting around the house all morning to quietly worry was not an option, especially once the interns had started packing up all the extra stuff I hadn't even asked for. Some would head to my home in Los Angeles, more still to my family home in Stockholm, but the staff would get their share too. Who else would do these crazy jobs with long hours and so much travel if they weren't getting some perks? All the sportswear, cool gadgets, and keychains a person could ask for.

The permanent staff I knew well by now. Most of them had been with "Team Larsson," as my mother infuriatingly called it, for more than five years. Some had come fresh from university, while others had been hanging in there for a professional tennis break that never came. They made my life pretty seamless, and most importantly, these people were my travelling family most of the year. We laughed, argued, played stupid games—anything to pass the time in a new country every other week. They made it fun to be in the gym or on court every day.

"When's the car?" I asked Parisa when she appeared bearing a smoothie and a bottle of water. Looking chic as ever in her tailored cream-coloured dress and fitted navy blazer, she had her glossy dark hair down in loose waves for a change instead of the professional buns and twists I was used to.

I was dressed for the day ahead too, only in my case that meant a pair of crisp white shorts and a matching white T-shirt, temporarily covered by what the kit maker called a 'presentation' jacket, but really it was just a tracksuit top with a few more splashes of colour. Only my shoes were waiting to be put on, from force of habit and maybe a little bit of superstition: I preferred to wear slider sandals until I got to the court area. Tennis shoes went on only in the locker room, along with my actual match kit. That was just a replica of my current shorts and shirt, but with the date and our names embroidered on the chest. I was honestly just glad I didn't have to do my own laundry with the amount I must have generated.

"Morning to you too, party animal. You know Britta is lying in wait to murder you for that, yes?"

Parisa's accent still carried a strong current of her native Pakistan, and her darker skin next to mine as she handed over my necessary drinks made my year-round tan seem to fade in an instant.

"Oh, let her. I went out for one drink, and I'm all ready to go today. It's not like I make a habit of it."

"Apparently there was some social-media buzz about you, from people on the street. Nobody got a clear enough shot, though, so you got lucky."

"If either of the men playing their final tomorrow went out tonight it would be 'look, he's just being a guy,'" I complained. "I don't mind people judging, but I mind when it's really about controlling what the little ladies are doing."

Parisa rolled her eyes and made no attempt to hide that was exactly what she was doing. "Lots of good luck messages and gifts coming in. You want to look before we go?"

I shook my head. Did I ever? It wasn't that I was ungrateful—quite the opposite. I just didn't like to weigh the whole day down in the expectations of others. A final should be nerve-wracking enough on its own, surely?

"You're going to make me do social media from the grounds, aren't you?"

"It's nice that you've stopped fighting it. Most people will never get to experience this, so you're shining a light on the sacred—"

I held my hand up to stop her. Parisa could wax poetic for hours if I set her off. I kept telling her she was wasted on my straightforward life. She owed the world a book of all her wonderful stories. To that, she usually snorted and started talking to me about photoshoots or personal appearances, knowing how much I hated them. "Were you able to fix that ticket I asked you about?"

"Not like you to be sending midnight texts, but yes. Darren in the box office is a sweetheart, totally in love with me, you know how it is. It helps that this woman already has security clearance as a player."

I don't know why I was so invested in Toni being there, not when there was still a good chance she'd think I was joking and not even show. Who'd brave the crowds on the last weekend of Wimbledon unless they were sure of a ticket? I should have asked for her number. Or maybe I should have learned how to flirt at least ten years ago.

With carefully timed lingering over my smoothie and a cowardly dash to the front door, I managed to get in the first car with Parisa and avoid my mother until we reached the Wimbledon grounds. From the moment we stepped out of the cars after the short drive, it was controlled chaos. Designated press areas allowed for photographs of each player's arrival, but there was also a gauntlet of VIPs and staff who all wanted to wish me luck, grab a quick picture, or generally say hello.

Although it didn't help my icy reputation, I kept the smiles polite and my earbuds firmly in place. Parisa and my mother ran interference on all the requests, and as silly as it sounded, I specifically had to refuse handshakes. Four years ago an overly enthusiastic billionaire sponsor had tried to shake my hand with both of his massive ones. He'd practically crushed bones in the attempt, and I still grumbled sometimes that he was the reason I hadn't won that particular US Open.

Lars, my fitness trainer, and Eziamaka, my physio, set to work getting my equipment and general area prepared once we entered the shared ladies' locker rooms. At that point I could avoid my mother no longer, and she pounced.

"Elin."

"Mamma? You know, Ezi looks almost ready to do some stretches with me..."

One glance from her shut that down fast. "Nice evening?" She switched to Swedish as soon as Lars left the room, a sure sign that she didn't want to be overheard or understood. "I'm sure I heard wrong about you looking for silly distractions before a final."

I rarely got to speak in my native tongue other than with my parents and the occasional meeting with old friends, but it was probably good to take a refresher. One way or another, I'd be meeting with the King and Queen of Sweden later today. They didn't always travel to my finals, but Wimbledon they had a soft spot for. Maybe they just liked the short flight.

"I was just stretching my legs," I said, finding a euphemism. "No harm, no pictures."

"There better not be. Just make sure you win today, then anything that might show up will only be a detail. They'll say it's impressive that you could be so irresponsible and still the best in the world."

"You know, Mamma, your compliments are a little hard to find sometimes."

She snorted, moving back to English effortlessly. "Elin, be serious. You're in touching distance of the all-time Slam record. Do you really want to lose your appetite for winning now?"

"Well, I'm thirty-two," I answered. "And some would say I've already won plenty. Maybe it's time to give someone else a chance."

"I don't think so. Even if it was, don't start today. I can't bear the thought of you losing to that woman."

That woman being Celeste Rutherford, ranked number three in the world and second seed for this tournament. Which, in case it wasn't obvious from those numbers, meant we spent a lot of time breathing down each other's necks. The reason for my mother's animosity wasn't rooted in that, though. No, we Larsson women respect a fellow competitor, and we understood that it wasn't personal when we were on court.

No, Celeste had the almost unique honour of being my ex-girlfriend, and though we'd never officially been outed or talked seriously about coming out as a couple, it had been a poorly kept secret for two years. Then she broke my heart, which turned out to be pretty easy to do, and we've been friendly rivals ever since. Which was a really short way of describing something that involved quite so much crying.

In our upcoming match, I was competing against her for what could be my twentieth Grand Slam title, or her fifth. A whole head taller than me, Celeste had a strength on top of her athleticism that my own frame would never be able to match. Our styles contrasted wildly, but it usually made for an entertaining spectacle.

Wimbledon crowds had claimed us both as their own at different points, even though I'm from Stockholm and Celeste is from Detroit. Maybe they just liked our attitude, but I was glad for both of us, especially after Celeste's first French Open win had been marred by a few racist shouts. She had risen above, classy as ever, but I had wanted to march into the stands and set about them with my racquet.

Like I said—wildly different styles.

Ezi approached with her exercise bands, ready to check on my now quite-recovered calf muscle that had bugged me through the Australian Open and almost until Paris. Despite my mother mellowing a little, physio was still preferable. I checked my kit was laid out and went over to start Ezi's exercises.

"What have you been up to?" she asked as soon as we were alone. "You know your mother blames us when you go off the rails."

"One drink is off the rails now? I was restless; I wanted to relax." It was hard to maintain dignified outrage with my legs in the air and my back pressed into a mat on the floor, but I attempted it anyway. "You're just mad I didn't invite you."

"I don't go drinking in fancy hotels, but thanks."

"I met someone." I blurted it out, not even sure what I meant. All I knew was that Ezi, who could inflict pain on me daily and still make me like her, was someone I could trust. "I mean, just socially. I don't know if it was…"

"This was the last-minute ticket? Smooth, Larsson."

"Hey, I might not have game, but I do get some cool freebies. Besides, she plays too."

Ezi pushed a little harder, making my hip grumble. "You mean she's a player?"

"No, literally. Plays tennis. Antonia Cortes…something."

"Ruiz. You might want to get better with names. Or she'll find out what a spoiled princess you are."

I laughed. She never was shy about calling me on my bullshit. "Come on, finish your torture session. I need to go play a warmup game after this."

All the routine and preparation didn't get me ready for that last stretch. Alone in the private dressing room with the screens all tuned to anything but tennis, it was always a little like what I thought a confessional would feel like. Would the umpire pull back a little curtain on the wall and ask about my sins? Apparently not.

At least the sponsors had picked out some great outfits for this tournament. Unlike the other slams, Wimbledon still insisted on its all-white dress code, dating back to the foundation of the All England club. While we could have a splash of colour and pattern, we all looked quite immaculate in our tennis whites. They even requested all our medical equipment be white too, if possible. From Band-Aids to knee supports. And the underwear too, of course, just in case we sweated through the top layer, which we almost always did.

Some of the players groused about it, but I liked looking so spotless. At least until the first lunge to return a low net shot, and then all bets were off. Grass stains didn't look good on anybody.

Even if I hadn't done this for a living, I'd probably still be into my trainers just as much. They've always been the biggest perk of the job, and these brand-new ones that I'd only worn for an hour or two to break in were practically moulded to my feet. I knew it was stupid to think they made me any lighter or faster, but it felt like they did. Sometimes silly little psychological edges like that made all the difference, like wings on my heels. I was Hermes or maybe Nike, but the shoes were all Adidas.

The wardrobe varied a lot over the season, but I relished being back in all white with the famous three lines down the side in black. It was a flattering look in the full-length mirrors. Moments like these, I actually got to confront my appearance. Most of the time, my body was more of a machine to me, something to push and prod at, to find out what more it could do. I knew I looked okay, even good sometimes. I just didn't let myself think about it once I was out in front of the crowd. I pushed the white sweatband into place on my forehead and snapped the matching wristbands. That and wearing sliders until changing into my match shoes was as close as I came to any kind of ritual.

After what seemed like an eternity, an usher came to knock on the door. "We're ready for you, Miss Larsson." Oh yeah, no *Ms* at Wimbledon. And the married women got changed to *Mrs* even if they hadn't changed their surnames. We'd only recently gotten them to stop calling married women by their husband's names on the scoreboards, and sometimes it really did feel like another century there.

Speaking of married women, I came face-to-face with Celeste who was waiting with her usher in the narrow hallway. I froze for a moment, unsure how to greet her. She took the lead, coming over to shake my hand and pulling me into a hug right after.

"It's been a while," she said, like we hadn't done a bunch of events together this year. So many of the smaller tournaments like a pre-event shoot with all the top seeds, and we still had one of our favourite charities in common. Oh, and did I mention I'd dumped her out in the quarterfinals in the Australian Open? Well, that too. It still hadn't evaporated the lingering awkwardness between us. If most groups of lesbian friends were incestuous, then double that for tennis.

"Best of luck out there," I replied, as we followed the head usher who would lead us out onto the hallowed ground of Centre Court. Behind us another pair of ushers carried our kit bags, stuffed full of racquets and tape, spare shoes and socks and a spare replica of this outfit in case I tore anything. I would have had drinks and towels, but we had our own fridges stocked on court, and using the provided regulation towels was required. As revenge, all the players liked to steal them as souvenirs. I'd left tournaments with an entire bag of contraband towels in the past.

As we made our way through the cream-coloured corridors, lined with tennis-themed art and various dignitaries, I nodded to each of the armed services personnel who manned each new stretch of floor. It felt like the least we could all do, invite them for a nice day out and some tennis—another stark reminder of my privileged existence.

Down a small, open staircase and the line of umpires and officials stood waiting for us. I was top seed, so I got to go out first. That also meant I was first to shake the Chairman's hand, and Celeste did the same right after me.

Even still, tucked in the belly of the building, I could feel the buzz of the crowd. It was more than a feeling, almost a tangible thing. The sheer presence of them seemed to resonate through the bricks and wood, though they were only restless and not even cheering yet.

Then the final stretch—which was apparently the right time to give us giant bouquets to carry out on court. Another tradition I'd never understood; they were taken off us moments later when we sat down, and most times I don't think I ever saw the bouquet again.

Exiting the door into the last little tunnel created by screens that shielded us from public view, I felt a familiar spike of panic. Nothing obvious, just my heart seemed to clench and I briefly tasted metal on my tongue. I glanced back at Celeste before we emerged into the crowd's hungry gaze, but she already had her game face on. I no longer existed to her as Elin the person, the one-time girlfriend. Now I was just The Opponent, that walking, talking obstacle between her and the prize she wanted.

Walking onto the grass brought a deafening roar from the first step, the dragon of anticipation yanked to life by the first person in thousands to react. Unlike after matches, I raised no hand in acknowledgement, and I didn't look around for familiar faces either. I did the required turn and curtsy to the Royal Box, populated by my own royal family as well as the younger members of the British one. Not a bad turnout, considering the men's final would pull a lot of focus the following day.

Just like Celeste had already done, I let my world shrink down to the challenge ahead. The grass felt springy beneath my feet, despite the dry sandy patches from two solid weeks of action. The sky above wasn't promising, a dull shade of grey that threatened rain before the afternoon was out. I hoped we'd be done before delays and the closing of the roof came into play.

I took my seat on the far side of the umpire's tower, nodding as my bags were set down, reaching for my first racquet as soon as someone whisked the flowers away. People liked to think we had a lucky one or some superstition like that. We didn't get the chance to get attached, not with how hard the modern game was on the kit. The strings were different almost every match, and when the strain started to show on a frame, it would be instantly and effortlessly replaced. I couldn't count how many I got through per season, but I wouldn't bet below fifty.

Finals were always slow to get started thanks to all the extra ceremony, so I got back on my feet and kept my weight shifting from one foot to the other, minimal activity so I didn't start to cool back down. The usual announcements rang out, and the crowd began to settle into their seats. Just the coin toss to come, a simple matter of which end to start and who would serve first. I'd long since stopped minding which of those I got. Winning meant starting strong regardless.

The umpire called us both to the net, where we earnestly shook hands again. The call was mine as the bronze coin flipped and twisted in the air.

Game on.

CHAPTER FOUR

OKAY, SO IT WASN'T SUPPOSED to go down that way. Forty-five minutes played and I was one set down, almost broken in the second game of the second set. Which in tennis terms was a polite way of saying I hadn't really got started and had somehow become even worse from there.

Not exactly the play expected from a champion.

Celeste, though, I had to give it to her. She'd always known my game well, but this time she'd come equipped to thwart me at every turn. Along with staying in close for every drop shot that barely cleared the net, she was somehow back on the baseline whenever I tried to drive a hard ball right past her. The one consolation was that her tactics had to be draining, and elite athlete or not, she'd be tiring if I could keep myself alive through this second set.

Which meant not letting her break me now, with 40 points to my 30. Serving had always been one of my strong points, but she seemed determined to return everything I hurled at her, like the concept of a nonreturnable ace hadn't been invented yet.

I realised in that moment, plucking the offered fresh ball from the ball girl's outstretched hand, that for all I'd claimed to be fatigued of winning, I really didn't enjoy the alternative very much. Everyone lost games, sets, and matches, no matter how strong or steady. But in a year where I hadn't gone all the way in either Australia or France, I was putting extra pressure on myself to win in London and New York. There was no point blaming that niggling calf injury either. At any given time, most of us were playing through some kind of pain or recovering from it.

My next mistake was glancing towards the boxes. Most attention in the ground and on television while there was a lull in play would be on the Royal box. I had met the King and Queen of Sweden countless times before, but it was always a polite, reserved conversation with them. They seemed happy in the company of the younger British royals, the ones who had famous weddings and very photogenic offspring. None of that was particularly distracting or unusual.

No, the mistake was making eye contact with my mother. She looked halfway out of her mind about how badly I was playing, her usually smooth blonde hair clutched until it was all out of place. When I met her gaze, she frowned, before hiding her face behind her hands. Great. It could be commitment to not illegally coaching me during the match, but I was pretty sure she was just pissed off.

But then came unexpected redemption. In the row behind her sat Toni, who was clearly in the middle of arguing some point of tennis with my father. Only when she saw me did she stop, making a gesture by pointing to the side of her head that basically translated to 'get your head in the game.' It wasn't expert-level coaching by any means, but it was enough to calm the rising sick feeling of panic that was sloshing around inside me.

Concentrate. Focus. All those useful words that had gotten me through every other time. I'd been distracted all week, in truth, and it was coming back to bite me on the butt.

Not anymore. Not with a pretty girl to impress. I mean, did anyone ever have better motivation than that? Other than a crushing will to win at all costs, but mine seemed to have taken the day off. In its place, I'd take anything that might work.

Celeste didn't see it coming. She seemed to think I was getting nervous about serving, since she was coming back so strong. Instead of my usual precise, calculated approach that some critics said belonged more to chess than tennis, I reverted to a style I hadn't played much since my first few years after breaking out.

An all-out assault, basically. I served like I was trying to put the ball into the Earth's crust, and I launched myself into leaps to hit forehands with deadly force. I had won intermittently by playing that way in my teens and twenties, overwhelming other players with force and speed. Having become so disciplined, it felt like being a kid again to just go for it.

It worked too. Celeste could play that way herself, but countering it wasn't easy. I'd switched to a more controlled style to minimise the toll it took on my body, reducing injuries and making matches quicker and more predictable. Then came this Saturday in July, and suddenly it was "anything goes."

My hair kept coming loose, and I was red in the face from exerting myself so recklessly, but as each muscle group burned and stretched that little bit harder, I only felt more alive.

Changing ends felt like a needless distraction, and so did every line call dispute or extra bounce between serves. I chugged down vitamin drinks at the appointed times and let that replenish my body as best it could. Turning the second set around finally pushed Celeste to abandon her game plan, but we were deep into the third and final set before she could get any traction on me again. Once or twice I caught her looking at me like we'd never met. She had never played me like this. Being a few years my junior, our paths hadn't crossed until I was well on my way to being the "Ice Princess," who was only ever cool.

I didn't look at anyone else until I heard the umpire call 40-love in the last game I needed to win in order to clinch the thing. *Championship point*, it would say on screens all around the world. Three championship points, in fact, meaning I could still afford to mess it up once or twice.

I could feel the air cooling. I wasn't waiting around again to get caught in the rain— not with the trophy almost in my grasp.

When I looked to my box, I saw Toni practically falling into the row in front, she was watching so intently. My mother had rescued herself from her slump and sat there with fists clenched, willing me across that final line.

I bounced the ball once, twice. Tested its weight in my hand and then gave its final bounce. Then it happened in that slow motion that I could never recapture outside of the moment. The ball, tossed to just the right height. My other arm arcing up to meet it, the sweet kiss of strings against racquet at exactly the position and speed I had asked of them both.

Ask anyone who hits things for a living and they'll tell you: You hear it when the contact is sweet, that perfect connection, where what happens next seems preordained by forces greater than anything you may or may not have done.

An ace. No return. Celeste's shoulders drooping as the ball hit the back wall of the court, utterly beyond her. My knees, how they gave way in sheer relief and maybe exhaustion. Falling to the dry, sandy ground, knees and shins barely registering the prickly grass. I let go of my racquet. I remember that much, but I didn't hear it land over the cheers that went up. If our entrance had been a dragon, this was a whole army of them.

Just one formality left: shaking Celeste's hand and the umpire's in turn. I made myself get up, and as soon as we exchanged those pleasantries, I was free to react, to enjoy the chaos around me.

I cried out, something primal and incoherent that wasn't a word. Just a feeling, the high of winning as potent and new as it had been that very first time. On and on the crowd cheered, and I felt the sudden compulsion to see what I'd seen so many others do over the years—never me, not rule-keeping, well-behaved me.

On shaking legs I got up and jogged towards the stands full of people, seeing the path to my destination as though it had been illuminated in neon. Used to it by now, most people either moved out of my way or tried to help me climb to that first level, over the wooden hoardings to where my family waited. I didn't feel any of the hands on me, helping and guiding. I was on a mission.

Moments later I reached them, and the little crowd of loved ones surged towards me. My father reached me first, ecstatic to pull me into a bear hug even though I knew he'd have been reading the newspaper on his phone during most of the match. He may not have loved the sport, but I knew he loved me. A kiss on the cheek from Parisa, and so many shouts of congratulations from my friends and colleagues. I'd name them all, but their faces were a blur at that point, and to most people it would just sound like reading an Ikea catalogue out loud anyway.

But somewhere in the clamour—and I needed to get back down on court; there were going to be presentations, and oh wow, this was not a safe place to be standing—Toni pushed her way through. She kissed me on the cheek, and my knees wanted to give out in an entirely different way.

"Well done," she muttered against my cheek, and it was a miracle I could hear anything at all.

A glance back at the court and I could see the usual presentation ceremony starting to form. With care and some helping hands, I turned around and bounced back down to floor level.

The loser—sorry, runner-up—always got their presentation first. Unlike when I started out, now the ceremony was conducted by the television presenters from the BBC. They had to address the people around the court on an echoing microphone while making the audience on television feel part of it all too. Celeste and I sat back in our chairs as the ball boys and girls formed a guard of honour. That was something that irked me in English—shouldn't they be ball children? There were countless questions I'd learned not to ask along the way.

Then, like almost all the other times, the adrenaline spiked and events got sort of fuzzy. I waited my turn, I lifted my big gold plate for the few minutes I got to hold it, and I drank in the applause. People say the British are reserved. I think those people have never seen them at a sporting event.

The on-court interview was short, my own voice echoing back at me like a nightmare as I thanked the fans and congratulated Celeste on making it a great final to play in. Then the final round of photos and cheers, signing a few giant tennis balls and posters as I escaped the court.

Not that it was much of an escape. While I had been blushing and bowing and celebrating, all the people who had paid thousands or been personally invited were waiting for their VIP moment. Any hope of a minute to gather myself or a quick shower was non-existent. I suppose royalty and other athletes were used to it, but I would still get self-conscious that I was shaking hands while wearing clothes partly soaked through with sweat. The neat presentation tracksuit jacket covered the worst of it, but I was relieved when the procession finally ended and I could duck into a bathroom and splash cold water on my face.

Celeste slipped in right behind me, and thanks to the red velvet ropes, not even the VIP guests had access to this players' area bathroom. Once upon a time this would have been our excuse for a post-match moment of misbehaving, and there was a way she looked at me like she was remembering that too.

"You got me. You got me good out there. I've never seen you play that way. Well, outside of watching your early matches online."

"I always had it in my locker. That's what they say, right?" Being near-fluent in English always left a few terms feeling strange on my tongue. "We're okay?"

Celeste gave me a long look in the ornate mirror hanging over the sinks. She took a step closer, placed her hand right next to mine. Not quite touching, but close enough.

"We could be more than okay, Elin. We've got this place all to ourselves, if you wanted a different kind of rematch."

I couldn't control the way my eyebrows shot up. Without thinking, I took a half-step back. "Uh, Celeste? We broke up. You married someone else. We—"

"Noticed the new girl in your box. You going back to doubles?" Celeste interrupted, changing the subject like she hadn't suggested anything at all. I sagged just a little in relief. She leaned against the sink next to me, her white wraparound skirt and vest top a perfect contrast against her deeply brown skin. Her muscle definition was as excellent as ever, but the pang of insecurity drowned quickly in my post-win adrenaline. "I thought she quit the circuit. Ruiz, right?"

I nodded, before jumping in to correct. "Just injuries, I think." I'd looked her up that morning when fighting boredom and mild jitters. "She's cracked the top one hundred again quickly enough, but no. No doubles, not at this stage of my career. The only way I'll go back to doubles is if—"

"You can't keep up in singles anymore. That's what I thought." Celeste leaned in to kiss me on the cheek. It had real tenderness, not the brisk continental both-cheeks kiss we'd exchanged over the net. "Come on, get back out and bask in your glory, woman."

"I had the good part; the only fun left for me now is the cheque. And we don't even get those anymore, just a nice soulless bank transfer."

"Your entire career is basically just torturing your introvert self for being amazing at something you can't do in private, isn't it?"

I laughed. Celeste always had been able to cut through the bullshit. She certainly could see right through me. "Save that quote for next time they want to make an inspirational montage about me, hmm?"

"Oh, they're probably cutting some right now. Dollars to donuts they're already showing it on the BBC, but it'll take ESPN an hour or so. I can't wait to never watch them."

"Will I see you in Cincinnati?"

"And the shoot for the... Wait, what's the next one? Watches, maybe? Or some kind of sports deodorant?"

Enough to make me groan. Endorsements were big money, but an even bigger pain in the ass. "I'll ask Parisa. She keeps all that stuff straight."

"Well done, seriously. See you out there."

I liked that about Celeste. Other people would retreat into solitary after losing, holed up in a hotel room to throw things around, or taking an hour-long shower just to cry. I'd had those kinds of finals myself. Instead, she'd be out there with the grace and composure of a champion, just one who didn't quite live up to her own standards on this particular afternoon.

Which meant I really could hide no longer. I was also starving. Winning tennis matches took a lot of energy, and I burned through calories even harder than I burned through racquets and tennis shoes. Taking evasive action from where my mother had cornered our King, I edged around part of the room to tackle the buffet table.

"Carbs before champagne?" asked a familiar voice, with its attractive Spanish lilt. "A woman after my own heart. But I brought you a drink all the same."

Toni handed over a flute of champagne, her own already half-empty. Thirsty despite my water and energy drinks downed between games and sets, I tipped the glass back and finished it in one big mouthful.

"Thank you. I think I needed that."

"Congratulations. That was…something. Although you're probably really sick of hearing that by now."

I couldn't help smirking as I confessed the truth. "Oh, I might look like it's all too much to bear, but you'd be surprised how much you want to keep hearing it. Trust me, try being on the other side of it, and you miss it a lot."

"Celeste gave you a good match. For a minute there…"

"Well." I found myself to eager to change the subject. "You scrub up nicely, out of tennis gear."

"I figured, being in VIP and all. Thanks for that, did I thank you already?"

I shook my head. "Not necessary, it's a nice perk. My civilian friends have all had a turn, and they only care so much about strawberries and champagne after a while." *Great. Way to sound like a lonely loser whose friends don't even like her.* "Is there anyone here you wanted to meet? I could introduce you."

"Nobody is going to want to talk to the girl ranked ninety-nine when the winner is in the room," Toni said, but she squeezed my arm to show she was joking. "I have a thing later, actually. But I'll see you tomorrow, at the Champions Dinner? My federation are sending me as their one guest."

"Spain only get one guest? But you have—"

"Oh no, I live in Spain now, and I train there. But I'm Mexican, so I play for Mexico."

"Ah, sorry. There's so many people to keep track of, and as you can see, I'm no social butterfly."

"You're doing great from where I'm standing."

My mother chose that moment to visibly wave me over to join her royal conversation.

"Excuse me, I have to go be very Swedish and downplay my achievements a lot."

"Not too much, you hear? See you tomorrow."

And before I could so much as shake her hand, she was gone. I couldn't blame Toni; I wanted nothing more than to leave myself. Instead, I made my way over, without food, to engage in more small talk, this time in the more relaxed form of Swedish.

"Do you have a dress, for tomorrow?" the queen asked me, bringing my attention back to the formal dinner that I usually did everything to duck out of after the official red-carpet photos.

"I do," I confirmed. "Blue, of course. I'm really looking forward to it."

"Well, that makes a change." My mother couldn't help commenting, since almost every big party was a battle of wills between us. "Every time I have to drag you there."

I gave an uneasy laugh, hoping the subject would change. An American news crew broke free of the press area and gave me an excuse to move on. So what if I walked to the huge windows overlooking the way out, hoping to catch a glimpse of Toni? It didn't mean anything. Well, not much of anything, anyway.

CHAPTER FIVE

PARISA YANKED HER BEDROOM DOOR open after I knocked for the third time. "You'd better be dying. Or have killed someone. It's barely eight. On a *Sunday*."

"I was thinking about my dress," I admitted, trying to catch her attention quickly. While I got up at six most days for my run, no one could ever accuse my personal assistant of doing the same. Usually I didn't mind; it gave me a couple of hours each day not talking about rankings and appearances and photoshoots.

"That's a first. I can't get you to think about your dresses when you're actually wearing them, so what gives?"

"It's just… You had a couple of other options that you said were better?"

"I said they were sexier, but yeah. There's a Carolina Herrera and a Givenchy somewhere in the pile I have to return. Why?"

"No harm in looking at our options, is there?"

"Are you going to wear it to watch the Men's Final or something?" Parisa had almost finished waking up. I had to get out of there before she got too curious. "Or do you want to change between the red carpet and the event? Because people keep asking if we're going to bring back the traditional dance…"

"Sure, I'll dance if you want." We both blinked at each other for a moment at that revelation. So what? I liked dancing. I'd taken classes before tennis swallowed my whole life at thirteen. I could even, to a point, keep the beat. The rhythm in most songs was just like varying the speed of a rally, to me. "What does that buy me?"

"I'll look out every dress option we have." Parisa pulled her hair up into a temporary bun, all business. "Does this mean I can get someone in for hair and make-up too?"

"Fine," I sighed. "Do your worst."

"If you're really in a good mood, you'll go with your mother to the match today."

"The last thing I feel like today is more tennis, but if I can convince her to come get a massage, then fine."

"The team thanks you."

Part one of my mission secured, I made my way downstairs to the kitchen. Naturally, Mother had beaten me there. She had the juicer running but most importantly a full cafetière of some insanely rich-smelling coffee. I swooped in to pour my own mug, but she batted my hand away and poured generous cups for both of us. Cream and sugar were already out, and she didn't grumble when I reached for both. Clearly the smudged mascara under her eyes, and the fact that she was still in pyjamas and robe, meant she had stayed out for a night worth this morning's calorific indulgence too.

"You don't have the papers out yet?" I asked. Usually the morning after a final, I'd be greeted with the papers sorted by favourable and unfavourable coverage laid out on the nearest surface. "Not like you, Mamma."

"It's still early," she replied, voice rasping a little. "And I already checked the important ones on my tablet. They're happy: You made it interesting for them."

"That's one way of saying it," I said with a snort. "The other would be that Celeste wiped the floor with me in the first set. We showed her, though, didn't we?"

These were the best times for my mother and I. Winning always gave her that temporary respite from the endless pushing she had devoted her life to. I shouldn't complain; all her energy and drive would have been for nothing if I hadn't wanted to do this. It was easy to forget that after all these years. At first she had wanted me to be any other teenager, not dropping out of school at fourteen to go professional and play in my first championships.

"I was worried about you out there," Mother said. "But you took control like I knew you could, Elin. Very good." The compliments were rare, and I wasn't ashamed to bask in them for a moment. "Of course it could have been a quicker start for you if Friday night had been spent in proper preparation."

"Mamma…"

"Fine, fine. You won; I have no case. But this is the critical time, dear daughter. You need to focus on breaking your records before you can even think about slowing down or retiring. You're so close to having the most Grand Slams of any player, ever. Don't let yourself fall short."

"And if I break that record I can just walk away?" I asked. "Who says I'll be any more ready then?"

"Only you can tell," she replied. "But until you do, I'm going to train you as hard as I ever have and keep planning for the next win. Now, how are you feeling after playing so differently yesterday?"

"Exhausted," I had to admit. "I was thinking of having a real massage this afternoon—not sports massage, something more relaxing. Can I book you one too? Call it my thank you."

She sipped at her coffee, eyes closed for a moment. "That might be nice, yes. Don't think this means you can skip the dinner."

Parisa showed up then to save me an argument, half-dressed with a bundle of couture bags over one arm. "Right, these are all the dresses you have to choose from, and I sent a text to a friend at Harvey Nicks to be on standby, in case you're feeling extra fussy."

My mother stared at Parisa, before a suspicious look made its way to me.

"This is…more enthusiastic than normal."

"I won!" I reminded them. "Really, it's ungrateful to be a bitch about a party being thrown half in my honour. I've decided to enjoy myself. You know, since I can go out drinking without a bunch of other adults tracking my movements?"

That shut them up, at least for a little while. I grabbed the dresses from Parisa, draining my coffee mug on the way out of the kitchen.

"Going to try these on! Won't be long!"

The red carpet wasn't as bad as in previous years. After all, it was a Sunday evening in a city with a hundred other cool things going on. The pressure was in winning the damn thing, not celebrating it.

I managed not to trip in the ridiculous heels Parisa picked out, and for once I felt like a bit of a princess in the navy satin dress we'd decided on. Strapless and cut in all the right places, it definitely showed off my arms. My one small tattoo—a rebellious souvenir from the first major tour that neither of my parents had been on with me—had a smudge of make-up covering it. When playing it was always covered by the racer back of my sports bras, but this dress left that whole section on display.

Did I mention that what I knew about fashion could be written on the white stripe running through a tennis ball? Honestly, if it wasn't about the newest rubber soles on tennis shoes, I had less than zero chance of knowing about it.

I knew that the dress looked good, though. If I had to play dress up, I liked garments that looked classic. The one good crossover between professional sport and fashion was that they liked you lean, so I had that going for me, although my thigh muscles made the skirt of the dress a little tighter than I think the designer intended. The split in the material certainly drew plenty of glances.

As was tradition, the Men's and Ladies' Singles winners were photographed together. Jürgen, the men's champ, was far better at all this press than me and better than most people on the tour. He was tall as all hell, and when the girl who's over a metre-seventy said that, it meant properly tall. With close-cropped dark curls atop stylised shaving on the sides, and some designer stubble, he often looked like a male model who'd wandered into a game of tennis by accident.

The press often seemed to think Sweden and Germany, where Jürgen hailed from, were basically the same country, not helped by the fact that we'd played mixed doubles together at a few tournaments when I still did that sort of thing.

That should have been the point where I got to say that despite his natural gifts, wealth, and success, Jürgen was a surprisingly kind and shy sort of guy.

Nope, in fact he was exactly the worst type of asshole that you'd expect. Entitled, smug, and prone to treating everyone around him like his personal property. He had made his way through the women's side of the tour like a dose of chlamydia, and rumour had it that he had in fact left some of the girls with an unwanted present like that. Those of us who didn't date men were usually beneath his notice, though it hadn't stopped him trying to "turn" us once or twice.

Only my success made him treat me with any kind of grudging respect, though I knew he told anyone who'd listen that it would be impossible to rack up career stats like mine in the men's competitions, since they were all so much more competitive. Point a television camera at him, though, and he was Prince Charming. Like I said: an asshole.

As usual he tried to pull me into an overly friendly hug, holding on too long and letting his hands drift just short of places that would trigger self-defence responses.

"Larsson, look at you. All dressed up like a real girl. Does this mean you're finally switching teams?"

"Not if you're what's waiting on the other side, no. You can let go, Jürgen. Otherwise the posse of models waiting for you might get the wrong idea."

That got him detangled from me quickly. We did the requisite press line—one question each, big smiles, and lots of candid shots. The trophies were wheeled back out for us to pose with. How strange to spend two weeks winning something only to hold it for less than ten minutes combined. We got replicas, of course, but those were already spirited away and packed for the journeys home.

I'd like to say I sensed her the moment she appeared on the red carpet, but the sporting press certainly recognised Toni quicker than I had at the bar. They didn't make as big of a fuss as they did over the top seeds, most of whom had been making the headlines for years. There was no denying Toni was gorgeous, though, and in my one—okay, maybe two—internet searches for her since Friday night, I had seen the modelling shots she'd done in her early career. A cursory look at the top stories suggested finding her in a bar on a Friday night hadn't been much of a coincidence.

The party girl of tennis? No wonder our paths hadn't crossed much. While Toni had been out in clubs with footballers and pop stars, I had been my usual boring self. In other sports, people would study their opponents to learn their weaknesses. I never had to do that. I played my way and they all came out trying to beat me. Sometimes the coaches would have me work on a specific shot or tactic, if the opponent had a particular weakness, but I didn't remember a lot of people outside of the matches as we played them. It was a handy excuse for not having recognised her right away, anyway.

All the same, before she was even free of the red carpet, I had handed back the trophy I'd sweated and strained for through all those matches and made my way right to her.

Of course our greeting with continental cheek kisses set off a flurry of clicks and flashes too, even though it was nothing more than friendly and I'd greeted a bunch of the other players that way already. We did the minimum of turning to pose together, before ducking through the doors into the ballroom set out for the occasion.

"You made it," I said, at a loss for anything more interesting.

"Yes, I got a taxi. I didn't have to swim the Thames or anything." She had that faintly amused look about her again. No doubt she found me a bit strange. Everyone else did. "Can I congratulate you again? Or will that just make you blush?"

"If you like. I'm more interested in what's for dinner, though. I have a week free from my tournament diet and I can't wait to eat something other than steamed protein."

"You wait for British catering to let yourself go?" Toni laughed for real that time. "That feels like a waste."

"Careful, you'll get us both thrown out." Nobody was close enough to overhear our conversation, though Jürgen was doing his best to leer at Toni from where he'd taken up his post at the open bar.

"I don't think they throw out the champ. Would leave the top table a little empty, no?"

"Oh, there's always an empty chair or two, after all the photo ops."

"Like your date? Only I didn't see you come in with anyone," Toni said, looking around as though I could be hiding someone in plain sight. "And there's no room in that dress to hide anyone else." Her look up and down was lingering, appreciative in a blatant sort of way. I liked it a whole lot better than when Jürgen had tried the same thing just minutes before.

"Yeah, I never quite got around to that. Not recently, anyway."

"Is that why you were out on Friday night?"

I laughed, but it came out with a funny little snort. The universe clearly wasn't going to give me any kind of a break.

"I really just wanted a dry martini. Anything else would be too much trouble."

"So you don't date? At all?"

I wanted to dodge the question altogether. Apart from anything else, it meant coming out all over again, even if I was pretty sure that Toni at least suspected the truth. Stalling for time, I gave her outfit the same appreciative once over that she had given mine. We all looked so different out of the unofficial uniform of T-shirts and tiny skirts.

Where I'd gone for a dark blue, she was human sunshine in a vibrant yellow that would look awful on me. I knew that much about fashion. Paired with subtle gold jewellery and her hair down in long dark curls, it was no wonder photographers had clamoured over her. I knew that a make-up team and stylists could bring out the best side of me when I did my endorsements for cars and watches and sportswear, but I'd never have that natural *wow* factor that kept drawing the attention of everyone who passed us.

I only realised I was staring, lost to the conversation, when Toni gave me a tentative smile. "Did I say something wrong?"

"Sorry, I'm so used to closing my mouth about my personal life that I think I've forgotten how to just talk about it."

"You don't have to—"

"No, I want to," I interrupted her. "I'm sure you know what this life is like. The practice schedule, the travel. I haven't really tried since my last breakup. It was just too much to..." I struggled to find the right word.

"Juggle?" Toni supplied. Her accent gave the *J* a soft *Y* sound, and I liked it a lot. "I get that. In fact it was the only upside of losing all that time to injury. I got to see what a normal life looked like again for a while. Keeping regular hours, being in one country for longer than a month. I can see why most people do that."

We were interrupted by the discreet bell calling us all to dinner. My mother was bearing down on me, still in a good mood from our relaxed day and all the positive attention. She hated when I wandered off at these things, and despite my change in attitude, she still didn't trust me to come and sit through dinner.

Worse, Jürgen had detached himself from the posse of beautiful girls and was making his way as though to escort me to dinner. That wasn't necessary, but he'd done it the other times we'd ended up champions together. I always suspected he didn't want me to make my own entrance and get any of the limelight to myself.

Only when he got to us, he found himself distracted by Toni.

"Ruiz, right?" He offered his hand to shake. "Didn't know you were back."

Oh. Of course he knew what had been happening with her.

"Yeah, only made it to the second round, though," Toni replied, shaking his hand so briefly I wasn't sure both hands had actually made contact. "Still, there's always the US Open."

"Oh, for sure. I plan on winning that one too. You in the mood, Larsson?"

I glared at him. Now we were back to his one-of-the-boys routine? God, he exhausted me.

"Right, let's go sit up front so everyone can stare at us." He offered his arm, which was at least gentlemanly. "My date's waiting in there, or I'd consider a last-minute trade," he added for Toni's benefit.

Well, that did it.

"Jürgen, there are actually women in this world not waiting around for your attention to land on them. Besides, Toni is here as my guest. She'll be sitting with me."

I gave her a pleading glance. No doubt she had her own table, probably with her friends from the circuit, and here I was yanking her up to the winners' table without even asking.

"Huh, I knew about you, Larsson, but I hadn't figured... You been recruiting?"

"For God's sake," I muttered, but I was relieved when Toni took my arm instead and we marched right into the main ballroom. Of course my entrance was greeted with applause—no different to coming on court, really; it's just polite—but there was a definite murmur around the room about me arriving with another woman. At least most people in the place would know who she was.

"Sorry for changing your plans for you," I said as we took our seats. My plus one's place card simply read *guest of Miss Larsson*. "I never do that. I hate bossy."

"I don't mind bossy," Toni said, leaning in closer to say it over the noise of the event. "Just for future reference." Then she turned to the person on her right, introducing herself and chatting to James, who was half of the winning Men's Doubles pair.

That left me to take a steadying sip of my water before launching into the pleasantries with the Chairman and host, who sat to my left.

Jürgen joined us, taking a seat next to his bored-looking date, and the lights dimmed across the room. Time for the speeches that would usher us into the meal and drinks.

Toni's thigh grazed mine, the long skirts of our dresses slipping against each other for a split-second as she turned back to face the stage. I felt that barest of contact like an electrical current through my leg.

It was going to be a long evening.

CHAPTER SIX

SOMEWHERE IN THE BUSTLE OF the evening, I lost track of Toni. I had forgotten how many people wanted to talk at these dinners, and at every break in the programme, a new person would drop by to congratulate or ask a question. The selfies took a lot of time too, and I wished after a while that I could politely decline. Unfortunately, this crowd was full of people who had paid a small fortune or donated to various charities to be there, and between them and my fellow pros looking for social-media buzz, my cheeks were starting to hurt from all the smiling.

And as for my speech? The less said about that, the better. If I had natural ability with my forehand and speed, someone had borrowed heavily from my public speaking ability to make up for it. Thankfully, I didn't have to say much beyond thanking people and making compliments about the organisation. That and always, always tell them that Wimbledon was your favourite tournament. Just like I said about the French Open in Paris and like I would hopefully say about the US Open in New York. Nobody minded a little white lie, as long as it was in their favour.

I hoped Toni had re-joined her friends at least or gone back to whatever plans she had before I hijacked her to piss off a misogynist with a great double-handed backhand. I scanned the room for her whenever I got a chance, and so many people offered to bring me drinks that I never needed to visit the bar myself.

A little high on champagne, given how rarely I got to drink, I sought out a quiet corner after the main courses had been served. Celeste was the one to join me.

"Having fun?" she asked. "When's the last time you stayed this late at one of these things?"

"You say that like I'm not a famous party animal," I teased her. "I remember us almost creating a scandal at the French Open dinner a few years back."

"That was too much champagne at work. In danger of that tonight?"

I shook my head. "Being sensible. Are you enjoying being gracious in defeat? Or are people avoiding you? I hate when they just do the pitying looks from afar."

"No, you hate losing," Celeste corrected with an easy smile. "Mostly compliments on a well-fought match. Could be worse."

I was pleased to see her, and Celeste had become a good friend in the way that only lesbian exes seem to manage, but the restlessness wouldn't leave me. I watched for every flash of bright colour in case it was Toni in her yellow dress.

"Mmm," I said to whatever Celeste continued with after that. It earned me a jab in the ribs.

"Distracted, much? Elin, are you seeing someone?"

"No," I answered, and it had the benefit of being the truth.

"Is there someone you wish you were seeing?" Celeste had never been a fan of my divided attention, and the end of our relationship had coincided with my most sustained period of consecutive wins. We didn't stand a chance in the face of that. "Only, I thought yesterday that you were... I don't know. Reminding me that married life isn't all it's cracked up to be?"

"What?" Now she had my attention. Celeste being open about her feelings was an unusual event. Eclipse levels of unusual. I heard that softness in her voice, and suddenly I wondered what I had missed.

"Nothing, it's just I've been thinking lately that we were good together. When it was good. Amy made all these promises that the travel wasn't a problem, that she'd come to as many tournaments as she could, and yeah, not so much in practice. I thought we'd get a few good years at least."

I reached for her hand as I struggled to find words, but she pulled hers away. Just like that, the walls went right back up.

"I know it's not my business, but you can always talk to me. You know that, right?"

"It's nothing, honestly. Forget I said anything."

"Celeste, it doesn't sound like nothing. I don't really know Amy, but maybe talking it out would help?"

"It's fine, Elin. I'll deal with it. Don't you dare pity me either. You didn't pity me when you whooped my ass on court yesterday, so don't do it over this. I'll be over it with a long run and a hot shower. And glad I didn't jeopardise my marriage for old time's sake."

"Nice to know, I guess?"

"Well, your ego really needed the help."

That time we both laughed, breaking some of the sudden tension. She gave me a casual, one-armed hug and leaned in to say one more thing. "Seriously, it's not going to be me, but whoever has your attention tonight... At least give her a chance? You do actually deserve to be happy, hon. A racquet and a bunch of trophies aren't going to keep you warm at night."

"No, but that's why I have blankets." I tried to crack the joke, but my heart wasn't in it. "And it's nothing, honestly. Just a pretty face turning my head for a moment. In two weeks, I'll be in Silicon Valley and I won't even remember I was distracted."

"You're playing that one?" Celeste seemed surprised. "I thought you were keeping it to a minimum outside of the slams."

"I have to make my quota," I reminded her, the unspoken part being to keep my world number-one ranking. "And I owe someone a favour. Then it's Cincinnati and the US Open. A few weeks of all things American."

"You do like some American things, it's true," Celeste said with a sigh. "Just not the right ones and—"

"Elin?" Suddenly Toni was there, and I hadn't even seen her approach. "I just wanted to say I have to go."

Damn if I didn't spring up from that comfortable velvet couch like it had caught fire. I spilled the remnants of my champagne in the process, though it avoided the silk of my dress. "So soon? I got caught up and abandoned you completely, I'm sorry."

"No problem, I did some wandering, and I know plenty of people here. In fact, we're going on to a club now, if you wanted to join us?"

Celeste's snort at the idea almost goaded me into doing it, but my true nature won out in the end. The heels were pinching, my mouth kept getting dry from talking five times as much as usual, and the early signs of a headache were starting to tickle behind my eyes. I smiled at Toni and led her across the room to the main exit.

"No, sorry. I think I'm all partied out for one weekend," I said, hoping she'd suddenly change her mind and stay now that she had my attention.

Maybe Celeste had a point about my damn ego.

"Going anywhere nice?" I asked.

"Some place where the trust fund kids and a couple of princes like to go, apparently." She rolled her eyes as she said it. "But I'm flying out tomorrow, so it's good to finish on a high note, right?"

"When do our paths cross again? Cincinnati?"

She shook her head. "Missed the rankings cut-off for that. I'll be in Toronto, mostly because they invited me. First though, a week at home."

"Me too. Well, both homes. We're going to Stockholm for a few days then on to my own place in LA from there. Makes sense since it's all-American for a while."

"That must be nice," Toni said. "I had a place in Florida for winter training for a couple of years, but I let it slide when I was out, and the federation don't want to pay for anything extra now. Maybe when I get my number a bit higher."

"Well, if you need some training space, you're welcome in LA. I don't really... I mean, there's a great hotel just down the road from my place, but I have the courts and my team will be there."

Toni stared at me like I'd forgotten to speak in English. "Did you just invite me to train with you?"

"Is that weird?"

She shook her head, but for the first time since we'd met at the bar, Toni wasn't looking me in the eye. "You do that often? Offer people their dream training situation like it's nothing?"

"What?" Damn, she had a point. I had never offered it to anyone. Even when we were together, Celeste and I had maintained our own places and our own training programs, entirely separate. I hadn't even thought about it before offering; I was just so intent on a chance to spend more time with this woman. I fumbled for a way to walk it back and make the gesture seem less than it was. "Is it so unusual? When I started on the circuit, a bunch of us used to rent places together. Well, the organisers did it for us. I'm not asking you to move in or anything, but the facilities are pretty great if you need them."

"You should write a brochure," Toni said, reaching out to squeeze my arm. "I'm sure there's already something in place, but let's swap numbers anyway. If you don't mind? I guess you don't give yours out a lot."

"Good guess." I hated it, but my personal number was given out to only a handful of people. Press and business were filtered through another line, one that Parisa kept the phone for. I'd had my share of scary experiences when it came to personal privacy. "I make exceptions for new friends, though. Tell me yours and I'll text you, then you'll have it."

"I promise not to sell it to the *National Enquirer*."

"Is that still going? Last time I read it I was pregnant with triplets and marrying someone from One Direction."

Toni snorted. "I'm sorry to have missed that." She rattled off her number, and I keyed it in faithfully. A quick 'hi' message and my number had officially been passed to another person, making it no more than fifteen in total.

"Okay, so call me if you want to train," I said. "Otherwise... Well, it's up to you."

Someone waved Toni down. "I really should go. Last chance to come with...?"

I shook my head.

"Okay, well enjoy the rest of being the champ." Toni took me by the wrists this time, as natural as though we did it every day. When she kissed my cheek, the touch lingered, the creamy press of freshly applied lipstick no doubt leaving its mark. "And say hi to the triplets from me, you know, when you tuck them in."

She was laughing as she left, and I found myself grinning like an idiot too. Moments later, Celeste was at my side again as though we'd never been interrupted.

"Isn't that—"

"Yeah, she's been injured. Back now, though."

I made damn sure not to stare at the door, trying not to give away how much I hoped she'd change her mind about the club and come back, even if just for a little while. Despite my best efforts, I was quickly rumbled.

"Oh Elin, sweetie. Don't tell me..."

"What?" I was straight on the defensive as though she had targeted my weaker backhand. "There's no harm in finding out a colleague is a nice person. So we might be friends? So what?"

"Friends, huh? Lot of wistful staring for just friends." Celeste had a fresh drink but hadn't brought me one. "Just as well, then, since everyone knows she's with her coach. That Xavi dude, who gave Jürgen a fright on clay a couple of times. You must have seen her with him; they're usually joined at the hip. Wonder where he got to tonight."

It shouldn't have been a disappointment. It shouldn't have mattered one bit, in the grand scheme of things. Yet I felt my stomach do that strange falling sensation, leaving me a little queasy.

Of course.

It figured, really. That when I finally pulled my attention from tennis to another person, she wasn't available. And probably straight, just to put the terrible icing on the crappy cake.

"Maybe that's who she was off to the club with," I suggested. It would make sense. A boyfriend who wanted time away from professional schmoozing but still wanted a fun night out with his beautiful girlfriend. Meanwhile, I'd been mentally inserting myself into a story where I was a bit part at best.

"You okay? You've got that look…"

"Tired," I said, because it wasn't lying. Being around this many people for this long really did exhaust me. "I'm going to head back."

"Sure? The night is young, and so are we. Relatively speaking, in your case."

I patted Celeste on the arm. Her teasing little digs always made me smile.

"Enjoy it. Go call your wife and feel better about all this."

She snorted, but I had every faith she'd leave in a little while and make that call. Celeste didn't give up on things, not until she absolutely had to. I left her to work the room, while I slipped out to the side entrance and hailed a cab. My mother could take the official tournament car home. She'd be out for hours yet.

When I got back to our rented home, the signs of our imminent departure were everywhere. I found my father in the dining room, supervising the last of the packing. By which I meant he had a glass of brandy, a brand-new hardback, and there were a few empty crates somewhere near him.

"Pappa."

"Elin." He looked up at me, peering over his reading glasses. "Or should I say *Askungen*, home before midnight again. Did your car turn into a pumpkin yet?"

My father had grown up in the States and spent most of his career as a diplomat until my tennis career began to blossom. We settled in Sweden then, in my mother's home city of Stockholm, and I began to train under the system that had produced greats like Bjorn Borg. It always made me smile that he spoke Swedish with a faintly American accent. The way he had just said Cinderella, for example, sounded uniquely like him, and I would always know his voice anywhere.

"I don't know when Mamma will make an appearance," I confessed. "She was having a lot of fun. You didn't want to go?"

"Not in my penguin suit, no," he huffed. The only one who liked getting dressed up even less than I did. "You know you have the BBC tomorrow? She was worried about that before she left."

I nodded. Another interview. Great. I'd have to think up some other not very interesting things to say about myself. "Yeah, and then straight to the airport. I'm looking forward to a quiet few days."

Unlike some places, there would be no great fanfare when I returned to Stockholm. At first there had been parades, or requests for them, but that was more common for players who come from small towns. Add in the Swedish need to be unassuming and never, ever to brag, and it made the perfect destination for an introvert like me. A few days in the family home, surrounded by familiar faces. I'd even have some of the salty liquorice that so horrified my foreign friends, just for the nostalgia of it all.

"You shouldn't forget to enjoy yourself, Elin." My father set his book aside and came across the room to give me one of his rare hugs. I think I must have looked like I needed it. "All this playing and winning... It's not supposed to be a burden. Plenty of people would kill for this life of yours. But I just want to see my girl happy."

He looked more exhausted than I did. Back when I'd started out, my father had been just as involved in my coaching. Driving me to tournaments, making sure I kept up with my studies once I went on the road for good.

He didn't miss a match for five years, easily, but then the rigours of always being on tour caught up with him. It meant I only saw him for the last few days of the Grand Slam tournaments and in the rare vacation spells.

"I'm happy, Pappa," I promised him. "But if I see a chance to get even happier, I'll take it."

"Good. Well, get off to bed if that's what you came home early for."

"Goodnight," I said, and I'm not ashamed to say I almost jogged all the way to the privacy of my bedroom.

I knew he was worried about me, the way everyone had been lately at some point or another. I always hoped keeping my feelings to myself would stop people from doing that, but eventually they had to poke and prod. I knew that was a sure sign I hadn't spoken to my therapist in too long, but I found I hated the video-call sessions on the road. I could never be sure if she was bored with me or if the screen had just frozen. Despite the known issues we'd been dealing with for years, what was she really going to do to help me? There was no cure for not feeling able to appreciate how lucky I was.

By the time I was ready for bed, face stripped of make-up and my hair brushed down from the contortions it had been through, the house had settled into quiet again. I dimly heard a car idling outside, the door downstairs. No doubt my mother coming home, followed by a muffled conversation. Too loud, but not loud enough for me to make out the words.

All I knew when I got down to breakfast in the morning was that my father had gone. I felt his absence like a hole in the wall, letting in a breeze that made the whole room uncomfortable.

"Did Pappa have an earlier flight?" I asked. How could he, when we were chartered on a jet for the short trip? It beat the pants off flying commercial, and it was one indulgence I jumped at every time it made sense.

My mother looked up from her coffee, ignoring the stack of newspapers that had been gathered as usual.

"No. He won't be joining us in Stockholm." Her Swedish was flat as she delivered the news, devoid of its usual comforting lilt. "Or anywhere, for a while."

"Mamma?"

"We're getting a divorce," she announced, picking up the nearest newspaper and opening it with a sharp flick. Clearly she considered that news to be the end of the subject. Another day I might have argued, called my father or just volleyed questions until my mother cracked and told me more. Instead, I just picked up a banana and methodically sliced it into my bowl of cereal.

The words would come; explanations, arguments. They always did. I ate in silence, considering how my father had most likely known last night, that his uncharacteristic hug had been a good-bye of sorts. I was sure I would still see him, but divorcing my mother seemed to carry an undertone of being done with tennis.

Which, by extension, meant me. Thirty-two years old and suddenly the child of divorce. I couldn't picture that reality, somehow. Already it just seemed as though my father was simply not on this part of the tour, waiting at home somewhere until our paths next crossed.

Slowly the house refilled with activity, everyone finishing their packing duties and leaving according to their schedules. Some would have time off before the next tournament, others would have other clients and other obligations to tend to in the off time.

When we were down to just my mother and me, I reached across the breakfast island and squeezed her hand. For a moment, I thought she was going to pull it away, but instead she let it rest there.

"Elin," she said, with a watery smile. "The important thing, the one fact we both still agree on is that—"

"Nothing distracts me from tennis," I finished. We'd been saying those words as a family for over twenty years. "I won't let it, but if you need some time off, Mamma—"

"Oh, shush." She dismissed the very idea. "If anything, I'll have more time and energy to focus on you. Won't that be nice?"

"*Absolut,*" I answered, letting go of her hand. "Let's get ready for the last of the press, okay?"

CHAPTER SEVEN

I HAD A LOT OF respect for the BBC. Their coverage of tennis had always been thoughtful and professional, and they were absolutely the first point of contact during the two weeks of Wimbledon, no matter where you came from. Those soothing British tones could tell the whole story, from hushed tension to the explosion of a match-winning shot.

They had the sensible policy of choosing all their tennis pundits from the pool of former players that grew every year. Any British ones who had ever made even a tiny splash were front of the line, followed by the biggest names who hadn't gone into coaching. Former champions, from the most decorated to the one-time winners with big personalities: It was really pleasant not to lose those people from the game. Familiar faces at tournaments made the constant travel and change less of a grind.

There was just one exception. When I won my first Grand Slam, fourteen years ago as a precocious teenager with overly straightened hair, it was something of an upset. I hadn't even made the Swedish Olympic team for Athens, but a good couple of months and a lucky draw got me off to a good start in New York. I rode that luck, with top seeds being off their game or recovering from injury, all the way to a shock berth in the final.

Where my luck seemed to have run out. I was drawn against the World Number One, the top seed, who had already won two of the four slams that year. I was a blip on her radar, a formality before another coronation. At least, according to the press. As the darling of the Global Tennis Association and as a competitor, Mira Sobotka had been too classy to dismiss me outright, but she hadn't brought the big guns when she played me either.

The crowd had gone wild for the scrappy newcomer, and I was all legs and quiet attitude back then, so it was like they'd just adopted a puppy.

One with a suspect backhand who somehow got away with it over three sets.

They always loved it when a dramatic shot clinched the championship, and my dive along the baseline to make a seemingly impossible return, landing hard only to look up and see I'd won the decisive point as the crowd went nuts. I'd rolled over onto my back and looked to the skies in disbelief and sheer joy.

That was the moment the commentator had announced, "The Queen is dead; long live the Queen!"

It was a little over the top. Well, a lot over the top, really. It was one of those clips destined to make it in every montage for the rest of my career. It would probably be projected on my tombstone.

I mean, I'd just won my first slam; there was no guarantee I'd ever win another. Mira had won the US Open three times already. Before me, she was on track to beat the same GTA record of twenty-two slams that my whole career had been built around smashing.

So although we kept a professional civility, it seemed from that point on that she had never quite forgiven me. That US Open was the closest she came, and she retired two years later on fifteen slams. Commentary had been her next step, and they just loved her at the BBC, since she'd been one of the greatest grass court players ever to grace Wimbledon. When she spoke about what it took to win there, everyone knew it was with absolute authority.

We met on the soundstage, comfortable chairs and favourable lighting set up for what Mira called her "intimate chat with a champion." I understood Jürgen would be in later for his turn in the spotlight. The handshake was brief, and until the cameras started rolling, Mira and I didn't exchange a word.

I always did these post-championship interviews in street clothes, something simple but classy from one of the designers that Parisa liked or was angling to get me some promotional work from. The black silk blouse felt like it had been sculpted specifically for me, and the smart white trousers to go with it felt as comfortable as my running gear to wear. With my hair down and make-up on, I felt a little more self-conscious, and I caught myself more than once playing with the pretty pendant necklace that sat perfectly in the vee of where my blouse was undone, "Just enough to tantalise," as Parisa said.

Mira, for her part, kept her hair short these days. It had been a precise pixie cut last time I'd seen her, but now she'd settled back into her familiar short bob. The hair that had once been coppery red had faded to the kind of silver that hairdressers could never replicate, one of those timeless looks that made ageing look not so bad after all. In her dark-green pencil skirt and pale sleeveless top, it was clear she'd kept in shape since giving up the game professionally. I knew she still played on the exhibition tours and for charity now and then, but I suspected it was her famous self-discipline at work.

"So," she began, glancing at the notes on her lap. Always meticulous, always prepared. "Elin Larsson, Wimbledon Champion. We've all heard those words many times before. There's a reason they call you 'the Volvo of tennis,' isn't there? Reliable, a safe bet. But tell us, how does it feel as to have come *so close* to losing, only to somehow win again?"

I kept my best professional smile firmly in place and tried not to answer through gritted teeth. Another hour of this and I could wash the heavy makeup from my face, get in the waiting car, and finally escape to the airport. I took a deep breath and began to respond.

"Well, Mira, you saw how Celeste gave me such a great match."

The biggest relief of finally making it to Los Angeles wasn't just that I got to spend a few weeks in the place I considered home, but that I arrived there alone, to a completely empty house.

My mother had stayed behind in Stockholm to deal with the divorce proceedings, and I was glad to be out of the house, which felt strangely empty without my father's presence. I had called him a few times, but each conversation had been brief, even by our standards.

The house echoed on my arrival, and once the driver had set my bags down for me in the foyer, I wandered around like a visitor for a few minutes. The fridge was stocked, the fruit bowls filled, and despite the fact that I'd been away for weeks, there wasn't a speck of dust or a thing out of place.

Sometimes I forgot how well looked after I was. Some would call it spoiled, though maybe not to my face.

Grabbing my personal bag from the stack by the door, I jogged upstairs to my bedroom. Now that, sadly, was even less disturbed than the other rooms. The lack of action practically announced itself in the crispness of the sheets and the stillness of the air. Rather than let my own furniture silently mock me, I went to wash off my lingering bad mood in the shower.

I've never understood people who can spend hours in the bathroom. Maybe it's because I usually showered two or three times a day, my one-woman quest to ruin the environment, but a necessary evil when your whole day is spent working up a sweat. It might have been nice one day to stand under the spray and zone out, sing whatever I'd heard on the radio that morning, but as soon as I was squeaky-clean, I jumped right out of there.

Just before I sank completely into a depressive funk, my phone rang to save me from myself.

"I need a really big plate for my dinner party Friday," said a familiar voice. "Gold, ideally. Know anyone who has one of those?"

"How many times do I have to tell you that we don't keep the trophy, huh? You'd know that if you ever watched my matches."

"Oh, I plan on blagging some tickets for... Is it next month? I know I want to come to New York, anyway. Glad to be home, big sis?"

Alice did like to come with me for the US Open, even if the very thought of tennis bored her into a coma and always had. With five years between us, I had just about picked up my first junior racquet when she came along. Between hitting balls against the garage wall and a screaming baby, there was no contest when it came to my attention.

She always said it was just as well. Those first few years, she wasn't interested in tennis or any of my athletic activities. Quite by mistake, my parents had announced that they were raising a son, my little brother. As soon as Alice learned to talk and dress herself, we were well on our way to finding out we had been wrong about that. It would be nice to say that the world had always been so easy, accepting Alice for who she really was and is, but that wasn't my story to tell.

All I knew was that I loved my sister, now a fancy sculptor and artist in her own right, and we frequently drove each other nuts. She would housesit for me sometimes but had bought her own place in Silverlake. Close enough to drop by, far enough that we could pretend not to live in the same city when it was convenient.

"Please tell me you have fun dinner plans you're going to drag me along to?" I answered. "Because this big empty house is bumming me out." Unlike with my parents, we never slipped into our native tongue with each other. Alice had found her home in America even before I had and defaulted to English whether I wanted to or not.

"I don't have plans, yet. Can we go somewhere that isn't the smoothie bar at a gym?"

"I don't want to see a gym this week," I half-lied. I'd be working out and training at home, so that didn't count. "So it's all up to you."

"I always said I should have absolute power," Alice fired right back. "Okay, let me clean up and I'll come get you. Or did you want to drive?"

"That sounds good, actually." I did spend most of my life being driven around, since tournaments usually supplied cars and drivers. "Is that your way of telling me you want to go out in the convertible?"

"Well, if you've bought something else boring, I don't want to know about it. Pick me up at seven?"

"Got it."

I smiled as I hung up the phone. Real food, fun company. Someone who would understand the weirdness of our parents divorcing—oh God, had they even told her yet?—and mock me for my new crush. If I told her about that, anyway.

After opening the closet, I took my time picking out something that wasn't made for playing sport in.

———

On a perfectly sunny LA evening, I switched off the engine outside my sister's house. Knowing her as I did, I knew there was no point in idling. Sure enough, it took almost ten minutes for her to appear. As soon as she slipped into the passenger seat, I teased her for wearing exactly the same sunglasses as I had picked out.

"Well, we have the same shaped face," she pointed out. "I see you're striving for butch points tonight, Elin."

While she'd gone with a pale blue summer dress, I'd opted for a grey linen pantsuit with a simple camisole under it. I had my hair down, partly because it was a relief not to tie it back and because a little part of my brain was always trying to be a bit less recognisable when out on the town. It helped that by Hollywood standards I was very minor news.

"Where to?"

Alice punched in a destination on the SatNav, and we headed off down the hill.

"So…elephant in the car time?" I began, enjoying the breeze through my hair from the motion of the car. "Did they tell you?"

"That the great house of Larsson will split?" she announced in her best *Game of Thrones* intro voice. "Yeah, Mamma filled me in on a video call. Most of which she spent arguing about some hotel booking for Cincinnati for you."

"And that doesn't upset you? You have no strong feelings? You're twenty-seven and suddenly your parents don't want to be together anymore?"

"Oh dear, here comes the Ibsen drama about Elin's existence," she started to mock. "What do you care? Wouldn't you rather they just be happy?"

"I… Well, yes, but…"

"Eloquent," Alice summarised. "Sounds like one of your press conferences. Congrats, though, on the win. She was very proud."

"The novelty really never wears off for her."

"Like it has for you, you mean?" Alice always could see right through me. "Oh, ignore the machine. Take a right up here. Mamma also said you'd been misbehaving in London. Going for drinks like an actual adult with free will."

"Yeah. Maybe the night before the final wasn't so smart, but I don't have to answer to her on that."

I felt the surprised glance without anything having to be said. Turned out I could still shock my little sister.

Even with the vagaries of LA traffic, it didn't take us long to find the sushi place. We took a small booth in back, nobody giving me a second glance. The refreshing feeling of being anonymous again let my shoulders drop the last inch, and I relaxed into catching up.

Somewhere between the eel and the salmon, Alice pointed her chopsticks at me in accusation. "There's something going on with you. Did you and Celeste have a little reunion after the match?"

"What? No." I sipped my wine, considering. "Although she did kind of suggest it? But no, we're not meant to be."

"Then it's someone else. Don't tell me, that pig from the men's tour finally wore you down and you switched teams."

"Ew. No. You might put up with dating men, but some of us have standards."

Alice flipped me off while finishing her own glass of red. "No, if this is a new thing for you then we have... What? A year of silent pining, minimum? It's not like you're going to make a move or really do anything about it."

For that, I balled up my napkin and threw it at her. "I have game."

"On the court, sure. If it was a case of hitting a ball at this new mystery woman, there's nobody better. But dating? I think maybe there's nobody worse."

"For that, you're buying dinner."

"The starving artist? I don't think so. I might not watch Wimbledon, but I know what they pay the winner."

Our parents would be horrified to hear us talking so openly about modest subjects like money. Not quite teenage rebellion, but close to our version of it.

"Speaking of romance and dating, I don't see you here with a plus one," I said.

"No, but maybe next time I could bring a certain someone. You'll like this one. He even has...wait for it...a real job."

"You mean he's not an 'aspiring' anything? Because I've lived through the actor, the dancer, the one who wouldn't wait tables just anywhere because he wanted to be a 'professional server.'"

"For that, I'm ordering dessert." Alice let it all bounce off her, secure as ever that in a comparison of our romantic success she'd come out in front. "And you don't get details until you spill about yours."

"Nothing to spill. This girl saved me from getting caught by the paparazzi, we maybe had a half a moment after I won the damn thing, and...yeah. She's probably straight—"

Alice groaned. I did have form on that front.

"And dating her coach. Because oh, she's another player. Which worked out so well before. To top it all off, I didn't even recognise her at first, so I probably look like an elitist asshole to her as well. Not exactly the start of a romantic comedy, is it?"

"I've heard worse. Although you can be married thirty-something years and throw it all away, as it turns out. Maybe we're both crazy to be looking for love?"

"You might be looking, but I'm not," I argued. "And I knew you couldn't just be that cool about the divorce. If we're going to talk feelings, though, it's going to take more than this wine."

"You mean a real bar?" Alice asked like she'd read my mind. "I know just the place."

I signalled for the check and patted Alice's hand. We weren't big on hugs and all that warm-blooded stuff, but it felt necessary in the circumstances.

"Come on, let's go drown our sorrows and get used to coming from a broken home."

The shrill ring of the phone woke me, or maybe it was the glaring sunlight through the bedroom window—I'd forgotten to close the drapes.

I fumbled for the evil noise-making machine like a drowning person clutching for a rope.

"Ms Larsson, your car will be with you in thirty."

I grunted some kind of acknowledgement, the spike of panic leaving words beyond my reach. What car? Why? I didn't even attempt the concept of 'thirty,' so I left that alone for a moment. Sitting up was the next grand plan, and I only felt slightly sick when I managed it.

Tequila. My sister could not be trusted around it, and neither could I. Water. I needed to get water and then maybe think about opening both eyes at the same time.

The promotional shoot for the US Open, that was the appointment. A long, repetitive day of shooting headshots that would be turned into giant posters and video clips they could use in animated titles. It was actually one of the few commercial projects I enjoyed. They always had a plan, no talking required, just follow instructions and enjoy the company of other pros and a loaded craft-services table. Pretty sweet day, if you weren't dying from a hangover.

I risked a look in the mirror. Ouch. Somewhere just north of "alive," but only just. I swear that never happened in my twenties. One benefit of being fit and having a good metabolism was that alcohol never used to do much damage on the way through. Since I'd turned thirty, some cosmic switch had flipped, and I paid in full for every drink the next day.

Alice came staggering in at that point, clutching two glasses of water.

"Wow, you look rough."

"Thanks, Alice. It's your fault, remember?" I took the water and chugged it down with increasing relief. Oh hydration, I would never overlook you again. "You want to tag along for promo shots today? I think it's at NBC."

"Burbank? No thanks," Alice scoffed in response. "Come on, let's try and get you looking human. The studio can do the rest."

CHAPTER EIGHT

WHEN I WAS SHOWN TO the soundstage, Celeste was almost dressed and ready. She looked great in her black and vibrant pink runner's-vest-and-shorts combo. After the strictness of Wimbledon, we were all looking forward to running through the other options for colour and fit. She had even toned the streaks of colour through her locs to be the same shade of pink. Celeste looked completely put together and ready to kick my ass in the name of revenge any time I liked.

I had changed into my own T-shirt-and-skirt outfit of navy and white with touches of gold. With one of my favoured white racquets in hand, I moved to join my colleagues who had gathered around the buffet of food and drink like a plague of well-paid locusts.

With the flurry of greetings and the lunge for a much-needed coffee, I wasn't really paying that much attention. Having my racquet tucked under my arm gave me a wider turning circle, and I managed to whack someone on the arm as I moved.

"Sorry, I... Toni?"

"Hola."

"I didn't know you were—I mean—"

She patted me on the arm, having snagged a coffee for herself already. "You didn't know the low ranks were allowed in? It's okay, me either. But Mexico is a big market, and Mexican-Americans... They want me on the promo shots. I think someone called in a favour, but hey. Free trip to LA, right? It's pretty nice on this coast."

"It's good to see you." I hoped the hair and make-up girls had worked their magic, because I didn't need to look as hellish as I had on waking up. "And sooner than expected."

"Like a bad penny, I just keep turning up. You didn't even know my name two weeks ago."

"Well, I did, somewhere in this brain of mine. How are you?"

"Good. Bit of a scare with my knee the other day, but all good. How about you?"

Celeste was watching us from where she was holding court—which I swear was no pun intended, ever—with most of the other top seeds.

"Well, my parents are getting divorced, my sister got me wasted, and this coffee is the only thing between me and sleeping standing up."

That stopped Toni in her tracks for a moment. She looked unfairly gorgeous, done up for the shoot as well, but especially comfortable in the peach-coloured dress, fitted to perfection with the collar popped.

"You've been...busy since Wimbledon, then?"

"I had some time in Sweden; now I'm home and doing this stuff. Weirdly, this is one of the quiet times in the year for me. I used to play everything going, now I'm pacing myself between London and New York."

"That was like me late last year, when I first came back. My specialist was so sure I was gonna throw my back every time I took a swing."

We were interrupted by her coach, and as soon as I saw him, I recognised him. Short, stocky, and with an expression like thunder most of the time. "Toni, *vamos.*"

"I don't think they're ready for us yet," I intervened. "Sorry, I don't think we've been introduced."

He had the sense not to completely dismiss me, although it looked like he wanted to. "Xavi," he said, extending his hand for the briefest of handshakes. "A pleasure, Miss Larsson."

Someone should have told his face it was a pleasure.

"I need to go get strapped up and taped up if we're doing the whole 'swing and jump and looking silly in front of the green screen' deal," Toni explained. "Usually I'd let it go, but they want some real action shots from us all, and there's no way I'm risking an injury doing something this dumb."

"See you out there," I said.

The director finally emerged at the front of the staging area, clapping her hands to get our attention.

"Ladies, our job today is to get people really excited for September. So let's get started! Is, uh—Can we start with Elin Larsson, please?"

I was almost disappointed. Going first meant I'd have no excuse to hang around and chat all day. I waved at the director and jogged across to start. Cameras began appearing everywhere, and all the players were ushered to different areas and backdrops.

I was careful not to look for Toni, in case it started any whispers. I told myself I wasn't bothered when she ended up being shot right next to me.

Alice had been right, and it made me crazy. Here I was, metres away from a woman I found intriguing, and I was doing exactly nothing about it. Then I caught Xavi lurking behind the camera and remembered why it was a dumb idea in the first place.

Maybe going first wouldn't be such a bad idea after all.

Those brief conversations with Toni had to sustain me for the best part of a month. Although she had my number, I got only a handful of texts. Clearly mass messages at that—updates on where she would be that week if anyone was looking for her. It felt like it meant something to be included, at least.

She kicked ass in Washington, though, while I was playing the Canadian Open. I paid more attention than I usually would have to a smaller tournament, but when Toni made it to the final, I was cheering her on via a stuttering, buffering stream that Parisa managed to bring up on my tablet for me. I sent my commiserations when she lost, pleased to even get a reply.

It was strange to play almost a whole tournament without my mother watching from the side-lines and managing my training schedule. It was easier in the one-week events, since warmups, matches, and cool downs were generally enough on their own. I played pretty much every day to make it to the final, accepting the cute trophy and the cheque with a bit of a spring in my step. No matter how jaded I had been lately, winning did still bring its own kind of high.

My mother showed up for Cincinnati, hitting the hotel reception at the same time as I did. Creepy, how she could time those things to perfection. She didn't offer much news about the divorce, beyond mentioning that they might sell the house, and I didn't ask any more than that either. We settled into our suite, only the lounge of it shared, and the routine of another tournament soon took over.

Until the third-round match on Wednesday, when I tossed the ball in the air for a second serve, like I'd done a thousand times before. The first serve had been a fault, something I'd been doing too many times since I first walked out on court. I hated that they called double faults "unforced errors." It was easier to admit I had just screwed it up.

The crowd weren't exactly on my side either, since my opponent was American. Sophie was classy enough not to work the home-crowd angle too much, but I didn't enjoy my every dumb moment being cheered like they couldn't wait to see a giant-killing moment. So much for tennis being a dignified sport where they only applauded the positive and politely ignored the things that went wrong.

Not that I made for much of a giant, that day.

Anyway. Bounce, bounce, toss it up in the air. Standard, one of the most repeated actions in my daily existence—hell, my whole life. Which was the perfect invitation for the... Okay, I didn't remember the name, but the big muscle running through my left hip.

It wasn't close to the worst ways I'd hurt myself trying to hit a ball, but it had me doubling up in pain and missing the ball entirely. At least until I realised that bending over was only hurting it more. Straightening up, I waved vaguely at the umpire. I walked like I'd only just learned how legs worked over to my chair, dropping my racquet on the ground and signalling for my physio, Ezi, to come running. She was already on her way, as the umpire called for a medical timeout, one of the few permitted breaks in play.

The tournament medical staff arrived right along with her, the doctor and nurse looking a little overwhelmed at being called into action in front of the large crowd. Usually, aches and pains were played through until the next natural break—change of ends on the court, the pause between sets. Acute injuries, though, anything that resulted from a fall or a sudden inability to move properly, meant immediate attention.

They had me stand and prodded at where I indicated until I hissed with pain. With the diagnosis made so quickly, I had the option for three minutes of physio treatment or to retire the match entirely. A forfeit, if you like.

I could already tell which it would be. While something like this would be easily fixed, it would take time and rest. Honestly, I'd had trouble with both of my hips on and off for at least ten years. A lot of players did damage in the early years of their career from playing too hard and too often, and that kind of niggling pain flared up again and again.

As Ezi offered me an arm to support me, I made my way to the umpire and announced that I would have to retire the match. The crowd at least had found some sympathy for me at that point and applauded me politely back to the locker room. Sophie, always the most sporting, came to shake my hand and propped me up on my other side, before running back out on court to retrieve her things and make the "victory" official.

"Mamma." I tried to head her off as soon as she made it down from the VIP seats. "It's okay, just that same damn muscle."

"I've called the hospital; they'll scan you and the specialist will be waiting."

"Not necessary," I protested, but I already knew it was a lost cause. I wondered whether it was worth trying to clean up and change. The transition from standing to sitting and the way my hip yelled at me said no, I'd be going in my match gear.

Hospitals, physio suites, doctor's offices: I was used to them all. They'd always been a part of the job, and sometimes a welcome respite from it. It troubled me a little, especially in countries like America, that wherever I went in the world the tour or my own money would always make sure I got the best of treatment. It felt decadent when I knew so many of the people who lived and worked there could barely afford insurance and too often didn't have real access to healthcare at all.

Still, at least my swanky doctors had nice offices. No squeaky floors and ugly lighting for me.

I always thought there was something a little off about anyone who went into sports medicine. Don't get me wrong, I was grateful for them. Over the years and in countless places, they'd patched me up and kept me on top of my game. Still, they were often a lot to take, personality-wise. Usually athletes in their own right, they often were more interested in my stats than my scans at first. Eventually, though, they all got past the jokes and trying to be friends right down to the medical nitty-gritty.

As I suspected, it was a bad muscle strain. Rest, painkillers, a change up in my physio to strengthen my core and the pelvis. I wasn't wild about a room full of people nodding about my pelvis, but I had gotten used to that and worse indignities. There was some warning about wear-and-tear on my hip joint itself, but I'd learned to deal only with the injuries I had at any given time.

"The important thing," my mother said, as we got back into the car, "is that you should be fit in plenty of time for New York."

"Good," I said with a sigh. "You know Alice wants to come this year? Maybe we could do something nice in New York, just the three of us."

"Winning a tournament isn't doing something nice? Come, Elin. Every slam counts now."

"Yes, Mamma."

I leaned back on the leather of the SUV's seat, watching the scenery fly by as we headed back to the hotel. Parisa had rearranged my schedule already, and I looked forward to some quiet time. Before I could get too complacent in my injured state, my phone bleeped for my attention.

You ok?

Toni. Well, that was unexpected.

Fine. Why? I replied. Surely it wasn't big news.

Toni's little bubbles seemed to stay on the screen for a long time as I waited for her response.

I saw you took an R. Nothing serious?

Had news really travelled that fast? Maybe she'd been watching the coverage, as we all did from time to time out of habit. Or had she been watching on purpose? Following my progress as I had been hers? Was that too much to hope for?

Old hip problem, likes to remind me who's really in charge sometimes.
Rest and physio, back in a week or two. How are you?

The bubbles loaded and loaded. Great. A slow texter. At least she finally had a flaw. The lack of them so far had been a little annoying.

*Training hard. Need to rack up some points before the season is out.
Glad you're ok.*

I plotted out some replies, but nothing seemed cool and breezy enough. Apparently my unusual interest in my phone had registered with my mother.

"Celeste?"

I shook my head, trying to avoid the scrutiny of her questioning look.

"Just to…uh, Ruiz—you know her, right? She heard I blew out today, was just sending good wishes."

"Hmm." Not much ever got past my mother, but what she chose to care about was a mystery until it happened. She seemed happy to let this one go. "Don't give too many details. Let people speculate on whether you'll be back or not."

I hadn't listened to her about what I should say publicly for most of my career, but that hadn't stopped her trying to tell me. In that spirit, I made a point of telling Toni I'd be back.

*Don't worry, you'll still be seeing me in Flushing Meadows. Whoever
plays first buys the smoothies, deal?*

No instant response that time. Was she already bored? Had she just wandered off already? Then, before I could get into a spiral over it, she started typing.

Sounds good to me.

Maybe the painkillers had finally kicked in, or the stress of the day had eased, but when I closed my eyes and let myself relax against the headrest, I was smiling.

CHAPTER NINE

ARRIVING IN NEW YORK WAS the usual whirlwind. Journalists would crowd into press conferences to ask us questions before opening day, about diet and training and the pure focus they all liked to write about. The US Open was big business, and as the last of the four Grand Slams in the year, it felt like an end-of-term party. Never mind that there were still a bunch of tournaments after it, including the GTA Finals in Singapore that finalised the rankings.

We did all work hard and train hard. Our diets were micromanaged by nutritionists and often personal chefs. But there was a reason we all arrived days before the tournament started: party time.

In London, we'd hidden away in the leafy suburbs, moments away from the stadium. For the US Open, the place to be was Manhattan. The hotels were huge and very fancy, with every kind of restaurant and entertainment right on the doorstep. It made for a fun life, in the days between being driven out to Queens, where we actually played.

My hip was much improved, but I was still working through some stiffness and pain. I hated playing in that not-quite-healed state, as it was basically asking to aggravate it into a worse injury that made me learn some new curse words. The bigger worry was that in trying to shield the hurt part of me, the unnatural movements would upset some other joint or muscle.

Ezi had been having the time of her life with my physio. Though she hated to see me injured, she knew it made me much more dedicated to my programme and eager to heal as fast as possible. It also made the work with her the entire focus of my time, instead of having to squeeze it in around matches and everything else.

She dropped by my suite as I was unpacking, imposing in the doorway at six feet tall even in her running shoes.

"You're not bending well," Ezi assessed in two seconds flat, with a soft tut of disappointment. "We might have to modify your serve, at least for the first match."

"We'll worry about that tomorrow," I said. "I'm just stiff from the plane."

That just earned me a stop-the-bullshit glare. Ezi could have had a gold medal in that, if the Olympics would only make it a sport. She was interrupted by the arrival of Alice, who'd be sharing the suite with me and our mother. Thank God for separate bedrooms.

"Sure these digs are fancy enough?" Alice asked, dropping a pile of bags on the floor of the shared living room. "I mean, is there anything in here that isn't sculpted from marble or gold?"

It was actually pretty tasteful, with lots of soft touches and very pleasant art on the walls. Only my sister could make it sound like Trump Tower.

"If you don't like it, I think there's a backpackers' hostel…somewhere. If you want to be so *authentic*."

"When are you all going to liven up and move to Brooklyn for this? It's a straighter shot to your little stadium, for a start."

"We can't all be ageing hipsters. Now, what do you want to do today? I want to actually see you while we're here."

"I thought Ezi would have you locked in the gym by now, honestly."

"No, she doesn't pay me enough to do bonus hours," Ezi complained. "I'm not officially on the clock until tomorrow morning. So I'm going to make the most of being in New York. You two should as well."

I plucked the plastic folder from my handbag without looking, knowing that Parisa would have placed it there while we were on the plane to Teterboro Airport. Sure enough, it was filled with a stack of invitations and printed requests for my attendance. Sponsors, both of me personally and the tournament, were always keen to have some splashy events. I dropped the pile on the coffee table and gestured for Alice to choose.

"Let's see…" She began to sift through them, discarding the bland corporate ones right away. "Oh, champagne? Maybe. Something with water polo?"

I shook my head. I wasn't doing anything that required exerting my hip or wearing a bikini.

"Well, tonight is sorted," she decided, setting aside a couple of fancy cards that seemed to be exclusively about cocktails. "Let's start with this little shindig; it's only a few blocks away. Anna Wintour's hosting, so you know it's going to be a good time."

I had met the infamous fashion editor a few times, since she liked to feature tennis in the magazine whenever she could. I wasn't hot on her radar in the same way as the girls who really did look like models, but she loved the sport enough to treat me with a great deal of respect. She'd made vague mentions about me doing a cover someday, but to my eternal relief nothing had ever come of it.

"Let's go," I said, knowing that if I started stressing about what to wear, we'd never get anywhere. It hadn't been a long flight, and I didn't look too crumpled. "What's the actual event?"

"Something about organic gin and…badminton?" Alice said as we headed down in the elevator. "That doesn't seem right. But hey, it's all hitting stuff, right?"

I groaned and fired off a text to Parisa. She would be thrilled that I'd finally shown up to some events without being bribed, coaxed, or dragged. Plus, I wanted her to relax and have some fun too. She could snag all the freebies and promotional stuff and actually use most of it too.

There were press in the lobby as we emerged, but as I'd stayed at the Palace every year for the past five years, I knew how to duck them by that point. After making a sharp turn, we entered a staff-only door by the elevator bank and followed the corridor out to the street.

"Not in the mood for the paparazzi?" Alice teased. "It's just the Euro press. The Americans don't really care that much."

"Still, cameras," I groaned. "There'll be plenty at the event, and tonight as well I bet."

"Good. Wouldn't want to miss a chance to embarrass you, Elin." There was just a hint of edge to her voice, like she thought her presence was the reason I'd given a full-body swerve to the public glare.

"You've been trying for twenty-seven years and haven't managed it yet," I said, and it sounded a lot softer than I meant it to. I just didn't ever want Alice to doubt that I was proud of her, since I knew beneath her mockery that she was always proud of me. Or I hoped, at least. "Although that winter you had green hair came pretty close."

"Well, if you ever get sick of blonde…"

"I'll know green doesn't suit us. Good note."

We strode down the sidewalk to the restaurant. The gin company sponsoring it had put up signs that could be seen from space, or at least New Jersey. At least we knew we had the right place.

Parisa caught up to us at the door, still an expert at running in impossible heels. She and Alice greeted each other with air kisses, and I got a quick hug for my trouble. Parisa had been the advance party, in town for two days already.

"You made it quickly," I said.

"Your mother was finding things for me to do," she replied with a shudder. "The only way to escape was if you needed something, so thank you. How come you're doing the press and promo?"

"Because she's still in pain, and she's worried she might crash out early," Alice answered, linking her arm with Parisa's and ushering me through the doors. "So she wants to get her face out there, make sure it's not a waste of time dragging you all here."

"Alice!" It was a warning and a protest at how quickly she had figured me out. "Not in public, okay? And I'm fine. Ezi has worked her magic."

I was sure my sister had more to say on the subject, but then she caught sight of a fellow artist in the crowd and was drawn away to talk clay or whatever sculptors actually discussed.

Anyway, she was wrong. I'd been a little sore for matches before, and it wouldn't make a bit of difference.

Two points. That's how close I came to losing my first-round match—to an unseeded twenty-year-old. From Belarus. A country even I hadn't visited, despite my considerable air miles.

And my hip was almost entirely to blame.

When I finally got off court after two hours, I relented on the painkilling shots I'd been leaving for a last resort. If I was going to get past anyone else, I was going to have to accept that additional help.

I spent the start of my next day off in the gym, headphones firmly in place. I knew what speculation would be going on, about my recent injury and the fact I'd come so close to losing to a relative unknown in the first round. Sports media was populated by sharks, and they had their first scent of blood in the water.

Don't get me wrong; I knew I was lucky to have had so many great headlines and back page splashes. I'd done well from magazines and even the big sports blogs, but it took a hell of a lot of work to get that kind of buzz. What they relished, and what probably sold more papers, was a shocking loss or a hint of scandal. Throw in the tragedy of injury or a personal feud, and the reporters after each match were practically salivating.

Back in the hotel suite, safe from prying eyes, I decided it was no kind of time to stay indoors and wallow. That used to be my preferred way of handling the tougher stuff, but with time I'd realised that I had to face my problems head on. Being up and being active made that much more possible. Besides, I had actually won, in the end.

I knew that the best part of big cities was that nobody paid close attention. With the entire tennis circus in town, attention would be spread across many famous faces, making me just one of many. It was the perfect environment to go out and get a little culture.

While I got dressed in my favourite jeans and a T-shirt not actually designed to play sport in, I flipped on the television coverage for the day. Having been so entrenched in all things recovery, I hadn't really paid attention to the tournament draw beyond my first-round opponent and whether Celeste was on the same side of the bracket or not.

Okay, fine, I had also checked to see who Toni was facing. She had a tricky match that day against Keiko Kobayashi, the thirteenth seed and one of my best friends on the tour. Most people hated that kind of draw when they were low in the rankings or just starting out. But if Toni was anything like me, she'd be thrilled to draw such a big challenge. An early chance to prove herself and a big name to take down if she won.

Was she any match for Keiko? The little I'd watched since becoming aware of Toni properly wasn't conclusive. For a moment, I considered calling the concierge and asking them to get me a seat in the players' section for it. Then I realised two things: It was on one of the outer courts, where there was no players' section, and the match had already started.

So I didn't make it any further than the couch for a while. I raided the mini bar for some juice and settled down to see if Toni would make any impact against Keiko. There was some chance, at least. Keiko had been out most of the previous season after knee surgery and wasn't yet back to her best. A year younger than me, she was clearly feeling the ravages of a long career too.

To listen to everyone's laundry list of injuries and complaints, it was easy to forget we were amongst some of the fittest people in the world. All sportspeople ended up the same, give or take a few lucky ones here and there. We got our bodies into the best physical condition, and then we pushed them past their limits time and again.

Keiko looked sharp and held her serve as seamlessly as ever. Having to break her was a challenge for anyone, but Toni managed it in the fifth game. The determination on her face was evident even with the camera zoomed out.

My phone lit up with a message from my mother. I ignored it.

I turned my attention back to the television. Keiko had settled into a kind of groove, flicking her long fringe out of her eyes. How she could play with that kind of irritation I had no idea, but most players' haircuts or style changes fell firmly in the superstition bracket. It had been a few years since Keiko had handed me my ass in Melbourne, reminding the tennis world I wasn't invincible after all. Coming off the year of my Golden Slam—winning all four majors in the same calendar year and polishing it off with a gold medal at the London Olympics—the media frenzy had been immense. Personally, I'd been relieved that people were talking about me like a human being again.

No matter what Keiko threw at her, Toni kept coming back. She was giving as good as she got and playing like she'd never been injured. I'd never missed more than a couple of months at a time, but even I had adapted my game to allow for wear and tear over the years. I envied that fearlessness, but I worried about it all the same.

Alice came back from whichever merry brunch she'd been at during the last set. I nodded in acknowledgement, unable to tear my eyes from the screen. Toni, much to her own obvious enjoyment, had almost broken

Keiko and in the enviable position of holding two match points. Which meant—in layman's terms—that she had two clear chances to win the thing before Keiko could draw even again or neutralise her.

It was also the kind of moment in which less experienced players tended to choke.

Some of the most accomplished players had come back from Keiko's position, even in major finals, to clean up and claim the match that seemed rightfully theirs on paper. I was one of them. My mother had told me early on that the points on the board didn't matter until the match was over. What mattered going into each point was who believed they could win it. Belief trumped a head start if it was strong enough.

"Who's got you so fascinated?" Alice teased, sitting on the couch opposite and kicking her feet up on the coffee table. "You missed a great breakfast, by the way."

"Shush!" I warned, as Keiko served again. The rally was short. Sharp. Fierce. And it ended with Toni smashing the ball into a corner that Keiko couldn't reach.

"Game, set, match, Ms Cortes Ruiz," said the umpire, his steady tones contrasting with the crowd erupting on all sides.

Toni was on the ground, prostrate in front of the crowd. In love with an underdog as always, they were raising the non-existent roof on her behalf. After scrambling back to her feet, Toni jogged to the net in a daze, shaking Keiko's hand and accepting muttered words of congratulation. They each shook the umpire's hand, and Toni raised her hands in acknowledgement of the crowd again.

"Well, that is a shocker," Mira's voice said, in post-match commentary. Awesome; she'd branched out from the BBC. No wonder, really, with her experience, but I dreaded to think what she'd be saying about me on television in the coming days. "A real first-round upset, a result that no one would have predicted looking at the draw."

"Jim," she addressed her co-commentator, both of them still off-screen as the cameras lingered on Toni and Keiko packing up and leaving court. "Does this mean Ruiz is back on track? Before her injury layoff, there was a lot of speculation that she was ready to step up and bag her first slam."

"Well, I don't think she's at that level yet, Mira."

Good for you, Jim, I thought. Too many people just agreed with every word she said out of deference. Clearly he had his own opinion.

"No, but has she rediscovered that potential?" Mira didn't sound pleased at being challenged.

"Oh, for sure, and beating a top seed is always a huge confidence boost. Still, the draw hasn't been kind to our new giant killer, because next round she faces... Well, let's have a look at the brackets, shall we?"

The screen brought up the draw and zoomed in on my collision course with Toni, just two rounds away.

"That's right, Jim, the reward for an unexpected victory—and she has every chance against a lower ranked player in the second round—is to face the top seed and world number one, Elin Larsson. Reward or punishment?"

I tossed the remote aside and leaned back on the cushions with a groan.

"Let's ask the lady herself," Jim said, approaching Toni who was coming into shot with her tracksuit top on and racquet bag over her shoulder. Her smile could have powered the Eastern seaboard, bright and beaming. "Antonia Cortes Ruiz, you've just knocked out the number thirteen seed, Keiko Kobayashi. How does that feel?"

"Honestly? Kind of amazing. I didn't know if I had a chance, but it just started going my way."

"Well, you looked very settled out there, very sure of yourself. Is this your real comeback from injury now? Can you get back to the level you were before?"

The crinkle of a frown between her eyebrows. Jim could have phrased that better.

"I hope so. I've worked really hard, and my coach and team have done everything they can to get me back here."

"In the next round, you have what many would call a winnable match against Sasha. You're certainly in with a chance."

"Well, I don't take anything for granted. She's been a great player for a long time, so I'll have to be at my best." Tactful, respectful. Nice.

Mira barged in with her microphone then. "Assuming you do progress, you get what many will call the toughest path through the tournament. Elin Larsson has been the brick wall for so many young players, the one obstacle they just cannot get past. Do you have a strategy in mind?"

"Well, I have to qualify to play her first," Toni said with a little laugh. "But bring it on, I say. If you don't want to test yourself against the best in the world, why play at all, you know? This is a huge tournament, and she's the goddess of tennis, so… But I need to win my next match and then I'll worry about Elin."

Alice threw a cushion at me for the goddess comment. Fair. It also gave me something to hide my blushes behind. I switched the television off, remembering I had planned to go out and be in the world. "You want to come gallery hopping?"

All I got from Alice was a groan.

"Fine, I'll go alone."

"You should. Being a *goddess* and all."

Okay, so I was never living that one down. Good to know, and somehow completely worth it. I grabbed my bag and some sunglasses, eager to be out on the streets of New York.

CHAPTER TEN

I CHANGED UP THE HABIT of the past few years and set my coaching team, under my mother's watchful eye, into doing some opposition research on one Antonia Cortes Ruiz.

"Why this girl?" my mother asked when I made the offhand request. "She got lucky with Keiko, and playing another nobody won't give her much of a warmup in the second round. You don't have to worry about anyone until the quarter-finals at the soonest."

"Mamma, trust me. It's just a hunch, a gut feeling."

"Fine, fine. I'm just glad you're taking something seriously this time around."

Parisa came back from booking my next car to the stadium for that afternoon. I didn't trust the traffic and liked to arrive plenty early for my matches.

"I did some digging on this Toni, personal stuff. Do you want that too?"

I froze for a second. I really didn't want this to turn into a whole situation. It felt like an unfair advantage somehow. Besides, if I was going to snoop around the woman before getting to know her better, I should really have done it by myself and stalked her social media like everyone else had to.

But hey, I had a match to prepare for and a ton of extra physio to be ready for it.

"I guess. It might help me get into her head a bit quicker."

"Um… Sure?" Parisa shot me a curious look once my mother wandered off to get everyone else working. "Elin, is this what I think it is?"

"Please don't think anything about it," I asked. "Just spill and see if there's anything useful."

"Okay, so she's been out for almost two years since she blew her back out at a Prem tournament somewhere in the Far East, I haven't checked which one yet. I want to say Shenzen? Funny though, it was actually a doubles match and she got hurt colliding with her partner. She didn't even play doubles before that season. Initial gossip was that she was out for good, right away."

Shit. That had to be a crushing blow for anyone in this sport. I knew there couldn't be a good explanation as such, but I'd been hoping for a slow recovery that just got delayed along the way.

"If we can find out more about how she hurt her back," I said, feeling pretty ashamed for bringing it up. "And how it's changed her game since she came back? Apparently I beat her in Paris before all that, but I don't remember the match at all. Vague flashes, but it's all just a mess of rallies apart from the finals."

Parisa added to her notes.

"Not married, no kids. I checked since that's usually the reason for an absence of more than six months. I think she had some funding issues when she first came back too, but she's more than breaking even again." Parisa was good, I had to admit it. "Current gossip is that she's sleeping with her coach, you remember Xavi? Him."

"But no confirmed couple sightings?"

That got me a knowing grin. "Nope. There's hope, then. You want me to come to the practice session with you? We have a bit of press after, previewing tomorrow's match."

"Oh, that, yeah," I had skipped ahead to the prospect of Toni so quickly I forgot I had another player to overcome, this time one of the lowest seeds from Poland. I tried to get to know my peers as far as possible, but the peppy young blondes were the hardest to keep track of. I suspect plenty of players felt the same about me when I was coming up. "Sure, keep me company if you don't mind."

"Alice not coming?"

"She says she won't be caught dead in Queens unless I make the final. And that when I do, she's bringing her own homemade signs. We'd better tip off Mother or there might be an international incident."

"Oh, let her have her fun," Parisa suggested. "It might be nice to go viral because your sister had some fun with a placard."

"Just remember you said that."

My second-round match went almost perfectly. My hip decided to let me play as though it had never been a problem. Then all I needed was for Toni to do her part against Sasha and meet me in the third round.

Good luck!

I sent the text a good hour before her match started, hoping she'd have a chance to see it before phones were tucked away. I wished we had some cuter way of saying it, like actors and breaking a leg. Definitely not one to try and make a thing of in professional sports.

Be careful what you wish for

Her reply might have sounded like a mild threat from anyone else, but it just made me smile. Of course she would be nervous at the prospect of playing me, only the cockiest player wouldn't these days.

I watched Toni's match through fresh eyes, with an intensity I hadn't had since my teens. Back then, I'd been trying to learn every trick and skill from Mira and the other greats. Now I was watching like an unofficial coach, cheering Toni on from afar. I held my breath when it looked like she wouldn't make it to the ball, then punched the air when she dived to make the backhand, winning the set in the process.

During the end changes, and the inescapable adverts on American television, I looked at the e-mail Parisa had sent with a bunch of relevant links. Thorough to a fault, that woman. A few were generic match reports, the kind of thing I wouldn't read about myself. Dry recounting of key shots and boring stats, almost never worth the time.

A few were interviews, though, and I found myself skipping straight to those. Sports media, never the most incisive, hadn't asked any deep questions. Generic enquiries about where young Antonia had grown up,

72

when she'd realised she loved tennis. The first one or two had one-sentence answers, short and snappy. I recognised that from my own. I'd been so terrified I'd say something wrong that I'd tried not to say anything at all.

But then the profiles got more in depth, and I found myself missing entire points to keep reading. Toni revealed a little more with each thoughtful question, and I found out how her parents had separated early, pulling her back and forth for years between Guadalajara and Malága.

Six years younger than me. Hardly insurmountable, but it was a little disheartening to have it confirmed. As age gaps went, it was hardly scandalous. No indication, though, anywhere, that she had any interest in women. Just those scalding looks, that blast of her full attention when it turned on me. Which could just have been good manners, after all. Maybe Toni was just kind of intense.

We wore clothes from different suppliers; her racquet brand was one of the newer ones I didn't entirely trust yet. Where I favoured the towel-material of sweatbands, always matching the accent colour of my outfit, Toni opted for a simple cotton bandanna twisted and tied around her head. The bands at her wrists never matched, to the point where it had to be intentional.

All that information, significant and not, just left me wanting more. Hadn't I asked these very questions? Why wasn't I satisfied to find out the answers? And then I realised: Reading about it second-hand wasn't half as interesting as potentially hearing those stories and details from Toni herself. I smiled at the thought. Would we get much chance to chat before the match if she made it through?

And just like that, her match came to an abrupt end. Her second-round opponent, Sasha, had been forced to retire with an injury. Just as I had in Cincinnati. The trouble with the grand slams was that the money just for showing up was too good to miss out on, so players forced themselves back before they were fit. Sasha had been struggling and Toni had taken the first set anyway, but the game was now handed to her in a forfeit.

She looked frustrated at winning that way. Not that I could blame her. Winning by forfeit never felt much like winning to me, either.

The pundits were waiting for her, especially since Sasha had gone straight off for treatment. Mira looked quite excited for once.

"So Antonia, you've made it through to face Elin Larsson in the third round as many predicted. Think you've got another giant-killing in you?"

Toni smiled and shrugged. "I can only try."

"Obviously Elin has a great rivalry with Celeste Rutherford and is fresh from winning Wimbledon. Still, there are rumours that she's playing through injury. Is this the best chance anyone has against her in a long while?"

I tried to tell myself Mira didn't sound too gleeful at the prospect. I did a quick set of side stretches recommended by the physios, almost out of spite.

The moment Toni escaped the clutches of television, she sent me a text.

Game on?

I smiled. She had confidence enough, I'd give her that.

I look forward to kicking your ass. Respectfully, of course.

Which only left me thinking about her ass. Damn it, brain. I didn't have to wait long for a distraction this time. Her texting speed had picked up. *Haven't you heard? I kill giants this year.*

I just wasn't loving the word 'giant' being thrown around so liberally. It made me feel huge and clumsy somehow, and not in the least attractive. *What happened to goddess? I think I preferred that title.*

My joy at quicker responses had been premature. The screen kept showing endless runs of those three little dots, but it took almost three whole minutes for those to give way to words.

Oh God you saw that? I never know what to say in these things. If anyone gets to be the goddess of tennis though, it's you.

Time to let her wait a bit. Too much instant replying might make me look a bit too interested. I had a gym session to get to. Running and stretching, nothing too fun.

Besides, I would see her tomorrow for our match, thanks to the relentless format of these tournaments. Better to play it cool.

I hadn't been nervous about a match in over a decade. Not in any noticeable, physical way. Those first few years I was a nervous wreck about everyone I played, either because they should crush me or then because I was the bright new thing that everyone wanted to tear down from her pedestal.

And okay, I still don't like talking about it, but anxiety attacks right before I needed to be in my best physical condition and mental sharpness? Not that helpful. I spoke to the most discreet therapists and tried what they prescribed, but the pills often left me foggy and lethargic. Maybe in another job, another life, I would have given them more time. Instead, I had to look around for alternatives, all the while terrified that someone would find out and splash my private life all over the news.

I'd learned, with my mother's constant coaching, to take that shaky adrenaline and use it channelled into strength and speed. If nerves made my body go all fight or flight, I could use flight to get my ass around the court that little bit quicker. A fraction of a second and a handful of millimetres could make all the difference on a vital point, and so I'd buried those human reactions deep beneath the surface to charge my reflexes and my motion.

Yet there I was, about to walk on court at the Arthur Ashe stadium. The biggest audience for any single tennis court in the world, I had played it countless times and had my share of big wins there. The friendly, raucous crowd were a delight to have on your side, and they treated the returning Open winners as their handpicked champions. If you won in New York, they'd always welcome you back.

Toni came bounding through the door from her private dressing room, another perk of playing on the big courts. She looked thrilled, but there was just the tiniest bit of tension at the edge of that broad smile.

"Ladies," the head usher greeted us, looking as sharp as ever in his tournament suit.

"Mohammed." I reached out to shake his hand. "It's nice to be back."

"I heard they had you on court in the Louis Armstrong for your first two," he said, as though it's some insider secret and not a matter of public record that also happened to be broadcast all over the world. He was clearly taking my turn on the second-largest court as a personal insult and not a quirk of scheduling.

"Well, we don't want to wear out the fresh paint too early, do we? You've met Toni before?" I gestured to her, not wanting to look like a snob by excluding her from our catch-up.

"Miss Cortes Ruiz." Mohammed bowed slightly before offering his hand, and she fumbled her racquet from one side of her body to the other in order to meet it with her own. "A pleasure. You were quite something in the first round."

"Thank you," she replied, shaking his hand with enthusiasm. Poor Mohammed looked a little startled.

I thought maybe I should distract them before his shoulder got dislocated. "Good crowd today?"

"Not bad for the end of the first week. There are some VIPs, of course. We'll introduce you around after the match."

The PA system from outside boomed into life, though we were insulated from the worst of it.

"Looks like they're playing our song," I said to Toni, whose smile wavered for the first time since she'd arrived.

"Yeah," she agreed. "Loser buys the first drink after?"

"You know how I like my martini."

We followed Mohammed down the corridor and out onto the court. Not quite the winding maze of Wimbledon, just gladiators thrown directly to the lions.

Hard courts made for fast, sometimes brutal, matches. We walked with slightly squeaking soles around the green section of the floor around the dark-blue court, taking our places either side of the umpire up on her elevated seat. I hadn't checked her name, but I remembered her face. The top-level umpires travelled with the tour, and she was relatively new. She'd told me off in Melbourne for smacking my racquet off the ground after a double fault, deducting a point for my temper.

Okay, maybe I had deserved that one. She gave me a knowing look as we moved to start the warmup rallies.

Once I saw Toni across the net from me, I started to remember our previous match in Paris. She'd come right after me, like we were both juniors with nothing to lose and not much difference in our rankings. The way she started to hit even in this loose warmup suggested she'd be bringing the same big hits. Her two-handed backhand came at me like I'd talked about her mother, and it had taken a quick adjustment to be able to return it.

All too soon the match was underway, the crowd a little restless given the early afternoon start. Fridays were always strange mid-tournament. The second week usually provided the big drama. I wasn't defending champion this year either: Celeste had kicked me out in the semis last year, on her way to winning the whole thing.

Toni won the toss and opted to serve first, which was common in players against me. They figured they'd have a chance to rack up the first game quickly, reduce the risk of me getting into my stride and leaving them with a zero for that set. I'd done that to more than a few players in my time, after all.

She looked good, with her cute little bandana, the same black and neon green as her shorts and tank top. Her dark hair was pulled up high in a ponytail, and on that front at least we matched. Thankfully, New York had gone for a bearable sort of grey day, far from the scorching heat of Australia in January. My navy-blue-and-gold dress felt good, felt almost like wearing nothing at all, which is really what you want in sportswear. The matching Lycra shorts underneath would be on display at moments I hadn't even considered, but that sort of thinking always melted away as soon as the first serve came at me.

She started with an ace.

Fifteen-love, the umpire confirmed. I had to get my head in the game, and quickly. Toni's smile was long gone, replaced by an expression of total concentration. Unfortunately for me, that was somehow even more attractive. I managed to stop staring long enough to return her serve the next time, but she took that point with a sneaky net shot I hadn't seen coming.

Okay, losing the first game was hardly a deal-breaker. I took a deep breath, the nagging tightness in the depths of my chest flaring at me, a reminder that I didn't always have this under control. I held my racquet loose and confident, bending forward in anticipation of what would come to my baseline next.

Toni tossed the ball in the air for her next serve, and from that moment she all but disappeared. Just a shape, just the blur moving behind the ball. All that mattered was beating that blur.

Game on.

CHAPTER ELEVEN

"Jesus!" Toni gasped as the locker room door closed behind us. The private dressing rooms were now the territory of whoever was playing on court after us. Our things had been thoughtfully relocated by Mohammed's ever-competent staff. I moved straight for my locker, tucked in the corner away from all the others. Number 19. Some people said it must be lucky; I just liked a little consistency in a life where I was somewhere different every other week.

I didn't know what to say to her.

I never did really, after matches like that. I considered some platitude or other, but as I turned to say it, she unleashed a torrent of Spanish with her head pressed against her own locker door, racquet bag still over her shoulder. Something about *madre* and then something else about *leche*. The speed and the furious tone made me glad that while I spoke fluent French, Swedish, and English, with a decent grasp of German, I had never been able to retain much in Spanish beyond *dos cervezas, por favor*. All the more annoying when I didn't even drink beer.

Hoping it wouldn't backfire, I dropped my things in the locker and turned to comfort her. "Hey, it was a good match."

"Are you kidding?" She faced me then, dark eyes flashing. "It's nice of you to patronise me, but that was a massacre out there."

I shrugged. "Sorry? I mean, you know how it is. We're all friends until the coin toss, then it's every woman for herself."

"6-1, 6-1 is not exactly a great match," Toni argued. "Damn, I knew you were good. You were great the last time we played, but at least I felt I was in it that time. At one point I thought the line judge was going to forfeit the match for me out of pity."

"Oh, come on," I said, reaching out to squeeze her arm. "It wasn't that bad. Sometimes when a rhythm builds up…"

"Well, if I had to have my ass handed to me, I'm glad it was by you." Toni's groan as she said it suggested 'glad' was still quite a way off. "Don't you have to go do your press conference now? Tell the world how you swept me aside?"

"In a few minutes." They'd come looking for me; Parisa would already be watching the clock. "If it's any consolation, I really didn't enjoy it."

"You didn't enjoy beating me?" Toni looked faintly amused. "Do you usually enjoy it? With other people?"

"Oh yes." I nodded my head harder than I needed to. "I mean, I wouldn't still be doing this if I didn't love crushing mere mortals, would I?" It was a joke, of course. Please, let her have taken it as one.

"I guess I did call you a goddess and all. Didn't realise it would go to your head."

God help me, she actually reached across and rapped her knuckles gently on my head, as though checking for a hollow sound. I think my knees were close to buckling.

"Elin!" Parisa called from the hallway.

I sighed. "Duty calls."

"Tell them I was gracious in defeat. And when you come back, you can tell me where we're getting that drink tonight."

"You really want to get a drink with me?"

"It might be nice to do it on purpose, instead of just finding you hiding in a bar, right?"

"Well, we could meet at my hotel—"

Toni raised an eyebrow.

"No, wait! I mean it has this fancy cocktail bar, on the roof? But you probably know a bunch of cooler places in Brooklyn or something, right?"

"Brooklyn?" Toni shuddered, and I mentally awarded myself a point over Alice. "If I wanted to drink out of jars and see men with terrible beards, there are cheaper ways. No, I like fancy. Where are you staying?"

"Elin!" Great. Mother had joined forces with Parisa in the hallway. There must have been some big-name journalists waiting instead of just the stringers.

"Coming! I'm at the Palace. If you're gone before I'm done, I'll see you there at seven?"

"Nice and early. I guess you do have a quarterfinal to prepare for."

"Oh, I didn't mean to—"

"It's all good," Toni assured me, and just to compound my state of panic, she leaned in to kiss me lightly on the cheek. No big deal. With my closer friends we did it all the time, over the net at the end of matches. Greeting each other at events. No. Big. Deal.

So why was my cheek tingling? Why did I feel myself blushing like I had a sudden, noticeable sunburn? If Toni noticed, she was classy enough not to say anything.

"Go knock 'em dead," she commanded, and I found myself on auto pilot towards the door. I pulled my sweatband off and shoved it in the pocket of my tracksuit. Fixing my fringe, I let my hair down and mussed it enough to make it look intentional before facing my mother and Parisa.

"Okay," I said, all business as the door closed behind me. "What am I saying out there?"

Alice was treating herself to an in-room massage when I returned.

"I think that was probably meant for me," I said, rotating my aching shoulders to drive the point home.

"Oh, Miss Larsson, there was a booking for two, so you can go right after."

I smiled at her. The girl looked barely twenty, even in her professional white scrubs.

"No problem," I said, throwing myself down on the sofa next to the massage table. "Make sure you really dig in on her lower back, though."

Alice flipped me off from where she looked perfectly blissed out under a white towel. "Ignore her, I have a disc problem there."

"O...kay?"

"Sorry," I said, not wanting to get our poor masseuse in trouble because of sisters and our endless games. "I'm Elin, by the way."

"Jasmine. And uh, I know. I'm a really big fan. When I played tennis in school, I used to always pretend to be you." She dipped her head at the admission. "Sorry, is that really sad?"

I shook my head. "No, it's sweet. Honestly."

"If you're going to keep talking and ruin my bliss, could you at least bring me some gossip?" Alice demanded. I stood up and started prowling the bedroom for something to keep me occupied. I was deliberately not looking at my phone, not for at least an hour. No matter how often it beeped.

"No gossip," I replied. "I mean, I won my match. But you don't usually care too much about that stuff."

Alice answered with a grunt as Jasmine finished up working on her shoulders.

"Then why are you pacing like a caged tiger? Usually after you win, you're the happiest girl on earth."

"I'm happy. Well, I didn't love beating Toni or anything, but that's the game, right?"

"Toni, is it?"

"Don't start."

Alice probably had more teasing in store, but when she looked over at me, I nodded at Jasmine, who moved off to clean her hands and pick out from fresh towels from her bag. Not in front of outsiders.

I sat back down on the sofa. "It wasn't personal. It's our job. My career. She understands."

"I think that's called being a good loser," Alice said. "I mean, if she hates you, she's hardly going to say so to your face, is she?"

"She doesn't hate me. If she did, why would we be going for drinks tonight?"

That got my sister up and off the table. I looked aside as she covered up, the deference to privacy I'd learned in her teen years, no matter how close we were.

When Jasmine returned with a towel for me, I shed my clothes quickly and got on the table. I was more than used to a brisk sports massage, and I needed it, having skipped the post-match ice bath.

Usually, Alice would wander off and leave me to it, but the promise of some juicy news kept her in place, pulling her robe on as she took my spot on the couch. "And are these drinks some big group event?"

"No...not that I know of. I invited her here. There's some privacy at least. And you've seen the drinks menu. It's pretty impressive."

"Should you even be drinking mid-tournament?"

"I'll have one or two. What? Are you going to tell on me to Mamma?"

"Tell me what?" Of course Mother chose that moment to return. She'd gone off to complain to the concierge about something when we got back from Queens.

"Nothing, Mamma," I assured her. "Could I have some peace for my massage, both of you? It doesn't exactly relax me to have to talk to you both like this."

Jasmine began working my calves, and I sighed in relief. I hadn't realised how tight those muscles where until her capable fingers started digging.

"Alice, *komma*."

There was no arguing with mother in that tone, so Alice got up from the sofa.

"Elin, we need to talk about your footwork later. You can't be that sloppy next time out."

"Yes, Mamma." Of course Britta Larsson still wasn't happy after a match that I'd won so decisively. That was why she made such a great coach, unfortunately for me. Maybe Toni would get a kick out of that when I told her later. Or maybe she'd find it a little sad, that at my age I was still saying "Yes, Mamma" just to keep the peace.

Soon Jasmine and I had the room to ourselves, and I found myself drifting pleasantly as she worked her way up each leg and down each arm. Slow and methodical, she pulled the tension from each overworked muscle, and by the time she got to work on my upper back I was halfway to a coma.

Only when she reached the dip in my back did she hesitate, speaking for the first time over the faint instrumental music that played in the background.

"Ezi told me when I got my booking that you're having a hip issue. Which side?"

I gestured weakly to the affected hip, and she gave it a tiny squeeze, barely perceptible. We were both relieved when it responded normally, no yelp of pain coming from me.

"I'll be careful," Jasmine promised. "Miss…Elin?"

"Mmm?" I asked.

"I would *never* normally… It's just this is maybe the one chance I have to be around you, okay?"

Was she seriously going to ask for an autograph? Or maybe a free ticket to my next match? These things did happen in the strangest situations. None of which had prepared me for what came next.

"I could lose my job for even suggesting it, but when I said I wanted to be you, before, what I really meant was I had this huge crush on you. And you know, here you are all gorgeous and naked, and I'm already—"

"Jasmine?" I was glad she couldn't see my face. If I looked as shocked as I felt, it wouldn't go well for either of us. "I'm very flattered, but that wouldn't be appropriate."

My mind began to whirl with possibilities. Was she some kind of honey trap? I never had come out publicly, no matter how many people seemed to know I was gay all the same. Or was she hoping to lead me to some misbehaviour and make me pay for it down the line? I knew a few people in the sport had paid off one-night stands and other compromising situations. I regretted ever asking Alice and my mother to leave. It wasn't the first time I'd been propositioned at a vulnerable moment, whether in the gym showers or in the glare of the public eye at some event, but it still always caught me off-guard.

"You sure?" She sounded so confident and was carrying on with my lower back like we were just discussing the weather. I wondered if I should tell her to stop touching me altogether, but I had to confess she was working magic on my sorest areas. I might have been tired of getting treated like some trophy that everyone wanted to get their hands on, but I didn't want to risk muscle strain by cutting the massage short.

"I'm sure. But um, thank you?" Smooth. So smooth.

"Okay."

The last few minutes of contact seemed to drag out for at least a week, but I could feel the benefit as soon as she stepped away to wash her hands and start packing up. I made a dash for the bedroom and the shower, hoping Jasmine would be gone by the time I had to start getting ready for my evening drinks.

It wasn't just the familiarity of the rooftop bar that I liked. It was how the subtle lighting made for lots of quiet, semi-dark corners and terrible conditions for selfie-seekers.

I took up position with my habitual martini. They made them perfectly here; the frosted glass and the spritz of lemon around the rim of the glass were a sharp contrast to the slightly sour drink. I'd never been into drinking alcohol for the sake of it, but this felt like an actual treat every time.

"Do you two need to be alone?" asked an increasingly familiar, slightly smoky voice at my shoulder before tapping me gently on bare skin.

The exhausted, sweating woman I'd left in the locker room was nowhere in evidence. Toni had dressed for the occasion, in a short dark-green dress that looked like it had been made specifically for her. Thin straps, the little purse tucked under one arm, and heels that pushed her over six feet. I could see all over again why there had been plenty of modelling offers, but she had that same slight awkwardness all us tennis girls had when moving around in anything other than sports clothes.

"You looked like you were really enjoying that drink. I wouldn't want to intrude."

"It's been a funny sort of day since I saw you."

"Oh, I bet you've had more fun than me. Less crying, for a start." She brushed a strand of hair from her face before it could snag on the minimal lip gloss she was wearing. I noticed her knuckles were red, a little swollen.

"You okay?" I didn't remember her catching a stray ball to the hand or landing roughly.

"Oh, just my bad mood," she said, shaking her head. "You really were gracious as hell, but I made the mistake of watching the match back with Xavi. He kept bitching about all the points I 'gave away' and it got heated."

Right. The coach. And presumably boyfriend. With the arguments that got heated.

"Oh...?"

"Don't worry, we didn't turn it into a boxing match. I did land a good one on my locker door, though. Pretty stupid, but I've got a week to heal now at least."

"On court, you don't seem like the punching type. You're the coolest person I've played."

"Well, I don't like the cliché of 'fiery,' for a start. And it takes a lot for my temper to tip over, but Xavi has a gift for it. He starts me simmering in the morning and... You know what? I don't want to talk about him. Do you mind?"

84

I shrugged. Not talking about men was always my preference.

"You were nice about me to the press," Toni continued, spotting an open table over in the corner. She took me by the wrist, and we snagged it before anyone else could drift that way. The server met us there, and I ordered a second martini while Toni opted for a Dark 'n' Stormy.

"I actually have no idea what that is," I admitted once we were alone. "But it sounds intriguing."

"Dark rum, ginger ale, and a splash of lime," Toni explained, looking after the server like he might be coming back already. "I think I earned it, don't you?"

"You sure did. This isn't too weird?"

"Why? Because you systematically destroyed me out there?" Toni laughed as she said it, reaching across to pat my hand because I must have looked a little worried. "I should know better by now, don't worry. You really are a machine on court, you know? And I mean that in the best way."

"Yeah, a machine. Elin Larsson the robot. I've heard that before." Maybe it wasn't cool to be pouting when you were the one who'd been victorious, but damn did I hate all those non-human comparisons. I had enough of a hard time convincing myself I was a regular person at the best of times. It tapped straight into the anxieties that kept me awake at night, but that wasn't Toni's fault.

"Hey, sorry," she said, when I didn't quite snap out of it. I wasn't sorry when it made her reach for my hand again, this time grabbing and squeezing both of them. Usually tactile people made me panic a little, but I found myself relaxing instead of just getting stiffer. "It really was a compliment."

"I guess that's why they call me the Volvo of tennis, huh? Safe, reliable, exactly what you expect..."

"Oh, come on." Our drinks came, and the server scurried off the moment they touched the table's surface. Clearly we were giving off some tension. Toni withdrew her hands, so I tucked mine safely back on my lap as we sat opposite each other on the high stools. The view out over Manhattan and its skyscrapers was impressive, familiar, but I couldn't keep my attention on it.

"What's really interesting, though," Toni continued, letting me focus on her again instead of sneaking glances, "is it feels like you don't even want it anymore, but you can pull it out like you did today and take it anyway. Same at Wimbledon."

"What…? Who said…? I mean, I don't…" I was sputtering, completely thrown by how quickly she'd seen through me. "Just because I don't turn cartwheels every time I win a match doesn't mean—"

"It's more than that, isn't it?" Toni leaned in, knowing what she said would be death for my reputation. "I'm not trying to be an asshole, I swear. I just wondered if everything was okay."

"Of course I'm okay. There are records to go for, more matches to play. I'm doing the thing I've loved since I was tiny. Who wouldn't be happy?"

Toni slipped off her stool, coming around to stand right next to me. "I thought my career was over, more than once these past two years. I know what it looks like, when things aren't right." Her perfume was light and floral, exactly right for her. I wanted to lean in, smell it more clearly against her light-brown skin. "And I've watched you for your whole career; we all do. Our coaches and our trainers say 'see how Elin does it' so we can learn. This isn't just you being quiet or humble."

For a moment I almost cracked and told her. The urge rose up in my chest like a wave cresting over the beach. All those things I could never have mentioned in an interview or to most of my fellow pros. The therapists and the prescriptions, the insomnia and the days when I cried through my workouts until enough endorphins kicked in to get me through. Learning breathing exercises to get me out on court when it felt like the crowd were going to break through the ceiling above me.

"Trust me, the more you get to know me, the more you'll see I'm just not very emotional about this stuff. It's nothing to worry about."

She didn't look like she wanted to drop it, but she startled me by leaning in for a hug.

"I meant to do that on court, but it's nicer when we're not all sweaty."

"And without twenty thousand people watching," I added, patting her back and hoping the hug wouldn't end too soon. Of course, it did, and she was back on her side of the table in a blink.

"Well, so long as you know how lucky you are." Toni went back to her original point seamlessly. "Boy, what I'd give to lift even one of those trophies, and you're on what, twenty? Twenty-one, if you go on and win next week."

I blinked at her. I didn't need my stats read back to me.

"Not to mention all the smaller ones in between. And two Olympic golds. I'm kind of geeking out here, sorry."

"They all count," I said. "Each and every one has been amazing, and I've worked really hard for them." I felt my back straighten, right into interview posture. I'd said these lines before, and I didn't have any fresh way left to sell them.

"Oh, I wasn't—"

"I know, everyone makes excuses. I didn't have a real rival until Celeste; it's been too easy for me. I've heard it all."

Toni leaned in again, her dark eyes drawing me in just as surely as her careful smile.

"Elin, I wasn't insulting you. Believe me, I see how hard you work. I just wanted to be sure you were enjoying it. You deserve that too."

I nodded, taking a long sip of my drink. The usual doubts and insecurities were trying to set me down a negative path again. As I watched Toni, she gave me an even sweeter smile, one I wanted to return.

"Let's change the subject," she decided. "You said you had a strange day. So what exactly happened after you escaped the reporters?"

"Well." I sighed, leaning back a little. "You're not gonna believe how my massage went…"

CHAPTER TWELVE

I WAS PLEASED WHEN TONI accepted my invitation to the US Open final, sitting in the box alongside my family again. The few times I glanced up there, I was both thrilled and terrified to see her and Alice getting on like a house on fire. Or at least talking in an animated sort of way.

I had learned not to look at specific parts of the crowd over the years, since coaching during the game is against the rules. With my mother being my coach, that meant I often had to ignore my own guests beyond a brief wave or nod here and there. The penalties were harsh, and it tended to ruin my mood when I got told off by the umpires.

So, anyway. I won.

Which Toni would probably say was another unenthusiastic reaction, but I really yanked at my healed hip muscles in the last game, so that took the fun right out of the whole thing. For a blinding moment I thought I was going to have to retire right before I pushed through three more serves and finished the damn thing.

Mira was waiting after the presentation for the exclusive ESPN interview, microphone shoved in my face.

"Elin, you've done it again. This is your twenty-first Grand Slam title, leaving you one away from equalling the all-time record." The crowd was going wild. I waved to them again, buying myself some time and a few deep breaths so I didn't talk through gritted teeth.

"Yes, wow!" I tried for enthusiasm. My smile was genuine, that much I could say for myself. The endorphins were fighting the shooting pain up my side, almost as effective as ibuprofen. "I can't quite believe it, but here we are."

"It took you the three sets again, just like Wimbledon. Was it slipping in the second set?" Something in the way Mira smiled felt almost shark-like. Had her teeth always been so big and white?

"No, sometimes against a very good opponent you have to take it to the wire. That's how it should be, no? As close as possible until someone breaks and wins."

I had seen Celeste off in the semi-finals, and my opponent that day was the number-three seed, Fatima, who happened to hate my breathing guts on a good day. She hadn't shown it on court, the consummate professional. I owed her the courtesy of recognising her achievement, and the match really could have gone to either of us at various points.

"Now our viewers at home may have missed it, but as you served for the match there, you pulled up on the second point." Fuck, Mira. Couldn't she have kept her observations to herself?

"Well, everyone knows I was out for a few weeks before the tournament. I've had to adjust some of my most routine moves to prevent aggravating that injury. When I forget, my body lets me know about it. No big deal."

"Yes, but—"

"I mean, I served after that and it seemed to work okay, right?" I laughed, forcing her to fake laugh along with me. I thought about Toni's accusation again, how she'd basically said I didn't want this enough anymore. Spiting Mira might be the motivation to get me over the line and through at least another season.

"Well, let's hope you enjoy your big win here today, and celebrate with the best New York City has to offer," Mira said, wrapping up. She sounded like she was working for the Tourist Office, but I was relieved to get the hell away from her and back to the locker room.

Parisa and my mother were waiting there, no sign of my sister or Toni. They'd be off in search of the buffet and free champagne in the official reception no doubt. Where I'd be expected to show my face pretty soon.

"Get Ezi?" I asked Parisa as soon as the door was closed. Fatima had apparently already raided her locker and hit the showers. I sat heavily on the wooden bench that ran down the middle of the room, hiking up my white presentation jacket and the tight tee beneath it. My muscles showed no sign of which one had betrayed me, maybe a faint hint of redness where the pain was worst. It felt like I'd torn something vital, and my brain expected to see blood or bruising, some reflection of its own pain receptors currently doing the mambo.

"Same muscle?" My mother came to sit beside me, touching gently but firmly with both hands. Despite her briskness, it didn't actually hurt more. She'd been a nurse before she'd quit to become my full-time coach. For a moment, I was back in our house in Stockholm, sitting on the stairs with a scraped knee and trying not to cry.

I nodded, and she started rooting around in her purse for something. A moment later, I hissed at the cold swipe of ibuprofen gel.

"*Tack*," I said, thanking her as it soaked in. The stuff worked fast. I was going to be fit for the winner's walkthrough then, with all the handshakes and polite cheek kisses that came with it. Less royalty this time, but still some pretty fancy names and the faces to go with them. The editor of *Vogue*, a couple of Oscar winners; I hadn't really been paying attention. No doubt a politician or two.

"It's okay," my mother insisted as I pulled my shirt and the light windbreaker-type jacket back into place. "Just get through this and you can have some time off. Nothing matters until Singapore."

"Right," I said through gritted teeth. "Singapore." She meant the end-of-year finals. The GTA held them at the end of every season to confirm the rankings that had been racked up and dropped over the calendar year. They used to make us go right through to the start of December, leaving us about two actual weeks off all year with no tournaments to play. Thankfully, some smart and organised female players had banded together and requested a shorter season; the men were still working on it, since their tournaments were a whole separate organisation.

In that moment, Singapore seemed a hundred years away, but I got myself back on my feet just as Ezi arrived.

"You want me to take a look now?"

"No, but as soon as I can get out of the glad-handing?"

Ezi gave me a quick hug and went to collect her things.

"Come on, Mamma, let's go do the rounds," I said. "Look, we made it to twenty-one."

I had taken my phone from the depths of my kit bag and it vibrated in my pocket as we walked over to the big reception in the stadium's impressive event space.

Congrats. You were great out there. Sorry for ever suggesting you don't want it enough. Guess that makes me the asshole.

I smiled. I had worked my ass off for it out there, it was true. The pain in my side had dampened the high of winning but not entirely.

Not such an asshole, but I forgive you anyway. I'll call you later when I'm done with the posing and the ass-kissing. They're all lined up and waiting.

I didn't get a chance to check the replies for a while after that, swept into the compliments and the room packed with VIPs waiting their turn and their exclusive snap for their social media. When I finally grabbed a drink and a seat later, I was a little concerned at how tired my legs felt just from the extra standing around. I really wasn't getting any younger, and these new aches and pains would keep cropping up when I went this hard.

"Good match," Fatima said as she breezed past, her handsome movie-star boyfriend, David, on her arm. I liked him a lot, and despite his own busy career where he headlined hundred-million-dollar movies, he made it to a lot of tournaments to support his woman. I owed David a reply about playing in a charity tournament for their foundation back in Trinidad.

I waved at them both in acknowledgement, hoping nobody else would notice my quiet corner. As I sat back in my chair, my pocket vibrated again.

So you have to get in line for that? Good to know.

Wait. Was that some kind of flirting? I mean, I'd been talking about my ass. Technically. I drank my glass of champagne in one gulp, and the bubbles tickled my nose.

Where are you? I asked, realising I hadn't seen her once in the chaos.

No immediate reply. I scanned the room as discreetly as I could without standing, but it was too packed to tell much.

I had to go, my flight is actually in a few hours but I couldn't miss the final. Your sis is lovely, she came out and got me a car and everything. She'll be back in now.

Sure enough, I looked up and saw Alice approaching with her own glass of champagne and a whole tray of canapés.

"Your little girlfriend is off to JFK."

"She's not my—"

"You sure about that?" Alice took the seat next to me, giving me the once over before extending the platter of crab puffs in my direction. "I was getting chapter and verse on how great you are, and how lucky she was to be there. And she's right, even I know you kicked seven kinds of ass out there. So what's up with you?"

I took my time stuffing the little puffs of pastry in my mouth so I didn't have to answer. I know, very classy for the tournament winner to be pulling faces with her cheeks full of crab, but sometimes Alice brought out the kid in me.

"Who's says anything's up?"

"You've got that pinched look, like you're sitting on broken glass but you don't want to cause a fuss." Always with the cute turn of phrase, my sister.

"Hip being a little bitch again. Nothing to worry about," I said, wrapped around a sigh. My mother was gesturing from where she was talking to someone who might have been a rock star or just really into leather and eyeliner. I turned just enough on my chair that I could plausibly ignore her. At least having Alice to talk to had stopped some of the hovering people glancing over to see if they could approach.

"Well, if you've got some time off to rest, that could work out very nicely." Alice had that glint in her eye, the one that said I was about to be sorry she'd ever come over. I envied how put together she looked—her eyelids perfectly toned to the pale blue jumpsuit she was wearing, her strappy sandals with heels that would have had me stumbling all over the place.

I stifled the groan. What favour would I be on the hook for?

"I'll still be training, still doing physio. And if it's not that bad, I'll be back on the road before you know it."

"Still getting your excuses in early. No, there's this new charity I've been working with. And you know—come on, Elin—you know that celebrity endorsements get the money coming in."

"Last I checked, Alice, you're a pretty famous artist in your own right."

"Oh please. When's the last time they put two weeks of sculpture on television around the world? Sure, I'm respected. I make money, which is more than a lot of artists can say right now, but I'm not face-on-the-side-of-a-bus famous. Not Adidas-named-sneakers-after-me famous."

I waved her off. I had a ton of charities I supported, some through the GTA and others because friends were ambassadors. Lately I'd been thinking about starting a foundation of some kind, like Fatima and David's. It could tackle a real problem out there in the world. Kids going hungry, or homelessness, or landmines maybe. There was no shortage of places looking for money and awareness-raising.

"Flattering me won't get me on board."

"Well, what about the fact that maybe it's time you did something for your community, hmm?" Alice had officially withdrawn her tray of crab puffs. We were down to the serious part now.

"Community?" I tried for a joke. "Tennis players? We make enough, thanks. Okay, we could do more for the semi-pros."

"Elin, that's not what I mean."

"Swedish-Americans? Alice, that's like double privilege. We might be immigrants but we're white and have money. Even Republicans like us."

I thought Alice might hit me over the head with the platter. I couldn't blame her. Deliberately obtuse was never a good look on anyone, and especially not me. I knew exactly what she was gunning for, and she wasn't about to miss.

"The project, as I suspect you already know, is aimed at helping LGBTQ youth. Do you want chapter and verse on the extra hardships, the extra risks they face? Bullying, homelessness... Think what it would mean to get someone like you as a patron. And not just the famous thing. You're a good person, Elin. You work hard. God help me for having to say it, but you're a role model."

I squirmed at the unexpected sincerity. "That's not what I'm... It's a branding sort of thing." It sounded hollow even to me. "Listen, I don't actually decide this stuff. You know Parisa controls my diary, the appearances, all of it. And every single place I show up has to be approved. There are sponsors, there are the GTA rules about regulated charities—"

"Oh please, they have you showing up for Wall Street banks and warmongers. You play exhibition matches in countries where people are still being stoned for being gay. And what's the only reason you can do that, Elin?"

Our mother must have sensed the rising tension. We'd kept our voices down, but she'd always had a radar for it. She peeled away from her conversation and was bearing down on us fast, in case we made a scene.

"Alice, back off. You know it's not that simple."

"No, it's exactly that simple. Some of us don't have a choice about when we come out." I winced. Alice being outed as trans hadn't been her choice; it had been dug up by tabloids looking for dirt on me. None of my ex-girlfriends would go on the record, but kids we'd been at school with had been too eager to talk about Alice. "So when you have all this power, and fame, and protection and money, to deliberately let people speculate which male player you're dating…that's a choice."

"Alice, please."

"No." She shot me right down, standing to leave. "I don't get to tell you when and how to come out, I know that. But in the meantime, you could at least do something for all the kids you won't be a role model to. All the people whose lives might be a little bit easier if they had another rich, successful, popular person to point to and say 'It's not so bad if she can do all that and still be gay.'"

I stood to continue the argument, but my mother had reached us by then.

"Whatever has you both in a mood, drop it. There's a journalist from the *New York Times* waiting to start the profile that Parisa arranged, and if one word of family trouble makes it in there—"

"Like your divorce, you mean?" I felt bad the moment I said it. My mother flinched ever so slightly, which was the equivalent of a more emotional person being slapped right across the face. "Mamma, I'm sorry."

"Use that if you have to, but you're both going to get smiles on your faces now. Or leave," she added, glaring at Alice. "I don't know why you can't learn not to discuss these things in public. You're the one, Elin, always complaining about the press and the intrusion. I raised you to keep fights out of the public square."

Poor Mother, all she'd ever wanted was for the two of us to behave. And break the decades-long record for the most Ladies' Singles Grand Slams in tennis. Other than that, her demands had been really quite reasonable. Oh, if one of us could have managed a successful personal relationship along the way too, she might have liked that. Still, as she liked to tell me in training when I could never quite get that extra bit of topspin on my backhand: We'd call the Vatican when we got a miracle.

"Can you get Parisa to rearrange the chat?" I asked. "Ezi's waiting."

"Take the reporter with you," my mother answered right back. "Obviously play it down, but it will get you some sympathy. Celeste isn't so far behind, and if your number-one spot slips over the next few weeks, it would be good to have a narrative."

This time I groaned out loud. Was anything not completely stage-managed?

"Yeah, run along," Alice said, back to bright and breezy. "Make sure you don't accidentally tell the journalist you're gay. Would hate that to become public knowledge."

"*Va' fan!*" My mother cursed under her breath. I knew what the end of her patience looked like and we were fast approaching it. "This is some gay thing? Drop it, both of you. Now."

I resisted the urge to stick my tongue out at Alice, but I came pretty close. Luckily for all of us, the *Times* journalist had found himself bored enough to approach our warring group just in that moment.

"Elin, hi!" Okay, clearly we'd met before. I wished I was better at faces. "We haven't met, but ninety minutes watching you clean up on court and I feel like I've known you forever." Just a bit too friendly then. I felt my straight-guy-defences activate and slide into place.

"Hi…" My mother mouthed *Frank* at me. "Frank. Thanks for taking the time. I have my physio waiting for me back in the locker rooms, if you want to grab a drink to go?"

"Sure, I can work with that," he said. I waited for him to ask what was wrong, but the question didn't come. Great, a real empathetic type. "So do you stick around tomorrow and watch the men's final too? Or is it more check out once you get the trophy?"

I summoned some patience and walked him out past a couple of servers so he could swipe a drink. This was going to be a long afternoon. For a moment I wished I was the kind of person who loved the crowd, so I could have stayed to soak up the attention and blown off the interview instead.

My phone vibrated as we approached the changing room, and I checked it despite my better judgment.

Hope you didn't mind me talking about your ass.

I smiled like a dopey idiot. *Why would I mind? Just try to keep it off ESPN.*

"Right in here, Frank. This is Ezi, the best physiotherapist in the world." They shook hands, letting me read the slowly typed reply.

That just sounds like a challenge. What do I win if I mention it in my next interview?

Suddenly the journalist and the poking and prodding from Ezi didn't seem so bad, not even when she ran through the initial checks and confirmed it would be another trip to the doctor.

Everything just seemed that bit more bearable with Toni's messages brightening up the day.

CHAPTER THIRTEEN

I MADE IT TO SINGAPORE, though only with a week of regular training behind me. At least my hip had healed good and proper this time, no rushing to be ready.

This would be our last year playing the finals in Singapore, with the next few years already booked up for China. I was almost sad to see the change, although the prospect of visiting somewhere new was one of the few things that tempted me to keep competing, at least for another year. As I made my way through Changi Airport, I stopped and blinked at the realisation. That was the first time in ages that I'd thought about next season before someone dragged me into talking about it.

Why did it feel like Toni's influence, however indirectly?

We'd been texting back and forth, nothing I could point to and say "Look, flirting," but I was glad to see her name on my phone almost every time I looked at it. Especially since Alice, still pissed about me letting her down for her queer charity drive, hadn't been talking to me at all.

"Ms Larsson?" The driver held up a sign. A small crowd had gathered, players arriving all around the same time despite the different corners we were arriving from.

Travelling first class definitely had its perks, including not having to handle the ton of luggage that I dragged with me from country to country all year. With just my backpack of essentials, I slipped into the waiting SUV and the airline porters loaded the bags for me. Parisa followed on, taking care of tips and everything else until we set off for the hotel. My phone vibrated into life as soon as I turned it on.

Landed?

I couldn't deny just seeing Toni's name on the screen had put a spring in my step as we crossed the hotel lobby.

At the St. Regis about to check in

She startled me by calling. What kind of person did that? Calls could be overheard and gave no time for thinking up witty things to say. I was bad at phones, but texting I could handle. I answered anyway, since thinking up an excuse would have taken even longer.

"Are you really staying at the St. Regis?" Toni said. "I thought you'd be in one of those crazy super hotels somewhere. We can breakfast together. I mean, if you wanted."

"I guess that means you're staying here..." I trailed off, spotting her on the opposite side of the marble lobby. Xavi stood a little way from her, surrounded by their bags and arguing with someone in a bellhop uniform. I decided to risk it and jogged over as soon as I hung up. "Hey."

"I didn't think you were going to make it. The girls were gossiping, and they said you wouldn't be back before Australia."

"And let Celeste sneak past me?" I acted like I'd never been so offended and probably looked like a complete idiot in the process. "You must be up in the rankings to make this. Congrats." I said it so smoothly no one could ever prove I'd been tracking her numbers relentlessly since Wimbledon.

Xavi interrupted, the Spanish far too fast for me even to pick out words, but Toni argued right back until he took off with one of their bags, the bellhop shuffling after him with the rest.

"You hungry?" Toni asked. "I slept the whole flight and now I'm starving."

"I could eat," I said, and although in my jeans and a tank top I wasn't technically dressed for dinner, I knew the staff here in the restaurants would accommodate me. Toni looked much smarter in her kicky blue dress and sandals. I looked for Parisa, but she was deep in conversation at reception. A text would do. "You stayed here before?"

"No, never made the finals before. The last time I was on track was the year I did my back. Is it always so humid here?"

"Pretty much," I admitted, although we were in the blissful cool of industrial-strength air conditioning as we walked through the lobby to where the restaurants were laid out. "We're right on the equator, so we don't linger outside for long. Not when we can be chilled like this. You okay with Italian? It means we can sit out by the pool, which is nice."

"I love Italian," Toni replied, falling in step with me like we went out all the time. "But what are my other options, just to see what I could have won?"

"Well, there's fantastic Chinese." I gestured towards the elevators that would take us there. "Or down here also French. They have these little... I forget the word, but it's like almost private dining? Which is nice when the press is around, but it might look a bit much. Or something."

"A bit much?" Toni asked, her smile teasing. "You mean it might look like a date?"

I managed to choke on air for fully five seconds. Thankfully I hadn't been drinking anything. "Right. Might look like that."

"Well, I know how you hate drawing attention, so let's see if we can have pasta by the pool."

The maître d', Mauro, greeted me like an old friend, even though I only spent a week here every year. I supposed in real terms that almost made him a constant in my life. Mauro chatted to Toni as he led us outside, and I was pleased to see the free table was the one tucked in at the far end, with some plants mostly obscuring us from view.

I declined the offer of wine, still feeling my way back into my regular schedule. I'd be up and in the gym by six a.m., so I decided to be kind to my future self. Toni was more adventurous, opting for a glass of red.

We didn't really get talking again until the drinks came out and we ordered our food. I caught myself fidgeting with the napkin, my cutlery, the seam down the side of my jeans. I'd chosen the seat with my back to other diners, not wanting the distraction if anyone did recognise me. It felt like some rare achievement, having Toni all to myself after weeks of just texting.

Her phone interrupted just then, prompting a quick but quiet torrent of Spanish. She ended the call with a dramatic roll of her eyes.

"Xavi," she explained, although I'd already worked that much out. "To warn me not to go wild tonight. Like I'd forget I have a doubles match tomorrow."

"Maybe he just misses you," I joked. I knew it would be polite to invite him down to join us, but the words stuck in my throat. "God, that pool looks nice."

"I think the other diners would notice if you dived in."

"So that's a no on skinny dipping?" I asked, taking a sip of my sparkling water. Awful stuff, but I'd made myself get used to it. "I've been swimming a lot lately, good for my busted hip."

I didn't miss the way Toni's eyes had widened at the mention of skinny dipping or how her smile got wider. Maybe I had finally learned how to play it cool.

"Any big plans for your vacation time?" she asked, taking a hearty mouthful of her wine and not quite looking at me.

I didn't have any. Usually I dragged my heels and then by the end of the finals picked something from the e-mails Parisa would send me. Some of them were favours or gifts from sponsors or friends, while others were just nice places she thought I might like. I was starting to realise I might be a little bit, well, spoiled.

"Part of me would like to just go home. We spend so much of the year on the road that it's nice to just be in one place, you know?" I ran a hand through my hair. She nodded, knowing the feeling all too well. "But then there's that quiet pressure to… Well, it's silly, but I feel as though if I don't have a real holiday then it adds to this idea that I'm this boring person who never has any fun."

Yikes. A little more honest than I intended to be.

Even Toni looked a little startled by it. She recovered quickly. "You really worry what people think, don't you?"

"I try not to. I've done every kind of meditation and therapy exercise, but the only time I can really drown it out is when I'm on court. There, I just have to win. My brain finally lets up on whether I was polite to my driver, or if my skirt is the right shade of white, or if the people in the third row think I'm dating Jürgen."

Toni took another long sip of her wine. "Maybe that's what makes you so good. That you need the peace you get out there."

"Maybe. I, for one, am thoroughly sick of talking about me, though. In case you thought I liked it. How was your week? You played the Kremlin Cup, right?"

"You pay attention to all that?" Toni laughed, playing with a strand of dark hair that had fallen forward over her face. We both defaulted to hair down on occasions like these, having to spend so much time with it tied up and pinned under sweatbands and bandanas. "Moscow is pretty cool, I got to do some sightseeing this time out."

"With Xavi?" Would I ever learn to stop picking at it like a scab?

"God, no. He barely leaves the hotel or the complex if he can help it. Put them both in the same place and he's in heaven. No, I went out with some of the other girls. Keiko asked me, which is pretty nice of her considering."

"I always meant to see more of Russia," I confessed. "When I was a little girl I was obsessed with the last Tsar. Even asked my dad a few times if I might be a lost princess."

That got another laugh from her. Toni was starting to make me feel like Ellen DeGeneres; nobody ever seemed to find me all that funny.

"I can't believe I made the final, though," Toni continued. "I know it's old hat for you, but it was like I finally got close. Made losing even more of a bitch, but hey, there's no shame in losing to Celeste."

"None," I assured her. Toni didn't perk up, though, so on impulse I reached out to squeeze her hand. "Trust me, you'll be back with other chances. But Celeste can take out anyone on her day."

"You guys are friends, right?"

"That's a complicated question." I wished I'd gone for the damn wine now. Still, it was hardly a secret. "You've probably heard it around the place anyway, but we dated for a while."

"Oh!" Toni blushed almost as dark as her wine for a moment. "I don't listen to rumours so... Well, so... That's cool. Cool, yes."

"You really didn't know?" I practically heard Alice taunting me inside my head. "I'm not exactly out, but I didn't think it was news."

"Hey, your personal life is your own. I didn't want to force you to tell me." Toni had recovered her composure, but something about her was a little off. Had I completely misread her? Did she think her mild flirtation was safe with a fellow straight girl and I had just blown that out of the water? We were saved by the arrival of our food.

I felt a little jealous of her risotto when they set it down, at least until my own pasta appeared and my stomach growled to remind me I hadn't eaten since my last snack on the plane. Burning through as much energy as we did, our bodies were always primed for more fuel to burn, and this was some damn delicious fuel in the form of a perfect puttanesca.

"Wow, that must be some damn good pasta," Toni teased as I moaned ever so slightly over the first bite. I hadn't meant to, but it really was delicious.

"How's yours?" I asked, and she nodded enthusiastically while taking another bite. "It's almost always good here." I said it with confidence, but honestly a lot of hotels and restaurants all blurred into one another at this point.

"We were talking about vacations, weren't we?" Toni said as we made our way through the respective dishes. "I think I might go back to Mexico this year."

"You still have a place in Spain though, right?"

"Mmm, but my dad's family are in Guadalajara." The way she said it was lovely, like the word itself was a happy memory. "My grandmother has a big old house south of the city, almost all the way to Lake Chapala. It's really beautiful there."

"Sounds like rest and relaxation to me," I said. "You must need it too, coming back from such a tough injury and playing a season like this. You've been in a lot more than I have."

"Yeah, but you know how it is. After you get injured, you're just so grateful to be playing again, you don't really mind how tough it is. Just so long as you can get out there."

"Right. Of course."

"Still, you could go anywhere I bet. The Maldives, or maybe one of those private islands somewhere. That must be cool."

"Sure, I mean there are options. It would just be nice to go visit someone, or with someone. Not my whole entourage with a training schedule and bags of spare racquets. Just…a real holiday. One bag and a camera around my neck, you know? Play tourist."

"Sounds nice, when you say it like this."

We ate the rest of our meal in companionable silence, and when Toni ordered a second glass of wine, I had them bring the bottle so I could join her.

"Sitting here, we could almost just be tourists," I said, realising we now had the pool patio to ourselves, candles lit silently by the staff while we had been oblivious. It was almost romantic, but I didn't dare think of it that way. Toni's dark eyes caught the candlelight beautifully, and I had even more trouble than usual not just staring at her. "Until you remember all our kit is upstairs, and the people to go with it."

"Have you ever been to Mexico?" Toni asked in return. "Other than playing the Open there."

"I haven't in a few years," I admitted. The prize wasn't on the higher end of the scale, and it always landed on a week where I'd had a more lucrative option. I shrugged off the vague sense of guilt. We all made those calculations. "And I haven't seen much of the country outside of a tournament, no. Oh! About ten years ago I had a long weekend in Cabo San Lucas. That counts, right?"

"Just about," Toni replied. "I mean, maybe it's weird of me to ask, but you could always come visit me for a vacation. There's plenty of room. It's not...you know, like this..." She gestured to the hotel in all its opulence. "But you'd be more than welcome. Abuela is always nagging me to bring friends, or a boyfriend."

Ah. Fresh confirmation. Still, friends wasn't such a hardship when it came to Toni. Despite my bubbling crush, I found her company much more pleasant that just about anyone else's.

"And you're not taking a boyfriend?"

"Why would I take some man there and ruin all my peace?" Toni scoffed. "It's the only time of year I can control exactly who I see and what I do. So Abuela can ask all she wants; that's never going to happen."

"Wouldn't I be intruding, then?"

"No, because I'm choosing to see you, to spend time with you. Listen, you probably have a hundred better offers, but it's there if you need it. *No importa*, right?"

She rarely lapsed into Spanish around me, but I appreciated the sentiment all the same.

"Let me check nobody made plans for me already—that happens sometimes—and I'll let you know tomorrow."

"Okay. You're not tired from your flight? I don't want to keep you out later than you should."

"No, I'm wide awake," I told her, and despite the long day it had the benefit of being true. "Tell me more about your grandmother's house."

I made it back to my suite just before midnight, unheard of at the start of a tournament. The Manhattan suite was everything I remembered but with a few new cool touches. My mother wouldn't arrive until the following morning, so I had the whole set of rooms to myself. Parisa was in her own room somewhere down the hall, and she'd left my key at reception for me.

The knock at the door startled me. Had Parisa ordered some kind of room service for when I got back? I checked my phone for missed calls or messages only to discover it wasn't in the pocket of my jeans. Great. I opened the door before I could get annoyed about that.

Only to find Toni standing there, my phone in hand.

"I figured you'd be on the top floor." She offered me the phone, and I took it gratefully. Not that it really held all my secrets, but the thought of it being out in the world without me had still made me panic a little.

I realised my chest was still tight and forced myself to relax. "Well, you know, they just call, and I guess this is what I was offered. Usually Mamma takes the other room, but she's not in yet."

"I should get back downstairs," Toni said, and the air between us was definitely shifting a little, something new and awkward there.

"Xavi will be looking for you, right?"

"Nah, he'll be sleeping by now."

"Nightcap?" I shouldn't. We both had matches early afternoon. "I think there's cognac."

Toni considered a moment, still half-turned back towards the elevator. "Sure, I could drink some cognac."

I ushered her in and nodded to the huge couch that dominated the sitting room. The bar was in the corner, so I tracked down the bottle and poured two measures into the ridiculously oversized glasses that let it breathe. The hotel staff had thoughtfully left some dark chocolate to go with it, so I brought the little plate of individually wrapped pieces along with our drinks.

"If my friends could see me now," Toni said once I'd set her glass down. "Late night drinking with the world number one."

"Your friends can see anything they like," I said. "It's just the press I stay away from."

"It's not like I can post a bunch of pics, though," Toni said. "I'm not complaining; I'm saying I get it."

"If you wanted a selfie you just had to ask," I pointed out. "It's so not the weirdest request."

"What is? The weirdest?"

"Um, the girl in Melbourne last year who asked me to sign her left boob? She wanted it tattooed. I mean, why not, right?"

"She's going to have fun explaining that to a doctor or a lover someday." Toni saw the funny side, lifting her glass in a silent toast. "But I just wanted you to know…this isn't about having a famous friend, for me. You must get a lot of fake people, and I wanted to make sure you knew there's no agenda here."

"That's sweet of you," I said, because it was. "Most people aren't that thoughtful. It's either full-blown creepy, or they do that thing where they insult you a lot to show how cool they are around a famous person. You, though, you can have your selfie anytime you like."

"Let's not show the world we're up late and drinking," Toni decided. "But when I see you on the warmup courts tomorrow, we'll get ourselves some social-media buzz. I want everyone pulling for you to finish the year on top."

"And I want you to jump as many ranking points as possible, so I guess that's fair. We can be cheerleaders for each other."

"That come with the cute little outfit?" Toni asked, and I felt that tingle again. "God, this sofa is comfortable."

I yawned, the day finally catching up to me.

"I knew I was keeping you up," she said. "Is it weird I want to just crash here?"

"There's a bed," I pointed out. "A spare bed, I mean." Blushing, great. What a smooth idiot I was. "All yours if you can move that far."

"Don't think I can," Toni said, her words more of a mumble. "Too tired."

"When you crash, you really crash, huh?"

Toni's response was to let her head fall back against the cushions with a soft little snore. I eased the glass from her grip before it dropped, and after a moment of debating myself, eased her down onto her side and placed a square pillow under her head. When she didn't stir, I went into the unused bedroom and brought a sheet to cover her with, smiling at the finished sight of a sleeping Toni all tucked in for the night.

It made it a little harder to get myself to bed. Part of me wanted to just watch her for a moment longer and revel in the peace. Instead, I stripped off and crawled under my own sheets, too tired even for pyjamas.

The world could wait for a few hours.

CHAPTER FOURTEEN

"ELIN, YOU COULD AT LEAST give the poor girl a bed."

I woke up with a start to find someone leaning over me, saying those words. It took longer than it should have to work out what the hell was going on.

Then I realised I was naked on top and the sheets were halfway down the bed. "Parisa!"

"Better me than your mother," she pointed out, completely unruffled by the nudity, pulling the curtains open to let some light in. "Your friend has gone back to her own room, by the way. Celeste wanted to know if you were free for breakfast—she's staying at the Raffles but is easy about where—and you've got an hour of press pushed up to before your first match. Sorry."

I lay back down and pulled the pillow over my head. Moments later, Parisa pulled it away. She looked as fresh as a daisy and like she'd been up for hours at the same time.

"Shower, please. Day's wasting," she scolded me, smoothing out the material of her Burberry check dress.

I grunted some kind of reply and made my way to the bathroom.

Celeste met me in the cafe closest to the venue, and it was a nice, familiar feeling to walk in and see her waiting at a table for me. We'd both gone for low-key looks around town, but there was no denying we were still dressed for sports.

"Hey, stranger."

"Sorry, Cee, injury and recovery wait for no woman. Fighting fit and ready to kick your ass, though."

She smothered a laugh with a sip of her coffee. "We'll see. I always have the edge on hard courts."

"So what's with the breakfast invite? You don't normally go for first-day catch ups." I knew Celeste too well by now to be anything other than blunt with her as I took the seat opposite.

"Has anyone approached you about performance enhancers? Someone within the tour, I mean. Not some random drug dealer."

"Me? No. I got a steroid injection in my hip, but that's all documented and cleared by the Tour's medical team. Why do you ask?"

"There are rumours doing the rounds again. And I've had more pee tests than I've had trophies lately. It's starting to feel like every other match. When I question why me again, they say there's definitely something going around out there."

"Beats me, but if I was on something performance enhancing, I don't think I'd be picking up these fickle injuries all year. Or at least, I wouldn't feel them so much." I sighed. "And I know you would never, so if anyone is insulting your character, you send them to me, okay?"

Celeste gave me her broadest smile. "You always did have my back. Looking forward to off-season? Mentally, I'm already on the beach."

"Where to this year?" I asked. Celeste took a joy in her vacations that I envied.

"Mauritius," she replied. "Assuming I make it to the final here, then the wife will fly out and meet me. Two weeks of no damn tennis, then some actual time at home. Might do us good."

"I'm glad to hear you're optimistic about it all again," I admitted.

"Yeah, I'm sorry about the summer. I respect you too much to be treating you like that, Elin. Forgive me?"

"Already have." I ordered my own coffee and the delicious-looking fruit salad when the waitress came over.

"What about you? Had enough of the sun this year? I still haven't recovered from when you invited me skiing in Sweden."

"It's not like we ever play in the cold! Ten and a half months of summer is more than enough for me. Anyway, I'm thinking of going to Mexico, staying with some friends who invited me."

Celeste took her time putting it together, but she was always much too sharp for me. "Mexico, huh? As in, where that Ruiz girl is from? Isn't that a coincidence?"

"She's the friend with the place there, yeah. And the boyfriend? So don't get all gossip mode with me. No story here."

She said more with the "Mmhmm" than most people could with a whole dictionary at their disposal.

"Do me a favour, could you?" Celeste went on to ask.

"Anything."

"Keep a record of all the times you get tested after matches. I just have this feeling that the pattern isn't as random as they say."

"Sure." I tried to think when I'd last been called for random testing. Usually once per tournament, but there hadn't been one in New York. When I'd first starting winning, knocking out bigger names and getting trophies, I used to get grabbed way more often after a match. That's when I learned to take my in-match hydration way more seriously. Nothing worse than being handed an empty cup when your body was three energy drinks short of being able to pee.

As our food arrived, a young girl broke off from her family who were at the counter settling their bill. Celeste tensed, even less comfortable with the public than I was. I couldn't blame her; she'd had plenty of negative experiences that I never would, not least because people could be racist idiots. Add to that her coming out when she met her wife, and she felt twice the need to be defensive.

"Hello," the little girl said, in her crisp little English accent. She looked Chinese, but I knew better than to assume her nationality on that alone. Singapore especially had a large Chinese population, a truly global city. "Are you here to play tennis today?"

She addressed the question to both of us, hands behind her back and sharing eye contact equally.

"We are," I answered with a smile. "Are you coming to watch?"

She nodded, as though I'd passed some test. Shooting Celeste an adoring look, she continued talking to me. "I want to play, when I'm older. I have my racquet with me."

I looked over to where a handsome man, presumably her father, was juggling a smaller child, a racquet slung over his shoulder, a backpack no doubt brimming with snacks and toys, all while trying to pay for their meal.

Celeste spoke up, rummaging in her purse. "Do you want to make your racquet lucky?"

The little girl nodded.

"What's your name?" I asked.

"Mai," she answered. "How do I make my racquet lucky?" she asked Celeste.

"Well, you bring it over here and we'll show you."

Mai darted off, liberating the Prince racquet in its slip holder from her dad's shoulder. He followed her over, seemingly resigned to another incident of her chatting to strangers. He stopped short when he saw us, which was pretty gratifying given the circumstances.

"Here." Mai offered the racquet to Celeste, watching like a hawk. "What are you going to do?"

"Well, my friend Elin here is the best player in the whole wide world. So if she signs her name, right here on your cover, then you'll play the best tennis you've ever played. It's like magic."

"Really?" Mai crossed her arms and gave me an appraising look. "You're very good, but magic isn't real. Also—" She asked her dad something in Chinese, and he replied with what sounded like a mild warning.

"You're my favourite," she said to Celeste. "Can you do magic too?"

"We'll both sign," I said, glancing around to make sure nobody else was getting ideas. I had the press gauntlet in twenty minutes, meeting my mother there. I didn't want to get stuck in an autograph line, but the rest of the customers remained oblivious. "Is that okay, Mai?"

"Yes, please!"

Celeste had unearthed a Sharpie, which would show up great on the white leather of the racquet's cover. We took our turns to sign, she with a *My favorite, Mai* and me with *Hit hard*. There, that should inspire the next generation, surely.

We extricated ourselves after the requisite family selfie, slipping our sunglasses back on and walking the short distance around to the arena entrance.

"Guess it's back to competitor mode now," Celeste said. "Keep track of the official peeing, though!"

I hugged her, even though we didn't do much of that anymore. "See you out there at some point."

"Ms Larsson?"

I looked up from fixing my laces. With a half hour still to kill before my match, I was only thinking about keeping warm, keeping my muscles loose and ready for a real workout. I had Keiko in the first round, the draw not so staggered here with only the top section of the rankings qualifying. Toni had scraped in second-last, mostly thanks to some injuries, but it would start off next season perfectly for her.

Of all the people I expected to see in the doorway, Toni's coach and boyfriend wasn't one of them.

"Xavi, right?"

"Yes, ma'am. I wondered if you had a minute to talk?" His accent was much thicker than Toni's, but his English just as impeccable. He had the build more of a wrestler than a former tennis pro, but we all settled differently in retirement.

"What about? Usually I don't see anyone right before a match."

"Of course. It's just... I figured if I don't ask now, maybe I never will. Are you happy with your coaching setup?"

I gave him a long, appraising look. "You mean with my mother? Who's coached me my entire career?"

"Lots of people change their coaches when they need a fresh approach. You've had some injuries too, that makes for big changes. I've been watching your progress closely this year, and I have some suggestions. If you were open to a change. I could work with Britta, or if she wanted a rest after getting you this far..."

"This far is twenty-one Grand Slams, yes?" I didn't like his brazenness, no matter how polite. I knew this sort of thing went on; some other players had a different coach every two seasons. I'd been tempted once or twice, when someone whose game I admired retired and went into coaching, but ultimately, success as a player had no bearing on what made a great coach.

111

My mother deserved credit for my achievements, especially when she'd learned so much on the job in those early years.

"And with my plan, you could not just grab the Open-era record, but hopefully smash it. You could easily have four, five more years, managed correctly."

And somehow that did it. It wasn't the disloyalty, not really. It was partly the realisation that coming to coach me would effectively be abandoning Toni, just when she was getting back on track. Much more than that, though, the length of time Xavi was talking about filled me with instant dread.

Five years? I'd barely talked myself into next season. Of course, I'd never really worked out *how* I would retire, outside of random dreams where I had to announce it on a cooking show or choose between retiring and doing a bungee jump from some impossibly tall building. My subconscious wasn't subtle and for many years had been doing my mother's work for her.

In that moment, though, I was sure of one thing: I didn't have five more years of this in me. Maybe the needle for my tank hadn't quite ticked over to empty, but it was in the range where any sane person would divert to the nearest petrol station. It was freeing, in a way. I didn't have an exact number, but the horizon was no longer endless.

"Thank you, Xavi, I'm flattered. But I'm perfectly happy with my current plan. You must be proud Toni made it here this year?"

"Antonia is very good," he said graciously. "For a while, I thought she wouldn't come back, but she proved us all wrong. Still, there are levels."

"And given the chance—given some expert coaching—she could reach the highest levels," I replied. "I'm no coach, but I know ability when it's hitting across the net from me. You should invest in her. I suspect she'll pay off."

"Right, but there's a difference—"

"She wants a slam like other people want to be able to breathe," I reminded him. "Pour your effort into that, not someone cruising for the nearest exit, okay?"

"Are you saying—"

It was tempting to say yes. To confirm it here first and hope word would spread. How long would it take me to extricate myself? Could my next muscle twang or joint creak be an excuse to finally walk?

"I'm saying I'm on the end of my journey. Toni's not even halfway. If you asked my mother, I'm sure she'd tell you the same. And she's a world-class coach."

The dig wasn't discreet, but I didn't want it to be. I loved my mother, for all her faults, and she'd given me everything. Toni? Well she deserved better, even if I couldn't give it to her.

"Good luck out there today," he said. "I'm sorry I disturbed you."

I waved him off without absolution and kicked my overstuffed racquet bag to one side. Restless, I started doing a modified kind of step aerobics on the bench I'd just been sitting on. Motion always calmed me, and I needed my head back in the game.

I waited for Keiko after the match—we'd hugged and kissed cheeks over the net as usual—but she was nowhere to be seen. Knowing she wasn't a sore loser, I asked one of the ball boys if he knew where she'd gone.

"Testing, I think?" He looked mortified to even be asked, but at smaller tournaments the ball boys and girls did more than just the on-court duties.

"Right," I replied, realising that even as the winner of the match I hadn't been asked. That was pretty strange in itself. With all possible respect, did it matter as much if someone was doping if they lost? Of course it did, integrity of the sport and all that, but Keiko was about the least likely suspect I could think of. I'd test myself before her, and I knew I hadn't taken a thing.

We finally crossed paths again in the players' restaurant, in this case just a small catering kitchen with a room attached to sit at long tables. It was private at least, so I made myself a fairly epic salad bowl and settled down across from her.

"You nearly had me there," I confessed. "Is it me, or is it getting closer each time?"

"Sure, if you discount me dumping you out in Paris. That wasn't close." Keiko winked at me. "Did I hear right? Ruiz's coach is shopping himself around and he came to you?"

"How the hell did you hear that?"

"I have sources."

"Well, uh…"

"Only I can't imagine how Britta would react to that. Tell me if she finds out; I'll pay for a ticket to watch."

I shoved some leaves in my mouth, buying myself a moment to think. "I said no, obviously."

"Weird that he'd only move now, right before off-season. He should have asked in the summer." Keiko knew more about the internal workings of our world than I ever would, so I nodded along. She'd probably be running the Global Tennis Association someday, and not as an honorary figurehead. "Does Antonia know?"

My stomach did an unhappy flip at the thought. If people completely unconnected to the situation already knew, it wouldn't be long until Toni heard. Assuming she believed it, there wasn't much hope for our friendship if she didn't hear it from me first.

I glanced at the schedule on the screen in the corner. She was on court, which bought me a little time. I finished my lunch while Keiko talked about her winter plans in Osaka and made my excuses as soon as I could.

My player's pass gave me access to the hospitality seating area, and on the first day not all the seats were occupied, making it easy to slip in for the remainder of Toni's match. Xavi was in the front row of the box, and I frowned when even from behind I could see him gesturing. Toni wasn't looking his way even between points, but it could still get her penalised for coaching during the game. I felt grateful for my mother's silent glares all over again.

I found myself ignoring Toni's opponent entirely, and for once I didn't force myself to do anything different. I was exhausted from pretending I wasn't interested, that Toni wasn't attractive. So what if she was with the punk in front of me? Maybe she wouldn't be once she learned what he was really like. That didn't mean she was into women, or me specifically, but I was tired of giving up before I even got in the game. Let the disappointments come if they were coming; I could take it.

I leaned forward in my chair, sensing the cameras on me, and kept my face as neutral as possible until Toni won the point with a powerful smash. I cheered along with the crowd and let the world speculate why.

All too soon she had won the second set and was striding off court after the requisite handshakes. I slipped out and through the restricted area to meet her in the space actors would call backstage. For the moment, Toni still looked pleased to see me, so I rode that good luck and tagged along with her to the changing area.

"Thought you'd be back at the hotel for a swim by now," she said. "Or maybe you should try your luck with a massage again?"

"Ha ha," I replied. "No, I saw you were on after and I wanted to cheer you on. Say thanks for New York."

"No match tomorrow, we could head out tonight," Toni suggested. "Everyone keeps saying you haven't done Singapore until you've had the actual Singapore Sling at the Raffles bar."

I scrunched my nose. "It's a little touristy, but if you want. The hotel itself is beautiful. I stayed there one year."

"You're the one who wants to be a tourist. Any more thoughts on Mexico?"

Having opened her locker, Toni started unzipping her tracksuit top. Oh crap. I hadn't really thought this through. It was one thing to admire from afar, but I'd always walked the tightrope when it came to communal spaces. Nobody wanted to be that predatory lesbian. So although it was temptation in a very real sense, I turned my back on Toni so she could change.

Clearly, her boundaries were not in the same place as mine. Once she had her T-shirt off and thrown in a laundry bag, she came around in front of me to ask again, this time in just her sports bra and skirt. Fine. I probably wasn't going to combust. If possible, she looked even more gorgeous, or it was the glow of winning that looked so good on her. Her hair was in a sort of side-braid, which would have annoyed the hell out of me on court, but it seemed to work for her.

"Hello?" She waved a hand in front of my face. "Mexico? Even just for a week, I'm not suggesting you give up all your time."

I realised in that moment I couldn't burden her with the Xavi news. One way or another, it was going to drive a wedge between us, and I just couldn't bear the thought. If the rumours reached Toni, I had every right to deny them if I wanted. Xavi would certainly do the same to save his relationship with her.

Not that I felt great about the choice, but I found myself saying, "Sure, just let me know the dates and the airport. I'll get it sorted out. You don't mind playing tour guide?"

"Not at all. Doesn't a week of great food sound perfect? Quiet places to read and sleep and just do nothing if you want. Or we can go out on the lake! Have some adventures maybe." Toni bounced back over to her locker, fuelled on pure enthusiasm again. She came back with a towel in one hand, her shoes and socks gone this time. "I need to shower, but can we ride back to the hotel together maybe? Make some plans."

"Of course. I'll have Parisa fix everything up once you fill me in. One condition, though."

"Name it."

"If you're giving me somewhere to stay, I'm paying for your flight. We can even go straight from here."

I knew Toni wasn't getting the best treatment from her federation, and we all paid most of our expenses out of pocket. This way I could treat her to first class, which was the only bearable way to do long haul after a season like this. The thought of maybe getting to do something nice for someone I actually cared about made earning this money seem worth it. I felt a surge of renewed lust for winning, like I was just starting.

"You don't have to do that."

"It's not a pride thing or whatever. I just really like to balance things out. I'll even use my miles if it's less...whatever."

"Well, I'm only just back to making real money, so I think I'll take you up on that. If you're sure?"

I nodded. "Go, shower, so we can get out of here."

She walked away, and I closed my eyes. If I concentrated very hard on my breathing, I could convince myself I wasn't picturing what she might look like under the spray.

CHAPTER FIFTEEN

WHILE I WAS RELIEVED TO take the finals trophy and end the season ranked number one, I was more pleased that Toni made the semi-finals. Her game had been improving by leaps and bounds, and she'd been watching all the other top players in their matches too, ever the willing student.

Parisa had been confused when I asked her to fix up travel plans for Mexico, and then she did the same mental mathematics as Celeste to work out why.

"Elin, are you dating this girl?"

"What? No! We're just friends. Honestly, Parisa. You of all people should know I'm perfectly capable of being friends with straight girls."

She held up her hands. "I know, I do know that. It's just I've got some crazy exclusive offers for you here, and you're saying the one vacation you want is a week at someone's grandma's house?"

"It might be good for me," was the only answer I had. "Anyway, we can't go straight from here because Toni is in Spain first for some charity event. I'm heading home to LA as planned, but these are the dates I want to be in Mexico. I told Toni I was arranging her flight too, so get her something connecting via Madrid, I guess? I've written down when she can leave, and I think we'll arrive fairly close together."

"Elin—"

"Can we just do the thing without all the questions? I know I'll get it from my mother, but I really don't want to make your life more difficult, I promise."

Parisa shrugged and started tapping on her tablet screen. I really would have been lost without her. I'd have to start thinking about that when it came to retiring. No doubt I'd still need an assistant, at least at first, but nothing like this level of organising and running my life. I'd be staying in one place a lot more for a start. I felt dizzy just thinking about it, that it could really happen sooner rather than later. Could Parisa tell? She didn't seem worried.

"Leave it with me," she said in the same comforting way she always did. "But you're telling your mother that you're not going to Sweden this year."

When my plane touched down in Guadalajara, I realised it had all been worth it. Arguing with my mother, not seeing my dad until closer to Christmas, even the continued radio silence from Alice that hurt more than it should.

If everything had gone to plan, Toni would already be landed and waiting for me somewhere in arrivals. I missed the whole private-jet thing, I could admit that, but first class from LAX hadn't exactly been slumming it. I grabbed my cabin bag and thanked the cabin crew as they let our section disembark first.

After that everything was a blur until I saw her, Starbucks cup in hand and earphones in. With her head down over whatever book she was reading, I had the chance to observe Toni for a long minute or two before she noticed me. My knees had a funny little moment when she finally looked up and smiled.

What was that annoying romcom about people and airports and everyone was sort of extremely English? It felt a little something like that.

"Wow, you really can travel light." Toni greeted me with one of her hugs that felt like she might squeeze the life out of a person. In board shorts and a scrappy tank top, she could have been any other gorgeous person on vacation here. Her skin had darkened further, from her time in Spain presumably, and her eyes twinkled with a relaxed kind of amusement that I found myself craving.

I had been true to my word and brought just one case and one bag. It had felt strange not to pack twenty pairs of shoes and multiple racquet bags, but it was a kind of strange I thought I could get used to.

"I rented a car, because we won't get around too well without our own wheels," said Toni. "I already got the keys, so unless you need anything in here?"

"Is the Starbucks on the way to the car?"

She nodded, hoisting her own backpack over one shoulder and wheeling her case that was slightly smaller than my own. Something in me liked the near symmetry of it. We looked coordinated, almost like, well, a couple. "Let's go."

I was expecting some compact car. Somehow that was all I ever pictured for rentals. Instead, Toni had rented a Jeep, one with a soft top that she instantly turned down with the press of a button. I sipped my iced coffee and slipped into the passenger seat.

"Don't judge me for using SatNav," she warned. "I know where I'm going, but I don't drive it myself very often. My *abuela* will be psyched we're making it for dinner too."

"I don't think I can judge—it's not like I know the way. Is it far?"

"Forty-five minutes, maybe an hour in traffic."

That I could definitely handle. I settled back, sunglasses on. "Driver picks the music," I said, the cardinal rule of my house growing up. My dad had always tortured us with jazz and my mother with sports shows presented by rude men mostly interested in football. Toni, to my relief, picked some kind of pop music. I bobbed my head vaguely in time to the music and found myself enjoying the scenery once we escaped the confines of the airport's seemingly endless parking lots.

"Can I suggest something?" Toni asked as we made short work of the highway.

"You're in control of the car and I don't know where I am, so… I guess you can suggest anything you like?"

Toni laughed at me, and I found I quite liked that. "No, but I thought maybe you deserved a real vacation. Shall we make a deal? No shop talk, all week. Abuela doesn't really follow it, beyond knowing if I win things and I'm making enough money. I thought it might do us both good."

It was something no one had ever suggested to me before.

"That sounds kind of perfect," I admitted. "I've been trying to pick up some Spanish in my downtime, so it would be nice to talk about normal things with normal people for a few days."

"Well, this part of Mexico is pretty popular with Americans and Canadians. You won't have to suddenly get fluent or anything. But good, tennis is off the table until we leave. This is gonna be fun."

119

I hadn't known exactly what to expect, despite my best attempts to snoop online. The Cortes family residence was set too far back from the road to show up on maps.

The long and winding driveway brought us to a gorgeous structure, a two-storey white building with balconies at almost every window and an inviting turquoise-blue pool in the courtyard. A part of me wanted to drop my bags at my feet and dive right in.

The torrent of Spanish was music to my ears, and every time Toni or her grandmother addressed me in English, I gave the most expansive answers I could think up on the spot. I got the whistle-stop tour of the property, and while I had been picturing a house full of aunts, uncles, and cousins, I was surprised to hear that for the most part, Maria lived alone. A slight woman, she had none of Toni's height or muscular build. On seeing a picture of her four strapping sons, including Toni's dearly missed father, I could see where her natural athlete's build had come from.

"Elin, *por favor*, my home is yours for as long as you stay. Anything you need, you just tell me. Or have this lazy girl get it for you." She gave Toni a playful slap on the arm. "I have my work, but you two must *relajar*, okay?"

And wow, did we relax.

The courtyard and its immaculate gardens were well-shaded by cypress-like trees, giving us an oasis of privacy only interrupted occasionally by the gardener or some insects that got a little rowdy. Like teenagers with the house to ourselves, we quickly discarded going sightseeing at first, opting to lounge by the pool with the stack of books we'd each brought with us, listening to the CDs and boom box that Toni had unearthed from someone's room. She found everything from salsa to Beethoven, via some truly awesome nineties pop that I somehow had retained all the words to.

I started my second day with a long leisurely swim, already being in the habit with my hip recovery. It wasn't quite the same as my own pool at home with its view out over the Hollywood Hills, but it was pretty special in its own way. Before the sun had fully risen, I was doing my lengths, and a sleepyhead Toni joined me about halfway through.

She stopped when I did, clearly more interested in keeping pace than racking up a fixed number of lengths. Maria called to us from the patio that she'd bring breakfast outside. The thought of some good strong coffee was the only thing that could have gotten me out of the water at that point.

Toni clambered out first, basically hoisting herself out on strong arms and ignoring the ladder altogether. I did the same, keen not to be outdone even if my biceps and triceps were burning lightly from a long swim. I noticed her scar then, just to the left of her spine. Before we pulled on our towelling robes to sit for breakfast, I found myself reaching out to trace it.

To her credit she didn't jump or even flinch.

"I wondered when you'd notice," she said. "From my back surgery. It's the only reason I made it back to playing. My surgeon was a miracle worker. Abuela here keeps telling me she prayed for him. So she gets all the credit."

"I knew it was bad, but that sounds…"

"Yeah. It wasn't just being able to play at that point. Everything was on the line—being able to walk normally, any chance of having kids… Way too much hanging in the balance for my liking."

"Wow, that's insane," I replied. "Is that something you're planning? Having kids, I mean?"

Toni shrugged. "I figure there's time when I retire. No way I'm taking time out voluntarily now. And y'know, I always wanted to do it with someone else, if I found the right one."

"So Xavi isn't on the baby-daddy list?"

That made Toni's eyebrows shoot up, and I rubbed my palms on my robe, worrying I'd messed up by mentioning him. She had to have at least considered it if they'd been together a while, surely?

"You mean as a donor?"

"What?"

"What?"

"Elin, do you think I'm sleeping with my coach?" Toni seemed to be processing fast, looking at me as though I might actually be stupid. Her voice rose as she continued. "Where did you get that idea?"

"It's what everyone says when I mention your name!" I protested. "And you two are pretty close. He's always with you."

"Because some of us don't have a ten-person team every time we step out of the house," Toni replied, and I thought she was teasing at first, but there was a definite edge to her words. "He runs a lot of interference with the federation for me. He's done the circuit himself, so he knows what's non-negotiable."

"I'm sorry, I just assumed." A little bubble of hope was rising in my chest.

"I thought you'd know better than to listen to rumours, is all," Toni said. "He'll laugh when I tell him, though."

That gave me a fresh stab of guilt about the rumours that had been doing the rounds in Singapore. It was the perfect opening to confess about Xavi shopping his coaching services to me, and probably other players, but the words died on my tongue as I realised it would ruin our holiday, which had been close to perfect so far.

"So, uh, babies?" I tried to change the subject back onto safer ground.

"Someday, sure. Sooner if I don't have to carry a baby myself." Another clue? Or was she talking about surrogacy? "What about you, Ms Larsson? Will the goddess of tennis be giving the world any… What's a baby god? Godlet?"

"I don't know if that's a word," I answered. "But sure, one day. I've been thinking about it more and more lately. Celeste, she wasn't interested, but I like to think that with the right person… Hell, I could do it myself. Like you said, I have the ten-person team, right?"

"I don't think Parisa signed on for diapers, somehow," Toni said.

Maria came out with breakfast then, the coffee pot and mugs a welcome sight. "Morning, girls. I've made *molletes*." I wasn't familiar with the dish, but everything we'd eaten so far had been delicious, so instead of micromanaging every calorie and gram of fat, I nodded in appreciation. Maria set the heavy tray down, and Toni got up to help her grandmother, the delicious scents of tomato and some spices wafting ahead towards me. My stomach rumbled gratefully.

"Gracias," I said as the egg-and-tomato dish was placed in front of me, sizzling cheese in evidence. My mouth watered at the sight. Getting back in shape for Australia was going to be an uphill climb after this week, and I found I didn't mind one bit. I did my part by pouring the coffee, and we all settled down to eat together.

We did venture out during the rest of the week, not least because Maria had a lot of charitable projects and social commitments that she preferred Toni to drive her to.

Lake Chapala was certainly as beautiful as promised, and we went out on boats to little towns full of local crafted goods and delicious treats. My favourite part was that no one seemed to recognise me at all, apart from a few double takes from the imported Americans. Toni was much more of a celebrity in in her home country, and everyone who recognised her wanted to talk either about Maria or the Mexican Open in February.

Most days, though, we spent at least some time in the pool or lying around it. I had brought some books that were long overdue for reading, and Toni turned out to be a total podcast addict. I'd never really found one I clicked with. Since my occasional insomnia was usually broken up by listening to people talking on the radio, most podcasts just made me feel sleepy before long.

"So," Toni said as we sipped at the mojitos she'd made after lunch on our second-to-last day. "This isn't shop talk, but kind of...what-about-after-the-shop talk. For some reason, I feel like your answer isn't going to be more of the T-word."

"It's true," I agreed. "I've never wanted to coach. The thought of going on television to talk about how other people are playing makes me want to hide under my bed. No, none of that is for me. Maybe—only maybe—some kind of ambassador role if it's for charity. I've been asked about that already."

"Right, but nobody expects you to retire yet. You'd have to stop winning everything first."

I snorted. "I don't know. It's not like I really have any other skills. I did okay in school but there's no degree or anything. Could I go back to college? It doesn't seem right somehow."

"What do you like doing? For fun, I mean."

"Haven't you heard? I'm too boring to have fun," I teased. "I really love taking photos. Not sure I could get to professional level, but I like my cameras."

"That makes perfect sense," Toni answered, playing with a mint leaf from the top of her drink.

"Why?"

"Because you've spent, what, twenty years almost in front of cameras? Not just the matches being on TV, but all the press calls, the adverts, the promos. It would be kind of cool if you ended up behind the camera after all that. Your introvert's dream."

"We can't all be show- offs, Antonia." It felt nice to use her whole name, the way it tripped off my tongue. I shifted on the lawn chair, my white bikini determined to wriggle into every crack and crevice. "Most likely I'll start a foundation. Pick something not so fashionable that really needs the help.

"I'm lucky, I know. Me personally? I'm set for life. I invested, I had good advice. I feel like I just want to quietly help people who didn't get that luck. Not for the pictures and the press. Just to…help. That's all."

"You're such a good person sometimes. It's kind of disgusting," Toni said, laughing around her straw. "But that's the dream. Now I'm back to playing regularly I'm trying to rack up the earnings. I've got a few years left in me; I know that. My back is better than before I hurt it, but there's just always that worry, you know? Back of your mind before you dive for a net shot or your knee doesn't like the landing on a jump."

"Oh, I know, trust me."

"This is getting kind of shop talk, isn't it? Sorry. I just really want a Slam. I want to get into contention this year. Is that crazy?"

I shook my head. Not if she wanted it enough, trained hard enough. The raw ability was clearly there.

"Anyway, afterwards I'm, like, the opposite of you. I'll go on TV. Give me pretty clothes and someone to do my make-up. I'll talk about anyone and how I could do it better. That seems to be what the guys do, anyway."

"Better you than Mira," I replied. "That woman really hates me. It wouldn't be so bad if she just worked for the BBC, but she gets everywhere. Australia is my only break from her, because she hates the long flight."

"She does not hate you," Toni said. "Anyway, I think it's cool how we balance each other. It means we won't be in competition, outside of playing. No fighting over jobs, no fighting over guys…"

"No fighting over girls?" I hid mostly behind my book as I said it, only so brave.

"Nah, I don't think we have the same taste," she answered. "I mean, you're not into blondes like I am, are you?"

I flicked my blonde—oh, I had never been so glad to be blonde—hair casually out of my eyes in response, saying nothing. Toni just smiled and popped her headphones back on, lost to some murder podcast or other.

I was starting to really like hanging out in Mexico.

———————

Our unofficial pact had been to ignore our phones as much as possible for the week, so I only caught up on my non-urgent messages when we were driving back to the airport. Toni didn't check hers until after she returned the hire car, and we made it through security.

"What the—" She stopped in her tracks.

"You okay?"

"No, I..."

"Toni?" She made her way to the nearest little metal bench and sat down, heavily. With her hair down, her sunglasses were like a hairband keeping it from her face. I could see that she was a moment away from bursting into tears. I sat next to her, careful not to touch or overstep.

"Is it true?" she asked, and I felt the ground shift underneath me.

"What?" I asked, although I knew. Surely our perfect week that had left us much closer, with the prospect of Toni dating women and definitely not dating the man who was about to wreck everything, would be immunity against my deciding not to tell her?

"About Xavi. Did he...? I heard a whisper in Singapore, but I dismissed it. Now he's blowing me up with messages saying he didn't do anything wrong, and he wants to be my coach more than anything. Meanwhile, half the girls on the tour are asking if I'm changing coach for next season, since you've poached mine?"

"I haven't. Toni, look at me. I have no interest in Xavi as my coach. You know how well I work with my mom. Why would that change now?"

"I don't know. Maybe she's stepping down. You said your parents are getting divorced..."

"That doesn't mean I steal coaches from other people. I wouldn't. And with all possible respect, even if I had a list of back-up options, I'm not sure I would have Xavi on it."

"Wow, I'm glad you didn't go with the disrespectful option."

"Toni—"

"Elin, did he ask you? Did he approach you?"

I nodded. "I was going to tell you, but then—"

"So he could have been out there asking everyone else, and I'd be blindsided. Left without a coach and scrambling around. You didn't warn me?"

"No, I would never have let that happen. I swear."

"*Let* it happen?" Toni stood then, as furious as I'd ever seen her. "I'm not one of your minions, Elin. You don't get to decide for me. You tell me the truth and I'll handle it. That's the only way it goes."

"I'm sorry." It was true, at least. Hot tears were just about blinding me, and I clasped my hands on my lap to hide how they were trembling. I knew how weak, how pleading that apology sounded, but it was all I had.

"Yeah, and what good does that do me? Just as well we're on separate flights."

"Toni, no. Wait!"

She started to march off towards her gate. I called her name, but she kept on going. I thought about running after her, but it felt too much like making a scene.

Great, truly spectacular. I'd really screwed it up this time.

CHAPTER SIXTEEN

THE YELLOW BLUR TOOK ME by surprise.

"Ow!" I yelled, rubbing my forehead.

"Elin! Focus!" My mother snapped at me from the side-lines, as if it was my fault.

Okay, maybe she had a little bit of a point. At this stage of my career, I really shouldn't have been getting beaned on the head by the ball machine. Still, she could have told me she had switched it on.

"Sorry, Mamma!"

"Don't give me sorry, give me your attention. You haven't had a good show in Melbourne for four years now. Let's get it together."

We'd arrived at the warmup tournament in Brisbane two days early, and my mother was intent on working off the last of my vacation-time moping. I'd played an exhibition match for charity just before New Year and, even with the annoyance of playing against Jürgen in doubles, I had been rusty and distracted. And I never played doubles, which really didn't help matters.

The practice court was good, a similar finish to the hard courts at the arena, much like the one in Melbourne too. I appreciated it when they kept things consistent.

"Alice wants to know if you're coming to her show, when you get back to LA?"

That was unlike my mother, to bring the personal into training time.

"Oh, does she want me there? Then she can ask me herself. Is Dad coming out for it too?"

"Maybe later in the week. He's busy with work, so he says. Wrapping up everything so he can start his retirement."

"He's retiring?"

Although tennis had become the unofficial family business, my dad had continued to work in his own importing and exporting business, a spin off from his days as a diplomat. He travelled almost as much as I did, and for years we'd tried to coordinate our schedules as far as possible. I hadn't realised how much I missed him until that moment.

Not that he was the only person I missed, but still.

"Yes, it's all coming out for the divorce paperwork. He wants to sell his boat and get a bigger one. I never thought he was such a cliché."

"Mamma, are you okay? This is a big change, especially at your age and—"

"I hear that boy Xavi wants to be your coach." She was good at catching me off guard. She did it on court to improve my footwork and reactions, and she did it even better in conversation. I considered her then, wondering if all girls really did turn into their mothers. We weren't so different to look at—she with her tidy blonde hair now cut short, her tracksuit worn like a suit of armour. With my ponytail and tennis dress from the same range, it certainly wasn't hard to tell we were related.

"And you know I'd go without a coach at all before I'd ever let him coach me. Please, Mamma. I don't want any other coach unless you're done with me. We're so close to finishing this up."

"Finishing?" Mamma shut the ball machine off, walking back over to me. We'd had most of our conversations at a distance, and it was disconcerting to have her zeroing in on me. "You're talking about it for real this time, aren't you?"

"I can't play forever. When my hip went, I worried… One of these days it's all going to slip. I don't want to keep playing when the next generation is knocking me out in the first rounds."

She sat on the bench on the side of the court and motioned for me to join her. For once we were all alone: no one sitting in to watch practice, no Ezi on hand in case I hurt something else. This week, players were scattered over Brisbane, Sydney, and Hobart depending on their tournament. All funnelling towards the big two weeks in Melbourne.

"First of all, I'd never let you play on that long. You have a reputation to uphold. But we also know you can't win every tournament every time. You never have. Maybe we start looking at a more targeted schedule. Jürgen is already doing this—focus only on the slams and the big prize money. Sit out everything but the minimum."

"Sure. Whatever you think." I couldn't hold my head up any longer, letting my chin drop to avoid my mother's gaze.

"Elin, what is it? You've never been the shiny happy one, but this is worse, even for you. Are you keeping up on your therapy?"

"Yes," I said, because it wasn't technically lying if we just kept rescheduling the same Skype call for weeks on end. I was sort of trying.

"I work you hard, *jag*?"

I nodded.

"Right, and look what you did. I just kept you on track to do all this. And you're so close to that record, it makes me crazy. I have dragged you through all of your doubts, and wasn't I right every time?"

"Yes," I sighed. I should have known my mother wouldn't deviate from the programme at this late stage.

"But nothing—nothing, *äskling*—is more important than you. If your heart has gone, we'll think of something else."

That did it. I burst into tears. Mamma pulled me close with one arm and let me sob on her shoulder. I felt like a pressure cooker who'd just blown the top clean off. She muttered something in Swedish that I didn't need to untangle, it sounded comforting all by itself.

"To be as talented as you are, Elin, it would have been a sin to keep it from the world. Do *not* think I haven't noticed what it's cost you too. I know how the attention and the expectations weigh on you, and I've tried to make myself a barrier. Are you really thinking about walking away so soon?"

I wiped the last of my tears and took a deep, shaky breath. Sitting forward again, I wiped my hands on my shorts. I studied the laces on my brand-new tennis shoes, available in stores right after the tournament, exclusively branded with the Australian Open logo and my signature, yet again in gold. What would walking away really do at this point? What if I regretted it in six months, when I got my head right again? Assuming I ever did.

"No, not yet. It's not some far-off mystery anymore, though. We're going to start talking about my last season soon. Hopefully right after I snag that last slam, wouldn't that be something? Break the record and retire in my acceptance speech?"

"A lot better than waiting for the next injury and issuing a press release from your surgeon's office," my mother admitted. "Then we need to get your head back in it for this. Okay?"

"Okay." I wiped my face with the towel poking out of my kit bag. I hadn't had time to work up a sweat yet, so it was still clean. "What about you, Mamma? If you don't have to coach me anymore?"

My mother shrugged, picking a ball from the floor and squeezing it in her left hand. I noticed her wedding ring was gone, a tan line under it fading fast.

"There are some interesting faces coming out of the juniors. I'll find someone, if it comes to it."

I should have known she wasn't done. Britta Larsson hadn't taken it easy a day in her life, and passing sixty clearly wasn't going to change that.

"They'll be lucky to have you," I said, bumping her shoulder with my own.

"There's something else going on with you," my mother said as I stood to resume my drills. "I know you'll tell me when you're ready."

I swallowed hard, not daring to mention Toni or Xavi. Everything about it made me feel like a perfect idiot. I whacked a ball over the net and told myself to focus on practice instead.

I was surprised to see the practice court was still fully lit, even though they were usually locked up this late in the day. I'd been in bed just after nine, but after two hours of tossing and turning I'd given up and made my way down there, looking for some staff I could charm into letting me in to hit for a while. When I got there, someone else had clearly had the same idea.

There was a ball machine firing mid-height lobs across the only strung net, a tall dark-haired woman returning each one with individual vigour, baseball cap pulled low. Of course. Of all the people to run into.

Toni didn't see me at first: She was deep in the zone and returning her shots with a relentless rhythm. When my soles squeaked against the floor, she was jarred from her concentration and looked over. As much as I hoped for some kind of acknowledgement, it stung when all she did was purse her lips in disapproval.

"I can turn around and leave," I called across the empty court to her. No reaction; she just lined up and thumped the next ball. "You're playing before me tomorrow, so you get dibs."

"Does your mother know you're out so late?" Toni asked when the machine finally ran out of balls. "Assuming she's still your coach."

"That's right, she is my coach. Always will be," I said. "That doesn't make her my keeper."

Whatever Toni's mumbled response was, she was smart enough to make sure I didn't hear it. It was time to change the subject, so I slipped my racquet bag from my shoulder. Not the giant match-day bag, just one of the countless spares left lying around in the crates of sponsor-provided kit.

"You want to hit?" I asked, but winced at how it sounded too formal, too imperious. Like I believed my own press, the tabloids who called me the Ice Princess. Or Toni herself, doing her level best to make 'goddess' catch on. "Or I can just stay over here and use the wall."

For a moment, it looked like she might ignore me altogether, but instead of reloading the ball machine, Toni tipped the unwieldy thing on an angle so she could wheel it well clear of the court. She strode back to her baseline like she was late for an appointment, before finally putting me out of my misery with a flick of the braid that hung over her shoulder.

"We can rally, sure."

"Well, if it's not too much trouble," I found myself saying. Not like I could really take the high ground. I sprinted over to the other end of the court, ditching my jacket on the way.

I was surprised when Toni came up to the net, glaring at my mini racquet bag that only held two.

"I want to try yours," she said. "Maybe that's what gives you the edge."

"Help yourself," I said. Sure, they were custom-made racquets that only I had in this exact colour. They weren't on sale anywhere. The big signature, again in gold, across the racquet cover made me feel sort of mortified as Toni looked it over.

"Why gold?" she asked. "Everything I see is gold, against black and white? Don't you get sick of it?"

"I didn't ask for it," I said, crossing my arms over my chest, bag dropped at my feet. "I guess the people who make the racquets at Wilson decided it, since I started winning stuff?"

"Actually, since your Golden Slam year," Toni corrected, pointing at me like a disappointed teacher. "It makes me nuts sometimes, that you don't keep track of all these amazing things you've done. It's almost ungrateful."

"Hey!"

"Well, it is," she said. "You realise you're the only woman to ever do a calendar year Grand Slam and top it off with the Olympic medal? But if anyone mentions that kind of thing, you act like they're insulting your ancestors."

"I'm not comfortable with compliments," I replied, which was painfully true. I shifted my weight from foot to foot. "Maybe I could learn to be more gracious. I *thought* I was being humble."

Toni was testing her grip on my racquet, so I pulled out the other and unzipped it. We matched.

"Humble is for people who win by accident, who only do it once. Anyway, what do I know?"

"More than me, apparently. You try doing the same thing, essentially, twenty times, and see if you have gracious words available. Or would you like to try finding paparazzi hiding in your garden? Outing your sister without her permission? I mean, I could go on."

"It's not like there's no good side. Like all the coaches wanting to throw over their people to come work for you."

"Which is also kinda shitty, since it costs you friends," I pointed out. "I know which I'd rather have, and now I have the same coach I always wanted and no friend. I'm not saying it's not privileged as hell, but that doesn't always make it fair. Or easy."

"Come on, let's get hitting," Toni said, bouncing from foot to foot to keep warm. The space was a little cool, but we'd be glad of that in ten minutes when we were sweating. "I mean, if you can handle it."

"Oh, I can handle schooling you again, yeah." I took my place at the baseline, posture bowing and bending to a natural receiving position. I shifted my weight from my heels to the balls of my feet, the tension moving to my calves, ready to propel me in the right direction. It was all so automatic, but the way Toni watched me, I felt conscious of every move and flex.

She plucked a ball from her pocket, palmed it and bounced it once, twice against the hard ground with its almost plastic veneer. God, I hated indoor courts. Why did I come looking for one?

Serving was an art form in its own right, and I always knew from my own initial toss of the ball whether it would be a good one or not. I could spot the signs in others too. If the height and weight of the ball in the air was just right, if the arm arcing up to meet it was fluid enough in its movement, and if the whoosh of air was just loud enough.

The tell, though, as a poker player might call it, was in the moment of contact. I'd been around my fellow pros in other sports for long enough to know the same was true in baseball, in cricket, in any sport requiring the application of a solid object to some kind of projectile.

When it hits right, you hear it.

Unfortunately, I was so busy paying attention to the sweet kiss of ball against racquet that I didn't leave myself time to react. Not that it would have mattered, because the cheeky little shit served an ace at me. It went whizzing past me like it had been launched by NASA. Who started a rally with an unreturnable strike across the bows?

Antonia Cortes Ruiz, apparently.

"Very funny," I called across the net. "For that, I'm taking next serve."

Toni shrugged, but she was grinning. She'd dressed with some thought, despite the late hour. I had thrown on the first shorts and tee I could find, nothing matching. Her runner's vest was a deep teal, cut away to show off those impressive arms and shoulders. She was lanky for a female player; the most successful were usually more compact and able to centre their power. Hers was more of a runner's build, but with glossy black hair pulled up in a high ponytail and cycling shorts to round out the look. She definitely looked more ready for a track event than a tennis court.

Leading by example, I rolled right into a friendlier serve, already in motion as Toni met it with a double-handed backhand that packed one hell of a punch.

We were off to the races then, hitting big and hard, making each other run for it. The huge room echoed with each smack of the ball, each solid bounce against the smooth floor overlapping with the squeak of our rubber soles as we darted around and slid to make the next shot.

Toni almost caught me out with a hefty shot to my weak side, one that a less nimble player would have no hope of getting to. But I had been in motion since the ball was hit, seeing the trajectory as though marked by neon lines through the air between us. I launched myself at the ball, connecting on the backhand well enough to drop the shot barely an inch over the net, leaving Toni stranded at the back of the court.

"Not bad," she called across, picking herself up. "And Elin?"

"Yeah?"

"You didn't lose a friend."

I picked myself up as Toni picked up another couple of tennis balls, shoving one in the waistband of her shorts since there were no pockets. It exposed a flash of sculpted hipbone that gave me a considerable moment to pause and let my gaze linger. I was no stranger to fit, toned women on a daily basis, but every so often, something exceptional knocked me out. Toni noticed me staring, and I forced myself not to look away.

I started the play again, because the world couldn't be allowed to intrude when I was lost in the rhythm of a rally. I hit with everything I had, and Toni returned with the same vigour. We were warming up properly, showing off when we could. Every time a ball flew outside the lines or bounced off a wall, a new one was fired across the net in its place. Relentless, and a hell of a lot of fun.

When was the last time I had played like this? Like tennis was just a game and the world didn't hinge on the outcome of a particular point? I was ashamed to admit I couldn't remember. Not that I got a chance to dwell, with Toni aiming a pile driver of a forehand almost directly at my chest. Reshaping myself, I enjoyed the fluid way my body reacted without any conscious thought on my part. Instead of twinging with aches and pains, I returned the shot with vicious relish.

If we had been playing for points, that one was worthy of winning a championship.

The rally continued, both of us working up a sweat. No more chatter was exchanged over the squeal of sliding feet on the smooth surface, and we were hitting hard enough for the grunts of exertion to hit levels that people tut at and call unladylike. Toni was much louder, including her exasperation when she missed a net shot or didn't get to the ball quite quickly enough. Her raw power was astounding up close, but it was her precision that impressed me most of all. More often than not, the ball was placed within millimetres of going out, but Toni never looked worried that she may have miscalculated.

She had been training hard, and it showed. A good showing over the next two weeks and she'd be seeded for the French Open.

I called mercy after a good half hour, in need of a drink. The vending machine spat out an energy something-or-other in orange, and I gulped it down while Toni fetched a drink from her bag. Her visit here had been planned, then.

"Is this how you always get ready?" Toni asked as we drained our drinks, sitting on opposite ends of a bench like we had to leave room for an umpire's chair between us. "I thought it would be all spa treatments and yoga chants today."

"Well, you know my track record on massages lately," I reminded her. "I'll take it easy this week, use the matches for most of my working out. The real work is next week, or if I get an easy draw, the week after."

"Must be cool, to just assume you'll see the second week every time," Toni said, her voice still a little tight. "When's the last time someone dumped your ass out before middle Sunday?"

"The way you're playing now, you could do it," I admitted. "I'll be hoping to avoid you and Celeste in the draw this time."

"You don't have to kiss up; I already forgave you," Toni scoffed.

"Toni, listen to me." I got up and walked the short distance to her. "There's no kissing up, I swear. You've upped your game, and if I wasn't as good as I am, I'd be worried you were coming for me. I'll let everyone else work it out on their own time. But you're going to play your way back into being seeded before long. From there, it's all yours."

She waved me off, but I saw the glint in her eye. Part of her, at least, believed me.

"Got another half hour in you, old timer?" she teased.

"I've only got six years on you, and if I can point out that I just won the last two slams?" I tried for arrogant and was surprised that I didn't entirely hate it.

"That's more like it," she said, patting me on the ass with her—my—racquet as she got back on court. "Will you tell me how you have this strung? I like how it hits."

"Sure," I said. "I need to hit the stringers soon anyway. I'm running out of ready-strung ones. Berti travels with the tour—make sure you always go to him."

"Okay, and while we're sharing, I'm splitting with Xavi. My new coach is signed, but we don't announce until the weekend."

I stopped short of the baseline and turned back to face her. Instead of letting Xavi embarrass her, Toni had cleaned house. I smiled. It was hard not to like that about her.

"Who?" I asked. Any number of retired pros would be eligible, strong choices in every direction.

She hesitated on the other side of the court. Maybe we weren't friends again after all, not quite. "Oh hell, who would you tell? It's Mira."

"Mira? As in Mira Sobotka? Who *hates* me?"

"I told you, she doesn't. She's a bit bored with just commentating. So she wants to get back into coaching. Apparently I have potential."

It was a smart choice, and Mira wouldn't give up television money for just anyone. She had to see real promise in Toni, which meant I officially wasn't the only one.

"Congratulations," I said, picking up a couple of discarded balls. "That's a big move. One that might make the difference when it comes to the trophies."

"Hope so," Toni said. "Now come on, I want to finish destroying you out here."

CHAPTER SEVENTEEN

I DIDN'T AVOID CELESTE FOR long at the Australian Open, and she promptly demolished me in the quarterfinals, playing some of the best tennis of her career. I didn't mind on balance; the Australian heat always sapped my energy in a way no other tournament did.

More importantly, her opponent in the semi-finals was none other than Toni. After the initial niggle of *I could have played her instead*, I re-dedicated myself to cheering Toni on. Sure, it was a little disloyal, but our newly repaired relationship deserved that much. Celeste and I had always been more traditional rivals, even when we'd been together. She'd never expect me to cheer for her success at the expense of my own. We just didn't work that way.

Toni took Celeste to three sets, which nobody saw coming. The talk of the arena was the difference Mira had already made to Toni's match management and how she played much more strategically. I might not have liked the woman, but I sure as hell respected her craft. I tried not to be jealous when I saw her hugging Toni as soon as she came off court.

I went to congratulate both women on a great match only to find they'd both been detained for drug testing, again. Unusual that both women from the same match would be called, but I supposed randomness must allow for that sometimes.

Celeste was less than thrilled when she finally got free of them. She almost took the door off its hinges when she stormed in.

"I am so sick of peeing in front of these weirdos in suits," she announced, scuffing her bag across the floor. "I'm starting to feel lonely when I go to the bathroom alone."

"Me too," Toni grumbled, following her in. "They made me redo mine when the first one was, like, a millilitre short. These people need to get a hobby."

"When did they start testing the person who lost?" I asked, leaning against the side of the lockers. "No offence, Toni."

"I'll try not to take any. You've never been tested except after a win?" she asked in return, her expression still thunderous.

I held my hands up. I didn't make the rules.

"Because madam here doesn't lose all that often," Celeste filled in the unsaid for us, quirking an eyebrow at me so I'd know she was mostly teasing. "Even so, the law of averages. Which round did you get tested in this time?"

"I, uh... Oh, wait." I'd done my out-of-competition test right before Brisbane, but nothing else. "I didn't get tested this time out. Maybe I was scheduled for this, if I'd gone through. Or the final."

"Keiko and Fatima were both tested after their QF too. Toni and Fatima were both called again, and I know they called Keiko in too, because her match was right before ours, Elin."

"I'm not really one for noticing patterns," I said, because someone had to. Toni and Celeste both looked up from where they were rooting around in their lockers. They were clearly waiting for me to say it. "But there's kind of a common thread here. I'm going through entire tournaments—ones that I've won, after publicly taking steroids in my recovery period and declaring it—and nobody is interested in testing me. Everyone who isn't as pale as me? They're doing multiple tests per tournament."

"There it is," Celeste said on a long exhale, sitting down on the bench. "I don't know that I've got another fight like this in me."

She had a fair point. As one of the few African-American women in the top of the rankings, and an out lesbian at that, Celeste had more than done her time when it came to winning over hearts and minds. She'd faced injustices that made my blood boil for her, and this felt like one too far.

"You guys really think the GTA... You're saying their drug-testing policy is racist?"

Celeste turned to Toni, who was clutching her towels. "You can't tell me the Mexican thing has never been an issue?"

"Of course it has," Toni replied, her brow furrowed. "I just… That always felt like more of an American problem. Okay, and a Spanish problem. But these big international bodies, they're supposed to represent us all."

"And where does the money come from?" Celeste demanded, gesturing with both hands in my direction. "Your Elins, your Jürgens. Look at the president of this and the chairman of that every time there's an official photo. Not a lot of melanin, is there? When's the last time you accepted an official handshake from someone who wasn't an old white dude?"

"There's Princess Michael of Kent at Wimbledon," I offered, only able to move the man part of the equation, not the white. "But then she doesn't even get to use her own name. This setup really is fucked."

"But if I point it out…" Celeste sounded so weary. I wanted to give her a hug, but I wasn't sure it would be appreciated. "I'm just another angry black woman. They'll back off for a couple of months, but nothing will really change. Maybe it's just the cost of doing business, and I gotta accept it."

"Celeste—" I tried, but she shut me down.

"I don't know how many wars I can fight in a day, Elin. Any time someone speaks out, they face some kind of punishment. Not to mention the terrible press coverage that suddenly happens."

"Well, if anyone is going to do anything, we need some figures," I said. I couldn't feel their pain, but I could do something to help and take the burden off my friends who had been fighting too much for too long. "With the cold, hard evidence it's harder to say anyone's just being some hysterical female."

"They won't release more than they already do," Toni said, nodding at my point. "That crappy scale they use, to make it look like everyone basically gets the same. There's a big difference between getting the minimum number of tests and the maximum, but they pass it off as all roughly the same. So some of us must be racking up ones that aren't being counted. Or they're not being shared, anyway."

"You both know Parisa, yes? Well one of the few good things about her being straight is that she has a boyfriend somewhere in the GTA. Now I'm sure they won't just have a pile of dodgy information sitting there, but he could look. I'm sure if I explained to Parisa, she would see how important it is."

"You mean, she'd get it 'cause she's brown too?" Celeste filled in the blanks again, getting up to head for the showers. "Hell, it's worth a try."

"Okay, I'll speak to her."

"Thanks, Elin. It might not change a thing, but we have to at least try. You hanging around after this?" Celeste asked.

I looked to Toni almost automatically. "No, I'm flying home tonight," I said. "Good luck for the final, though."

"See you in Qatar, then?" Toni asked, heading for the showers.

"Ah, you won't, actually." They both looked at me. I wasn't injured, and the big prizes in the Middle Eastern tournaments were always a draw, especially with no more slams until the French in May. "Or Dubai."

"Wait, you're not—"

"No!" I interrupted Toni, not wanting Celeste to know I'd been thinking about leaving the game for good. "I'm just doing a whole targeted thing for this season. Focus on the slams. My mother's idea."

"Well, if Britta has a plan..." Celeste said. "We'll miss you out there, but not the competition."

"Gotta go," I replied. My phone had vibrated before I made it to the exit.

Sure you're okay?

Toni's text was predictable in a way that made my heart skip just a little. I should have known she wouldn't accept a non-answer like that.

Definitely okay. It really is my mother's plan.

I put my phone away until I had made it to the car that was waiting for me, the driver ready to take me to the airport. Parisa and my mother had flown out right after I lost, taking care of most of my luggage in the process. This whole travelling-light thing was starting to grow on me.

But is it political? Some kind of human rights thing? Gay rights?

That was my back-pocket excuse for not going, but I didn't think it would fly with having played there often enough in recent years. It almost reminded me of another pressing conversation waiting for me when I made it back to the States.

Partly. I need more breaks, like the one we had in Mexico. No serious tennis for me until Indian Wells. You?

I was halfway to the airport before she replied.

I'm playing Qatar, then back for the Mexican Open. Let me know if you get bored with all that free time, I can probably score you some tickets.

The offer, and what it meant for us being back on good terms, was everything I'd wanted to hear. I'd hear about it from Parisa, and from my mother, but I was already mentally blocking out that week to travel down to Acapulco.

Might take you up on that.

I willed myself to switch the phone off, so as to not get dragged into another round of reading too much into her words. If I was going to get myself on track for retiring, the last thing I needed was a romantic distraction. Not that it would even get romantic, probably. Toni might not even be interested in that kind of thing; we'd only just cleared up she wasn't dating Xavi.

I pulled the book I'd been getting lost in from my purse and read it the rest of the way to the airport.

"So you want me to ask Sean—who I broke up with three months ago, by the way—to sneak out confidential medical data on all the female players?"

Parisa stared at me over her Niçoise salad as she summarised what I'd just asked of her. I nodded in confirmation and she took a long sip of her Diet Coke.

"One of these days you're going to ask me for a *cool* favour," Parisa continued. "Like, 'hey Parisa, my six friends and I are going to rob the Met Gala, but we need a lucky eighth person to smuggle the diamonds out. You in?' And I'll say, 'Sure, Elin, it beats arranging your travel plans for Indian Wells. Why not?'"

"Are you done being dramatic? And okay, so you broke up. Are you telling me the poor guy isn't still in love with you?"

Parisa raised an eyebrow at that, but she didn't deny it. She picked at her salad a little longer, feet up on the desk in my home office. I sat behind it, like I had a real job or something.

"Fine. I'll see what I can find out. But please don't do anything that gives me a PR headache. Pass it off to someone actually affected. Nobody needs a white-saviour routine here."

"Agreed." I flipped the television on using the remote I didn't entirely recognise. "Any idea where I can watch the Qatar matches?"

"Keeping an eye on Celeste? Or has someone else caught your attention? I see things, you know. Obvious things. Antonia-shaped things."

"Not now, okay? Am I all done with signing and saying yes to stuff for today? I wanted to go catch Alice at the gallery before she disappears for the day."

"Sure she wants to see you?" Parisa asked, and it was a fair question.

"She's my sister," I said with a shrug. "If I want to make things right with her, she's just going to have to put up with it."

"With an approach like that, I don't see how it could go wrong," Parisa replied, completely deadpan. "Take the nice car; Alice much prefers the convertible."

"Thanks for the tip. You'll text me when you hear something from Sean?"

"Already on the case."

"This is why you're the best, P." I kissed her on the cheek as I grabbed my keys and headed out. We'd have to talk soon, about what my changed plans were going to mean for her and her career, but having already broken it to my mother, I was holding off on telling everyone else.

The sun was shining, and my car purred like a contented tiger as I backed it out of the gates, ready for the open road. Sure, Los Angeles traffic would have me crawling in no time, but for a moment it felt like I could just put my foot down and soar.

That kind of mood? No way would Alice hold out on me. We were as good as reconciled.

It took three hours to even get her to talk to me. She had clients in for a private viewing at the gallery, which I respected. Then when I returned after their appointment she had suddenly disappeared for 'supplies.' Only when I tracked her down to the coffee shop across the street did Alice finally relent.

"What is it, Elin? I'm in the middle of a busy day."

"Yeah, ducking out mid-afternoon for a flat white screams 'slammed.'"

"Oh, sit down. And shut up."

I sat opposite her, the chair a little uneven beneath me. "Alice, listen—"

"If this is another round of excuses, save your breath," Alice warned me. "I would never force anyone to come out, but your excuses are just that: excuses. You have all the support, money, and protection you could ever need. You won't lose your job. So anything you do at this point is a choice."

"You're right." It felt good to let that one finally drop. "I've been a coward. Most of my sponsors would still grab at the whole LGBTQ thing anyway, because it makes them look good. Maybe I'd skip a few smaller tournaments, like I'm doing right now. But ultimately, yes, Elin Larsson— the brand and the person—can survive coming out."

"Why change your tune now?" Alice was right to be suspicious. In a way, I did have selfish intentions.

We'd never looked less alike. She had her hair dyed a coppery red and cut into a short, flicked-up style. I'd never tried anything so stylish. While I was quite happy in my jeans and a simple white shirt, she looked flawless in a pinstriped jumpsuit and heels.

"I'm tired of being so careful," I said. "Of missing out on meeting great women because everyone assumes I'm straight. Of watching my pronouns and never confirming anything. I can't tell you the last time I went on a proper date. I...I want that to change."

"Good. Now who's the little floozy who's finally turned your head?"

"Alice!"

"No wait, I know. It's that hot one who called you a goddess. Then you beat her and... I don't think I know what happened after that?"

She flagged down the waiter and ordered a fresh coffee. I added an iced tea for myself.

"Well, if you hadn't been sulking with me, you'd know we went to Mexico together, stayed with her family."

"Elin, that's so not like you."

I watched a couple outside on the sidewalk, arguing about something as their happy little dog bounced around their legs.

"It wasn't... It took me the whole trip to find out she's not totally straight. Then it all got messy because her coach tried to poach me as a client. For a while there, nobody would talk to me. Including you."

Alice folded her arms over her chest. Fine, so I'd deserved it in her case.

"Anyway, it's not just about chasing some girl. I spoke to Mamma about retiring, for real. That's why I'm not playing so much this year; I'm putting all my focus on the slams. Injury permitting, I'll play until I break the record. Then I'll bow out, see what comes next."

"What does come next? No way you're going to make small talk in the commentary box like the other ex-pros."

"You've got me there," I said. "I haven't ironed out all the details yet, but I'd like to start my own charity, maybe a foundation. And while there are a hundred causes that could use my help, I thought it was about time I gave back to my community. As you would say."

"What would that look like?" Alice leaned in, intrigued.

"Building on the smaller projects you work with—helping with homelessness, bullying, making sure schools teach healthy things about our sexualities and genders. But maybe more, globally. Lobbying governments where it's still illegal, helping with asylum for queer people from those countries... I don't know how big we can go, but I'd like to try. You're always complaining about Corporate Gay and how the biggest organisations sell out and settle for the minimum. What if we could do more?"

"We?"

"I know you have a career, but you also care about this stuff. Maybe you could consult, share some contacts? Totally up to you."

"Well, well. I never thought I'd see the day, but here we are. Elin Larsson is ready to change the world. You might even get the L, B, T, and Q on equal billing if you carry on like this." Alice leaned the rest of the way over the table and pulled me into a hug, not letting go until our drinks arrived.

"See? That sounds like a project. And maybe we can make it easier and safer, so that nobody has to wait until their thirties to come out. Unless they want to."

"Or until they meet some pretty Mexican chick and can't contain the gay any longer," Alice teased. "If you're playing less, does that mean even fewer chances to stammer at her and not ask her out?"

I finally had something to surprise my sister with. "I'm actually going down for the Mexican Open in a week or so. Not playing, just to cheer her on. And if, uh, people ask me when I'm there, then I'm going to tell them that's why. She invited me, so maybe it's time I took the next step. Right?"

Alice smiled as she blew on her coffee. "Go get her."

"Not, like, right now. Weren't you listening when I said in a week?"

"At least that gives us time to teach you how to flirt. I'll bring in my best people."

The offer was a good one, but I'd already made up my mind. "Nope. No tricks, no smooth moves, no borrowing from cheesy movies. Just me, as I am. And if she's interested in that, great. If not? Actually, I can't think about not. I get queasy."

"Oh yeah, there's our Romeo," Alice said with a snicker. "Please tell me there's a way to get this whole disaster on video."

CHAPTER EIGHTEEN

"I CAN'T BELIEVE YOU CAME!" Toni greeted me as if we hadn't seen each other in a decade, when in reality it had barely been three weeks. It seemed like a promising sign when she hugged me so tightly I felt like we were skydivers who'd just jumped out of a plane together. Actually, we were still standing in the lobby of her hotel in Acapulco.

"Mexico and California aren't really that far apart, you know. At least compared to the air miles we rack up every year."

I'd let Alice pick my outfit, and she had me in skinny ripped jeans, acid washed within an inch of their structural integrity, topped off with a low-cut white V-neck tee that felt sort of translucent, and a tailored white blazer that I did really like. I didn't usually bother with jewellery at tournaments—one more thing to stash in the locker and risk losing somehow—but since I didn't have to change and play, I had opted for some long necklaces that Alice insisted set off the whole look. Mostly, I felt like there was a giant clock ticking until someone spilled something on me. I was basically a walking stain magnet.

"Still, you're taking time off. And this isn't a tournament you usually bother with." Toni was dressed for her first match, in a peach strappy top with a white skirt, her tracksuit top open and matching her tennis shoes exactly.

"I had to come cheer on the local girl. It's a rule, or something." I'd already checked in and organised myself before meeting her, and the tournament was held on hotel grounds so we didn't have far to go. "Can I get you a drink before you head out?"

"No thanks, but if you want to walk with me, maybe that will settle my nerves?"

I agreed with a nod, slipping my shades back on as we moved towards the tournament area. A lot of familiar faces, a few waves and shouts, but mostly we were left alone to do a lap of the perimeter. I was glad I'd opted for flat sandals.

"I thought the whole Cortes Ruiz brand was about not getting nervous?" I asked, only teasing a little. "Or is the scrappy underdog thing changing as you get back up the rankings?"

"It just means more, being here. I know it's not even on your radar, but it's the first pro tennis my dad ever brought me to see."

"Does it make me spoiled if mine was at Wimbledon?"

"Yes!" Toni smacked my arm. "I got a bunch of messages from Xavi saying he'd like to talk, but screw him. Mira's great, I know you're scared of her but—"

"I'm not *scared* of her!" Okay, so maybe I wouldn't have challenged her to a fist fight, exactly, but I was more offended by her dislike of me. "You looked good in Qatar."

"I just need to get these nerves fixed, then nothing can touch me. You'll have to teach me your secrets someday."

"But then they won't be secrets anymore." We circled around to the players' area, and I sent her off with a kiss to the cheek and went to find the bar. I had half an idea for how to make the suggestion about dating now. I just had to wait until the match was over.

Toni wasn't kidding about those nerves, and she dropped the first set against an opponent she could have dispatched with her eyes shut. Although she won in the end, it took her a long while to get done with showering and doing post-match with Mira.

Who was the first one of the two to appear while I waited at the bar, and I couldn't exactly ignore her.

"Missing television yet?" I asked, hoping it sounded polite enough.

"I'll still be doing slam coverage, don't you worry. Maybe now I'm coaching I'll find a way to get you to answer questions without looking like you've been held hostage, Elin."

Ouch. Fair, but ouch.

"You're doing good work with Toni. She's much more optimistic about this season."

"Thank you. Can I buy you a drink?" That was way more civil than expected.

"Actually, Elin and I have plans," Toni said, arriving in her civilian wear. "I promise, I'll be on the courts at seven to practice what we talked about."

"See that you do," Mira said, giving me what looked suspiciously like a warning glare. "No distractions, Antonia."

We walked off, and I left my half-finished soda and lime on the bar.

"*Antonia*," I teased in my best Mira impression. "Aren't you two professional?"

"She's not so bad," Toni said. "But I let her down today. That first set was a mess. It still takes me too long to take control of the game."

"I might be able to help with that. We just need some quiet, and some privacy."

"Oh yeah?" Toni said, leading us back into the main body of the hotel. "Your room or mine?"

It took me the entire elevator ride to compose myself after the way she said that, wink and all. Somewhere in there we must have decided on her room, and it turned out to be a pretty decent junior suite.

"Coming up in the world," I remarked, shrugging my blazer off and draping it over the back of the sofa. "But come on, sit here with me."

"This better not be hypnosis," Toni grumbled, but she came to take a seat beside me all the same. She looked more relaxed in her tight T-shirt and running leggings, her hair still a little damp from the shower. It was distracting too, how good she smelled. But I had a favour to grant.

"I'm going to tell you something that I've never told anyone, outside of Parisa and my immediate family. Okay?"

She shifted a little, turning towards me a little more. Serious face, which was sweet considering we'd just been joking around.

"I know it's not exactly a secret that I don't love attention, crowds, all of that. It's not just a picky little preference. I was diagnosed with a generalised anxiety disorder years ago, before I even went pro. And yes, it's

148

difficult sometimes. I manage, though, and the discipline of this whole life actually helps in a lot of ways."

"Oh. Elin, I had no idea—" She reached out and squeezed my shoulder. I couldn't help liking how tactile she was, how it all came so easily to her to comfort others.

I waved away the concern. "It's not as bad as it could be. Lots of people have it way worse. But I manage it with therapy and all the healthy crap we have to do anyway. Which makes me useful to you."

"Useful?" Toni asked with a smile. "You mean, I'm not just in this to steal your racquets?"

"It's cute that you think you could get them off me. But seriously, just trust me, okay? I'm not trying to get in on Mira's job or anything. I don't want to be your coach."

"No, because if you were my coach, people would assume we're sleeping together. Like they did with Xavi, and already with Mira."

"Mira's straight," I pointed out.

Toni shook her head at me, her expression saying I was way behind on this one. "How did you miss that?"

"Anyway. I'm not sleeping with you."

"Why is that, by the way?" Toni asked, brown eyes sparkling as she leaned a little closer.

I panicked a little, I couldn't lie. Instead of blurting out any old thing, I simply held her gaze for a moment or two. Then I indicated she should sit on the floor in front of me, and she did.

"I didn't know that was an option," I finally answered. "For a while there, I thought you were taken. And since then I wanted to respect our friendship. Right now, though, the most important reason is because I want to show you this."

"Then go ahead." Toni crossed her legs in an easy yoga pose, sitting with perfectly straight posture between my thighs, facing away from me. Like this, I could be a little braver.

"All you have to do, and maybe it's not so easy at first, but you have to find that feeling, the one thing that's making you panic. Now, it might seem like ten things all at once, but usually there's one central problem. In your case, it's feeling out of your depth when you start a match, I think. You can adjust that, but let's use that as a baseline."

"This therapist role-play is working for you," Toni whispered, but she squared her shoulders and seemed to focus all the same.

"It's kind of a positive-visualisation thing." I laid one tentative hand on Toni's shoulder, warm to the touch even through her tracksuit top. "You focus on that negative thing, the one that's causing all the trouble, and you push all your settled, positive feelings towards it."

"Mmm."

"So instead of that weird feeling where everything is chaos, and decisions are hard, and you're always rushing, you get the calm. You can shut out all that noise and turn the world down to what it needs to be. Just one person on the other side of the net. One point at a time, one ball coming at you."

"You're good at this."

I risked placing my other hand on her other shoulder, anchoring Toni to the moment.

"It should feel like this. Like something gently holding you in place. Just the moment, just the ball, just the point. You start the first game like that and it won't slip."

Toni laid her hands on top of mine, squeezing gently. I didn't dare to speak, for fear of disturbing the moment. I wanted so badly for her to get it, to have the same weapon in her arsenal against nerves.

"Well," she said after the quiet had really settled between us. "Simple, but it works. I already feel like I could beat someone. Even you."

"Right?" I dipped my head a little to speak the words in a whisper, closer to her ear. "With little tricks like that, you can do anything you put your mind to."

"Anything?"

"Anything."

She moved so quickly, with such easy grace that I didn't even see it coming. In less than a blink my hands were slipping from her shoulders, coming to a rest on her upper arms. Instead of the back of her head, I had that stunning face just inches from my own, eyes trained on my lips.

This part? Yeah, this part I could handle.

"Is this when I say that this could affect our friendship?" I whispered, and thankfully Toni's only answer was to press her lips against mine.

I'd like to say my brain made some pretty description for it, compare how she kissed to how she played on court, but at that point my last two brain cells were basically high-fiving each other and I was doing my best to kiss back as well as I knew how.

There was that initial nervousness. Not one of those movie kisses where everything magically lines up first time, where both people have the exact same idea about who moves when, and how. Instead, we both moved to the same side at the same time, making Toni laugh softly into the kiss as she corrected, tilting her face the other way.

The kiss got deeper then. Her fingers were suddenly teasing at the nape of my neck, before tangling in my hair and tugging gently.

"Huh," she said when we finally paused for a moment. "So that's what that's like."

"That doesn't sound like a complaint..." That ego of mine chose the worst moments to desert me.

"Definitely not." As we kissed again, and again, Toni made her way from the floor to straddling my lap, fingertips skimming the low vee of my shirt, making the three hours of agonising over what to wear infinitely worth it. Just when I started to wonder how far this was going to get, one of our phones started ringing. Not mine, as if it mattered. The moment had officially been interrupted.

"Sorry, sorry," Toni muttered, and some impressive cursing in Spanish followed right after. "You know what? Let me take this. It's the federation."

"Maybe you didn't fill out all your forms," I suggested as she answered, the conversation far too rapid for me to even get the subject matter.

What did become clear was that someone was making Toni very angry, very quickly. I leaned back against the cushions, watching with concern. Eventually enough was repeated for me to start making out some words. *Droga* instantly had me on alert, and so did *acusasión.* I was practically levitating off the couch by the time she ended the call.

"What the hell?"

"Oh, trust me, you do not want to know."

"You're being accused of something? Drugs?" I had pieced that much together but nothing else. Toni began to pace on the other side of the coffee table, running her hands through her hair.

"Not me, not yet. Xavi—there's going to be an investigation." She stopped, texting much faster than her usual pace. "He took on someone new to coach—some kid who's just gone pro from Mexico City, and apparently he offered him some kind of…amphetamines? Something? I never even heard of the stuff."

"Shit. Sounds like you got away from him just in time." I stood up, wondering if I should try to comfort her. The last thing I wanted was to look like I was trying to nudge things back to making out. I had more tact that that, at least.

"No, it's too recent. People are going to assume things. If I thought I got a lot of tests before then this… Fuck!"

"Wait, wait!" I called after her as she started dialling someone. "Toni, wait! You can't say anything to anyone, not yet."

"What?" She turned to look at me as though I had lost my mind. I pulled my phone from my pocket.

"Wait, please. Anything you say is going to be public record from now, so no calls, no conversations about it. Not even with me. Your *only* comment is through press releases and prepared statements."

I hit Parisa in my favourites list and was glad she picked up in two rings. "Hey, I need a PR genius. Do you know any?"

"I can block your number any time I want, you know. What did you do in Mexico, Elin? You've been gone five minutes."

"Not me, but I need a favour for my friend. Can you talk to Toni about something if I hand her the phone? She needs some advice. And probably a lawyer, but we'll get to that."

"Great, you've found someone more trouble than you are. Put her on."

I handed the phone to Toni, who seemed set on refusing. I pressed a quick kiss to her cheek. "Please, let me help."

"Hi, Parisa," she said. She listened for a moment. "I've heard a lot about you as well."

⁂

A flurry of calls, a bunch of e-mails, and one room-service order later, Toni and I were finally left alone in front of a standard competition-week meal. That meant lots of steamed vegetables and salmon that seemed to be measured by the slab.

"Sorry," she said as I uncovered the plates and poured the sparkling water. "What the hell happened to the day, huh?"

"Well, a bomb got dropped on your head right after a match, so…"

"And then there was our interesting development."

I sipped at my water. "Is that what the kids are calling it now?"

Toni rolled her eyes, just a little, but it seemed affectionate. "Listen…"

Ah. I saw what was coming as surely as I could have predicted her serve coming at me. "I know." I took her hand and rubbed my thumb gently over her knuckles. "This is no time for what would hopefully be a really fun distraction. It's going to be hard enough to focus on your tennis. But Parisa will help, anything you need. And I'll hang out the rest of the week. Non-distractingly."

"You don't have to do that. What about your training? Indian Wells is around the corner."

She, unfortunately, had a point.

"I'm still hitting the gym. Know anyone who could loan me a racquet to keep my swing up to speed?"

"Elin, I want to say upfront that I had nothing to do with anything. It's going to be a pain in the ass for a while, but—"

"Hey, hey, come on. I know you don't. You've worked so hard to come back from injury. Maybe I don't know every little thing about you, but I know you're not doping. You don't ever have to explain yourself."

"You're the best, you know that?" Toni came around the table to lay another kiss on me. "But yes, you're right about the distraction. We'll call that one for the road and see how things are in California."

"Sure."

"It's not going to be easy though, I'll tell you that. I'm getting impatient already."

"Then get back over there and eat your food," I suggested, although I would much rather have put the table to more interesting use. "Or we're never going to stick to the no distracting rule."

"Fi-ine," Toni said, groaning as she pulled herself away. "But you'd better find something really boring to talk about for the next little while."

"How interested are you in Swedish history?"

"Not even slightly?"

"Then Antonia, sit back and relax. Because I am going to bore you senseless."

Training with Toni that week in between her matches was a particular kind of hell. I certainly wouldn't have traded my usual prep for it, especially when Mira was there to coach one-on-one. It made me nostalgic for the worst of my mother's moods when coaching me through one of my slumps.

The freedom was pleasant, though. I got used to doing things for myself again—shopping when I needed something, making my own calls, and generally being in charge of my own day. I worked out for the same number of hours and spent time with Toni until one or both of us felt that line approaching, and then I would retreat to read or watch bad movies in my own hotel suite.

So when she made it to the final, I knew the self-restraint had been worth it. Even if the thought of 'restraint' in the same sentence as Toni made me worry, I'd need yet another cold shower. At this rate, I'd be fine to go scuba diving in the Antarctic.

There was a short line to access the VIP section; typical for any final with all the first-timers and day-trippers. I scrolled through my phone as I waited, only to feel the distinct chill down my spine that only one person caused.

"Hi, Mira," I said without looking up. "I hope you're not hiding a camera and microphone."

"Shouldn't you be heading back for Indian Wells?"

"Tomorrow morning. It's not such a long flight. Toni's playing well."

She gave a little huff. "Yes, I worked that out when she made it to the final. She's a talented player."

"You're helping her. You could take the compliment."

Mira ignored me until we took our seats. Since we were both from Toni's allocation, of course we were sitting next to each other. My disappointment at that discovery was wiped out by seeing my other seat mate. "Maria! You made it!"

Toni had organised everything, but her grandmother had been ill and the plans were up in the air. I knew this final boost would ease the last of Toni's nerves.

"Elin, *guapa*! It's so good you came back to Mexico. You're not playing?" Maria was dressed for a state occasion, in a beautiful twinset and pearls. Her short salt-and-pepper hair was immaculately styled, and her bright smile was so like Toni's that I had to hug her in that moment.

I shook my head. "Not my tournament this year. But Antonia has been fantastic. Have you seen her other matches?"

"Oh, yes."

Mira cleared her throat next to me. I just about resisted the urge to roll my eyes. "Maria, this is Mira. She's Toni's new coach. She's making her even better."

The two started talking over the top of my lap, and of course Mira had more than passable Spanish. By the time the umpire called for silence for the first set to begin, I was starting to feel almost left out.

Until Toni caught my eye from the baseline and winked at me, anyway.

She'd won the toss and opted to serve. I watched her take slow, deliberate breaths. Centring herself, just like we talked about. She bounced the ball a few times and tossed it up like it weighed nothing at all.

There was no mistaking the sweet crack of perfect contact, and the serve sailed past her opponent as an ace.

Game on, Antonia Cortes Ruiz.

CHAPTER NINETEEN

TONI WON HER FIRST PROFESSIONAL trophy since her comeback in straight sets, which was better than even she could have hoped for.

The whole crowd were on their feet as she jumped and punched the air in celebration, jogging to the net and shaking hands like every gracious winner. No interviews on court this time, but I knew she'd be running a gamut, with national and international press out in force in the staging area.

I passed a pleasant while with Maria, introducing her to everyone I recognised, and enjoying her pride as the federation officials and sponsors fawned over their winner's family. I didn't wait in the receiving line as Toni entered with her trophy—in the shape of a giant silver tennis ball—but we exchanged smiles so she knew I was hanging around for her.

"*Dios mio*, how have you done this a million times?" she asked when we finally met in the corner of the arena's huge restaurant area, at least an hour after the match ended. "The aftermath is harder on you than the match."

"Now you finally see what I've been saying all this time?"

"Yeah, but it's a pretty great high all the same. I just didn't think it would be so exhausting with the handshakes and the cameras."

"Well, hometown advantage. Wait until you get one of the big four—and you will, I know it."

She hugged me, hanging on just a moment too long. "Thank you. For being here."

"It was worth it to get to sit next to your *abuela*. She's so happy."

"And worn out, she's gone to lie down now she's chatted with everyone from Mira to the mayor."

"She's staying with you, in your suite?"

"Mmm," Toni confirmed. "I need to hand this trophy back, then there's a cheque to collect apparently. What I really want is…"

"Yes?"

"A shower. It's barbaric that we come straight from court without getting properly cleaned up."

"Well, the locker room is that way, of course." I pointed, like she hadn't been in there every day of the past week. "Or, and this is just a suggestion, my room also has a very nice shower. Much more private too."

"Is it rude to sneak out this early?" Toni asked.

"You know the best part about being the champ? You can pretty much do whatever you want."

"Really?"

Anywhere else, I might have risked kissing her, at least on the cheek. The room was still far too busy for that.

"If you want to do one more tour, get all your praise, then go ahead. I…will be upstairs."

"That sounds very distracting," Toni replied.

"It does," I agreed. "Luckily for you, the tournament is over and there's nothing left to pull focus from. So really, it's up to you."

And for once I didn't trip over my words, I didn't fail to say what I wanted; I just said enough and left on the perfect note. All that remained was to see if Toni would take me up on my offer.

Half an hour later, I began to doubt if I'd told her my room number at any point during the week. Then I remembered that I must have, because she'd called for me for morning gym sessions at least twice.

After an hour, I began to consider that she had misunderstood and had gone to shower somewhere else, and that the well-wishers must have held her up again along the way.

Thirty minutes after that, I had run down half of my phone battery from constantly making it light up to check for messages. Someone less proud might have just sent a message asking if everything was okay, but I had put myself completely on the line for this one. I dreaded to think how desperate it would have sounded if Toni had simply changed her mind.

When my phone did ring, it was my mother confirming the arrangements for Monday. Indian Wells was close enough to Los Angeles that I could technically commute, but for maximum relaxation we'd be staying locally. I couldn't care less about the details, other than the news that Alice was going to come for the end of the second week, assuming I made the finals.

I got off the call as quickly as I could, but when I ended and saw there were still no messages, I tossed the damn thing at the nearest wall. Since phones were basically overpriced pieces of plastic, it cracked badly and mocked me silently from where it landed just by the en suite bathroom.

Not really the Saturday night I'd had in mind, so I ordered room service for one and put the television on the first mindless music channel I could find, cranking up the volume as I started to pack my things. Even that didn't take long, not with one bag and one case, so I ended up taking everything out and packing all over again.

In between times, I paced, helping myself to something from the minibar on each circuit of the place. I couldn't remember the last time I'd felt so damn claustrophobic.

I had dinner, put the tray out for collection, showered and dressed for bed. Still no sign. I put out every light but the tiny reading one over the bed. Although I tried to flip through a magazine, all too soon I felt my eyes slipping closed.

Some time later, I jolted awake. Had I just heard my name? I waited to see if someone was at the door, if they would knock again. When nothing came, I stumbled out of bed to check, but there was only an empty hallway.

I made my way back to bed, sighing into my pillow as I let sleep pull me back under.

———

By the time I reached the airport, I had a replacement phone, but there were no new messages from Toni when the SIM pinged back to life. It still bothered me that she might have come to the door and I missed her by being asleep. Then again, if she really wanted to talk to me there had been other opportunities.

I didn't pick up a paper, and I ignored every other alert on my phone. It was only when we landed in LA that a headline caught my eye from the kiosk. Even my bad mood couldn't erase the habit of picking out Toni's name whenever it cropped up, and there it was, splashed all over the news about Xavi being busted for doping. My heart started to thump against my ribcage as I took in the whole impact of it. A scandal like that could burn down everything. Anyone tainted by it could be out of tennis for life.

Jogging over to the newsstand, I paid for a copy of the *LA Times* and flipped over to the sports section. A quick skim of the opening paragraphs confirmed that Toni had been kept for hours for extended testing. Which also explained why she wouldn't have had access to her phone. While I'd been thinking the worst of her—that she would deliberately blow me off— she had been having a terrible experience that had most likely tarnished her whole victory. My mouth went dry as I read it all.

The glimmer of hope was that Toni had been cleared since she received a negative test result, but it said that further tests were still pending. It had completely reduced her win to a punchline in the overall scandal, and I wanted to hit something on her behalf.

They'd brought my car around for me, so as soon as I was clear of the maze of LAX, I called her on hands-free.

"Toni, I'm so sorry," I blurted out as soon as she picked up. I got a stifled sob in response. "Listen, I know you've done nothing wrong. So do the media; they're just burying that fact halfway down the page. Are you okay?"

"It's ruined everything," Toni said, her voice hoarse. "I was so happy, and I just went to pick up my bag before I came to your room. They were waiting for me like... I feel like a criminal."

When I replied it was through clenched teeth. "Parisa will know what to do. Interviews or dignified silence, whatever she comes up with will be the right move."

"I'm not talking to anyone. I wasn't even going to answer your call."

"You still coming to California?"

"My flight is in three hours. But Elin—"

"Come to mine first, okay? I'll text you my address. We can travel down together Tuesday morning."

"No, I'm toxic right now. I think Parisa's advice would be..."

I gripped the steering wheel tighter, glad that traffic was moving pretty smoothly. My car was straining at the speed limit, and I had to resist the urge to just floor it.

"If she told you to stay away from me, I'll fire her." Parisa had been with me six years, had improved my life and my career at every turn, but I wouldn't stand by and let Toni be thrown to the wolves. "Okay, maybe I'll just sulk with her for a really long time, but if she said anything like that, it's just reflex. She's always trying to protect me. I don't need to be protected from you."

"That's the first thing anyone's said that makes me feel any better," Toni admitted, snuffling a little. "Abuela tried, but she had to get home."

"Well, in a few hours you'll be here. I'll have a car service at the airport for you, just look for the sign. Actually, I'll have the sign say Larsson in case the press are lurking. Okay? Just look for it."

"Thank you."

"It's no problem. Just come get some privacy and get back to enjoying your win. We'll deal with the media and the ex-coaches and everything else tomorrow."

Alice popped over not long after I returned home, to drop off a piece I'd admired at her gallery on my last visit. In return, she got to laugh herself silly at my attempts to tidy an already spotless house and staged an intervention when I got carried away setting up one of the guest rooms.

"For the love of… Elin, when she gets here, please don't have the fact you set up a separate room be the first thing you mention. I am amazed sometimes that you're not still a virgin."

"Excuse me, Toni is having a professional crisis."

"All the more reason to have some personal fun, wouldn't you say?" Alice closed the guest room door behind us and ushered me back downstairs. "Especially on the same day as she has to deal with LAX. That saps the life from anyone who passes through it. Wait, how is she here already?"

I looked to the driveway and groaned. Car service, yes, but not bringing Toni to me.

"Mamma," I told her, and Alice took up residence on the sofa. "She was supposed to be going straight to the club."

"Then you'd probably better get us a drink. Oh, did you hear it's supposed to rain later in the week?" Los Angeles residents were usually rendered useless by rain, the city grinding to a halt. Southern California was sunny and dry, and we liked it that way for a reason.

"It never rains at Indian Wells," I reminded my sister, grabbing a bottle of white from the wine fridge and a couple of glasses. I was sticking to juice, with play picking up tomorrow.

"Elin!" my mother called, and I temporarily regretted giving her the keypad combination. No, actually, nothing all that temporary about the regret. "I let you go to Mexico on the condition you train well and stay out of the headlines. What the hell is going on?"

"First of all, you didn't *let* me do anything."

My mother strode past me with a pronounced sigh.

"What I was doing is supporting a friend. Someone who's very important to me, who hasn't done anything wrong when it comes to doping or cheating. She'll be here in a couple of hours, and I want you to remember I said that and treat her accordingly."

"Plenty of people cheat without knowing, especially if the coaches are the ones bending the rules," my mother replied. "If they don't ask what's in the smoothie, they can't get in trouble. Or so they think. What do they call that? Denying it?"

"Plausible deniability," Alice supplied, being not helpful at all from behind the pages of the *Sports Illustrated* she was flicking through. In a minute, she'd find my swimsuit shot in there and ruin it for her completely. In a better mood, I might have warned her.

"Mamma, what does that even mean? If you've been secretly putting speed in my vitamin supplements, now would be a terrible time to mention it."

My mother fixed me with a look before muttering something in Swedish. I didn't catch all of it, but the word *otacksam*—ungrateful—featured heavily.

The afternoon stretched out into general chatter. Limited updates on the divorce from my mother, who seemed offended that we'd even bring up the subject. Instead, she nagged me to get out on the court out back and do some positional work. I politely refused, and let Alice tell us all about her latest gallery patron, who seemed to think buying one small sculpture meant he owned the place.

"Whatever happened to the boyfriend?" my mother asked, earning a groan from my sister.

"He wasn't quite right for me," Alice admitted. "Maybe I should give this new patron a go instead. Teach him how to be rich without being a douche."

"And Elin? When is your little girlfriend arriving? If she's in a fit state, you can get that hour of training done after all."

I considered my options. We were way past sputtering refusal. "She's not, yet, but if Toni becomes my girlfriend...is that going to be a problem? Are we going to fight for two years like we did about Celeste? Or with Hanna before her? Or—"

"Elin, stop rhyming these girls off like I committed some crime against you. Have I ever had a problem with you being gay?"

Alice sat up straighter, paying attention again. Either of our parents directly acknowledging this subject was a rare thing.

"No, but you might have if I told everyone and suddenly got dropped by Adidas, or Morgan Stanley, or—"

My mother dismissed that with a wave. "You've named two who would never drop you. It's all about diversity now. If any had left, we would have replaced them. My concern about your dating life was never the girls, but your concentration whenever you got crazy about one. And don't think I don't see the timing on this either."

"What's that supposed to mean?"

"We've just had a chat about how tennis makes you bored, you're ready to walk away. We agree we're going to try for the record before you quit, as long as you feel okay. Then suddenly with just two slams left to win, there's a new pretty girl on the scene? It's so like you, Elin."

Before I could argue back, we all heard the distinct sound of a car pulling into the drive again.

"Behave, both of you. And make sure to focus on Toni's win. That's what's important, not some tinpot scandal."

I was waiting by the door as she stepped out, the driver insisting on bringing her bags into the hallway for her.

"Hey," I said with a hug. "Sorry, I have visitors, but I can get rid of them in a heartbeat."

"Nah, people is good. I'm the extrovert, remember? It fuels me."

To hell with Mamma and Alice no doubt staring at us. I gave Toni the most reassuring kiss I could conjure up, brief but firm in purpose as

I placed my lips over hers. "That, we can talk about whenever. For now, there's wine and a fresh audience."

"Hello!" Toni called out, going over to greet my family. Within moments they were all laughing together, and I leaned against the edge of the staircase, trying not to think about how well they all fit together.

My mother insisted on cooking, pulling fresh things I didn't know I had from my fridge. Since her making anything other than open sandwiches was about as rare as a comet almost hitting the Earth, Alice and I were inclined to shut up and let her.

Luckily, they left soon after dinner, leaving Toni and I with a large, echoing space and some dishes to do. We stood side by side at the sink, some music playing quietly from the speakers in the living room.

"Your home is beautiful," she said, and I looked around imagining her fresh perspective on it. The giant windows and stripped floors, the light that touched every corner. Furniture that Parisa and Alice had helped me pick, after I threatened to "just do an Ikea run." Of course, the view out over the hills sealed the deal, and when we dried our hands, I led her out to the deck.

"This is my favourite part," I told her. "As the sun sets, you can only just see the lines of the court, and the breeze sometimes makes the water in the pool splash a bit like the sea. Once it's dark, it's like being all alone on the mountain top. Even though it's not like that in real life at all."

"Well, it's a home fit for a champion. Sorry, goddess. Thank you for inviting me over. A hotel tonight would just have left me alone and crying again. Mira might be improving my game, but she's not exactly into the cuddling part of it all."

"Better to have a hard-ass for your coach than a cuddler," I replied, slipping an arm around her shoulders. "You can always find someone else for the cuddling part."

She didn't entirely lean into it. "Listen, it's not just because of Parisa, but I don't think we can take this anywhere until everything is cleared. I can't speak out about the biased testing now, and the last thing I need is being accused of sleeping my way to the top. Everyone knows you're untouchable when it comes to the authorities, and I'd hate for even one person to think I was using you for some kind of immunity."

"Oh, Toni..." I wanted so badly to argue, but I understood only too well what she was wrestling with. "You're right. Of course. I had no expectations, so you know. The guest room is already made up."

"Right, good." She looked disappointed, at least. "Sorry, it was an awkward conversation and I didn't think we should wait any longer to have it. The minute all this is calm, though..."

She kissed me soundly before I could ask what, then pulled away with real reluctance.

"We should turn in," I suggested. "Big couple of weeks coming up."

Parisa and Celeste were waiting for me after my first-round match, which I'd won without too much of a sweat. I hated getting the wildcard in the early rounds, it always seemed to overwhelm them to come up against a name so soon.

"I got the data," Parisa explained, waving printed pages briefly under my nose.

"And it's actually worse than the anecdotal evidence," Celeste finished the thought for her. "But we don't know what the next step should be. From me, it sounds like just being angry. Cortes Ruiz they'll say she's covering her ass after finally getting back in the trophies. Keiko doesn't feel confident about leading some kind of movement."

I considered them both for a moment, scanning the information but not taking much in. The vague feeling that had been nagging at me since Celeste first mentioned it crystallised in that moment. I knew what I had to do, even though the thought of doing it made me feel weak in the knees.

"It should be me," I said. "Making it very clear I don't speak for women of colour, because they're more than capable of doing so. But as a white, cis woman and world number one in the sport, I have a responsibility to take the heat when a whistle needs to be blown."

"Are you sure?" Celeste asked. She had her hands on her hips, almost challenging me. "I know you wouldn't talk over us, but there's a real chance the GTA won't take it well. It could affect your prize money or even your endorsements."

"Sure, because I haven't made enough money already from this sport," I replied, biting back a laugh. Parisa smiled at me, but with a hint of warning. She didn't want me to stop bringing in the money yet.

"Elin, they really don't want this story to happen," Parisa said, tapping her foot on the floor, impatient with our sudden enthusiasm. "There's a chance they'll make an example of you."

"So let them," I said, lifting my chin and squaring my shoulders to show I wasn't intimidated. I almost convinced myself. "I have nothing to lose, and everything to win. This sport has been changed and improved, time and time again, by women who stood up and said 'enough.' Do better. Be fairer. That's all we'd be doing—continuing that great tradition."

Celeste nodded, her rigid posture relaxing at last. If this had been some kind of test on her part, I seemed to have passed. I clenched my fist in silent resolve not to let anyone down.

"Okay." Parisa held her hands up, accepting my decision. "Celeste, let's go through what we already talked about."

CHAPTER TWENTY

TENNIS BECAME ALMOST THE SECONDARY concern as that first week at Indian Wells wore on. Every hour seemed to bring a new piece of gossip, new confirmation of someone being over-tested, and along the way some actual matches were played too.

Toni practically confined herself to her room once we checked in for the tournament. I didn't get to spend much time with her, but in competitive mode I had a busy schedule to stick to anyway. As angry as events off-court were making me, it had been years since I'd enjoyed my tennis this much.

Was I trying to make up for everyone else having a rough time? Or was it just one of those purple patches with no nagging injuries, no tricky opposition, and just general good luck? It felt like every ball I hit landed exactly where I imagined and nothing was out of my reach to return. Even in fairly routine wins there was usually a moment of panic, a pushback that I wasn't expecting, but I went two full matches without any of that drama.

I met with Celeste for lunch in the players' dining room, a welcome respite from wandering the grounds and trying to remain unnoticed. Although the grounds held two huge stadiums, the country club feel could be a little too intimate most days.

"Hey." She greeted me with a kiss on the cheek, looking smart and relaxed in her lemon-coloured shift dress. Her hair was expertly styled in short twists, and Celeste managed to look both strong and elegant as she took the seat opposite me. "You all set for later?"

"Think so," I said. My next match, third round, was scheduled for the main stadium late afternoon—the prime-time slot. "So assuming I win, and they don't call me in for testing, I'll take the first shot in the post-match."

"It won't be a lot of press, though," Celeste warned. "But enough, probably."

"It's going to take more than one mention. Every match we play is just adding to the stats at this point. So I'll try—they may not even listen to me. I just don't want someone else being cracked down on if I can do it with a little protection."

"White privilege had to be good for something eventually," Celeste teased. "Mentioning it now is going to bring up the whole doping mess, and Toni. You want to get entangled with that?"

"I'm already kind of entangled with part of that anyway," I admitted. "Since the rumours are already doing the rounds, I thought I might as well tell you. Not that a scandal is exactly making for prime dating conditions."

I wanted so badly for Celeste to be happy for me, but there was no smile forthcoming. Just a half-nod of acknowledgement. "Okay. Well, good luck with that."

"I know, we have to focus on bigger problems than my love life." I raised a glass to her. "You want to be at my press conference, then?"

"I'll hang around to watch in back, unless that puts you off?"

"It's okay, C. You know nothing distracts me."

I didn't quite carry that much swagger into my post-match press conference. While the first two rounds only merited a brief chat with one or two reporters, now the gaggle was starting to gather after each match. Journalists wanted to speculate on how I'd fare in the quarterfinal, which it turned out would be some rising star from Canada whose name I couldn't seem to retain.

They wanted, essentially, to ask the same questions as every other time. I bit my tongue, kept my answers brief, and waited for an opening. If nobody dared bring up Xavi and the doping, I'd have to force it into the conversation myself. Not exactly my strong point.

It took a little help from home in the end. Ulrika from C More Sports, who brought sports coverage to most of Scandinavia, started her question with a familiar "*Hej.*"

"Elin, you must have seen the coverage that at least one coach has been suspended for offering to supply weight-loss pills containing a banned substance."

"Yes, I know who you mean."

"Is it true this man, Xavi Arrigo, approached you as well?"

That sent the room into a frenzy. Thanks for nothing, Ulrika.

"No, he did not approach me about any kind of pills or substance. He did offer his services as a coach, which, as you can see, I had no interest in. I happen to think I have the best coach working in tennis today. And no, my mother didn't order me to say that."

Some polite laughter.

"I want to address the larger issue, though, here on the women's tour. There's information out there to support what many of us have suspected for a while now. There's an unfair selection process when it comes to in-competition testing."

"Are you saying you get tested too much?" Ulrika asked, coming right along with me even as others clamoured to ask their questions.

"No, quite the opposite. I've won entire tournaments without being tested once. I've had some tests, sure, but I've since found out that other players are being tested after every round, even if they've lost the match. And sadly, there's a pattern."

"What's the pattern, Elin?" The guy from ESPN asked. I looked up, catching Celeste's eye.

"Well, white players like me are skipping through with minimal testing, almost none. Women of colour are being tested heavily, too much probably, and it's happening too much to be a coincidence."

"Elin—" He started again, but I stood to leave.

"It's not just gossip between players; the numbers are out there if you investigate. I know you guys can do that, so you can tell the story, okay?"

I left with the room in uproar. It might not even make a headline, but I hoped they'd at least start looking.

I was settling down for the evening with my one glass of wine and a mindless action movie cued up on the television in my hotel room. I could have driven home again, all two or three hours of it depending on traffic, but it quickly got too tiring during the hustle and bustle of the championship, so I'd taken up the suite set aside for me at the Hyatt. I'd had plenty of offers to go to dinner, to hang out with some of the other girls, but I'd blown it off in favour of a long bath and a few hours with my brain hopefully in neutral.

So, of course, then came the knock at my door. Getting on to this floor meant getting a special key card, and hotel security had a very short list of who was allowed one. I debated not answering, since almost all the lights were off in preparation for the film. Still, what the hell. If someone needed to interrupt me, they'd have to live with my pyjamas-and-robe combination.

"You did it," Toni said, pushing right past me as soon as I opened the door. "I can't believe you actually did it."

"Called out people being racist? Yeah, I did. I'm not expecting a medal for it."

She stopped long enough to glare at me. "I mean, you're going to get tangled up in my mess. They all think it's just a matter of time until something shows up in one of my tests, and then someone's going to start asking why you're getting involved at all."

"Because my friends are being targeted," I replied. "It's not just about you, but I'm glad your ego is surviving this difficult time in one piece."

"It's already online, you know that? It's making all the other stuff come right back to the front. I don't want to be a story, Elin."

"I'm not making you one," I pointed out. "I'm okay just running this through Celeste and Keiko and anyone else who wants it out there. You can stay out of it. It's not my story to tell; I'm just stepping out first to take any early shots. Once we prove this is happening, nobody can say it's being a sore loser when Celeste takes over talking about it."

"Elin—"

"So congrats on making the quarters, is what we should be saying to each other. Glad I avoided you in the draw this time, all that shit."

Toni circled the sofa and came back around to where I was standing. "You're dressed for bed. I'm interrupting."

"Did I complain?" I reached for her, brushing my fingertips along her upper arm, bare beneath the short sleeve of her running top. She was dressed for the gym but didn't appear to have worked out yet. If she pulled away, I would respect that.

Instead, she reached for the ends of the belt on my robe and toyed with them a little. "You looked good on TV. Righteous anger works for you."

"I suppose this is where I have to point out that we're in the middle of a competition and still avoiding distractions?" I had never sounded less sincere in my life. Toni's only response was a smile that had a downright predatory quality. A very pleasant shiver went down my spine.

Slowly, deliberately, she untied the loose knot at my waist, slipping her hands beneath the cotton of the robe to take hold of my hips.

"It's lucky you taught me your trick for shutting out distractions, really. Isn't it?" Her voice had dropped to something approaching husky, and if I had been weak before, I was absolutely defenceless by now.

"I was, uh, happy to share."

"I should thank you properly. Instead of yelling at you for standing up for me in public. Just so you can't tell how touched I was to see you out there defending all of us."

"Oh." I didn't get a chance to comment further. Toni kissed me this time like she'd been waiting ten years to do it, like if we stopped we'd never be allowed to start again. I already knew I couldn't let that be an option, so I kissed her back with the same fervour.

We made short work of our clothes, and Toni had me naked while she was just down to her underwear. She pushed me down onto the couch, straddling my hips as she stripped off her sports bra, tossing it somewhere across the room. My hands were already wandering, but as her breasts bounced ever so slightly with the motion, I couldn't focus on anything else. I had to touch her, had to cup each one in my hands and feel the slight weight of them, rounder and fuller than my own.

Not that she seemed disappointed, taking her own touches in turn. More direct, she grazed her thumbs over my nipples, working them quickly into harder peaks. Each touch sent a low-level current through me, ramped up my excitement by one more notch until I thought I might burst from anticipation.

"Let me," she said, maybe because she could tell I was overwhelmed. She stood just long enough to slip off the last piece of clothing, kicking her underwear away as soon as it hit the floor. Fully naked, she was like something out of a fantasy, but a moment later we were lying together, our fronts pressed against each other like we'd fit that way a hundred times before.

We took our time about kissing each other, letting our fingertips trace and squeeze and massage. I wanted to remember every touch, even though I knew it wasn't possible. Taking charge without being bossy, Toni directed my hands until our touches mirrored one another. One hand between each other's legs, revelling in the wetness we both found there. The other trapped between us, and the way she rolled my nipple between thumb and finger worked so well for me, making my back arch. She urged me to be a little rougher, pinching hard enough to make her gasp against my lips as we continued to kiss.

It was almost too intimate, to touch each other that way for the first time, but when I came under her hand it took away the last tiny whisper of fear. She climaxed moments later, my fingers still thrusting inside her. Only when we'd ridden out a second orgasm each did I relent, wrapping my leg over her and caressing her cheek with damp fingers.

She laughed softly, kissing me all over my face in a dizzy, distracted sort of way. "I thought it would be different, the first time. More throwing each other around."

"Oh?"

"But this was so much better, don't you think?"

I nodded, utterly high on the endorphins. Any way would be perfect, if we ended up like this. "You know, there's a bed with a lot more room than this," I reminded her. "Plenty of space for throwing around if you want to compare."

"Hmm, maybe in a minute," Toni muttered, her voice a little raspy. We should drink something. Pull something over us to prevent a chill. Later. Neither one of us wanted to move, not when being this close was an option.

"Morning," I whispered as Toni finally shifted in my arms. "We should probably think about how you're going to sneak back to your room. I'm not playing today, are you?"

"Later," she said, grumbling into my side. We had made it back to bed in the end, with a much more physical round that had been every bit as enjoyable. I didn't think I'd dislike any way of being with her at this point. "No sneaking. No hiding."

"Really?" I felt the familiar flip of panic go over like a pancake in my stomach, and yet just as suddenly the feeling passed. I didn't have to hide, and more importantly I no longer wanted to. Let people talk. How could I be anything other than proud to be with someone like Toni?

"If you're okay with it," she lifted her head enough that I could see one dark brown eye watching me from beneath her messy fringe. "I'm not pushing, but from what you said last night…"

"I'm ready," I said. "There might be a bit of attention, I don't know. They kind of gave up on getting anything on my love life, so let's hope they don't care."

"Or…" Toni suggested, sitting up fully and letting me drink in the lines of her back. I traced the short line of her scar with one finger, before bending a little to place a kiss over it. "We could just take a shower and worry about the press later. If we have to. There are no cameras in here, babe."

"Babe? Really? That's all I get promoted to after last night's performance?"

"Keep up the good work and all kinds of nicknames can happen." Toni slipped out from beneath the sheets, pulling me along with her. I thought about token resistance, but she was strong enough to carry me in there if she put her mind to it.

"I'll settle for babe," I said, following her into the white-tiled room and whacking the shower into life. "Now let's get wet, shall we?"

CHAPTER TWENTY-ONE

THE QUARTERFINAL SNUCK UP ON me quickly, having spent a second night with Toni, this time in her room. Although we hadn't really been out in public together yet, or had much chance to show any public affection, I still felt the whispers whenever I moved around the complex. They would only grow. When Celeste and I had first started dating, it felt like everyone else knew before even we had.

I walked out to the court with an unfamiliar young woman in my wake, clearly still in her teens. It took a moment to register that this was my opponent, and not someone I'd once briefly met and forgotten. She looked like she should still be in the Juniors, those awkward years before the real winning kicked in. Had I looked that young when I'd started out?

"Elin," I said as we waited to be announced, extending my right hand. She didn't take it. "Yeah, I know. Everyone knows."

"Sorry, but I don't think we've been introduced?" I withdrew my hand, a little embarrassed.

"Sarah," she said, like I'd asked for a kidney rather than her name.

"Well, it's great to meet you, Sarah," I said, offering my hand again. She just stared it down without staying anything at first. I resisted the urge to flip her off instead, but she finally relented, and our hands met for a limp split-second.

"I don't really go in for the touchy-feely crap," she replied, before turning and marching out ahead of me.

I saw a distressing amount of myself in her at that age, that almost impossibly young age, right down to the flippy blonde ponytail. I had never been rude, at least not on purpose, but my awkwardness had been taken as thinking too much of myself by some people. Especially Mira, who should have understood my situation as a young champion suddenly in the world's spotlight, still struggling a little in my second language. I still carried those feelings with me, so I was determined not to write Sarah off the way others had with me.

Despite the attitude over a simple handshake, she was perfectly meek during the coin toss and the warmup. But the minute the umpire called our match to begin, she came out of the traps like one of those angry little devils they have in Australia. I weathered the initial storm, but damn if she didn't make me work for it.

As we changed ends, I muttered a genuine, "Well played, Sarah," but whether she misheard or thought it was sarcasm, her mood seemed to darken. From that point on, she started losing her temper at double faults or missed shots. First it was just groans of annoyance or stamping a foot, but the cursing soon got close to being audible. I didn't mind so much, since it broke her concentration and made my march to winning the first set more of a procession.

Then I started to worry for her. I'd seen plenty of promising young players burn out or rage their way out of the rankings and out of the sport before they ever really got going. When she spoke back to the umpire, we were both called over for a warning word. I resented that a little, as though blame were somehow to be shared here. Bill, an umpire who'd been on the tour longer than I had, gave me a brief wink to mollify me, the joint warning being for the kid's benefit.

Sarah didn't calm down.

She got into an argument with one of the line judges next and had a point deducted for her trouble. I fudged a couple of winnable points, trying to let her play her way through it, but the red mist had truly descended.

The ball boy didn't get out of her way quickly enough, and as he scurried back to take position at the net, Sarah started telling him off. Enough. I would take it directed at me, and the umpires were more than used to it. Upsetting the kids was a step too far. The crowd had grown restless with her bad behaviour, so I intervened.

"Do you want to talk? Or are we going to play tennis?"

Some of the crowd laughed, which I hoped would diffuse the tension. Others seemed to dissent, as though I was part of the problem. Bill leaned into the microphone at his umpire's chair.

"Quiet, please. Players and spectators."

We played more of the second set, but Sarah in all her spiky rage had decided the ball boy was the root of all her problems. He scurried across my side of the net to pick up a shot that hadn't made it over, and she shouted something at him. The kids who staffed all the tournaments—usually for free or just the promise of some nice sports gear—were almost always the best-behaved, polite little people, and they really didn't deserve to be yelled at.

"Hey!" I called back at her. "Leave him alone." The crowd applauded, but I didn't really care what they thought anymore. This was something primal, to the point where I moved across the court and placed myself between the boy and Sarah. Just as well, since she'd picked up a stray ball to hit in his direction. This damn match was going to make sports news the world over.

"Get out of the way!" she snapped at me. "If he wants to catch every last ball, he can have it."

"Sarah, don't!"

Where the hell were the officials in all this? Everyone was just standing there watching.

Luckily she thought better of swinging her racquet, letting that arm drop, but the temper stayed with her just long enough to hurl the ball towards the poor kid, only it bounced off my hip as I turned to shield him better.

That did it. The place was in an uproar. I vaulted the net in one stride, ready to challenge her, but catching my mother's eye in the stand stopped me short. The damage was done. I didn't need my own disciplinary problems, especially not if I was going to help the other girls on the drug testing problem.

Some of the line judges had surrounded Sarah, so I looked back to comfort the boy. He'd been taken care of by some other officials, so I stood there by the net, hands on hips and waited for Bill to call it.

"Code violation. Unsporting conduct. Default, Miss Harrow. Game, set, match Miss Larsson."

The crowd cheered, but it had a nasty, ironic tone to it. I shook my head, jogged over to shake Bill's hand, and gathered up my things. No need to sit and drink, put on my jacket, or even put the racquet back in its cover.

I wanted off court, and away from all those eyes on me. It was a crappy way to win, but the rules were clear. Any unwanted physical contact with anyone in the court area was a disqualification. Sarah was probably in a world of trouble, even as I heard her still making her case to unsympathetic officials.

I felt my phone vibrate as soon as I got out of the shower and read Toni's blow-by-blow commentary with a smile as I sat there in my towel.

Is she really doing this?

Someone get the kid her pacifier, this is wild.

My hero, saving the children. Tell me, Miss Larsson, does that outfit come with a cape?

I rolled my eyes and fired off a reply.

If that's your way of saying you're into role play, I'll consider it. Good luck for yours. See you back at my room.

What better way to roll off the stress of the day than with some quality time in bed, or on any other piece of furniture for that matter, with Toni? I could hardly wait.

Of course, I watched her match and was both relieved and proud she'd made it through. Her reward was yet another matchup against Celeste in the semis, while I would be facing Keiko.

I expected her first demands on walking through the door would be either dinner or a full breakdown of what the hell happened, but Toni's first priority turned out to be backing me up onto the bar in the corner and going down on me until I practically had to beg for mercy. It turned out I was going to like her post-win routine very much, and I made sure to repay the favour once I got her as far as the edge of the bed.

We paused long enough to order room service, although we took dessert to bed. The strawberries and cream might have been a nice little joke from the chef, but the way we used them would definitely have resulted in us being thrown out of Wimbledon.

"Will you have to talk to the media tomorrow?" Toni asked. "Only I checked and you missed them entirely today."

"I slipped away in all the chaos," I told her. "Officially, the statement was that I didn't want to comment on a volatile situation, but at some point I'll have to do some questions, yeah."

"When's the last time someone got a match penalty? I've seen games get taken for busting up racquets or swearing, but this was straight to maximum."

"It doesn't happen often; I've certainly never seen it in person before. I don't know what made her that mad. She's young, I know, but this isn't such an insane pressure here. Nice to win, sure, and competitive. But she might have blown up her whole career unless she finds someone who can teach her to control that."

"I'm just glad it was punished," Toni admitted. "I spent a lot of time fighting that 'fiery Latina' bullshit, and too often you see white girls get away with so much more. At least your umpire was in no mood."

"Bill's okay," I said. "The one time I cursed at him he put the fear of God in me, and I haven't misbehaved since."

"Before all your drama, I heard there's some kind of leak with the testing data. That some newspaper will run that the testing has been biased."

I sat up at that news, dragging Toni with me.

"Seriously? You wait until now to tell me?"

"They won't run it now, not with footage of the disqualification to play with," Toni pointed out, and she had a point. "But it's out there, it's working. You got it started."

"Okay, good." I reached for the water by the bed, dealing with my thirst. "Now, where were we?" I asked, dealing with another kind of thirst entirely.

I ran Keiko close in the semi-final on that Thursday of the second week, when a lot of people were already letting their attention drift to the Miami Open the following week. I had no excuse but to join them when I went out after three sets, having been broken twice in the last one. Not my finest hour, and yet the new, fragile happiness with Toni was almost enough to offset it.

"Be careful in there," Parisa warned as we approached the press room. "Leave the drug stuff for Celeste and Toni if it comes up, okay?"

"But—"

"There's a difference between taking the first shot to protect your friends and speaking over them when they deserve to be heard. Stand by them every step of the way, I know you will, but don't be that white lady who hogs the spotlight on it. Stick to the Sarah debacle and anything else you can think of."

Parisa was right, as always. I took up my spot at the table, far more microphones and recorders on it that time. We were at the business end of the tournament, after all.

I got a softball question from the BBC woman about how disappointed I was to go out at this stage, and it was a chance to get warmed up.

"Obviously I would rather be in the final," I wrapped up. "But Keiko played a smart match and deserves to be there. Depending on the other semi-final result, I might even be cheering her on."

There. That would both inflame and confuse the gossipmongers.

Ulrika popped up again. "With word from the GTA being that they may consider a ban for Sarah Harrow, do you support that decision?"

Shit, I hadn't heard about that. I had been in kind of a cocoon since the match, though, doing the absolute minimum of activities that were outside of a hotel room.

"Well, the rules are clear, I think. I'm not sure we should be adding special penalties on top of that. We didn't, for example, when Jürgen threw his racquet in the Australian Open a while back and it hit a line judge."

Ulrika persisted, as she always did. "So you think there's a problem in women's tennis? You've already mentioned the drug testing."

"Yes, any organisation should be investigated if found to not be applying their own rules or acting in ways that are wrong. When it comes to Sarah's case, I don't know her. But I know the tour is a lot of pressure when you're young, and we as a sport have to provide the support for all players. Not just physical but mental health too."

Wow, I had never talked so much in a conference. It was like I'd traded jobs and become Prime Minister of Sweden for the day. What next, was I going to raise taxes?

The rest of the questions were familiar ground—was I going to play in Miami, was I looking ahead to the French Open? I handled them all with my customary short answers and left the room quite untroubled.

Toni joined me on the loser's bench that evening. While she wasn't quite so happy on arrival, I was pleased to discover she liked to process her feelings about a loss with just as much enthusiasm as for a win, maybe even more so.

I was quickly getting used to her staying over. So much so that I didn't panic when the loud knock at the door came in the morning. I pulled the sheets up higher, reaching to reassure her, but that side of the bed was empty. A moment later, I heard the running water and grumbled the whole way to the door that I could have been joining her in the shower again instead. Checking before taking the door off the chain, I wasn't entirely surprised to see my mother. I decided to let her in, but not without complaining a little.

"Mamma, I booked us separate rooms this time for a reason," I said, but she brushed past me without a care, ready for the day in another spotless navy blue tracksuit, her short hair pinned back and her sunglasses pushed up on top of her head. I felt a sudden rush of love for her in that moment, even though she was clearly there to complain about something I'd done. She really had devoted so much of her life to helping me have all this. Despite our usual distance, I followed her in my fluffy robe and pulled her into a hug.

"Yes, you might very well cling to me," she said, patting my arm absently. "I've just been told that before you start at Miami on Tuesday, the GTA want to call you in for a meeting."

"*Va' fan!*" It was my turn to curse, and my mother only nodded instead of correcting me. I let her go and started to pace. "What are they pissed about? That I protected a kid from Sarah Harrow? I won't apologise for that."

"Oh, I'm sure they're going to bring something about that to be a problem for you, but no, the main issue is that you are, and I quote, 'bringing the women's game into disrepute.'"

For a horrifying moment I thought she meant my fling with Toni, just started though it was. I felt the same sickening dizziness I always did when confronted with the prospect of blatant homophobia, but then I realised that couldn't be it, no matter how paranoid I got.

"The drug testing? They're saying I'm slandering the association? I deliberately didn't say more in the last press conference."

"You still made reference to it, about applying the rules. And you already claimed they're racist or deliberately fixing results, when they say it's all blind and fair and objective."

I began to pace. "If they're so sure of that, why do they want to shut me up? See, this is why I had to be the one to do it. This sort of quiet intimidation would make someone less protected back down. Well, they can screw their tap on the wrist. I'm not going."

"Elin, come on," my mother warned, helping herself to an apple from the bowl on the table. "What does a meeting cost? They'll come to Miami to meet with you."

"And I won't be available." I pulled my phone from my pocket. "I'm telling Parisa now that I'm not agreeing to any meeting, and that I'll continue to speak out if anything seems unfair to me."

My mother turned on me, and I'd rarely seen her so angry. It stopped the rest of my rant right there in my throat, like something I might choke on.

"Enough! Why have you chosen this year to become a crusader? You don't usually stand up for yourself, never mind your competitors."

"They're my friends too, Mamma." I folded my arms in disapproval, standing my ground.

"From someone Sarah Harrow's age I might expect it. Hell, you were a handful then too in your quiet way. But I have put up with everything from the retirement talk to fighting off new coaches, and now to the girlfriend hidden in the bathroom. Now you're picking fights with the people who decide if you play this game, and if you get to win prize money."

"She's not hiding. You just showed up unannounced."

With perfect timing, Toni chose to open the bathroom door, emerging in just a short towel and a cloud of steam. She barely flinched on seeing my mother. "Morning, Mrs Larsson. I hope Elin isn't late for training."

"No, no, now that she's out she gets a day or two off," my mother replied, back to being perfectly pleasant as if a switch had been flipped. "Have you girls had breakfast yet?"

Toni shook her head. "I'll just get dressed real quick, if you have plans."

"Join us," my mother insisted, full charming Britta mode like Toni was some big sponsor. "Elin, get yourself together too, and I'll see you both downstairs.

"Lobby or terrace?" I asked, since both those restaurants served breakfast.

"The private dining room," Mamma replied. "Parisa will meet us there too."

With a brisk wave, my mother left the suite and Toni just smiled at me.

"Man, I never quite realised what it must be like having your mom in charge of your professional life. Mine would love this much involvement, if only she gave a damn about tennis."

"Not even now you're winning stuff?" I hadn't mentioned her mother's absence in Mexico, since it was a small tournament and a hell of a journey there from Spain.

"Maybe I can talk her into Paris or Wimbledon, if I stay fit for them."

"That would be nice. Now, as much as I'd rather you dropped that towel, we'll get no peace until my mother gives me her lecture over breakfast. I'll make it up to you after, I promise."

Toni dropped the towel anyway, revealing all that bronzed, toned skin that would make a professional sculptor weep with anticipation. She grinned as she saw my newly stunned reaction. This wasn't going to get boring anytime soon. I was a hopeless lesbian, and she knew it. By some stroke of luck, she seemed just as into me, and I hoped harder than I ever had before that I wasn't wrong about that.

"You know, if we're really quick, people will just assume we were slow picking out clothes."

"You're a terrible influence," I pretended to complain, but she silenced me with a searing kiss, minty-fresh from just brushing her teeth.

She had a point. Breakfast could wait a little longer.

CHAPTER TWENTY-TWO

I SHOULD HAVE BEEN ANNOYED that Parisa and my mother were conspiring by calling a meeting, but they had still invited Celeste to join us for breakfast, and she showed up despite being in preparation mode for another final.

The private dining room meant we could all talk freely, but it didn't take long for tempers and voices to rise.

"I agree with Elin," Celeste finally told the room, sipping at the coffee my mother had poured for her. "So what if they want to rap her on the knuckles? If anything, it shows they're rattled for a reason. And this wussy non-threat is only happening because of who she is. Anyone else and it would be a full disciplinary. If they can't come after her, I say she tells them to kiss her ass. Respectfully, ma'am."

Celeste had handled racism, sexism, and homophobia her whole life. She had gone toe-to-toe with some seriously tough people and always held her own. But she was unfailingly polite, and I maintained that some small part of the fearless woman was actually scared of my mother. Certainly about cursing in front of her.

"Mamma, the worst they can do to me is issue a press release saying they disagree. They could do that without a meeting, so they clearly don't want to make a big deal." Toni's fingers grazed my thigh under the table and my breath caught in my throat. "If I don't make myself available, they're not going to chase me on court, are they?"

"You might be lucky, if they're more interested in this ex-coach of yours, Antonia," my mother said. "If that story keeps blowing up, you can all say what you like and no one will mind. But out of interest, were you all tested after your semi-finals?"

I shook my head, but Celeste and Toni both nodded. The door opened then, and Mira entered. For a moment, I was surprised to see her, but that was years of avoiding her interviews at work. Of course she should be here if this affected Toni's career.

Parisa and my mother greeted Mira warmly, since they'd always been on good terms. It was just difficult me who didn't like the media side of it all. Parisa took over the informal presentation.

"Toni, you've been a blast to work with and I'm happy to do it as a favour as long as Elin asks me, but your federation should be supporting you through all this. I know a lot of women on the tour don't get full-time assistants or publicists until they're secure in the rankings or have a couple of slams. I don't think you're going to have the luxury of waiting that long."

"Well, the federation handles all my paperwork and press releases," Toni replied, squeezing my thigh now through my track pants. She was going to pay for her teasing just as soon as we could get out of there. "I don't do that much press outside of the official promos. I mean, I guess I could ask my old publicist back. She handled the modelling I did before?"

"Perfect," Mira answered. "And if she's good, she can work directly with Parisa going forward. Anything you're not sure of on the tennis side, ask me. I have a unique perspective, after all." Her glossy bob was a sparkling silver, and despite the move to coaching, she was still dressed for television in a deep red pantsuit rather than activewear. There was a time she could have outplayed any of us at the table, even in her three-inch heels.

Still, if we had to have a strategy session, I was proud that it was exclusively strong, independent women all at the top of their games. The problems were more likely in a room full of GTA suits, too many of whom were still entitled white men, who hadn't ever been involved in the game. I hoped that would change over the next few years too. Wow, I really must be happier if I was sitting there plotting all the ways to make the world a better place. I laid my hand on top of Toni's where it still rested on my thigh. One last thing was nagging at me.

"Wait, why are we all coordinating? This drug-testing thing could die out in a week. If it carries on then Celeste will be the next person to go public, so…"

"Uh, I think that's more to do with 'us,'" Toni answered, finger quotes and all. She looked around the table for confirmation, getting a shrug from

Celeste and nodded confirmation from everyone else. "Nobody here wants us being a couple to get mixed up in these other issues because it'll pull all the attention. So we let the publicists do our talking for a while."

I found myself blushing, but where in the past I would have denied it or played down any need for coordination, the simple act of touching Toni in that moment confirmed that I was serious about her. At least about trying to make it work, travel and competition and all. She might see sense and dump me before we got back out of Miami, but right now I didn't want to consider any setup where we didn't at least have the option to see each other every day.

Our timing was pretty great too, since March was one of the more settled parts of the calendar. April was a mess, with little tournaments everywhere until we settled into some of the nicer European venues to get ready for the French Open.

"Well, I appreciate everyone's help," I said. "But if we're done for now, then I think I'd like to take Toni for lunch somewhere that isn't decorated with tennis balls."

"I'll e-mail what they say about you not taking the meeting," Parisa replied. "So go have fun, you crazy kids."

I felt like a teenager being allowed to go to prom at the last minute, but since I'd been a teenager who played in junior pro tournaments instead of going to anything like a prom, I decided to lean the hell into the feeling and enjoy it.

Judging from the soft giggle as I dragged Toni out of that room, she was on the same page.

There was one downside to Miami, and every year it gave me pause to check every joint and muscle, just in case a tiny injury might be developing to keep me out of it.

Not the weather; I'd played in dry and humid heat all over the world. There was a reason they called it and Indian Wells the Sunshine Double. I certainly didn't mind the city with its amazing restaurants and beach culture. I was actually looking forward to seeing more of the Spanish-speaking side with Toni to demystify some of it. It wasn't remarkably different as a tournament, one way or another.

No, the one thing that put me off the second competition was Miami Airport. It was at least a little more bearable flying private, so I had insisted when Parisa made the arrangements.

Celeste had triumphed in California and was now seeded favourite to do the same in Miami. The urge to not allow that, to claim the title for myself, thrummed in my veins from the moment we set foot on the plane.

Toni had initially refused to travel by private jet, horrified by the environmental impact, but ultimately our slightly sickening desire not to be apart won her over. She was an official convert when she didn't have to take her week's worth of kit through security and baggage claim, kicking back with some champagne almost right away.

As an additional bonus, Alice had driven down to fly with us. She had some big collectors in Miami, and I'd been happy to give her whatever tickets she needed to impress them. While she couldn't give a damn about tennis, a lot of other people did, and it was an easy way to kiss up to rich art buyers and have some fun in the evenings too.

"You're late," I told Alice as she stepped on board. "Honestly, we're taking so many people it's starting to feel like coach in here."

"Don't be ridiculous, Elin," my mother scolded on her way past to help herself to the champagne. "And have a drink. It might make you better at sharing."

"Is that official coaching advice?" I asked, doing exactly as I was told. "To increase my chances of winning the Miami Masters, drink more alcohol?"

"Wow, you're showing your age, lady," Alice warned. "Even I know it's not called the Masters anymore."

I gave her a little smack on the back of the head as I passed, taking the seat next to Toni.

"This isn't too much, right?" I asked quietly. "The family, the travelling together... If we need to slow down, just tell me."

"Nah, dragging things out and pretending not to like each other as much as we do? That's for straight people. I much prefer it our way. As long as I'm not cramping your style."

"Darling, I have no style," I reminded her, leaning across for a kiss without caring that other people were around. It was freeing in a way I could easily get addicted to, so I did it again for good measure.

"Okay, you two," Alice warned. "I didn't sign up for the Love Boat, so chill."

I smirked at her but sat back in my own seat ready for take-off.

Celeste retired in the third round with a hamstring problem, and Toni made it to the quarters before Fatima put her out in straight sets. The crowds had been in party mode for all the first week, so I was only a little jealous when I had to stay serious and focused going into the second week, while everyone else seemed to get into the almost carnival atmosphere. I'd even spotted my own mother with a flower in her hair, flirting her little heart out with some pop star half her age. If she knew he was gay, it didn't slow her down one bit.

The Hard Rock Stadium was a pretty fun place to play in the end, and the day of the final felt like spring break for grown-ups. I couldn't remember the last time I felt so relaxed going into a big match, and the credit was mostly Toni's.

"You keep playing like this," she told me, "and you'll break the record this year, you know that? You only need two, and you'll walk it in Paris if you play this well."

"No, that's over-confidence," I warned her. "You can think it all you want, but I can't let myself believe you. Besides, you're on track for your all-important first slam if you keep this up. And get past me, duh."

Mostly, I didn't want our Miami bubble to pop. Next week, Toni was off to play in Charleston, and I had a week at home. Alice had already started drawing up the plans for my foundation, so time would be taken up on that. A first real step to life after tennis, which I couldn't wait for.

Because although I was enjoying my tennis again, playing well and hopefully about to chalk up another trophy, most of all I wanted to find out what was on the other side of all this. Part of me knew that staying on the tour would keep my path crossing with Toni's more often than not. But then there would be months like this one coming, where I could be in Lugano while she was in Bogotá, meeting up again in Stuttgart for a week only to split again for Prague and Morocco. That was before we counted the skippable tournaments for me, or the few that inevitably fell to injury here and there, even for the less serious aches and pains.

A little voice somewhere in the back of my head, the kind that only spoke up in the middle of the night when I was struggling to find sleep, kept suggesting that if only one of us was still playing, the other would be free to just follow that one schedule. It was way too soon to think about living together, about big commitments, but the touring life had the benefit of all that togetherness without exactly having to make it official.

Not that I brought up the subject. If I missed Stuttgart, we'd miss each other for most of a month until reuniting in Madrid at the start of May. Hardly unbearable, but it would certainly be a test.

"What are you thinking about?" Toni asked as I pulled on my socks and trainers, ready for the match.

"Babies," I blurted out without thinking. "Um, I mean. Someone asked the other day if I wanted kids. So I was thinking about babies."

I expected her to laugh at me like she usually did. I had a habit of just saying my first thought around her already.

"Really? Is that part of the whole walk-away-from-tennis thing? Or are you going to have a baby and come back?"

"Woah, woah, wait. Nobody said anything about having one, not for a long while. But yeah, I've realised it's probably something I want to do. Or at least think about. I've never let myself do that before."

Toni walked over to the window, even though we'd probably memorised the view by this point.

"Yeah, me either. And Elin, I know we're not... I mean, nobody is even thinking about... But I'm not there yet. I'm not where you are on the whole career thing. If I can play until I hit thirty-two, or longer, I want to stay in as long as I can."

"I know." I stood, shoes tied just right, and went over to hug her from behind. "We're at two different stages, and a lot of the time we'll be in two different places. But maybe there's no reason, once we work out our own part, why we can't try to combine the two. Sometimes. A lot of times."

"I'd like that," Toni whispered, leaning back against me, her eyes closed. I kissed her neck gently, leaving her room to talk. "But I worry. You're so... you. The best at this, and you're halfway done with it. I worry that when you leave tennis, you're going to leave me with it. Which—again—way too much assuming and jumping ahead."

"Trust me, if there's one thing I've learned these past few weeks, it's that this damn sport can't be so bad as long as you're in it. The rest is details. We work those out as we go. And if things get serious, we make serious decisions."

"I should go," Toni replied, and I could feel her pulling away before she even attempted to actually leave my arms. Something inside her had closed down to me, and I had no idea what.

"Will you still come cheer me on?" I asked, confused and unable to hide it from her.

"Of course," she said. "Now get out there and win yourself another trophy."

So I did. It would be rude to refuse a lady's request, right?

The celebrations in Miami were wilder too, and I was actually looking forward to the fancy dinner and maybe dancing afterwards. The clubs here had something for everyone, and I could spend a late night out with salsa music quite happily. That had been the plan anyway, until Toni pulled me aside during the post-match handshakes.

"Listen, I didn't check my flights until this afternoon, I actually have to go."

"Wait, we can rebook—"

"I can't, there's a photo call in the morning with the mayor, it's a whole big deal. I'll call you, okay? And congratulations, gorgeous."

"Toni, wait!"

She leaned across to kiss my cheek, barely lingering. A moment later, she was gone, lost in the crowd. Even if I could spot her I couldn't have followed; there were still a bunch of people waiting to meet me including a couple of kids who'd won a contest. I kept checking my phone, but no more explanation came.

Just when I thought I could finally sneak off, maybe head to the airport and see if I could still catch up to Toni, I felt an irritating tap on my shoulder.

"Elin."

"Mira. You know, it actually hurts when you dig at a collarbone that way." I folded my arms, our alliance fragile in the absence of Toni.

"Yes, I'll try to remember you're so breakable. I know Antonia already left, but in a moment you're going to be asked to step into a room with some representatives from the GTA. They're not happy you've been avoiding them since last week, so take this meeting. Understood?"

"Mira, I'm not going because they click their fingers. They know where I am."

"Oh, for the love of... They're angry with you, can't you see that? Otherwise it would have been dropped. So make nice, just enough for the issue to carry on. Is that so much to ask?"

"We'll see," I replied. I didn't enjoy being told what to do, and even less by Mira. Before I could complain to her, I was being approached by a little posse of men in suits. Something the press in the room noticed almost instantly, despite the fact I'd been shaking hands with all kinds of people for over an hour.

"Miss Larsson, we really do need to talk. You haven't collected your prize money yet, so why don't we do both at once?"

It wasn't like I still had to pick up a cheque. I simply went in to sign and the money went by wire transfer. All one million and something dollars of it.

Mira glared at me from the side, and so I relented. "Okay, but I don't have long. My sponsors are expecting me for a reception."

Both true and not. They'd be cracking the champagne because I'd won again with their logos on my sleeve, beamed to screens and printed on pages all over the world.

They ushered me into a faceless office, occupied by one large desk and a couple of chairs. I stood tall despite still being in my match clothes, hands on my hips to stop me from fidgeting.

"I'm not sure what you need to talk to me about, but—"

"Miss Larsson, we need to inform you that recent remarks you made at Indian Wells are considered by the disciplinary committee to be bringing the game into disrepute."

Okay. That shut me up. At least for a minute. I just stared, waiting for some kind of explanation.

189

"I'm sorry, what?"

"In recognition of your incredible career and excellent disciplinary record, the committee also decided that it would be acceptable to offer you a warning in private. That would give you the chance to retract and apologise, with no further action being taken."

"Now hold on one minute. Why would I take back what I said?"

"Elin, please." The guy talking seemed to think we knew each other. Maybe we did, but he was unremarkable. Was it possible I had that face blindness I read about on a long plane journey once? Or just terminally bad with names? More likely. "This can all go away. You're not even affected by the accusation you made."

"And yet you're already looking to punish me," I pointed out. "How much more would you crack down on someone whose career wasn't *incredible* and whose disciplinary record wasn't *excellent?*"

"All you have to do is mention at one of your next press conferences—it doesn't have to be today—that you wanted to withdraw your remarks. The company who provide our drug testing and other medical services are one of our most important partners. Without them, we'd end up with less money for prize money and other important things." Another suit explained it like I didn't know how our corporate world worked.

"And if I don't?" I had to ask. If I was going to stand up for the people who mattered to me, I was going to know the consequences. "What if someone else raises the same complaint? Because others are angry too, including the women treated unfairly."

"Further disciplinary action. Including considerable fines and possible suspension from competition."

"Suspension from what? A week in some minor tournament?" I scoffed.

"For up to three months," the first man replied. "Including the French Open."

CHAPTER TWENTY-THREE

I DIDN'T TELL ANYONE WHAT the meeting had been about for days. Maybe it was stupid to sit on the threat, but I hadn't tried to retract my statement at the press conference either. One thing was sure: I really didn't want to do that. It would be selling out my friends on an issue I believed was a genuine injustice.

Maybe if I'd been around Toni I would have spilled sooner, but with her in Charleston and me moping around at home in Los Angeles, the opportunity didn't come up. Our calls were brief, and I could feel the slight chill between us even in texts. I should have been diving in to solve that issue, but the black cloud hanging over my career consumed too much time and effort.

Over lunch with Alice at Beverly Glen Deli, we talked about our plan for a global LGBTQ charity. I had to hand it to my sister—she'd taken half a sentence of an idea and turned it into something real seemingly in a couple of weeks.

"So what's up with you, Elin? I know you're not playing much this month, but straight into the comfort food?"

I'd ordered a grilled cheese that came with scrambled egg inside it, something of a diner special. It also tended to put unsuspecting diners into a food coma, but I could handle it. I'd have to put an extra half hour on my workout that afternoon, but it would be worth it.

"Toni's being distant."

"Isn't she literally a great distance away in...not here?"

I nodded. "It's just awkward, that's all. Once we're in Europe again, when the flights are two hours instead of half a day, it'll be easier to hang out."

"Did you guys have a fight, or did you call it off for the different countries and now you're regretting it? You shouldn't be so hung up on monogamy; you just met the girl. By your standards."

"No, I wasn't... We haven't even talked about that. She caught me off guard, though, and I blurted out something about babies and she started stressing about how we're at different career stages and...ugh."

Alice let her head thud against the table. "What are we going to do with you?" She sat up again to point at me. "You have truly achieved peak lesbian this time. Are you sure U-Haul aren't one of your sponsors?"

"It was just a conversation! I wasn't asking her to knock me up!"

Tilting her head, Alice tutted at me. "You have got to learn to be cool. Anyway, text her about it and say you were joking. Break the ice in case she thinks next time she sees you will be with a turkey baster."

"Any more lesbian-pregnancy material to come? Or is your stand-up routine done for today?"

Alice reached across and patted me on the head. "All done. So when do you play next?"

"Madrid. Mamma didn't enter me for Stuttgart, and it's too late now. So I'm going to head back to Stockholm on Monday, spend some time with Dad. I haven't really seen him since Wimbledon in July, and you know how bad he is on the phone."

"Oh, yeah. He was over for my show, but then it was something in New York. If he can get off the boat long enough you might even see him."

"Come with me!" I said. "We've never been back all as a family, and with the house on the market, this might genuinely be the last time. Actually, when is the last time you went back?"

"Are you paying for the food or am I? I should get back to work."

"No you don't," I replied. "You know, most of the time I just swing by between tournaments, but it's pretty weird you never come for Christmas, or even just when you know we'll all be there after Wimbledon. What is that about, huh?"

"Okay, so you're paying. Read that plan, and if you like it, get your attorney on board. We'll have to appoint a foundation manager first to get everything up and running. Bye, Elin."

I had officially had enough of people making sharp exits on me. Throwing down some bills on the table, I made sure to leave a generous tip before jogging out after my sister. Her heels were no match for my legs over short distances.

"Hey!"

"Back off, Elin. I told you, work."

Alice had parked her jeep two spaces down from my car, so I wasn't really going anywhere.

"Okay, I'm going to tell you something I didn't say in there," I said. "The powers that be have told me to withdraw my accusation, apologise and deny there was ever a problem. If I don't? Fines, for sure. Maybe even banned for the French."

"Well, who really wants to go to Paris in July?" Alice asked, still not facing me.

"May," I corrected. "I told you my secret. So now you tell me what you weren't saying back there."

Alice fiddled with her keys, sighing before she turned around and made her admission.

"There's a reason I insist on English, El. Same reason I don't want to go back to Sweden if I can avoid it. Back there I have this little shadow following me around, the hint of everyone else's memories of someone I never really was."

"Alice..."

"No, it's okay. Here I've only ever been Alice. Everyone has only known me as I am, as I should be. It wasn't so bad going back at first, but then that nasty tabloid ran their story on me and everything I thought I had left behind was thrown in my face."

I reached out to her, pulling her into a hug that I hoped would say more than my words. "We all know who you are, Alice. Who you were always meant to be. And if anyone, anyone ever said anything—"

"That's the thing. If it happens, you get to have the fight. You're ready for the fight over it. I like my life here, where I don't have to be on guard, where I don't have to be insulted or deadnamed or have anything bad happen to me, just so someone can step in and prove what a great ally they are."

I understood in that moment what I had been asking Alice to give up just for the sake of a holiday. "I'm sorry," I said. "I hope no one ever says anything that needs me to smack them in the mouth, because I don't want you to have to hear it. Just know if they ever did, I would have your back. Every time."

"You're not such a bad sister, sometimes," Alice admitted, pulling away from me. "But maybe this is what happened with Toni, a little bit. You said something harmless to you, but you didn't realise what it sounded like to her? It's just an idea; I'm not saying you're in the wrong."

I pressed the button to unlock my car and walked towards it. "I think you might have a point. Come over before I leave, yeah?"

"If I have time. I have a date tomorrow. But you'll get details on that later," Alice told me. We each reversed out in our separate cars and headed out the same direction until I turned down onto Mulholland and enjoyed the rolling hills with their killer views all the way home.

***

I got a friendly reminder e-mail from the shirts at the GTA after I officially registered for the Madrid Open. I silently told them to go screw themselves and finished packing for my trip home.

***

Toni stayed in touch; I had to give her that much credit. But by the time I landed in Stockholm, it all felt a little too strained. I decided to let her off the hook, as much as it pained me to type every word.

Going to sea with my dad for a few days, will be out of contact. Kick butt in Colombia, see you in Madrid x

Of course, she didn't reply all that quickly, but when she did it was about the best reply I could have hoped for, considering.

I really miss you Elin

What else could I tell her but the truth?

I miss you too

I left it at that, because there was no way to change what was happening over the next few weeks anyway. It would give me time and space to work out what to do about the drug testing problem and also check in on my parents and how their divorce was progressing. My mother had told me very little beyond checking I was sticking to my non-competition training schedule.

Spring in Sweden was a bracing slap in the face after months in tropical climates. I came out of the gate at Arlanda to find my father waiting for me, bundled up in a sensible coat and carrying one for me. He knew by now I was never quite adjusted enough, and I pulled it on gladly as we walked to the car.

"I'm glad you came, *äskling*."

"Me too, Pappa. Hey, did you ever speak to Alice about why she doesn't like to come home?"

He nodded. "It's not a problem, as long as we're fit enough to travel. One day when we're not, she agreed we'll talk about it then."

"I didn't know," I replied. "Am I a bad person? A bad sister to not realise?"

"No, no. Alice is happy, her life is good. She doesn't dwell on the little things that might still bring her down. And honey, you're busy. Now, do you want to choose the radio station?"

I reached out to press the buttons and scan for something, but my father playfully knocked my hand away. "Remember, Elin. If you want to pick the music, you have to be driving the car."

I groaned. Some things really didn't change.

———————

After one of my gym sessions the following week, we met up at the *Kulturhuset*, the cinema and arts centre that I used to hang around in the little free time I had as a teenager. My dad had it in mind to see some German movie that he'd heard about, and I was in the mood to humour him since my mother had gone to some coaches' retreat in Spain. I tried not to think about how much closer that probably put her to Toni now that she'd be done with her South American tournament. It was going to be the best part of a month before I would seeing her again.

"Now Elin, I made sure they have subtitles since I know your German is terrible these days."

"I can follow along," I said, lying only a little. "Actually, could we just grab coffee for now? Maybe catch a later showing?" The glass-walled building made a busy but pleasant spot to sit and watch the world go by. I didn't get to do that very often.

He still guided me through crowds with a protective hand at my back. When I'd first started playing in front of big crowds, he'd been my unofficial bodyguard. What I liked most about being back here was how little anyone cared about celebrity, that even when they recognised me they almost never reacted. It was as close to anonymity as I got, and I felt so much better for it.

We found a table for two with a view out over the square and the bustle of the cafe behind us.

"Your mother tells me you have a new woman on the scene," he began, stirring his hot chocolate. "Do I know her?"

"You and Mamma still talk?"

"We're getting divorced, not going to war. We talk. The house is going to sell, it's fine."

I sipped my coffee. "Well, as long as you still gossip about us kids, I suppose it's okay. You don't know Toni, but you'd like her. Assuming she is still dating me. I guess we'll find out in Madrid." The texts had tapered out again, and I was feeling sorry for myself.

"You know, I have instructions to tell you that retirement is not so fun. That you'll miss your world when you leave it, that you won't know what to do with your days."

I couldn't help but smile. My mother really did work every angle.

"I think the time's coming," I said. "Not quite yet, but the next injury, the next bad run… I don't see me coming back from that. Which is fine; I have plans. But I got it into my head, thinking about a family of my own…"

My father's face lit up. Great, I'd just started the "when do I get grandchildren" countdown. Rookie mistake.

"Anyway, I probably scared Toni off by thinking out loud."

"If she's meant to be, she won't scare so easily," my father said. "And you retire when you're ready. There's always a space for you on the boat."

"Oh great, that fixes everything," I said. "You won't be disappointed? I know you don't come to all the matches now, but you got me into all this, just as much as Mamma."

He took my hand, all reassurance and gruff affection. "You'll never disappoint me, Elin. Now, I'm going to browse the stores downstairs. Why don't you call this lady friend of yours and make things a little less distant, hmm?"

"That might not be enough."

"No way my girl gives up that easily," he insisted. "Now, don't come downstairs until you feel better about it all."

What choice did I have?

I called Toni without second guessing or checking her playing schedule. I just tapped her name and made it happen. Direct action—that was the right idea. What had taken me so long?

It rang for almost too long, but just before I gave up the line clicked into life.

"Toni, hi, I know it's going to be a while before I see you, but I was just thinking—"

"Antonia is in for her sports massage," Mira responded. "And she's trying very hard to improve her ranking before May, so if you care for her Elin, you'll keep it to minimum contact.

"Did she ask you to field calls from me?" I would rather the call had just gone to voicemail.

"Yes, we're developing a good system, just the two of us. She just wants to focus on tennis, nothing else too serious."

Wow. That had to be a reaction to my stupid rambling about the future and my plans. Toni had been so freaked out she had Mira running interference between us.

"It's just a chat, Mira." I tried to brush it off. "Wish her luck from me and I'll…see her whenever."

Making my way downstairs, I saw my father waiting by the doors. Only then did I notice that he'd aged, that the tall stocky man I was used to had begun to stoop a little, his shoulders seemed a little less broad. When he noticed me, I forced myself to plaster a smile on my face and gave him a thumbs up. No need to disappoint him the way I'd ruined things for myself.

The call came on the Friday, the day before I left for the Madrid Open.

"Miss Larsson, we have you scheduled for your press conference on Monday at 11 a.m.," the man from the GTA told me. "We'd appreciate if you could issue that apology before your first match commences."

They had realised how little tennis I was playing, despite being fit. Madrid was going to be my last warmup for the French Open too, so they'd have a limited window to get a punishment approved. Sink or swim time.

Which didn't mean I had to let them in on my plans.

"Of course, that would be a perfect venue for my statement," I agreed. Not that I had decided what that statement might be. Parisa was on the trail of some kind of e-mail or memo that confirmed the extra testing of players who weren't white. "Thanks for the reminder."

"We really would like to put all this behind us. I'm sure you understand." I understood all too well. Their office politics also didn't bother me anywhere near as much as the prospect of being around Toni again.

"Oh, I understand completely. Do watch for my comments."

It wasn't career suicide if I did it for good reasons, surely?

CHAPTER TWENTY-FOUR

I WENT INTO A KIND of hibernation mode, insisting on no visitors once I checked in to my Madrid hotel, and I booked private sessions as early as possible on the practice courts. My mother was thrilled, but Parisa pulled me aside on the Sunday.

"You know Toni left messages for you at reception. Something about changing her number."

Well, that was something. Not exactly an explanation for why I'd heard nothing since Mira picked up, but close enough. I shrugged off Toni's concerns, ignored the messages, and threw myself into a daily routine of exercise, meditation, and shutting the world out with my headphones. Lonely, sure, but I'd never felt more focused on the task ahead.

It was fun to be back on clay. Most of the courts year-round were hard like at the US and Australian Opens, but the distinctive red dirt gave a bounce and a way of playing that challenged all of us. There were specialists who kicked ass every year in France and Spain, only to wilt on grass at Wimbledon soon after. I was lucky enough to be an all-surface kind of player, but I couldn't rely on speed here like I usually did. I had to be much more strategic, and even then, weird things would still happen that I couldn't account for.

More than the tennis, I was keyed up for the press conference. Others would talk before and after me, the first glimpse of the top seeds before we launched into a fast and furious week where winning meant playing a full match every day.

I kept the music playing in my ears until the last possible moment, removing my headphones only once I was seated. The same inane questions started us off: How was I playing, was I fit, did I think I could win the tournament? I gave routine answers that didn't require much thought. I wondered how far the GTA would go in forcing me to talk about the drug-testing problem. I hadn't discussed anything even close to it, and my allocated time was ticking down.

Sure enough, a man I didn't recognise shot his hand up and asked his question even though I was calling on someone in front of him. I watched him, the camera flashes and noise of the crowd fading out for me.

"Miss Larsson, before you took some time off you raised some questions about the tour's drug testing. Is there anything else you want to say on that?"

There was the engineered opportunity, and all I had to do was take it.

"I did mention that, because the women affected by unfair and biased testing were right to fear that they would face retribution for mentioning it in public. I offered to raise the subject because I have a certain amount of privilege and I wanted to use it for good, but not to speak for those women."

The murmurs went around the room.

"It turns out they were right to be worried about that. I've already been threatened with fines and a playing ban just for asking the question. Which makes you think, doesn't it? If there's no problem, no racist policy, then why would anyone warn me not to talk about it?"

Faking innocence wasn't going to convince anyone, so I said it about as straight and sarcastic as it felt. The room knew what was up, and I got sympathetic looks from some of the regular journalists who'd been covering me for years.

"So I guess I'd just ask the GTA to release some figures that clear this whole mess up. If there's no problem, they shouldn't have any problem. Now, if you'll excuse me, I have a match to get warmed up for."

I left the room with my phone already ringing, vibrating away in my pocket it. I ignored it for the short walk to the practice courts, where I hit the crap out of any ball unlucky enough to get near me. After that, my first-round opponent didn't know what hit her. She retired in the second set, and it felt like a mercy killing.

I repeated the process on the Tuesday, swapping the press conference for coffee with Celeste and Keiko, the most social I'd been since hanging around Stockholm with my dad.

"They really came for you in Miami?" Celeste asked, frowning at her kale smoothie.

"I'm surprised I wasn't handcuffed with the trophy still in my hands," I said. "You know this just means you were right. I'm happy to be the target if it means you get actual justice for this. I didn't get tested after winning yesterday. You?"

Celeste nodded but Keiko shook her head. "I bet I get pulled in today, though. I can't tell you the last time I got more than two matches without a test."

"And I got one test in Miami, despite winning the whole thing. What are they up to?" I wondered out loud.

"You have to figure they're protecting someone, in this case another one of the white players getting tested as little as you. Or they suspect someone after Xavi, and all they know it's the coach of one of the women of colour, so they want to flush that out." Celeste laid out the options nice and clear. "Or it's a random pattern that's somehow going wrong, and they don't want to fix it even though they have to know about it by now."

"That about sums it up," Keiko agrees. "I really don't need this bullshit; my year has already been up and down like a yo-yo. Hey, where's the plus one? Celeste told me you and Ruiz are a thing now."

I glanced around the lounge on instinct, but Toni was nowhere to be seen. She wasn't on until the evening match. At least I thought so; I had deliberately avoided looking at the brackets this time out.

"Yeah, well, we're not joined at the hip. And it's... You know, it's nothing serious so don't start with me, you two. Shouldn't we be...saving the sport or something?"

We cracked up laughing at that. "Anyway, I haven't heard anything since they called about the press conference. No shady suits showing up at my door. Let them investigate and maybe all the extra testing will stop." Toni appeared then, with Mira at her side. Nobody else had brought their coach into the players' lounge with them, and I took it as my cue to leave.

And like I said, it was just like the day before. This time we made it through the whole second set, but I was done with the match in less than an hour. It was rare I got the chance to double-bagel someone, but sure enough it finished 6-0, 6-0. Efficiency felt good, and I resigned myself to another quiet night in. It wouldn't make me particularly happy, but it was going to be great for my ranking points and my bank balance.

Wednesday brought the third round and the chance to watch Sarah Harrow in the match before mine. She kept her temper this time and disposed of Fatima over the full three sets, shocking just about everyone. I was glad to have avoided her so far, and I really didn't fancy a rematch when the little punk had the wind in her sails. Luckily, we couldn't meet before the semis on Friday.

I didn't get such an easy run, but I did get a win. When I was asked to step aside on the way to the locker room, I thought I might finally be getting a drugs test. For a moment I panicked, wondering if someone would falsify my result to get me in real trouble. That was a paranoid thought too far.

Instead of a bored-looking nurse and a plastic cup, I was brought into another sort of storage room where the same three suits from Miami were waiting for me. Clearly the Global Tennis Association let its staff rack up the miles along with the players and umpires.

"You didn't retract your statement," the tallest one says, his comb-over a little tragic under the fluorescent lights. "In fact, Miss Larsson, you doubled down."

"I did." I pulled myself onto the desk to sit, in the absence of any chairs. "Why? Because nobody has answered the original questions I raised. We want proof the testing is fair, and that women of colour are not being targeted. It's that simple."

"You'll be invited to a meeting next week," the short, rounder version of Mr Suit interrupted. "At which a fine will be levied. Can we assume you won't attend?"

I pointed at him and winked, full of confidence I didn't entirely feel. "You've been paying attention."

"Then we will proceed with further disciplinary action immediately. Regardless of where you finish in this competition, it will be announced on Saturday that you are suspended from all GTA Tour events for thirty days. Ninety if there are further incidents."

"On what charge?"

"Bringing the game into disrepute. We'll also be consulting our legal team on the libellous nature of your comments."

"It's not libel if they're true," I argued, hoping that was right. "Also, shouldn't this be some long process? Lots of answering to a panel of people in different locations, then it takes two months to even decide when the decision will be?"

"We can take decisive action when the behaviour merits it," Tall Suit said, enjoying himself far too much. "You'll have an opportunity to appeal, of course."

"In the meantime you can deny me the chance to earn? To defend my titles or win new ones? No way, you can't do this."

"The rules and by-laws are very clear," Tall Suit continued. "Now, if you'll proceed next door, you've been selected for testing. Not so racist now, is it?"

I didn't bother to argue. I could feel the temper rising in me like lava shooting through my veins, and I'd only make it worse. Unlike Sarah, I had enough experience to control the outbursts just long enough to make them in private. Maybe I could put that on my resume as a life skill once I retired.

I tried counting under my breath as I pushed my way out into the corridor, but it wasn't distracting me enough.

"Miss Larsson?" A door opened further along the corridor, and a small woman in at least her sixties emerged, lab coat in place. "No rush, dear. Do you need a drink?"

I shook my head. I'd just polished off a full bottle of energy drink coming off court. Tamping down a sarcastic remark, I realised I might be able to get something useful out of the tester.

"I can come in now," I said. "I'm sorry, I didn't catch your name?"

"Doris," she replied, ushering me into the bland space with its sink and singular toilet cubicle—no door. "Now let's get this over with, shall we?"

My phone had been vibrating on and off since I left court, but I only thought to check it when I got back to my room. Flopping down on the bed in my clean tracksuit, I saw I had something from an unknown number. That wasn't usual, given how few times I gave my number out.

Any panic about the number having leaked was wiped out by opening the text to see it was signed 'T xx.' Parisa must have taken pity on her and given her my number again. I saved the new number before I could think better of it and focused on reading the rest of what she'd sent.

Sorry for silence, phone died on me. Guess I'll see you tomorrow? T xx

What did she mean about tomorrow? I scrambled for the player's welcome pack on my nightstand and checked my schedule. The only thing I had was the quarterfinal match which meant... Oh damn, why hadn't I looked at the whole bracket?

I'd be playing Toni in less than twenty-four hours, and she'd only just started talking to me again. There was a saying for that in English; I just couldn't think of it for a moment. Oh yeah. *Fuck my entire life.*

Sleep? Forget it. I grabbed a restless hour here and there, but it wasn't really worth the effort of lying down in the first place. I went through all my daily routine as though it was any other match, but on the practice court, the other players gave me a wide berth. Must have been something about how I looked as I served ball after ball towards Ezi, stepping in as my rally partner for the day.

It was more frustrating that we were the fourth of the four women's matches that day, and my ranking meant we were on the biggest of the three courts—the Manolo Santana. Twelve thousand people would get to see every step, every facial expression. I was so used to tuning out crowds, but now that number was horrifying. Would they be able to tell? Was there anything for them to tell? Hadn't I effectively been ghosted the moment I let her walk away in Miami?

At least I managed a nap in the afternoon, before my final warmup. When I made it down to the locker room, I found Mira waiting. For once she didn't pass comment on me, concerning herself with whatever was so fascinating on her tablet. Coaching instructions to shake the world, knowing her.

Toni didn't appear until moments before we were due to walk out. There was much less fuss than at the four slams, but it was still an occasion here in Madrid. The third quarterfinal had just finished in Stadium Two, meaning the winner here would get to play Jodie, a tour stalwart from the US who everyone liked. She didn't win much in terms of finals, but she was usually in the reckoning most times. Still, it was a potentially simple path to the final, one I would make short work of.

Just had to beat Toni first. Which was fine, as long as I didn't look directly at her. Or think. Or feel.

If she had looked good when I last saw her in person, Toni was unfairly gorgeous today. Seeing too much of it had generally left me immune to the charms of a woman in tennis gear, but it turned out my libido was ready to make an exception. With her hot pink and navy shorts and vest, it felt like neon arrows to point out her stunning legs and defined arms. The one indicator she might be affected by my presence was her matching baseball cap, all the better to try to hide behind. Toni's tan had deepened with another round of sunshine tournaments behind her, and she looked all the better for being without me.

We left Mira in the locker room and walked the short distance until red clay was underfoot.

"Have a good game," Toni said as we lined ready for the handshakes and coin toss. "You look great, by the way."

"I looked good last month too," I said, not moving my lips too much in case the cameras picked us up. "Which, you know, I could have shown you if you'd kept in touch."

"Elin—"

The umpire interrupted us and there was no chance to say more. We shed our jackets on our respective chairs and I took my end to start the final warmup rally. I kicked the ground in quiet frustration at letting Toni know how hurt I'd been. So much for rising above it.

When the match started, I dug deep, reaching for that competitive boost to start things off with a sting. Instead, I found myself watching Toni shift position on the baseline, her hips swinging smoothly from side-to-side as she awaited my serve. I bounced the ball a little too long and she noticed it, giving me a wink from across the court.

Oh yeah. I was screwed.

As with most of the venues we played, there was a huge general locker room for all the women upstairs in the Caja Mágica, but the actual match participants had smaller changing rooms near the court itself. The lockers and the showers were a shared space there, with a private dressing room either side.

I should have guessed she'd come storming right in after me.

"What the fuck was that?" she almost spat the words, catching me off guard and backing me against the wall.

"Excuse me?" I might have been crazy about this woman, but nobody talked to me that way. "Oh, are we talking now?" I felt sick, I didn't want to fight with Toni, but now it seemed inevitable. I could no sooner stop it than I could have stopped a speeding train.

"What do you mean are we talking? You're the one who disappeared on me. Went home to California and then cancelled Stuttgart. What was I supposed to think?" Toni asked. We were inches apart, but it didn't much look like she planned to kiss me this time. I felt her height advantage so acutely in that moment, her dark eyes trained on me as I fumbled for a response.

"You stopped calling! The messages dropped off. I can take a hint, Toni. I wasn't going to make a fool of myself, not again."

"Again?"

I didn't reply, turning my head away. I tried to sidestep her, but she didn't give an inch, planting her palms on the white brick wall behind me and effectively trapping me in place. I could get out if I wanted, we both knew that, but it gave me the excuse I needed to finally confront the whole mess.

"Fine. I started blabbing about babies because you caught me in a weak moment, and instead of listening to context, that it's all some far-off future thing, you freaked out." I willed myself to stare her down on this point. I was in the right. "I didn't mean to scare you, but you handled it very badly."

"So what if I did?" she snapped. "Anyone would freak. What you didn't bother to ask was what kind of freaking out was I doing? Because that, Elin, is the difference. I didn't want to run a mile from you. You started talking about the future like I could be part of it, and I didn't panic for a second. Not until I realised how much I wanted that, how much I liked maybe being in that picture for you. We'd barely been together five minutes, and there I was, ready to grab my U-Haul like some big fucking cliché!"

I squinted at her in confusion as I tried to put it together. "You're saying you flipped out because you didn't flip out at the idea of marriage and babies? That's... That's pretty dumb?"

"Yeah, well, I'm beginning to see why you don't date so much, if you start talking about your future kid's college tuition on a first date."

"Ha ha," I replied, patting her on the arm but still making no attempt to move. "If we had just talked...and then when I thought we would, before coming here, you suddenly disappeared!"

"I broke my phone, I told you. It took a while to get a new one—I was on the road."

"And making Mira your secretary?"

Toni pulled back a little. "What are you talking about?"

"She fields your calls, tells me when you're too busy? Like you didn't put her up to it when you realised you wanted out. Please, give me some credit."

"I...I didn't know. I never asked her to do that." Toni let her hand slip down the wall, taking mine instead. "Elin, come on. I would never do that. I know how you feel about Mira, for a start. She's an excellent coach, but I wouldn't use her to hide from you."

"But you did hide from me." I wasn't letting her away with this one. I pulled my hand free and shoved past Toni. She caught me and pulled me close. Damn, I really had missed that closeness. I felt her breath on my cheek.

"Of course I hid. You, this... I'm terrified. You don't know what this is like for me. I have idolised you, looked up to you like my personal goddess for years now. It got me through recovery and coming back. And then I find out not only are you gay, but you actually like me? It's like shit, maybe Santa was real all this time?"

I couldn't help it. When she started to cry, the first tear rolling down her cheek, I reached up to stroke it away with my thumb. We were basically holding each other up, and I didn't know how we'd found ourselves at this point at all.

"I don't think I want to be an old man in a red suit." I had to at least try teasing her. "And I'm not asking anything of you, Toni. I just really like you, and I want to see what this is between us. As long as you want that too. I never wanted to scare you."

She kissed me, soft and gentle and maybe just a hint of salt from her tears, but I felt the tightness in my chest ease for the first time in weeks. I didn't care that we were both in sweaty clothes, that her hair was damp when I ran my fingers through it. I kissed her and kissed her and damn she kissed me back until I was backed against that wall again, this time with the promise of much more than a conversation.

"But one more thing," Toni said, pulling herself away with obvious regret. "I just, I just have to know. For sure."

"Anything," I replied. "Ask me."

"I just… Elin, did you let me win out there today?"

CHAPTER TWENTY-FIVE

"Did I *what*?"

There was a strange ringing sound in my ears. Had she really just said that to me? It wasn't bad enough she'd clawed her way to victory in the third set at my expense, but now she was checking I hadn't thrown the match? Just to, what, get back in her pants?

"I need to know," she said, having the decency to look down at her feet in something like shame. "That my win today was legit. That I earned it."

"Did you score more points than me?" She nodded. "Did you win two sets?" Another nod. "Did I do anything other than play you full strength? Full speed?" She shook her head that time.

"Elin—"

"Then you have your answer. How can you even ask me that?"

"Well, last time I played you, I barely made it off the court alive." Toni moved across to sit on the chair by the door.

"You've improved," I replied, softening as I saw the lack of belief in her own potential. "Working with Mira has been good for you."

"I've dreamed about this day, you know?" She looked like she might cry again. "Only now I don't want it to affect any chance I might have for...us. Can we do this and still compete? I know you're thinking about stepping down, but—"

"I'm not gone yet," I reminded her. "And I should hide your racquets for ever accusing me of going easy on you. On anyone. If and when I retire, it won't be because I stopped trying to win. Now will you hurry up and get to the part where you get to be smug?"

"Because I finally beat the best player in the world?" Toni replied.

I flipped her off, but I did it with a really big smile. "Exactly. Now you've got Jodie next round, which should mean you're in the final on Saturday. So start enjoying that. How did you want to celebrate?"

She dragged a look up and down my body that made me feel like my clothes had just been torn off. Before she could put what that look suggested into words, the sound of Mira's voice interrupted us.

"Antonia?"

"I have to go check in. See you in the showers in a minute?"

I grinned at her like a fool, because that's exactly what I was when it came to all this. "Don't take too long. I might start without you once the water hits me."

She left with a spring in her step. Good.

As much as I wanted Toni to myself the next day, when she woke up in my bed all sleep-tousled and out of sorts, I sent her back to her own room to get ready for her semi-final. I would watch from the stands, even though it was still unusual behaviour for me to hang around after I'd been put out. Let them talk; I was officially past caring.

What I did have to care about was the threat of suspension hanging over my head. I needed two slams to equal the record and three to break it. With the French Open being one of the remaining three, I had to play in it to have any hope of wrapping up my goal in one season. Maybe I'd still play on for at least one more year, but the sooner I got the numbers, the sooner it would feel like fully my choice again.

I met with my co-conspirators in the players' lounge, my mother and Parisa rounding out our numbers.

"I have more data," Parisa said, brandishing some printouts. "The shift definitely started four years ago."

We looked around for a moment until Celeste did the maths. "The season I won my first slam."

Keiko gave a low whistle. "Shit, you know people are racist and then they still surprise you. I remember the crappy coverage you got at the time too."

"They didn't exactly love you winning in Paris last time either. But with me it's always this implication that I'm cheating just by being built this way. Who knew all this time they were actually testing for it?"

"I'm sorry," my mother said to them both. "If I'd had any idea this was going on…"

"They've kept it pretty quiet," Celeste said. "I suspect what the tour wants is to maximise the slender blondes who spend half the year modelling and don't hit the ball too hard. In case it puts any men off, that sort of thing."

"Well, this skinny blonde hits as hard as any of you," Parisa said, in a compliment I wasn't sure I wanted. "But yeah, I suspect you're right, Celeste. I've heard some borderline shady things from the marketing people now and then, but that's just the risk of doing business sometimes—too many of them speak before they think."

"Just so you all know, they invited me to a disciplinary meeting which I already refused." I had to get it out while I could still summon the words to talk about it. "And I've been told there'll be an announcement Saturday that I'm being fined and suspended for 30 days."

That started the uproar. Parisa's string of curse words was like shouted poetry, and my mother practically turned furniture over, on her feet and ranting in Swedish. Celeste and Keiko were talking over both of them, listing more incidents of potential racism. By the time Celeste got to where they could shove their damn trophy, I didn't know whether to laugh or hide under the table. The whole room was staring at us, or at least trying to catch a glimpse.

"Calm down!" I hissed, smothering the laugh that was definitely trying to escape. "This is why I painted the little target on my back, it's okay. I don't like to think what they would have done to you, Celeste. It almost feels like they were trying to…I don't know, provoke you?"

"We'll find out soon enough, because no way are we letting them away with this. It would mean you miss Paris!"

That set my mother off, predictably. Through a flurry of muttered curses, she took out her phone and started sending out frantic messages. "Like hell will you miss a slam, Elin."

"Mamma, they haven't done anything yet. It could be a few guys trying to intimidate me into shutting up." I didn't believe that; I had seen how serious they were. Maybe that pissed me off most of all, that they expected me to be scared of them. Well, the tennis world would cope without three random assholes in suits, but they might not be so quick to go and play tournaments with their top players boycotting. Talking people into not earning money would be a struggle, but most of us could afford to take the hit.

"When will you know if they're serious?" Keiko asked, pulling her long dark hair back into a ponytail.

"Tomorrow, I guess. That's what they said."

"Then we'll decide tomorrow. None of us are going to Rome next week, right?" Celeste asked. We all shook our heads. "Okay, let's go deal with the semi-finals. Sorry, Elin."

"I'll have fun watching," I said, and for once I actually meant it.

I was wrong about it being fun.

Watching Toni in Mexico had been a breeze compared to this match. I played every point with her in my head, tried to look completely unmoved whenever she notched up another point, another game. Doing well here would look good for her going into Paris. Even though I had my eye on the big prize there, I wanted Toni to get as close as possible.

Mira ignored me again, unsurprisingly. Any attempt she'd made as a media personality to disguise her bitterness towards me was well and truly over. I was glad a few people sat between us in the VIP section, and I struck up conversation with some of my fellow pros who'd come to soak up the action and talk shop about the upcoming tournaments.

Somewhere in the middle Toni lost focus, like the trick I'd taught her had stopped working. I knew she must have other coping mechanisms, but I worried for her when the shots and the decisions started being just a little out of step with what Jodie was throwing at her. Before I could get too upset, though, something clicked again, and Toni saw the match out like her life depended on it.

She was going to another final.

I applauded as hard as anyone, but let Jürgen commandeer me to brag for a while so that when the cameras swept over us all, I'd look disinterested: just another working holiday. I knew there'd be some commentary on me being a good sport, staying to cheer on the person who'd vanquished me. What a professional, huh? If only they knew.

Friday night felt like an excuse to have dinner out, and Toni insisted even with the final hanging over her. Seeing her wandering the streets of Madrid at my side, I was seeing her in her element. She had visited the city many times with her mother, not just for tennis, and took great delight in pointing out funny little stores and hidden side streets.

"I had no idea you were so hot on your history," I admitted when we finally made it to the hole-in-the-wall tapas place that looked like nothing much outside but had a six-month waiting list for reservations. "And how did you get us a table here, anyway?"

"Elin! Señorita Larsson!" The maître d' almost fell over himself rushing to greet us. "And Señorita Cortes Ruiz, *por favor*."

"I dropped your name like a hot potato," Toni admitted, whispering in my ear. "It's incredibly sexy how well that works. I intend to do it a lot from now on."

Well. How could I complain about that?

"Keep this up and my name won't be the only thing dropping tonight," I whispered back as we took our seats at a table tucked into an alcove. A little privacy, then. "Assuming I'm wearing anything that can be dropped, of course."

She almost spilled her water at that. Good to know I wasn't the only one so easily flustered.

I didn't look around for once to see if we were noticed. For a few minutes, it seemed like every member of staff dropped by to wait on us personally, but eventually my wine was ordered—Toni stuck to water.

"So tomorrow, I'm going to have an extra guest for the match," Toni told me, leaning back in her chair, the candles on the table lighting her like a painting. "In the seat next to you, in fact."

"If this is some ex-girlfriend…" It turned out that for all the speculation and rumours around Xavi, and despite a few failed attempts in high school, Toni had never properly dated any men. Not that it mattered to me one way or another, as long as we were attracted to each other, but it was a reminder for me not to run around making assumptions.

"No, it's my mother. She decided maybe she can care a little bit for a final. She keeps saying I'll be like 'the Spanish champion' if I win, which isn't… Still, she's not normally so enthusiastic."

"This is a big deal for you, isn't it? Do you need me to be just a friend?" I reached for her hand, entwining our fingers. "I can do that, for you. You know my history with being out, so…"

"I think I'd like to tell her who you are to me," Toni confessed. "I mean, she already knows there's someone on the scene. And that I almost blew the whole thing."

"But you didn't," I assured her. "It doesn't have to be such a big deal. You've met my mother."

"She travels with you. You work together every day. And she gets it, Elin. From what you've told me, there was no big adjustment. One gay daughter, one trans daughter—Britta just rolls with it and loves you both the same. My mom? It's not like that."

"She knows you're gay, though?"

Toni nods, sipping at her water. "But she told me she doesn't want to know all the details, not in her face, all of that. If she has to meet 'some woman' I better be serious about her."

"And you didn't tell her what lesbians are like for serial monogamy?" I tried to lighten the mood, but my heart was doing a strange kind of pitter-patter that would have set alarms beeping if I had my treadmill heart monitor on. "Sounds as though you really like me, if you're going through all this."

"That's what I'm saying," Toni said, heaving a sigh of relief. "So yeah, you enjoy that tomorrow. Me? I'm glad my ass will be on court."

"It is a very nice one," I agreed. "You know, if we just ordered dessert we could be back at the hotel in less than an hour."

"I'm hungry," Toni protested. "But okay, we'll skip the first course. You're a bad influence."

"Oh, I know." I wanted to make a joke about how the GTA would agree with her, and we'd find out tomorrow, but the words just wouldn't form. She deserved a night with no stress, no interference with her preparation. We'd talk about it after the match. "And I'm really happy you want me to meet your mother."

We smiled at each other in the candlelight, and my heartbeat settled down to something quick and happy.

My plan to shield Toni was obliterated by the morning headlines. Alerts had started appearing on my phone in the wee small hours, thanks to Parisa forwarding them, and it seemed the GTA were going all out for the suspension.

What pissed me off almost as much as the thought of Toni waking up to be distracted by it all was the way the official statement implied I'd done something wrong when it came to doping. No mention that I had spoken out against injustice, just the vague implication about me, drugs, and suspension. Only at the very end did the statement mention I had never tested positive for any banned substance.

I went back to bed and waited for Toni's alarm to rouse her. She had one of those sunrise alarm clocks and took it with her to every hotel and house throughout the year. Slowly, the fake sunlight woke her up with a smile on her face.

Like the lovesick idiot I was, I thought maybe she had never looked more beautiful. I said good morning with a soft kiss instead of words.

"Hey," she said, voice still husky with sleep and deep enough to hit me right between the thighs. "What are you waiting so patiently for?"

I wished it was for something as fun as sex.

"Listen, it's not a big deal, but I made some headlines today. You're almost definitely going to get pulled in for testing whether you win or not, so don't let anything affect your focus."

"Can we go for a swim?" She was checking her phone, catching up on reality swipe by swipe. I braved myself for her anger at me not having told her sooner.

"If you want to, sure. I'm apparently a real troublemaker, though, so you might not want to be seen in public with me. Or let me meet your mother."

"Elin, you're taking a stand to protect the sport we all devoted our lives to. You don't take illegal steroids or speed or anything to cheat, and no funny little men from the GTA can intimidate you. Especially not with a press release, no?"

"Right. You saw the part where I'm going to be fined and suspended once the president approves it?"

Toni kicked off the covers and slipped out of bed, coming around to stand on my side. In her tiny cami and shorts, dark hair tumbling wild over her shoulders, it took all my strength not to yank her onto the mattress there and then.

"Well, that you have to appeal. Reps, attorneys; hell, why not set your mother on them?" Toni kissed me on the end of my nose. "Other people I might worry, but babe, you can take on anyone."

I felt ten pounds lighter by the time we brushed our teeth and picked up our swim gear. Who knew that talking it through with Toni, and her boundless confidence in me, that I would feel better than if I just silently fretted over it? Okay, when I put it like that, I saw exactly how obvious it was, but the very pleasant feeling remained. I felt like I could take on the world, not just the stuffed shirts of the GTA. Let them ban me. I'd sue my way into the French Open and bring the glare of public opinion right along with me.

The pool was mostly empty, save for a few men thrashing out lengths in the fast lane. Usually I'd go threaten their egos with my killer front crawl, but I was more in the mood for lazy backstroke with frequent interruptions for making out in the shallow end. Toni indulged me for a while before going to splash around in her real workout, teaching the fast-lane boys a lesson in the process. At least until Jürgen showed up. With his arms, he had the edge on all of us.

He eventually came across to disturb me after zipping around like Flipper with a fake tan, wearing Speedos that had to be threatening his circulation.

"Larsson. That bikini is almost obscene by your standards."

Usually, I opted for a one-piece, but my kit sponsor had offloaded a bunch of their new summer line on me, including this pale blue bikini that was probably more skinny straps than actual fabric. It covered everything essential, and it was comfortable to swim in, so what did I care beyond the way it made Toni stare like she was trying to memorise me for a test.

"We can't all... What do our Aussie pals call it? Smuggle little birds?"

"I heard you've gone all communist on us. So bored of winning you've picked a fight you must lose?" I swept a little wave at him with my arm to express my annoyance. He took it in stride and kept at me, wading in my direction till I was backed into a corner of the pool. "Hey, I get it. I like to mess with the suits whenever I can. I think sometimes they forget who makes them all this money. Nobody ever bought two grand hospitality tickets to watch some accounting."

"Careful, boy wonder. I might start thinking you're on my side."

"Oh, I'm not on any side that doesn't make me money. Still, you're my white whale, the one that got away. I should do something nice for you."

"Jürgen, you didn't ever stand a chance. I'm gay."

His smile was almost blinding. "What? I thought that was just bitching from all the guys you knocked back. Including me."

"Charming." Okay, it was a little funny how relieved he looked. Had I really been such a hit job on his masculinity?

"So who's the lucky lady? There must be one on the scene now or you would have told me sooner."

Which naturally, was Toni's cue to swim over.

"Babe?" She gave Jürgen the once over. "Is he bothering you?"

"We're all friends here, Ruiz. Congrats on making the final, by the way. Keep this up and you might even win a big one. Although since you've melted the Ice Princess, maybe that's the only prize that matters, hmm?"

"We should go." Toni pointed to the huge clock on the wall. "My mother will be landing at Barajas any minute."

Jürgen wasn't impressed by her dismissal, but he turned to me once more. "Anyway, something nice. I heard some of the boys' chat in the locker room, and they think there might be the same problem in the men's testing. I asked if they had proof and someone can get it. You want a copy? I can have the guy hand it right over to you."

"Why would you help me?" I asked, feeling Toni's arm slip around my waist under the water. A united front.

"Like I said, I stick it to the man when it amuses me. Give them hell, see what happens next. He'll leave an envelope at reception for you. This afternoon sometime."

"Thanks," I called back to him, following Toni's lead towards the ladder and dry land. Maybe I did have legs to stand on after all.

CHAPTER TWENTY-SIX

I COULDN'T TELL TONI, BUT while we got ready for her mother's arrival, I felt very queasy. Not because I thought I'd make a bad impression, although there was a reason my lingering nickname was the Ice Princess. Not just because I was cool under pressure. No, this was one area where my lack of real-world experience tripped me up. I hadn't really done meet-the-parents in any real way, apart from a couple of nice parties at Celeste's home back in Michigan. Then there was the complicating factor that Gabriela didn't care much for tennis. When I ran out of things to talk about, I could usually fall back on that.

At least Toni seemed nervous too, right up until her mother strolled into the hotel lobby, and then every bit of tension evaporated in a massive hug and a torrent of Spanish that seemed like a mutual compliment fest.

"Mama, this is Elin."

"*Por dios*, Antonia, I know who she is. This lady is on television and magazines more than the Pope. It's very nice to meet you. I've been hearing for at least ten years that you are the greatest thing to ever happen to tennis."

I shook Gabriela's offered hand, a little dumbstruck. Toni had the good grace to blush.

"It's very nice to meet you," I said. "And your English is fantastic. Does that run in the family?"

"If you live in the part of Spain that the English have invaded, you learn," she replied. "Although I always say your people have the right idea: raise all the kids bilingual. God knows the English never will."

"Toni will have to go and get ready soon, but we have time for some coffee," I suggested. "I could take your things up to her room and then join you both?"

"No, no, leave it to the bellboy. I might not be so good talking about your little yellow balls you all care so much about, but I do want to talk to the woman who has Antonia so...well. I'm sure you know."

Gabriela linked her arm with mine, and the other with Toni's.

"Come on, girls, there's a lot to talk about."

I let Gabriela hang back with the officials and players in the lounge, soaking up the praise for her daughter, and made my way to the seats a little early. We had survived her interrogation, but I was still a little stunned. I'd never been so relieved as when Toni got her call to go start the official warmup.

Taking my seat, I was pleased to note that the court was pristine, freshly raked, and just the hint of a breeze had the net rippling lightly. Clay courts slowed play down considerably, took away the advantage of big servers like Celeste.

Perfect conditions for Toni's style of play. She could do this.

When someone came to sit beside me, I assumed it was Gabriela. Then I recognised the perfume and turned to discover Mira. Like I just had been, she was focused on the court out in front of us, never turning her head to look at me as she spoke.

"I really thought you'd have taken the hint by now, Elin. Your presence is only going to hold her back."

"She's in her second final in a matter of weeks, how am I holding her back? She just beat me, for God's sake." I gripped the free chair on my other side, not wanting my temper to flare too high. "Which is still pretty hard, even if I'm not nineteen anymore." Okay, that was a cheap dig about how she never again beat me after I took that final from her, but Mira had irritated me into it.

"So this week you want to have a girlfriend, you want to be out. Then it'll get tricky and you'll get right back in the closet. How much time will Toni lose to a broken heart, hmm? While you're pretending you never had anything to do with her."

"Is this before or after the GTA ban me for questioning their drug-testing policy? I have enough problems without ruining my relationship."

"Then break it off now, while it's still barely a relationship. You two almost managed it after Miami, hardly talking. Just let that happen again and let her have a real shot at winning some slams."

I put it together then. Toni's confusion about missing my calls. Mira's reputation as a control freak. I almost smacked my forehead as it all fell into place. Hadn't Toni herself told me Mira was batting for our team? Despite the anger rising in my chest, I forced myself to stay neutral. Well, the icy side of neutral anyway. "When you answered the phone that time…was that the only time you kept us apart? Or what, deleted a few messages here and there? Didn't pass along the notes from reception? Is that how it is?"

Mira just watched the court, saying nothing.

"Nobody is that invested in their client's success, not really. Even my mother has never sabotaged a relationship of mine, and she literally gave me the life I'm using to play this game with. So it begs the question, Mira… Do you want me gone because I'm a distraction? Or because you want to take a run at Toni yourself?"

"Oh please," Mira made a scoffing sound. "You think very highly of yourself. Always have. That's why you get those nicknames, isn't it? But if I wanted Antonia in that way, well. You wouldn't stop me. All you've done is confirm she'll date an older woman."

Mira had ten years on me, maybe more. If she'd ever been nice to me, I'm sure I would have developed a raging crush, and she'd definitely been the object of my fascination before I'd ever joined the tour. How sad to think we might still be competing after all this time. Only one thing was for sure: Toni was worth it, so in any contest I'd make sure to win.

Then the judges and the umpire came out, followed soon after by the players. Gabriela slipped into her seat, but I didn't notice at first, too intent on watching Toni come out on court. When she looked up and waved, the eye contact unmistakably just for me, I realised I had already won.

Now she just needed to do the same on court, and to hell with Mira either way.

The GTA, or at least a small clutch of people in power there, had decided to go on an all-out offensive. As concerned as I was about the prospect of missing the French Open, I also had something much more pressing to deal with: a whole week off that Toni wasn't playing either.

She needed a break after the sheer volume of travel she'd done while I'd been bumming around the Stockholm with my dad. Not for the first time, I wondered how nice it might be to stay in one place for weeks on end, to have a routine that wasn't punctuated by ever-changing airline reservations depending on whether I was fit to play in the next tournament or not. It sounded pretty damn pleasant, and those seven days we'd had together in the south of Spain were more precious than either of us wanted to admit.

All too soon it was back to business. I needed one slam to equal the record and a second to break it. Three left this year, otherwise I'd be chasing again in Australia come January. For me, that meant I had to play in the French Open, and it was just over a week away. Smaller tournaments were running, and Toni had gone to play in Strasbourg.

"I think Paris was the right choice for the press conference," Parisa said for the third time that morning, as we drove to the hotel. She was right. Checking in a week early made it look like I was especially committed to the tournament, and with so many tennis fans converging on one place, it would tap into both the fan and media attention perfectly.

"I just want to get it over with," I admitted, smoothing down my blazer, a smart black one that seemed serious enough for the occasion. I'd opted for a pale blue shirt underneath and jeans to calm things down a little. No point looking like a court defendant with a full suit.

The hotel function room was much like every other I'd ever given a press conference in. No matter how fancy the frescoes or expensive the hanging art, the rooms always had that temporary feel to them. Something about rearranging the furniture into so many different events made it feel like it couldn't be one particular thing.

I saw many friendly faces in the gathered press. Parisa's monitoring of the online debate said most people were on my side, but it was always preferable to be talking to the nicer journalists in this kind of situation. I'd seen one too many comments telling me to sit down and shut up, because if there was one thing every woman could look forward to, even at the top of her game, it was that she'd be treated like she had no idea what she was talking about.

I called on Ulrika for the first question. She got right to the point. "Elin, have you paid the fine? And are you currently suspended?"

"I haven't paid, no. Turns out they don't take PayPal." I got a mild ripple of laughter. "As far as I know I can't play this week, or next week, which of course is here at Roland-Garros. I'm here and ready to play, but I've been banned for asking a question."

A French journalist spoke up next, and although I could mostly follow, I waited for the translation to filter through to be sure. "Elin, have you broken the rules? Are you sorry?"

"No, I haven't broken any rules. My players' representative and my lawyers are very sure about that. It's why we want to appeal, but because there was no process followed, it's hard to do that."

A woman from the BBC next, who looked about twelve. Her question was long and rambling, but I found my answer quickly enough.

"The body in charge of tennis has a racist, unfair policy. Instead of taking this chance to fix it, they're punishing me. The reason I spoke up was to protect my fellow players, women of colour, who would likely have been punished more harshly. I have a certain profile, and I want to use it to help their cause. As soon as they're safe from retaliation, I will step aside because it's not my place to talk over these women. Once this is resolved, please direct all questions to my friend and colleague, Celeste Rutherford."

A few cameras were still flashing, and the overheard lights were starting to feel hot. I didn't envy people who had to be on television every day.

Ulrika chimed in again. "Elin, is it true that you're doing this because you're in a romantic relationship with Antonia Cortes Ruiz? Until recently, she was coached by someone who has been suspended for drugs violations. Isn't it possible any targeted testing was based on that information, and not on race?"

Well. Here it was, the golden opportunity of an opening. I wiped my palms on the tablecloth, shocked at how quickly they'd started to sweat. My mouth was dry, and every thought I tried to form was drowned out by the thundering of my heartbeat, which seemed to fill my whole head. I thought I'd been nervous in my first professional match, in my first final. Those had nothing on the moment right in front of me.

"I didn't come here to discuss my personal life." The room's anticipation deflated a little, along with my own. I really thought I could do it that time, just open my mouth and have the words come out. I glanced down at my phone, saw a message from Toni had lit up the screen just before I said it. Was she watching? Was anywhere carrying it live? "And the patterns go back four years, in both the men's and women's competitions. The information has been released widely now, so you'll just have to look for yourselves. I'm a tennis player, not a journalist."

The BBC journalist jumped back in and tried to ask another question, but I shook my head. "No, sorry. I want to add something to that answer."

The murmurs went round. It was usually effort enough to get me to answer a question once, never mind twice. I smiled, and from somewhere the peace slipped over me, the same way it had after telling my parents, after the first time I kissed another girl. The sense of rightness, that I knew exactly who I was, and more importantly who I wanted to be to the world.

"I wasn't deflecting before, about my relationship with Toni. We are together, although she's playing today in Strasbourg. I just wanted to be clear that it isn't why I'm asking these questions or taking this position on the unfair testing procedures."

A hundred questions came at me then: How long and how did we meet? Did I identify as a lesbian? I just sat there, letting it bubble over and over until it finally died down.

"Elin, what do you want the GTA to do now?" Ulrika asked, giving me a discreet thumbs up that I was more than grateful for.

"I want them to admit they're wrong to punish me, just for pointing out a problem. I want them to investigate that problem, and I want women of colour to be treated equally to white women when we play tennis. Anytime, anywhere. I want those women who have been unfairly treated to be listened to and apologised to."

They dutifully nodded along.

"And I want to play in the damn French Open!" I added, grinning as I thumped the table for emphasis. "Thank you, everyone."

I was sort of amazed my legs worked when I stood up, and that I made it out of there step by step without just dropping to the floor. The moment I was in the anteroom, I tapped on Toni's name until the phone started ringing.

"Oh my God!" she greeted me, her voice in a register that could make ears bleed. "Did you know that was going out live, like, everywhere? BBC, Eurosport, ESPN? Babe, you just came out to the world. Are you okay?"

Well, when she put it like that... "You know what? I am. I really am. I should have done that a long time ago. But actually, no. This was the right time for me. I got to confirm it, got to tell people, because I have you in my life. I got to tell people I'm gay because it's also the reason that I'm happy. That's all thanks to you."

Toni was quiet for a long moment. "Yeah, I'm pretty great."

We both cracked up laughing, and the last of my tension ebbed away. "Thank you," I told her. "For everything."

"Don't thank me yet—do you think they'll let you play?"

"We'll see," I replied, looking around to see if Parisa had followed me out. No sign yet. "You sure you don't mind us being outed in the media? I know your family know about us, but this could be a big deal for a while."

"I'll say," Parisa agreed, appearing out of nowhere in her smart grey pantsuit. "You two could be the Ellen and Portia of tennis, if you play your cards right."

I groaned and slid down the wall a little way bracing at the knees to hold myself up. "I should have known you already have a marketing strategy."

"Wait until the first time you're drawn against each other. The 'love match' headlines will be insane," Parisa said. "Now come on, we have places to be, Elin."

"Gotta go," I told Toni. "I look forward to our next love match."

"Me too," she replied, voice warm and welcoming as ever in my ear. "Love you, bye."

I heard the stuttering little breath after she said it, felt her panic like a palpable thing.

"Just as well," I whispered. "Since I love you too."

Too soon? To hell with it. I'd spent my life waiting for someone I couldn't wait to say it to, and there she was in the form of Toni. I already knew how I felt, and I was officially over hiding how I felt. It was too important.

We'd talk later; I already knew that much. Parisa had some new endorsement deal lined up for me, and we were going to sign the paperwork at their Paris office. After that? Well, the TGV train took less than two hours to Strasbourg, I'd already checked.

Maybe next time I said 'I love you' it would be in person.

Toni was still on court when I arrived, but she'd told reception to get me a key card. I let myself into her room, trying not to laugh at the post-hurricane levels of mess she left lying around when she was on her own. Maybe I really was lovesick, but I liked her chaos more than my own sterile overly organised life. It felt like part of her personality was coming at me from every direction, and who wouldn't like that?

I dropped my overnight bag on a chair and considered my options. The adrenaline of the day was starting to wear off, and the bed itself looked all too inviting. I'd never been one for taking naps, but the pillows were practically calling out to me.

When I woke up, the room was much darker and someone was stroking my cheek with the back of their fingers. "I really hope that's you, but if not, then housekeeping is getting a big tip for friendliness."

"You look good like this, very peaceful," Toni said. "You wouldn't know you just did a very brave thing."

"Brave, sure," I said, opening one eye. "Some would say stupid, but I like that you think it was brave."

"I'm proud of you, you know?"

"Why?" I woke up properly at that, wriggling up into a sitting position. "I mean, thank you, but why specifically?"

"I suppose it could be because you're *so* good at tennis," Toni began, her tone as serious as her face was grinning. "And there's all those things you do for charity. Starting up your own, even. I suppose I could be proud of you being gorgeous, and funny, and really kind even though you don't want anyone to know it."

"Toni..."

"But no, I'm proud that you told the world today that I'm the lucky woman who gets to date you. That was a really nice moment for me."

I bent forward a little, kissing her soundly. "It was pretty nice for me too. Well, when the panic attack calmed down, anyway."

"Did you—"

I shouldn't have made light of it. I'd explained a lot over the past week together, about anxiety and how I'd been dealing with it. "No, just an expression. You're sweet to worry, though. I have to say, being with you and all this happiness has helped with it a lot. It won't ever go away, but my head is full of positive things, so it's easier."

Her phone beeped. "Sorry, let me just… Oh, we should put the news on."

She went looking for the remote, and the screen blinked into life. We cuddled up and watched the TV-5 coverage of my press conference. I had to put my hands over my eyes. I could just about handle watching myself on court when my mother pointed out mistakes as part of her coaching, but promos and interviews, I never even looked at.

"You following?" Toni asked, her arm around my shoulders. "My French is lousy."

"Mmm, they're saying something about me being defiant. Oh, and also the shock news that I'm in a lesbian relationship. Okay, so…"

The footage cut to the GTA European headquarters in London. Some senior executive, not one of the three suits who'd been on my case, was being asked something while the French newscaster talked over it. Only when he spoke did she shut up long enough to let me hear the English.

"We're very concerned that this has become a public matter, but of course the GTA has nothing to hide and we welcome questions and scrutiny. Especially from the world number one and one of the finest players the women's game has ever seen."

Another off-camera question I didn't catch.

"No, absolutely, and aside from injuries it's very important to us that the best players play in our most prestigious competitions. Elin Larsson will be very welcome at Roland-Garros, and at Wimbledon in late June, for that matter."

Oh, the relief almost knocked me back against the headboard. Taking a stand had mattered so much, but the punishment had been weighing on me more than I could tell anyone. Beside me, Toni punched the air before kissing me on the cheek.

"You did it!" she said. "They were bluffing and you called them on it."

"They still need to actually investigate now," I replied, but even my pessimism couldn't spoil the winning feeling. "What time do you play tomorrow?"

"Ah." Toni looked a little sheepish. "My head wasn't really in it today, and it was a rough draw—that angry little Canadian? Anyway, I kind of got dumped out in the first round."

"So what you're saying is you're free to come back to Paris with me? And we can train for the Open together?"

Toni nodded in confirmation, and I wrangled her into my lap for a celebratory kiss.

"Yes to all of that," she said. "I love you. Sorry for letting that slip on the phone."

"I love you too," I told her. "On the phone, in person, anywhere…"

"Good," Toni said, pulling the sheets out of our way. "Now let me show you just how much."

CHAPTER TWENTY-SEVEN

IT WOULD HAVE BEEN A little easier if we could have stayed in our bubble, but the arrival of the French Open proper meant an avalanche of press for both of us.

"Do you want to do a joint interview?" Parisa asked over lunch, on the Sunday before the first round began. "It won't sound like you, which means it'll pull focus from the actual tennis. On the other hand, it's a lot of press coverage."

"Not all of the reaction will be positive," I pointed out over my plate of pasta. "I don't want to end up with protests and boycotts, not after I just made a big deal about how I need to play and the tournament needs me. Us."

Toni smirked a little from across the table. We had been intending to eat alone, but Parisa had tracked us down easily enough, with my mother and Mira in tow. They'd just pulled chairs over, much to the waitstaff's horror.

"It might be a good thing, then, that you can't meet each other before the semi-finals. If you do cross paths, I'll handle the headlines, but it's going to mean at least one sit-down with TV. That work?" Parisa had her planner out, various plans and contacts sketched out all over the page. Not for the first time, I was in awe of how she kept track of it all.

"So now we can focus on tennis?" my mother asked, getting an approving nod from Mira. Great, those two joining forces could only spell disaster for me. Retirement suddenly looked like a great option all over again.

But first: two more slams.

Winning the early rounds wasn't too strenuous, which was its own kind of relief. Everyone at the top of the field had improved in the few weeks I'd taken off, and between them, Celeste, Toni, and Keiko were playing some phenomenal tennis. So too were Fatima and even the young upstart Sarah, who seemed to be keeping her temper in check. Her presence came in handy too: The longer she stayed in the competition, the more headlines focused on her and kept some of the heat from Toni and me.

There was definitely something to be said for having every other day without a match in Paris, even if we were mostly confined to the hotel and the practice facility. We would come back with reddish smudges of clay in all sorts of places, clean up, and spend our evenings together back in that bubble the outside world hadn't quite popped yet.

"This is nice," Toni said, from where she was already soaking in the bathtub. She'd called down to have some fancy bath oils and rose petals sent up, only to beat me into the tub because I was taking too long over my evening Pilates. By the time I slipped into the water, facing her across the steaming water, she was grumbling that the oils just made the flowers stick to her skin.

There was nowhere in the world I'd rather be, and I supposed it was only fair I tell her that.

"Me too," she agreed. "I wish it could always be like this. We're both playing well, you seem happier on court than you were when we met, maybe longer than that."

"Mmm. There'll be some times where it doesn't line up, but with your ranking climbing like this you'll be qualifying for everything that I am. It's just…"

"Yeah?"

"If I can wrap it up with two out of the three left this season, I think that might be it for me."

She sat up, splashing her hands and making the water surge up on my chest like a warm wave.

"Seriously? I thought that was about being unhappy. So soon? Elin, really?"

"I am happy, with you. I don't need the tennis, even though you're right, it has been coming easier for me. But I think I can enjoy it more

229

because it doesn't feel like forever now. It feels like the exit might finally be in sight."

"Wow." Toni shimmied forward, causing more little waves. She was tucked snugly between my thighs at that point. "I mean, it would be insane. Going out on top like that. You could win all three, you know that, don't you?"

"Unlikely. But I think I have enough in the tank for two. Then there would be a kind of long, public farewell, I guess? If I can't do it, then I'll play next season. But I don't want to play until I'm too old for it."

"Mmm, that's right, your birthday is next week. At thirty-three you're my older woman." Toni gave me a wink, her grin downright cheeky. "Oh, I'm not complaining."

"Well, you young ones are always coming for my crown," I teased, even though we were both well aware she'd be twenty-seven the day before Wimbledon. "I thought I should start having some fun with that."

"Are you telling me there's a line outside?" She dragged her fingertips down the inside of my thigh, her nails short and blunt, but enough to spark a reaction all the way down. "Because I was planning on taking my time tonight."

"I think you're already more than I can handle," I confessed. "I'm not looking for anyone else."

"Good," Toni replied, shifting position so she could kiss me, her fingers slipping beneath the water. "Because neither am I."

Toni lost to Celeste in the semi-finals and didn't take it well. I had to leave her stewing in her hurt and anger, taking up my part in the second semi and playing for the chance to meet Celeste. Maybe the worry forced me to be efficient, or maybe Fatima was off her game that day, but I booked my berth in the final as if it had been written in the stars, just waiting for me to show up and fulfil the prophecy. Winning felt like that sometimes, as though forces beyond a simple ball and racquet were at play.

It made for a quiet evening, one where Toni eventually asked to be alone and I was happy to comply. I found my mother in the hotel bar, nursing the one glass of Scotch she allowed herself on a match day, and she motioned for me to join her. For once, we talked in our native tongue, no guests and no Alice around to give us pause.

"How is she?"

"Pissed off with the world," I replied. "She really thought she was in with a chance, after Madrid. There's no telling her that this was still a good showing."

"Hmm." My mother sipped at her drink. "I didn't know if she had it in her, but she's like you. It's not obvious, but this level of investment will pay off for her. If she can stay fit. I remember how bad her back was; she was supposed to be done for good."

"Still." I waved down the waiter and asked for some juice. "It's one less motivated person in my way. I want to have a good summer."

"I hope you didn't say that to her."

"Of course not. We don't... My success is not at the expense of hers. And vice versa. I can be happy for her, if I win on Saturday, she'll be thrilled for me. It's healthy, Mamma. It's good."

She watched me for a long time, considering. "Yes, I think it is. And no 'if,' Elin. When. Celeste is strong again this season, but you have the edge. Without her serve here she's relying on everything else."

"I know, we'll go over it all tomorrow. You've found me some weak spots?"

My mother nodded. Always ready to help me win. "Since you want to save the tennis for tomorrow, I should probably tell you...your father called. We have a buyer for the house."

That startled me, just as the waiter brought my juice. I almost spilled it over him in his starched uniform, and the apologies took a minute or two. "That's really it? Just gone?"

"Yes, and we can sign the divorce papers the same week. It won't be until after Wimbledon, don't worry. Are you coming back in July with me?"

"I don't think so. I don't want to watch that, sorry. Dividing up our lives, I mean. I know you two are so adjusted, but it's weird for me. It was weird being home with Pappa and not you, honestly."

"It's okay," my mother assured me. "Here I am, ending the great love story of my life, and it seems yours is just starting."

I blushed, furiously. My mother didn't talk about things like love. If asked, I would have said she loved her children, loved her job, and yes, eventually she would have mentioned my father. I'd never seen him as her great love, and I realised in that moment how much children missed. I had taken for granted our safe and welcoming home, no screaming fights or dark clouds hanging over it. Once we started to travel with the tour, that family life had been my oasis, my safe place to land.

I saw in that moment that I hadn't been picturing that anymore, when I thought about home and peace and contentment. I'd been picturing my own, high in those Hollywood Hills. Completing the picture? Toni at my side. I wanted to ask her to move in with me, even if she kept her own place in Spain.

"Yes," I finally said, although maybe we'd both forgotten the question by then. I raised my glass in an ironic toast. "To the great loves of our lives."

My mother clinked her glass against mine. "Be happy, Elin. Two out of three now, yes?"

I nodded.

"One, after this."

"Then let's try to make it Wimbledon," she replied. "You always were at your best on grass."

Was this really my last French Open? It was still hard to imagine, even as I soaked in the details on the day of the final. I had always loved this event, even just the subtle changes of the umpires speaking only in French, from the *silence, s'il vous plaît* to saying *égalité* instead of deuce. Would I miss the red clay stains on my shoes and, more embarrassingly, on my shorts? Most years I avoided that, but I'd had my share of lunging for seemingly impossible returns and even the odd fall.

I got to the locker room early, long before Celeste showed up. I had one little addition to make in my first final played as an openly gay woman. I was no seamstress, but I had brought the handy little sewing kit from my hotel room. I laid out my kit for the match on the bench beside me, my bag packed exactly as I liked it, my skirt and shoes laid out as though ready for the first day of school. I changed quickly into everything but my brand-new T-shirt, already embroidered over the heart with the tournament, the date, and my opponent.

I sat on the bench in my bra and skirt, threading the needle with clumsy fingers. I'd tape them up for the match when I was done, more superstition than for any noticeable difference in my grip. I checked the various sponsor logos and found the perfect spaces I was looking for on each sleeve.

I hadn't done this since my first Grand Slam final win, the one where I'd beaten Mira and pissed her off for a lifetime with the hyperbolic commentary of "The Queen is dead; long live the Queen." Back then, I had picked up a last-minute sponsor during the tournament when they realised I was going to make the final.

This was before I had Parisa or Ezi or any kind of team beyond my parents and a well-meaning woman from the Swedish tennis federation. I only realised on the day of the match that I hadn't added my sponsor's logos to my shirt, and they'd paid specifically to be on my sleeves. Since those got a lot of camera attention during the game, I already knew they would be a big deal to forget. With no one around to ask, I'd borrowed a sewing kit from the locker-room assistants, and the sponsors had been very happy to see their name all over the footage of my shock win.

Today, I wasn't sewing to keep the sponsors happy, but I wasn't going out there in front of the world again without something important in place. Not just for me, or for Toni, but for who knew how many kids watching on television?

Parisa had sourced these patches who knew where, but she got them to me on time. The two rectangular rainbows fit perfectly between my official sponsors' logos, drawing the eye right to the spot as I stitched them as neatly as I could with white thread.

Celeste came in then, and if she thought it was weird to find me sewing, she said nothing. We wished each other a good game and retreated to our private dressing rooms.

Three tries left. Time to go.

Four games into the second set, the ball girl on my side of the net did what they were all terrified of doing: She tripped when scuttling across to retrieve the ball. The crowd gasped, because she really did look tiny in the huge arena. It was so unusual for one to even stumble that the officials froze for a moment in indecision.

I didn't really think about it, but the instinct borne of countless scraped knees and stumbles had me jogging over to her, dropping my racquet so I could check for injuries.

"You okay?" I asked. The crowd were murmuring that I had gone over, and I could feel the officials approaching behind me. The little girl looked terrified, assuming they were coming to scold her and pull her off court for messing up. She was struggling not to cry, so I summoned the best French I could fumble together.

"*Ça va?*"

Her lip trembled and she pointed to her left knee, already trickling blood down her shin for her socks to absorb. The apologies tumbled out next, in perfect English, that she didn't mean to ruin my concentration.

"We're okay. Can I tell you a secret?"

"What?"

"When you've played the final lots of times, you don't need to concentrate anymore. Come on, let's get you fixed up. Ready?"

She nodded, and I stood up while taking her hand. "What's your name?"

"Olivia."

"Okay, Olivia, go get that cleaned up. Nobody is mad, I promise."

I handed her over to the head of the ball boys and girls. The umpire called my name over the microphone, and I looked back at him in confusion. Was he going to call me out for some kind of violation? Screw that.

I watched Olivia get helped back towards the changing areas and picked up my racquet, only to shove it under my arm and start clapping for her. The crowd finally got the hint and joined in, Celeste too. I saw Olivia smile at that, and satisfied at last, I walked back to the baseline ready to receive service again.

I found myself struggling to keep my usual neutral expression. Olivia. That was a nice name for a little girl.

No, I had taken the first set, and I was still on track for the second. No wandering thoughts, no distractions. Olivia's scraped knee would be fine, and she'd no doubt be back at it next summer. Celeste bounced the ball, ready to launch it at me, and I readied myself all over again.

Celeste seemed to be flagging when I broke her serve in the second set. We never made real eye contact during a match, but I recognised the frustration in the set of her impressive shoulders, in how her feet seemed just a little more bound to the clay than her usual constant motion. All I had to do from there was hold my own serve, and the trophy was mine.

The replicas we got to take home were pretty enough in their own right, but that wasn't my incentive. Winning now meant equalling a decades-old record and setting myself alongside the greats of the game. It wasn't what I pictured starting out. I hadn't dared dream of this even at my most arrogant.

Then, at thirty-love, the little bastard went. That same hip muscle that had disrupted so much of the last season just failed to extend and stretch like it had a thousand times before. I managed to cover the initial tearing pain by thumping the failed serve into the net, a cry of frustration echoing around the stadium. I couldn't step off at that point, not within two points of the Championship. Whether through adrenaline or sheer bloody-mindedness, I got the next ball over the net and played out the rally without having to hold my side. Celeste got the best of me on my backhand and pulled it back to 30-15.

Shit.

I wish I could say exactly how I claimed those next two points, but I went after them like they were a couple of painkillers: something I was badly in need of. I knew I wasn't holding myself correctly, that I was likely making it worse, but I knew interrupting for medical treatment would be fatal to my chances. Give Celeste a chance to get back into it and she'd come for me.

It took a cheeky drop shot to clinch it, but when I fell to my knees it looked like celebration.

"*Jeu, set, match, mademoiselle Larsson,*" came the announcement. The crowd were whipped up for the award ceremony to follow, but when I looked for Toni and my mother in the box, I found only their concern radiating back at me. Nobody else seemed to have noticed, and I went through the ritual of shaking hands and briefly commiserating with Celeste as we waited for the presentation. She went first as runner-up, and after what seemed to be a small eternity, I got to walk up over and receive my trophy. Holding it up for the crowd gave me fresh jolts down my side. It wasn't light, and the width of its base meant the damn thing took two hands.

The moment I could tuck it down at my hip, I did, and I had the chance to address the crowd. Asked how it felt to win again, to equal the record, I just babbled a little in French about how happy and proud I was. It seemed to be what everyone was expecting.

I counted the minutes until I could get away from all the attention, even though I'd spent the day trying to drink in every second of it. The pain had abated as I held the Suzanne-Lengler cup down low, but once the interviewers let me go, I had another round of lifting it and smiling for the press to do.

By the time I escaped, I was fighting back tears. Celeste walked me back and neither of us said a word, I knew enough to give her space after a loss, and she clearly didn't want to crowd me either. Once I'd handed the trophy back and slipped into my private dressing room, I finally sat down and tried an experimental stretch of my left side. The tears fell then, and they brought the cursing with them.

That was when my mother and Toni came spilling in, with Parisa and Ezi hot on their heels.

"Tell me where it hurts," Ezi teased gently, stepping in to investigate. "Yeah, that's gonna take a scan, Elin. I think you've really torn it this time."

"Son of a bitch." I dropped my head in my hands. Had I really managed to wreck my body right when I pulled level on the record?

"Hey, hey." Toni came to sit beside me on the bench, laying her arm over my back where I'd hunched forward. "Babe, it's okay. You've hurt it before and bounced right back. I know you're on a roll here, but another season to nail it… You could do it in Australia if you can't play any sooner."

My heart sank at the thought. I'd been holding on so tightly to this being my last season that the thought of going on felt like breaking a promise to myself, one that really counted. All my new dreams about kids, about doing work that wasn't just hitting balls around all week, they seemed as far away as they had ever been.

"It's fine, I'll be fine," I said, wiping the tears and pulling myself together. My mother was watching me with her arms crossed, a little apart from the fuss around me. "Can I get something to get me through all the handshakes and hugs? Then I'll need to get to hospital, but somewhere discreet, okay? No kidding, I don't want everyone to know. Not this time."

They all nodded in agreement, Parisa stepping out to start making calls. Ezi started rooting through her bag, pulling out a bottle of something promising and some sprays.

"I'm going to blast you like I'm tranquillising a horse, okay?" Ezi's hands were steady and gentle, and I trusted her completely. "Then we'll get someone with an MD to really show you a good time."

"I'd kill any of you right now for some Percocet," I confessed. "But give me what you've got. Toni, you okay to hold me up if it gets too much?"

She flexed to make me laugh, and it worked. Her arms looked as great as ever in the sleeveless creamy blouse she'd worn with tailored trousers. But for the definition, she didn't look too much like an athlete, just a normal person dressed up for a day at the tennis. I liked the look on her a lot.

"Let's get this over with," I said, swallowing the pills and pulling my shirt back down over the ice gel pack that Ezi had taped in place, covering the cooling spray that was already starting to work. It would minimise the damage, and I could get out of there.

The rest? I'd deal with that later.

CHAPTER TWENTY-EIGHT

IT PROVED TO BE A late night at the hospital, but they let me slip in through a side entrance and treated me in a completely private room. Toni stayed by my side apart from coffee runs and producing a haul of junk food that I couldn't believe she'd found in France, never mind near a hospital.

"You burned up a shit ton of calories today, babe, and canapés won't replace it. One cheeseburger won't kill you. The milkshake? Maybe, but hey, it's strawberry."

"What kind of maniac brings me a meal from Death Row and chooses strawberry over chocolate?"

Toni shrugged from her seat next to my bed. I really didn't need to be admitted, but lying propped up on a body pillow was way more comfortable than just about anything else. That and the fact that they'd given me the good stuff in an IV. I could have run through the brick wall and not felt it at that point.

"The kind of maniac you're dating." Toni looked up as my mother re-joined our little party, busy with her phone. I expected her to at least try to hide our unhealthy feast, but to my shock Toni offered a bag to my mother and she accepted it without complaint.

"Mamma, I don't think I've ever seen you eat fries," I said, as she picked a few from the bag and chewed them with dainty little bites. She muttered something in Swedish and ignored me.

"When is the doctor coming?" I asked, sipping at my milkshake. The strawberry was actually pretty nice. "I don't want to sleep here if I don't have to."

"You just don't like that the gown shows everyone your ass," my mother chimed in, helpful as ever.

"You would think a place as fancy as this would have gowns that go all the way around," Toni said. "And the nurse said the doctor would be in at nine, so any minute now."

As though she heard, Dr Huppert appeared in the doorway of my room.

"I will pretend not to see your diet," she began, with a tight little smile. One of the world's leading Sports Medicine specialists, she came as highly recommended as any human person could be. She'd treated everyone from golfers and boxers to the world's most expensive footballers. She'd resurrected careers that were supposed to be finished. It was hard not to feel like she held my future in her hands.

At least they were slender, tidy hands, with the elegant fingers I'd expect of a surgeon. She looked entirely put together, rather like we'd interrupted her Saturday evening. The shift dress she wore beneath her lab coat was black, elegant enough for any Parisian restaurant. Her coppery hair was pulled back in an elegant bun, diamonds sparkling at her ears.

"Congratulations, mademoiselle, on your record. Do you want the audience?" she asked me with a brisk gesture to my mother and Toni, clearly used to wading through the entourage of professional sportspeople. "I don't want you moving more than you have to right now, or we'd be having this consult in my office."

Toni moved ever so slightly, as though to leave, while my mother didn't so much as flinch.

"They can stay," I said. "Then I don't have to repeat every word you say. Saves time. And please, call me Elin."

"Well, Elin, I don't know how to coat it in sugar. You've really done it this time. You mentioned the pain is different to last time, more intense?"

"Yeah, it feels like it's coming from somewhere deeper. And it's making my leg feel weak, like my thigh is trembling when I put weight on it?"

"If you weren't so fit, with thighs that can, hmm...probably crack rocks, you wouldn't have been able to walk at all. You see, you have not just injured the muscle this time, you have hip impingement. The ball of the hip isn't fitting in the socket properly. So you get a lot of pain and much less movement."

"Told you, you have great thighs," Toni said, slapping me gently on the one on my uninjured side.

"You really should have come straight in, instead of staying to shake hands and all that. Anyway, your options. I assume that's what you want to hear most? Skip to the important part?"

"Yes, doc." This woman I liked. She could slice or dice me any way she wanted. "Hit me."

"Surgery. Usually for people much older than you, but this kind of damage will only deteriorate. We put some metal in, everything fits again and no bones scraping. Which means no swelling, no pain."

I huffed out a breath and leaned back against the pillows. Anything surgical meant a recovery time in months, not weeks.

"Will I be able to play at full strength after that?"

Dr Huppert lifted her shoulders in a gesture too elegant to be a shrug. "It is possible, but not likely. You'll regain full range of motion and stop the pain, but high-impact sport like this? It could be too much for the joint to sustain. You could hit around with friends. I don't think you could play a two-hour match."

That landed like a bomb in the silence of the room. I had been expecting some damage, maybe a lecture about not playing like I was still in my early twenties, but not anything quite so bleak.

"Is that it? Surgery or nothing? You did say options."

"I did," Dr Huppert continued. "I know your schedule, that Wimbledon is barely weeks away and that you might have been counting on it. With plenty of rest, some permitted steroids and painkillers and a *lot* of physiotherapy, you could make it through to, say, August. But ideally, you would take up surgical treatment right after the tournament ends."

"What about doing that until the end of the season?" I didn't want all the pressure resting on Wimbledon, not if I'd be at less than full fitness. "Through the US Open, at least. Maybe not all the way to end of year finals?"

Dr Huppert shook her head. "No, your body won't hold you up for that long. Not with the damage increasing by the day. Of course you will have complete discretion from us here. How you manage it is your business, but I can't promise you beyond August. Even then you'll be playing through the pain."

"Thank you." Was that the right thing to say? What did you say to someone who'd thrown your grand plan for happiness into disarray? I'd been ready to walk away for so long that I hadn't realised how much I wanted the damn record in my own right. To know that even surgery might not mean I could come back? I felt like throwing up.

"I'll leave you to think, but the staff will put your call through to me if you have more questions tonight. If not, we'll keep on with the treatment plan and have a meeting Monday morning."

"So," my mother said as the doctor left the three of us with our bombshell. "Elin, what the hell are you going to do?"

Staying in the hospital drove me nuts, but it was definitely less of a threat to my privacy. Checking out of the hotel, all the chaos, I didn't miss that one bit. Mostly, I wanted the time alone. Ezi came by to check on my treatment plan so she could make her own arrangements, but we were used to working in companionable silence. I got to watch the men's final on Sunday from the couch in my room with her—I had to move periodically, but not too far. She sipped at some mint tea and left as soon as she was confident I had been looked after.

Toni came back to join me after I insisted she use her ticket to see the match in person.

"Hey, you look about five minutes from breaking out of this place," she said as I eased myself back onto the bed. "You pack your bag, and I'll carry you on my back."

I pulled her closer for a kiss. "What's the hospital equivalent of the Mile-High Club? Want to join?"

"That would be so cute, if you could actually move." She was still dressed up from the final, in a nice dress and blazer that I told myself I'd borrow next time I had to go to something formal.

"Cute, huh?" Always so ready with the compliments, even the silly ones. "I'm legally high right now; I could probably do the splits if I wanted."

"Tempting, but you would pay for it later. I can be patient, and so can you," Toni said. "Also, I think this flirting is a way not to talk about your plans."

"I've planned not to make any more plans," I replied. "Do you think it's karma? I've spent all this time bitching about having to keep playing, and now the universe is punishing me?"

She shook her head. "I don't think that's how it works. You don't deserve that, just for feeling stuck."

"I don't know if this will be much of a surprise, but I want to try. I want to do the injections and the physio, see if I can get over the line in London. And if I don't, I'll have the surgery and try to come back next season. I did some reading this morning, and with some changes to my game it should be possible."

"Elin, if this is just panic because they said it's a bad injury, don't do it to yourself. You can walk away today, now. You're a champion; you matched the record. Part of you wants to be done already. I'll support you whatever you decide. Just don't put yourself through agony for the sake of it."

Toni sat on the side of my bed, taking my hand. "You know how much I respect you, how much I would kill for your stats. But I love you, Elin. I can't stand watching you in pain, especially if you don't have to be."

"It won't be so bad, with the plan they have. I'll stop if the painkillers stop working, but I want it. I need it, I think. Otherwise I'll spend the rest of my life wondering 'what if' about playing one more slam."

"I get it," she said, and for the first time in my life, it felt like someone truly did. "I was planning on making Wimbledon my first slam, but hey, I can let you play."

"Very kind of you."

"That's me," Toni said. "Listen, I told Mira I'm out of Nottingham this week. I don't think I can get out of Mallorca, but I'll be back for Eastbourne. Did they say whether you can do that as part of your Wimbledon plan?"

I shook my head. "Rest and targeted workouts until the tournament starts. Anything else is too hard on the hip joint." I'd woken up to a comprehensive report from Dr Huppert with the specifics of each option. "There's no way I can win this fucked up, is there?"

"Don't say that," she replied. "You carrying an injury is worth most players at full strength. I'd drag you across the line myself if I could." She took my hand up to her lips and kissed it. "And I know what all this is like, so talk to me okay? When you want to cry, or scream, or throw things, I'll be right here."

"At least with you I got lucky." I moved over to kiss her again, resting my forehead against Toni's. "They're letting me out of here tomorrow after my meeting, where do you want to spend the week? You'll have to keep your practice up for Mallorca."

"Here? London? I don't mind. I just want to make sure you're okay."

"You know they pay people to do that, right? Actually, I pay people to do that. The last thing I want is to get in the way of your career, especially now."

"Oh, shut up and accept that I'm not going anywhere. Not this week, anyway."

"I just had to fall for the stubborn one, didn't I?"

"Yes, you did," my mother added from the doorway. "Are you two behaving or do I have to go away again?"

"You're fine, Britta," Toni said, moving a few inches down the bed from me. "Should I go get coffees?"

"No need," my mother produced a tray of takeaway cups. "I see Jürgen lost. You must be happy about that, Elin."

"Mamma, I'm going with the shots. I need to try, for Wimbledon. Can we do it?"

She set the coffees on the table by my bed and took the hand that Toni wasn't holding. For a horrifying moment I thought she was going to cry, something I couldn't remember ever seeing before.

"We can do anything you want. You can, *äskling*. Tell us what you want and we'll get you there."

"Do you think Pappa and Alice will come to Wimbledon? Just in case it's my last one?"

She nodded. "Of course. We'll arrange everything; just focus on getting better. Ezi will tell me what we can work on, but I'm not going easy on you now."

"Didn't expect anything less. Do you think Parisa can find us somewhere to stay in London until the tournament? Dr Huppert recommended a specialist there, and there's a leaflet for some physio place too."

We got lost in the chatter of travel arrangements and plans, but Toni held my hand through the whole conversation. The longer she stayed, the more sure I felt that I could do it.

I just hoped that gut feeling was right.

The apartment in London was a perfect hideaway. Minutes from the Harley Street specialists watching over me, close to everything in the city I usually missed when in town for Wimbledon. With Toni heading off to Mallorca on the Sunday, I was determined to make the most of Saturday night.

Heels were out of the question, so I picked out a black suit with a crisp white shirt.

"You're really not going to tell me where we're going?" Toni asked for the hundredth time. She was dressed to kill in a little black dress. We looked good together, I couldn't deny it. "You know, what if I had plans for us tonight?"

"Let me do this," I said, kissing the side of her neck. "And come on, there's a car waiting for us downstairs."

I worried the whole journey that my idea was cheesy, maybe even too childish. Then the car rolled to a stop outside the hotel where we met almost a year before, and Toni turned to me with that killer smile.

"Elin Larsson, you're a closet romantic."

"I thought it would be a nice way to see you off. I know it's only for a week, but I do find that I miss you more each time."

We walked into the bar arm-in-arm, taking up a table with a great view of the room. For once, I didn't care what view everyone else had of us.

"So here's the thing," Toni said as I sipped the one martini I could allow myself on the painkiller cocktail that was getting me through the physio. "I actually did have a little plan for us tonight. Or I started to make one."

"But now you're drinking Lagvulin, you don't mind?" I tried, hoping I hadn't steamrollered her whole evening.

"Well, mostly. Anyway, I know you shouldn't be walking long distances, but will you come somewhere with me? I had to improvise a little."

"Sure." I took her hand and followed her towards the bar. She leaned across to the bartender and he nodded to the door disguised in the wall, the same one we'd made our escape through last summer.

This time we didn't run down the corridor, but Toni led me instead to a service elevator. I had a hundred questions, but I stuck to my default of keeping quiet and letting Toni show me whatever she was up to. From the elevator we took a turn towards an open fire exit, propped open by a crate of some wine or other. The floor didn't seem to be one with guests, but when we went through the fire exit, we found ourselves on the roof.

"Okay," Toni said, gesturing vaguely to the London skyline. "I kind of guessed what you had in mind when you were so fixed on choosing our date tonight. So I called ahead and asked a little favour."

We walked along the roof, edged by a stone balcony and punctuated by old-fashioned chimneys. Around the second one, a little table and two chairs had been set up, candles lit and flowers decorating the little scene. I swallowed around a sudden lump in my throat. This was romance, and I'd never been happier to be bested.

"Antonia, what are you up to?"

"Come over here and find out," she said, beckoning with one finger. "God, I'm so nervous... Sorry."

"Don't be." I kissed her softly on the mouth. I could hear the faint sounds of the street below: the car horns, the shouts, the bustle of London at its most vibrant. Compared to that, being alone with Toni was an oasis, so much calm and contentment just from standing there in front of her. I hoped I made her feel the same way. "There's nothing you can't say to me."

"You're going through so much, and I know we haven't been together so very long, but Elin... I'm crazy about you. I don't want to drift in different directions all year, all over the world. I want to have a plan, that's about both of us. I want to be there, with you, for everything that comes next."

In that moment, as I started to realise that this conversation was about much more than a quick drink on the rooftop, I felt elation far beyond even my first big win had given me. The painkillers I'd been relying on had nothing on that pure surge of happiness, and it felt like I'd never been in pain at all.

"Toni, are you..." I couldn't finish the thought; the tears were suddenly welling up and my throat wouldn't let the words come out. I wanted to hear it from her. Nothing else could compare.

"Will you be my wife?" Toni asked with a sudden certainty, taking my hands in hers and looking me straight in the eye. She'd never looked more beautiful than she did in that moment, the twilight and the candles making her almost glow with loveliness. "I love you so much, and it's okay if you don't want to, not yet, but I just had to ask and—"

"Yes," I said, with another kiss to silence the rambling, however much I enjoyed it. "Yes, Toni. Of course I will. I was going to ask you to move in with me, make your base in LA. But this is even better."

"We can do both," she said, kissing me again. "It's pretty nice up here, right?"

"You picked the perfect spot," I told her, pulling the two chairs together so we could sit and watch the city start to light up for the evening. "Wait, did you get a ring?"

"Oh God, yes!" She plucked the little velvet box from her cleavage, which cracked me up laughing.

"You're lucky I didn't find it before you had a chance to ask," I said. "I was getting a little handsy in the car earlier."

"Yes, I noticed," Toni replied, totally deadpan. "It's almost like it's hard to surprise you."

"I'm going to miss you this week, did I tell you that?" I leaned into Toni as she put her arm around me.

"Of course you are," she replied. "But now we're going to be in the same place whenever we get the chance. Pretty nice, right?"

"Right," I agreed, that sweet contented feeling I was almost getting used to slipping right into place again.

CHAPTER TWENTY-NINE

HIDING MY INJURY PROVED IMPOSSIBLE by the end of the first week at Wimbledon. I'd had to disclose everything I was taking, none of it illegal by the game's standards. I checked in with the drug-testing staff if they'd had any change in procedures, but all I got in response was a glare. Good.

Shots before the game, shots after the game—it affected me in the strangest ways. Sometimes my body didn't feel like my own, and my usual precision was shot to hell. In a weird way, the early matches became more fun. I got to rely on my killer forehand, which always made me feel powerful. I had weakness, or maybe just a lack of confidence, on my serve and on the backhand, but people tended to target that anyway.

I tried desperately not to view everything about the tournament as some heavy milestone, but it did weigh on me. Smiling through interviews and press conferences had become second nature, but this time I hung on every word, considered every answer like it might be the last time I was ever quoted.

Not having to face Mira in front of a camera certainly helped, and her replacement at the BBC was much kinder in her questioning. A former champion in her own right, she'd wrapped up her career in the early nineties, long before I ever burst on the scene. When she asked me about equalling the record that had stood for thirty years, I found myself opening up in a way I hadn't before.

"It's not the only important thing, I know that. But every time you get closer, when you win the fifteenth slam and then the sixteenth and you still have years left to play, it becomes an obsession," I admitted. "I realised this year I've let it define my career, and that was wrong. Maybe the next person to equal it, to break it even, is already playing today. There's so much talent out there."

"Like your good friend, Celeste."

"She could do it, sure. She has years ahead of her, and she's great on every surface. I'll certainly be cheering her on for as long as she plays." I had come dangerously close to revealing my imminent retirement, and I was not ready for that.

"Speaking of other players." Here it came. I hadn't worn the ring on court or on playing days at all, but this interview between the third round and quarterfinals was on my off day. The diamond sparkled on my left hand, catching the studio lights over and over. I resolved in that moment that I had to find something every bit as gorgeous for Toni to wear.

"Yes?" I said.

"You announced before the French Open that you and Antonia Cortes Ruiz are dating, and now, forgive me for prying, but you seem to have updated your accessories."

I looked down at my clothes and my shoes to toy with her a moment, before lifting my hand. "Yes, I have. We got engaged here in London, in fact. Wimbledon will always be very special to us."

"Of course." It wasn't live, so asides like that would be edited out. "Do you want Wimbledon to be The One? Where you finally break the Grand Slam record? Could it really happen next Saturday?"

"That would mean a lot to me." I couldn't tell her how much. "But hey, there's a lot of tennis between now and then."

Toni was having a fantastic Wimbledon, and with the luck of the bracket, we couldn't meet each other before the final itself. Assuming we both got there.

"It doesn't feel right," she said, as we lay on the couch in our suite after the round of sixteen matches. It had been the busiest day of the tournament; there was a reason they called it Manic Monday. My head was swimming a little from the painkillers. "Being out there and enjoying my tennis while you're in agony."

"It's not all bad," I tried to reassure her, even as her hand skimmed the inflamed area around my hip and made me suck in a quick breath through my teeth. "Just a few more matches. Then they can fix me for good."

"I think…" she trailed off. Much like with her texts, I had learned some patience. Toni was particular about how she shared her thoughts, and this was going to be no exception. "A part of me is still worried that when you're done with playing, you'll be done with me. You're not in it yet, but there's a grieving process. There might be times when you don't even want to know the sport exists."

I mulled that over for a moment. "Then those are the weeks that I'll stay home. I can be on my own without resenting you, I promise. If it gets hard, we'll just have to talk about it. You did, you know, put a ring on it."

"Ah, so you did take that seriously? Good to know." She kissed my shoulder. "Need another gel pack? You don't feel so cold there anymore."

"No, it can wait a while," I said, confident the pain wouldn't come roaring back. "Don't move just yet."

The one thing working against me was that I had been bracketed into the first quarterfinal, meaning I played again the next day in the early afternoon. I was going to get screwed one way or another; having Tuesday off would mean playing the quarter and semi back-to-back instead.

It was really starting to make sense, how many of us succumbed to injury. The exertion I'd taken for granted now felt like climbing Everest, only to win a shot at scaling Kilimanjaro the very next day.

From the moment the umpire called "Game, set, match" in my name, I was wiped. I didn't remember the aftermath at all, apart from Ezi's arm holding me up as soon as I made it behind the green wall at the back of the court.

"You did it," she told me. "You damn near killed yourself to do it, but you're through."

"My future involves a lot of ice and anti-inflammatories, doesn't it?"

Ezi guided me into the medical suite, having commandeered it already. I wouldn't be able to hide out for long. The press speculation about me playing through injury had reached a fever pitch, and they wanted details, yesterday. I still wasn't sure how much to tell them, but I'd worry about that when there was a press conference in front of me.

Toni wasn't playing until tomorrow, so she was hanging around in the locker room once I'd had my shots and had ice packs strapped around me again. They'd have dunked me in an ice bath, if the motion of getting in and out wouldn't cause more stretching damage.

"You're pushing too hard," Toni said, coming to sit beside me, helping me get out of my tennis dress, the zipper coming in handy on that particular style. Even the sports bra underneath had one in front. What next, Velcro for my shoes? "Can you promise me something?"

"You mean other than to marry you? God, Toni, you're getting pretty demanding these days."

She kissed me, mostly in exasperation as far as I could tell. "If it gets any worse than this, you'll retire. And *please* use your in-match medical treatment better. No more toughing it out until the end."

"She happens to be right, this almost-wife of yours," Ezi joined in, standing over me with her arms crossed, face as stern as ever. "They don't give out extra medals for being a martyr. And I would think you have enough of the regular kind as it is."

"Just one more," I promised. "Get me through two more matches, okay?"

"Come along, Elin." My mother interrupted our bonding moment, clapping her hands in that brisk way of hers. For the first time, I realised she looked like a woman old enough to have a daughter in her thirties. When had that sneaked up on us? If I closed my eyes and had to recall her, I'd picture my mother much as she always was. My memory didn't take into account that she wasn't in her forties anymore, that time had marched on for everyone, not just me and all these years on the courts under my belt.

"Let's get the press done. Mamma, you want to come face them with me? You know that always makes them happy." It happened to be true. My mother, who had patience for almost no one, was somehow the darling of the touring press who followed us around for most of the year.

"Fine, but if their questions are stupid, I will tell them so."

I almost felt sorry for the journalists.

I spent my off day at the doctor's office instead of watching Toni play, and I didn't make for the most cooperative patient. Eventually, one of the brusque nurses took pity on me and handed me a tablet with the match live-streaming. Celeste put up a good fight, and on another day, she'd have had the strength and stamina advantage, but Toni was playing like a woman possessed. I suspected I knew why: She wanted to get to the final so she could give me an easier time of it than anyone else might.

I still had a semi-final against Keiko to get through, but apparently Toni and I had to talk. Before I could start to plot about how to handle telling her to go out there and still attempt to kick my ass like anyone else would, I was being called in to see the doctor.

To my surprise, Dr Huppert sat there with her British counterpart, both of them frowning over the scans I'd just had taken.

"Twice the doctors, half the bad news?" I tried for weak jokes, opting not to leverage myself down into the bucket chairs set out for patients. I wondered how an orthopaedic specialist got by with such low, impractical chairs. Instead, I stood, leaning over and gripping the back of the ugly leather thing.

"Elin, it's good to see you again. Dr Sattar asked me to come in today and consult since I was in town anyway." Dr Huppert looked as runway ready as ever in her chic sky-blue dress, the glossy red hair down over her shoulders today. "Congratulations on making the semi-finals."

"Your achievement so far hasn't been without its costs," Dr Sattar jumped right in, every bit as stylish in his monogrammed white shirt and silk tie. "As you can see here, the damage to the socket has increased compared to your last check-up in Paris."

"I'm playing through it, though? I mean, it's not ideal but the temporary measures have dragged me this far. You're not going to try and tell me to quit now, are you?"

They exchanged a look. That was exactly what they had intended. I was glad I hadn't sat down.

"I would like to revise my earlier advice," Dr Huppert began. "The deterioration we've seen, it seems I underestimated just what you put yourself through in just a handful of matches."

"It's Wimbledon," I said with a shrug. "It's a particularly good year. I'm doing everything I can to play smart instead of hard, and I plan to do it right through Saturday afternoon. But I don't want to wait any longer on the surgery—can we get it booked for Monday? Or if you can refer me to someone in LA, I'll take Tuesday. Just…done. We'll get it done."

"The recovery period means Los Angeles might make things more comfortable for you, to be at your home base," Dr Sattar said. He'd treated me in previous years for calf strains and a shoulder issue that dogged me in my early twenties. I trusted him and was sure he understood the demands and my schedule. It would be so easy to tell them I knew I wasn't coming back after the procedure, but I didn't need a lecture about focusing on positive outcomes.

"Right, if that's everything?" I turned to leave.

"Actually…" Dr Huppert called after me, her accent wrapped around the word like a burgundy vine. For the first time she looked something other than completely composed. Was she…? She was blushing! "Since I'm in town until Monday, I wondered if you had any way to see about a ticket for your matches? With all the uncertainty… It is just I've never seen you play, in person."

I laughed, shaking my head just a little. It had always been this way, and something about the familiar ridiculousness comforted me.

"I'll leave two in your name for collection at the box office tomorrow. Not sure I'll be able to for the final."

"If you make it," Dr Sattar cautioned.

"I will," I said, grasping the door handle and letting myself out of there.

———

"You were fantastic today," I said, sitting quite comfortably for once at the small dining table. The painkillers had kicked in, the inflammation was down, and I could think clearly. "You'd better keep that up if you make it to the final."

"Of course." Toni answered just a little too quickly. "I mean, I'll try."

"Sweetheart?" It was a new one to try, no pet name for her had settled yet. Maybe some people just didn't suit one? The closest I'd come was hearing her name like a little chorus in the back of my mind sometimes: *Toni Toni Toni.* "If I somehow pull this off, if we both make the final and I'm still walking come Saturday…"

She did try to keep a straight face, to seem as neutral as a man in an online comment section playing devil's advocate. Three seconds later, Toni caved. "Okay, but if I get there I can protect you! It wouldn't be throwing anything; it would just be playing you more carefully, so you don't get hurt any more than you already are."

I watched her come closer but held myself back. "And you think I want that?"

"I don't mean—"

"If you're going to play me with anything less than everything you've got, then do me a favour and let Fatima win tomorrow."

"Listen, I might lose anyway. And even if I make the final, there'll be other slams. I can try again in September, it's no big deal."

"Does it feel right when you say it? Because to me, you look queasy. It will kill you if you go out there and half-ass it just to help me. And you, even more than me, know that it's not guaranteed. A twinge tomorrow, a tear the next day, and it's all over. Or that level is. You've given everything to get back here, to be within spitting distance of your first slam. But if it means retiring without my record, I'll do it right now to make sure you can't go soft on me."

"You realise this is probably unhealthy for people who are supposed to be getting married?" Toni yelled back at me. "Are we going to put it in the vows? I promise to risk your health just to soothe your ego?"

"I don't have an ego!" Yeah, nobody was buying that one. "I have one shot, and if it doesn't work, fine. But it won't count for shit if you hand it me, or try to convince anyone else to, in case that's your backup plan."

"You're impossible, you know that?" Toni was up in my face now, and it felt a lot like we were sparring on court. This was the argumentative, competitive side of her I needed to come through.

"I do know that," I said, reaching across to stroke her cheek with my thumb. "Please do this one thing for me. It's as important to me as any wedding vow, and I think you know that. I think you'd want the same from me in return."

"What if I really hurt you somehow? Worse, I mean?" Toni looked terrified. "How would I forgive myself?"

"You won't. When the pills all work, and the injections, I'm flying out there like nothing's wrong. And if you find yourself changing your mind, going easy on me…just remember how it felt when you hurt your back. If that happened again and you didn't have a slam that you could have won, how will that feel? Don't make me do that to you, either."

She kissed me, furious and deep and her way of making the promise I'd asked of her.

"You know I'll give you everything you want. Including the game of your life. Want to hit the hydro pool while you're still pain free?"

"Any excuse to get me in a bikini," I sighed, but I pulled up my top to show I was already dressed for exactly that. "Then an early night. We've got matches to win."

<hr>

Toni was gone when I woke up, her side of the bed neat, almost as though she hadn't been there at all. For a moment I let myself forget the semi-finals, that we were in my favourite house in South-west London instead of Los Angeles, that any minute now I'd move and the rumbles of pain would start to reverberate up and down my side. I closed my eyes, feeling the slight glow from where the sun had peeked through the heavy curtains, and stretched out my arms to cover both sides of the pillows.

Would it feel like this? Toni off at some smaller tournament, racking up her ranking points and another cheque between slams? Warm and content and knowing she was just there. Maybe the nursery across the hall, maybe a day full of events for my charity ahead. Maybe no bigger plans than going for a hike up to the Griffith Observatory, without the phone ringing or an appointment to restring some racquets or sign for a new delivery of sportswear.

I was going to be fine, however the next three days turned out. That realisation, the certainty that came with it, felt something like flying.

Rolling over carefully, I grabbed the pills and water left out for me, swallowing them as I eased my way out of bed and towards the bathroom. Ezi would be in any moment with my injection, so no point rushing around just yet.

Toni would spend the best part of the morning and early afternoon warming up and keeping warm, while I'd know my fate soon enough, the benefit of playing first.

I sipped some more water, wondering at the churning sensation in my stomach. Reaction to pills before breakfast? No, as I sat down to take a few deep breaths I recognised it.

Nerves. I was actually nervous.

Well, wasn't that adorable?

CHAPTER THIRTY

I GOT BACK FROM BEATING Celeste, thankfully in just the two sets, to find Alice waiting in my hotel suite.

"I really need to tell security to up their game," I said, trying not to hold my side as I walked in.

Alice moved to hug me, then reconsidered when she saw the grimace on my face. "What the fuck have you done to yourself this time? At least tell me it's from having too much sex."

"I talked to you from hospital. I *know* Mamma explained this to you more than once. I don't expect you to care what the average serve speed is, or whether the seeding system has flaws, but can you at least try to hold on to details about whether your only sister is in massive amounts of pain daily?"

"That's fair," Alice conceded after a moment. "I'll do better. But I'm here, at your request. How much tennis is there left to sit through?"

"Just the final. On Saturday."

"Who are you playing?"

"My girlfriend, if things go well. Sorry, fiancée. Can't quite get used to that."

Alice flopped out on the sofa, picking up the remote and turning the TV on. "Sorry, I just love listening to the news in British. They sound way less like the world is on fire. It soothes me. Plus, no Fox News."

"It's fine," I said, taking a seat myself and propping up my leg to give my hip a rest. "Thanks for coming. You get this is a big deal for me, right? I don't need to draw a diagram?"

"Hmm? Oh yeah, big deal. Break record, make Mamma happy, and you might retire. I'm on it, Elin."

"Not might. Will retire. As in this is my last final, my last match. And outside of family and my doctors, nobody knows that yet. It might be a big deal come Saturday, win or lose."

"Your wife-to-be is gonna beat your ass in your last ever game? Puh-lease."

"If it's her, yes. She's going to try. I made her promise. I don't want some pity win that won't count stacked against the others."

Alice snorted. "I always said there was something wrong with you. Now you've finally found someone as batshit competitive as you are. It's kind of sweet. Will she carry you off court if she breaks you?"

"She probably would," I replied. "Now you're going to have to flip to the BBC. Her match is about to start."

"Okay, that was me giving it my all," Toni announced as she walked in three hours later. "Alice! Hi!"

"Yes, I don't think Fatima knew what hit her," I agreed. "Apart from that point in the third set where you literally hit her. With the ball."

"She dived in the way of a smash! It wasn't my fault!"

Toni and Alice hugged each other hello, cheek kisses and all. Eventually Toni made her way to my side, and I felt an instant lift as she folded herself into the armchair with me, all shower fresh and a little flustered from rushing around.

"Hey," I murmured, patting her thigh. "I missed you today. Sorry I couldn't come watch in person."

"It's okay, you missed Mira shouting my head off after, so probably for the best. She says I can beat you Saturday if I 'sort my head out.' Little does she know, right?"

"You two are really going to play each other and fight it out, aren't you? The media must be having a fit with the engagement and all."

"Yeah, about that. I got so many questions," Toni said. "And Parisa says we have a bunch of joint interviews tomorrow on top of the other things. Should we talk about what we're going to talk about?"

I gave a brief nod. "Later. We don't have to get our stories straight; they're not the police. I trust you not to completely embarrass me on television."

"Cool, because I don't trust myself. Can we eat in tonight? I know we have to be apart tomorrow, so I want to make the most of it. Alice, did you want to join us?"

Alice was watching us with an odd, fond little smile. I hadn't seen her look at me that way in a long time; it seemed like something left over from our childhood. "Are you nerds actually separating the night before your final, like it's a wedding?"

We both just stared at her. Of course we were.

"Okay, you should just tell people that story. Then anyone who has any doubts about you being made for each other will be totally sold. And don't worry, I won't crash your dinner. I'll take Mamma out on the town so she can stop stressing about your leg exploding."

"Hip," I corrected automatically. "And thank you for that. I suspect it's only a matter of time before she comes in here to talk the same strategy that we've been talking for two weeks. Like I don't already know how to beat this one."

"Hey!" Toni protested. "Just for that I'm going to beat you in three instead of doing it in straight sets." She followed up with a kiss, and I let her get away with it. It was a good sign she could joke around.

Alice got up to leave, picking up her jacket and bag from where they'd been abandoned on the coffee table.

"Have fun, you two. Can't wait to see you all over the sports pages."

———

Where had joint interviews been all my life? With Toni at my side I actually enjoyed the experience. I was relaxed, I cracked jokes, no question felt too repetitive or too intrusive. It was unheard of.

She, on the other hand, got adorably flustered. "Well, uh, we haven't really planned the wedding? Have we?"

I shook my head, smiling at the idea she might have just missed the entire planning somehow.

"I mean, I wasn't thinking about that when I asked. Yes, I did ask! Okay, uh..." Toni trailed off, her eyes silently begging me for help.

I stepped in to save her, turning the conversation back to the match ahead.

"So I'm guessing this is a first? A couple playing against each other?" I asked, as if we hadn't already been told a hundred times.

"Well, in doubles, actually," the presenter answered. She picked up her notes and carried on, letting us both silently heave a sigh of relief.

"We could just do it, you know," I said, as we sat to one side in the media centre, waiting for the setup of the next promo spot. Most had been done at the start of the Wimbledon fortnight, but there was always an extra bunch of footage to hype up the finals. Some years they had the finalists read poems and other times dressed up in ridiculous costumes—it was really whatever the BBC felt like putting us through.

"Do what?" Toni asked, missing her mouth yet again with the raisins she'd been tossing up and trying to catch. Hard to believe she had a career built around her coordination.

"Get married," I said, as calmly as I could manage. "I need to go home for surgery next week, once I'm up and walking again we could just...go do it. Before New York, even."

"Wow." Toni bumped my shoulder with hers. "Do you mean it?"

"I'm not changing my mind about you," I said, turning to face her. "Win, lose, playing, retired. When you asked me, all I wanted to be was your wife. I've never seen the point in waiting around once I know what I want."

"People will say we're nuts. That it's fast." Toni was trying to argue, but her grin matched my own. "But I think I'm learning not to care what people say."

"Then we'll make a plan," I said, kissing her softly. "After the match."

"After the match," she agreed. We were still smiling when they called us for closeups.

We stuck to our plan, spending the night before the final in separate houses. With all the pre-final activity, I didn't set eyes on Toni again until we were ready to be led out on court. Just as I had with Celeste the year before, I got to lead us out.

But there was time for a quick word first, as the announcements got the crowd settled.

"Hey," I said, not quite able to reach out and touch her. Match mode was quickly descending, and I wanted to get a little human moment in before it settled in. "You look good. Ready."

"Elin?" She looked panicked for a second. "I know how important today is for you, but I spent last night thinking how right you are. This might be my only chance."

I smiled. "I knew you'd get it. Whatever happens, may the best woman win."

Toni gave a curt nod, her shoulders dropping a little in relief. Before we could say anything else, we were being led out, bouquets in our arms like every other year.

By the time we were hitting back and forth over the net, it was almost as though we didn't recognise each other. The buzz in the crowd was different to other times, the notes of gossip underlying the cheers and applause. We were a novelty, and unless some other seeds were hooking up, it was likely to be a one-off situation. Partner versus partner, fiancée versus fiancée.

The umpire called time on our warmup rally, and I rolled my shoulders one more time. Toni had won the toss and chosen to serve first, so I got to the baseline and took up position. My hip felt good as I moved a little in anticipation, or at least it didn't feel much of anything, which was all I could hope for.

The crowd simmered down, ready for the first play to begin. Breaking the record was in my grasp, but Toni's stance across the net radiated a danger I wasn't familiar with. The ball came rushing towards me, and the old instincts kicked right in. The worry and the moralising disappeared, and I swung my racquet to make the return.

***

Toni wasn't kidding about her change of heart, or her commitment to what we'd agreed. She played me like she hated me and gave me one of the biggest challenges of my career. Short of the engagement ring safely stowed in my racquet bag, it was the greatest gift anyone had ever given me.

She took the first set, which got the ripples of surprise rolling around the stadium. It took a tiebreak, but she pulled it off. I was as proud of her as I was angry at myself. I should have nailed down that first set to rein her in and given myself a chance to win the match in two. No, it was destined to go to three; I could sense it the way other people could tell when it was about to rain.

The first twinge from my hip came deep in that second set, right after I broke Toni for the first time all match. She'd been serving much harder and faster, part of Mira's coaching no doubt. If she noticed me pull up for a second, Toni gave no indication. The blankness of her expression said she was deep in the zone by that point, and I was relieved.

When I clinched the second set to level matters between us, I took advantage of the natural break to call for a medical timeout. After a cursory examination, I got my painkilling injection topped up, a ton of Ezi's magical ice spray, and a change to rehydrate without rushing. Toni glanced over a few times, but I was too busy making sure the pain had subsided to watch her reactions.

I'd know how it affected her by how she came out serving to start the third set. I retied my laces and swapped out my racquet for good measure. It was all coming down to this.

Maybe I was imagining it, but the crowd seemed to be living and breathing every hit with us. My worries about Toni being rattled by my treatment were misplaced. She kept sending rockets across the net at me like she was sponsored by NASA, and we forced each other to every corner of that green grass to win each point.

At one point, having only just rescued my service game with a dangerous sliced return that had me on the ground, I almost wished I'd let her go easy on me. Then the competitive demon that lived somewhere in me took charge again, and all I cared about was winning the next point at all costs. And the one after that.

On a sunny Saturday in July, we were really leaving it all out there. Sweating through our shirts, grunting with effort, it wasn't going to win points for attractiveness. It was, as the excitement in the ground proved, some excellent tennis. Some matches didn't seem that way at the time, but this one had been an epic from the first game.

We made it to 4-4, and it already felt like the longest match I'd ever played, though the time on the scoreboard said it couldn't be. The atmosphere crackled like a storm was coming in, but that was just the anticipation in the crowd.

It took every trick in my personal arsenal, but I broke Toni's serve just when I thought I might be outplayed. I saw the moment her head went, used to spotting the signs from across the net in just about everyone I'd ever played. Had I been watching her from the stands, I think my heart might have broken. As it was, her obvious slump only lifted my spirits. It was in sight at last. The fucking record. The win to end it all on.

The crowd's wave of support crested then. They smelled blood and threw their fickle love behind me and my slim advantage. That was the Wimbledon I knew and loved. I let it lift the ball as I threw it up to start serving out what might well be my last game in my last match.

Which, naturally, was the point my body decided the pain in my hip was strong enough to push through the fog of painkillers. It wasn't so bad through the first point, but it made me stumble by the time I got to 30-0.

I couldn't take another medical timeout for the same issue. I could fake a second injury, but I hated that unsporting bullshit. Even if I had a legitimate cause, it would give Toni every chance to recover from the rhythm rolling my way, meaning she might well claw her way back after any break.

No, just like with the French, I was going to have to play through it. In my distraction, Toni pulled a point back.

Shit.

How I got to 40-15 I couldn't remember. I just knew my serve was weaker than milky tea, and it took angling myself in a weird way to misdirect Toni where my shot was going to land. But I was there. The Promised Land. Serving for the match, with a two-point cushion.

Which led to a double fault at the worst possible moment. On the second serve I felt the pain radiating up my side. I wasn't going to be able to serve again. I wasn't. But I absolutely couldn't retire the match there. It would be snatching defeat from the jaws of victory. Even thinking it made me want to throw up. I tried lifting my serving arm, careful as I could be. Even that gentle motion made me almost black out. It wasn't going to happen.

The crowd were hushed like a congregation, but my delay meant a few nervous coughs were creeping through. The service clock had almost ticked down when it hit me: my last hope.

I took up my serving stance as normal, as if simply willing it would make my body cooperate. Toni was ready to receive, but she had already felt the match slipping from her. The hope had all but died in her eyes, and I needed that to get through, as awful as it was to see.

To her surprise, and the crowd's shock, I served my last point underarm. Nobody had done that in decades, because it lacked power and precision. It was something ladies at a garden party used to do or kids at the beach.

It fell well short of where a normal serve would hit, but it landed within bounds. Toni scrambled once she realised what was happening, but the lack of power in my shot meant she only fluffed it into the net.

The crowd roared so loudly it felt like an explosion. No one seemed to believe what they'd just seen, and I couldn't believe I'd just done it. The noise alone wasn't confirmation though. I needed the umpire to do his final job of the day.

"*Game, set, match, Miss Larsson. 6-7, 7-6, 6-4.*"

I didn't fall to my knees this time, just stood there with my head dropped forward, letting it all crash over me. I shoved my racquet under the arm on my good side and clutched at my hip as though it would help.

The moment absorbed, I looked up to see Toni approaching the net. I tried jogging across to meet her, but my hip insisted I go slower than that. She leaned in for the customary cheek kiss. and I let my racquet drop as I grabbed for her, clutching her shoulders.

"Is it bad?" she asked, our foreheads pressed against each other's. "Oh Elin, please tell me you're okay."

"It's over," I whispered back. "Get me through this?"

The kiss we shared wasn't exactly chaste this time, but we kept it mostly PG all the same. The crowd went wild for that too, and Toni rushed around the net to support me as we shook hands with the umpire. She gathered both our racquets and shoved them next to my chair before helping me sit down. Usually the runner-up would retreat to her own chair, maybe hide her head and her tears behind an official towel. Instead, Toni sat on the grass by my side, motioning for the medical team to come back out to me.

The head of the presentation ceremony noticed right away and came over as the preparations kept unfolding, all of it live on television around the world.

"Ladies?" was all he asked. Ezi had her miracle spray out again, and that gave me some instant relief. There was some arguing over whether I could have another injection so soon, but I grabbed the doctor who was wavering and told him to give me anything he had.

"I'll be fine in a minute," I told the official through gritted teeth. "Give Toni her moment and I'll be ready for mine."

The show really had to go on. No way was I missing my twenty-third one of these because I was off in a treatment room somewhere. There'd be plenty of time to recover once this ceremony was over.

I was cheering and applauding as loudly as anyone by the time they finally got to presenting Toni with her runner-up's trophy. They didn't linger over it, knowing nobody truly wanted second place, but I had tears in my eyes as I watched it all unfold. How lucky I was, not just to have made it through this day, but to have done it all with this magnificent woman right there with me.

The guard of honour seemed a mile long when they called my name, but I stood on slightly shaky legs to walk through it, just like every other time. The pain was receding with every second, and the end was finally in my grasp.

Step by careful step, I made my way towards the end of an era, and my future.

CHAPTER THIRTY-ONE

THE COVERAGE OF THE FINAL was absolutely nuts, and I knew it had to piss off the guys that it so completely overshadowed the men's final on Sunday. By that point, I was all tucked up in my private hospital room, full of opiates and sleeping as if it had just been invented.

Toni was by my side the whole time, which probably made her a far better person than me. If I'd gone through the day she had, I would have taken at least a day alone to deal with most of it. Her only concern had been making sure I hadn't pushed myself too far in sealing that record-breaking win.

"It would have been okay," I told her in one of my more lucid spells. "If you had won. I would have been okay with it being you."

"Yeah?" Toni had asked, peering at me over her magazine. She had folded herself into the chair at my bedside, soft and relaxed in her shorts and T-shirt. "I think you'd have thrown your racquet at my head, you big liar."

Celeste and Keiko dropped by to see me before they headed home on Monday and updated me on all the gossip from the Champions' Dinner that I'd missed.

"I knew something was off with you," Celeste said, squeezing my hand for a minute. "That speech sounded like you were bowing out, but you were just injury-freaked. You gonna make it back for Melbourne?"

I tried to shake my head, but it just made me dizzy. I wasn't ready to have the full conversation with my fellow pros yet, even if my acceptance speech had been full of very big hints about last times and looking back at my career. "I'm done, C. Bowing out on top. I knew going in that it was my last one."

She looked at Keiko in surprise, and I let them have a moment to react. We'd talk again; it was inevitable. I'd also have to do a ton of exit interviews to keep all my sponsors and everyone else happy too. God, that sounded exhausting. I could feel the pull of sleep tugging at me again. It was good to give into it.

"Elin, are you feeling up to talking?" Dr Huppert was leaning over me, immaculate as ever. I opened my eyes, and that was encouragement enough for her. "Thank you for the tickets, mmm? Those were two fantastic matches I saw you play. I feel very lucky."

"You're complimenting me," I realised. "Which means you have bad news."

"Ah, yes. The hip is very angry with you. We're going to operate here, today, so no long flight for a few weeks."

"Will I… Oh, wait." I'd been about to ask her if I'd make it back in time for the US Open. Force of habit, or at least half a lifetime of conditioning at work. I didn't have to do that anymore. I cast around a little for Toni, absent from my room for the first time since I checked in.

"I sent her to get some lunch," Dr Huppert explained. "She has been here too much without looking after herself. Not good after all that exertion on Saturday."

"When do I go under?" I asked.

"Soon. One more round of tests and then we've booked you into the private wing of a much bigger hospital. Safer that way, better facilities. Have a think about questions. You can ask them all then."

Toni came back then, a salad bowl in hand and some bottled juices tucked under her arm.

"You're awake," she said. "They want to operate today. Parisa is already on it, making plans."

"You're so pretty," I told her, and let myself drift back off.

I got clearance to fly to New York just in time for the final, a journey beset by delays and strikes and unexpected closures. Despite all that, despite still walking on crutches, I was there in the players' box at Flushing Meadows to watch my soon-to-be-wife lift her first Grand Slam trophy. I couldn't have been happier if I'd won the damn thing myself, and it was like a dam bursting somewhere inside me. I could have all that competitiveness, all that will to win, but I could relay it through Toni as a healthy outlet for it.

The photographers couldn't get enough of us together at the reception afterwards, and Toni barely left my side. I hadn't told her I'd be there, just told her in our calls to focus on winning, to get the slam that was rightfully hers. Her face when she'd first seen me courtside was one I could never forget.

I pulled her close when the crowd around us finally calmed, almost everyone having already expressed their congratulations.

"I'm so proud of you," I said, and we both heard the 'I love you' that was woven right through it.

***

"All packed?" I asked from the doorway of our bedroom, watching Toni move the same three pairs of shorts back and forth between two bags. "Or do we need to get a professional in here?"

"It's fine, it's ready. I'm not going until next week," Toni pointed out.

"Yes, but I don't want a week of boxes lying around our bedroom," I replied. "It's great that your kit sponsors love you so much, but that is a lot of clothing for one human lady."

"Melbourne is really far away," Toni said, pouting at a hoodie. "You sure you don't want to come?"

"I'll be out for the second week," I reminded her. "You make sure and stay in for that. Is there any chance you're fixating on the packing because you're nervous about tomorrow?"

Toni got up off the floor quickly when I said that, vaulting over the bed to join me. "No way, not even a little bit. Tomorrow is the good part. Everything else feels like the big distraction right now."

"Good." I kissed her, sweet and tender. "You should feel that way about our wedding. I like that you do."

"And the honeymoon is all booked for after?" she asked, fussing with the strap of my tank top. "We leave straight from Melbourne?"

"Mmhmm. Just a little delay to play the tournament in between. Think how much more you'll enjoy the honeymoon with your first Aussie in the bank, right?"

"Well, it's a long way to twenty-three, so I better start racking them up," she teased. "No, wait. Twenty-four, if I'm going to break it. Equalling is for runners-up. I win slams now."

"It's just a relief New York didn't go to your head. Have you cleared enough space in here yet for us actually to have sex in our own bedroom? Not that I minded the kitchen, bathroom, or either of the guest rooms, but really."

"I was just testing that your hip has fully healed," Toni argued. "Can't do that in just one location. Science, babe."

I groaned. I was marrying a nerd. But a damn cute one, it had to be said.

The opening ceremony in Melbourne included a brief statement, read by Celeste. In it, she thanked the GTA for their new drug-testing policy, a system that would be transparent and fair for all players. It was followed by the president making his apology for the unfair treatment in recent years and promising to do better in the future.

It wasn't perfect, but it was a victory for Celeste, Keiko, and so many more of our friends. Toni still felt uneasy on the subject, but Xavi had been banned from the sport for life once the doping allegations were proven true.

I watched Toni's first-round match on television over dinner with Alice and Todd, her latest boyfriend. This one seemed completely head over heels, so there was a chance he'd stick for a year or two at least. Maybe we'd even double date the weeks Toni wasn't on the road. I saw her wedding ring, or more accurately the white tape covering it, and touched my matching one with my thumb. We were so far apart, and yet I'd never felt closer.

This was the first major tournament since I'd finished my recovery, when technically I might have been fit enough to explore playing again. I wondered if the regrets would finally come. I held my breath as the first serve flew across the net, fresh from Toni's racquet, and waited to see what my heart would do to me.

Nothing. Relief, more than anything. A jolt of pleasure as Toni claimed her first point. I didn't miss it, not like I thought I might, but I didn't hate it either. I could be a fan, an interested party, and no longer pick up a racquet every day.

"Did you want to grab a drink when she's done?" Alice asked, paying more attention to the screen than she would have any other time.

"Okay," I said. "That sounds good."

When Toni won, we slipped out to the bar across the street and I ordered a martini while Alice and Todd bickered about what to have. Taking a sip, I raised the glass for a moment in a silent toast to my wife.

"Just one drink," I whispered under my breath. "And look what it got me."

ACKNOWLEDGMENTS

First and foremost, to my wife Kaite. Not just for literary inspiration and being generally amazing, but for riding out the 6-month resurgence of my teenage crush on Steffi Graf. If only I'd known that's what it was at the time…

A big theme in this book is family, and I'm so grateful for the support from my mum and dad. I've been thrilled while writing this to meet my newest niece, Beatrice, and to see James become a lovely big brother to her.

I don't know where I'd be without my friends, who've also been my biggest supporters. I hope Lande will appreciate this book most of all, since she's lived through daily Wimbledon and French Open chats with me this year and so many years before.

Writing buddies and advisers have kept me sane, including Annie, James, Michael, and Ricky. The Discord squad of Ashton, Bianca, Rachel, Molly, Urska, Andrea, Shad, and Kendrick have pushed me to new levels and been the best of company. Love always to Laura and Jo for making me laugh every time we talk.

As with so many things, this wouldn't be possible without the support of the good folks at Ylva. To Astrid, Zee, Sandra, Alex, and Amanda: Thank you for all that you do.

And to the four cats that have interrupted, sat on my laptop, cried for food, and generally tried to halt all progress? You're lucky you're cute!

ABOUT LOLA KEELEY

Lola Keeley is a writer and coder. After moving to London to pursue her love of theatre, she later wound up living every five-year-old's dream of being a train driver on the London Underground. She has since emerged, blinking into the sunlight, to find herself writing books. She now lives in Edinburgh, Scotland, with her wife and four cats.

CONNECT WITH LOLA
Website: www.lolakeeley.co.uk
Facebook: www.facebook.com/lolakeeley
E-Mail: divalola@gmail.com

OTHER BOOKS FROM
YLVA PUBLISHING

www.ylva-publishing.com

MAJOR SURGERY
Lola Keeley

ISBN: 978-3-96324-145-1
Length: 198 pages (69,000 words)

Surgeon and department head Veronica has life perfectly ordered...until the arrival of a new Head of Trauma. Cassie is a brash ex-army surgeon, all action and sharp edges, not interested in rules or playing nice with icy Veronica. However when they're forced to work together to uncover a scandal, things get a little heated in surprising ways.

A lesbian romance about cutting to the heart of matters.

CODE OF CONDUCT
Cheyenne Blue

ISBN: 978-3-96324-030-0
Length: 264 pages (91,000 words)

Top ten tennis player Viva Jones had the world at her feet. Then a lineswoman's bad call knocked her out of the US Open, and injury crushed her career. While battling to return to the game, a chance meeting with the same sexy lineswoman forces Viva to rethink the past...and the present. There's just one problem: players and officials can't date.

A lesbian romance about breaking all the rules.

DEFENSIVE MINDSET
Wendy Temple

ISBN: 978-3-95533-837-4
Length: 276 pages (100,000 words)

Star footballer and successful businesswoman Jessie Grainger has her life set, and doesn't need anything getting in the way. That includes rebellious rival player Fran Docherty, a burnt-out barmaid with a past as messed up as her attitude. So when the clashing pair find themselves on the same Edinburgh women's football team, how will they survive each other, let alone play to win?

ROMANCING THE KICKER
Catherine Lane

ISBN: 978-3-96324-129-1
Length: 314 pages (86,000 words)

Parker Sherbourne, the new rookie kicker for the High Rollers, Las Vegas's pro football team, is hot property. When athletic trainer Carly Bartlett signs on, her boss has one warning: don't get involved with a player. That's no problem—until Carly has to treat seductive Parker and sparks fly. With the macho world of football against them, can they beat the odds in this lesbian sports romance?

Slammed
© 2019 by Lola Keeley

ISBN: 978-3-96324-275-5

Also available as e-book.

Published by Ylva Publishing, legal entity of Ylva Verlag, e.Kfr.

Ylva Verlag, e.Kfr.
Owner: Astrid Ohletz
Am Kirschgarten 2
65830 Kriftel
Germany

www.ylva-publishing.com

First edition: 2019

Credits
Edited by Zee Ahmad and Amber Williams
Cover Design and Print Layout by Streetlight Graphics

Made in the USA
Coppell, TX
24 August 2022

82009437R10173